Shadows of a Dark Past

A JESSICA MINTON MYSTERY
BOOK 4

SHARON HEALY-YANG

SHADOWS OF A DARK PAST
A Jessica Minton Mystery, Book 4

By Sharon Healy-Yang

Cover Design: Sharon Yang (concept); De-Ping Yang (compilation)

First Edition, 2024
Print: ISBN: 978-1-956851-96-0

Second Edition, 2025
Print: ISBN: 979-8-9920155-0-8

Published by Sharon R. Yang

Printed in the United States of America

www.sharonhealyyang.com

Jessica Minton Mystery Series

Bait and Switch
Letter from a Dead Man
Always Play the Dark Horse
Shadows of a Dark Past

Shadows of
a Dark Past

Jessica Minton, her sister Liz, and her husband James join the cast of her mystery radio program on an isolated New England island for remote broadcasts at a reputedly haunted mansion. Unfortunately, the mansion lives up to its reputation as dark secrets from the past of the island's leading families lead to frightening midnight somnambulism, ghostly possession, madness, murder, and a séance gone horribly wrong. Worse, James Crawford's own past rises up to stalk him under the mansion's shadowy influence. Will the quick wits of the Minton sisters and James Crawford be enough to unravel the mysteries of Birdsong Island in time? A tale of mystery and the supernatural in the mode of *The Uninvited*.

Chapter One
Wednesday, October 15th, 1947

A rattling jolt snapped Jessica Minton out of the daze that had almost put her under. Even before her eyes had quite focused in the grim, dim illumination, her hand reached to the train seat to her left.

No James.

Blinking herself more awake, Jessica straightened up. Her momentary disappointment flickered out as she remembered that at least James wasn't missing behind enemy lines, on the run from German soldiers. This time, he only had to avoid dust, silverfish, and mice while pouring through recently discovered letters at Ballard College in upstate New York. Junior sabbatical work was hardly a cause for trepidation—although he might appreciate help from Dusty with those mice.

They were both separated by their work for two weeks or so: James in Florence, New York and she on the bumpy train ride to Portsmouth, New Hampshire to join her colleagues on the Wellstone Mystery Hour at an island with an allegedly haunted mansion. *Boy, when people say two careers are murder on a marriage, they don't know the half of it!*

The powerful coastal wind rocked the carriage, forcing Jessica to steady herself again. Her gaze fell to the window on her right. The gorgeous colors of fall were now absorbed by total darkness, while her pale, strained features were reflected back by the cold, weak lighting in the car.

At least she wasn't alone. Across from her, hidden behind a *New York Times*, rather worse for the wear of a full day's travel, was her sister Liz.

Another jolt, and from behind the fashion section of the paper came Elizabeth's dry observation, "Hope that wasn't anyone we know."

Jess smiled, amending, "Or at least anyone we like." She straightened her yellow-gold swing jacket with its black Persian-lamb collar. Smoothing back wisps of dark hair that had escaped her bun after a long day's travel, Jess added warmly, "Liz, I really appreciate your coming on this trip with me. I think we can have some fun. Time away could be good for both of us."

Elizabeth lowered her paper, revealing a stylish woman in a black skirt and fitted hounds-tooth jacket with Chesterfield collar. A small black velvet béret nestled in her dark hair, caught in a smart French roll. Liz's earlier quip had proved that "smart" described her brain as much as her fashion sense.

"So, kid sister, is that a tactful way of saying you think I need some peace and quiet to think long and hard about Leo McLaughlan and the rest of my life before I snafu things up but good—again?"

"Liz," Jessica began, a bit exasperated, "sure, you had some bad breaks, but it's not as if you're a foul-up. Maybe you did pick the wrong guy . . ."

"Twice."

"Well, I made plenty of mistakes in the romance department before I met James. I even made one of the same ones as you."

"You broke that off for the right guy. I went from the fire into the frying pan. Not as bad as the other way around, but it still cost me, cost you *and* me, cost too many people."

Elizabeth wasn't being a cry-baby or bitter, just reflective.

"Look, Liz, Leo McLaughlan is a stand-up guy. You know that, I know that—even James knows that."

"Oh right, James, my go-to guy for romantic advice. Did you forget, kiddo, he's one of the reasons I'm divorced?"

This had been a sore spot for Elizabeth from the get-go. Yet Jessica also knew that prickliness had softened over the past two years as Liz saw how happy James made her.

"I like Leo—and so do you. What's the real problem, Elizabeth?"

The wind seemed almost to shove the train from the tracks, forcing both sisters to grab their armrests. Liz quipped, "We may be making a side trip to Oz."

"Never mind the wisecracks. We both know that Leo McLaughlan is nothing like your last two fellas. Answer my question: why are you afraid to say 'yes' to his marriage proposal?"

Folding her arms, Elizabeth asserted, "Because when it comes to romance, *I'm* a jinx."

"Jinx?! *You?* No, Liz! You can't believe that!"

"Oh no? So how did my ex-husband and my ex-fiancé end up?" Liz challenged.

"You can't think that way," Jessica argued, hesitating as the wind once more rattled their carriage. "These guys made their own choices. We have free will, you know."

"Pardon me, Thomasina Aquinas, but, well, the first one, maybe . . . but Larry . . . he'd still be—"

"Liz, no," Jessica insisted. "Don't blame yourself. He made his own choices. You've got to know that. Besides, Leo is a different kind of guy. You know that as much as he loves you, he won't do wrong. Period."

Her sister muttered, "I don't know. Maybe you're right. Maybe I'm wrong. I just don't want to make another mistake, for *Leo's* sake. He deserves better."

Jessica shook her head and smiled. "Admit it. You're crazy about the guy. And this beautiful mansion on a gorgeous island is just the place to bring you to your senses."

"Right, a creepy old house where you and your chums are going to re-enact an unsolved murder for your spooky radio show: just the place for a nice, peaceful, contemplative retreat."

Jessica shook her head. She picked up her black conical cap from beside her and bouncing it on her lap continued, "None of which involves you. You're there to stroll the woods or the beach, poke around the village, slip over to Portsmouth, read, and sleep late—maybe even take a swim!"

"It has been an unusually gorgeous, warm autumn," Elizabeth allowed, a smile playing on her lips. Then she looked impishly at Jess and teased, "Just why do *you* need to get away? You love your fella and your work. How 'relaxed' are you going to be, immersed in all this ghost mumbo-jumbo?"

"I won't be working all the time," Jess laughed. "When I'm free, you and I can have a ball doing everything I just mentioned. Anyway, to be honest, doing a radio show about fictional ghosts and goblins and murders is a darned sight less frightening than all this Red Scare business in the news," Jessica answered, nodding at her sister's newspaper.

Glancing down, Elizabeth grimaced and agreed, "I'll say. All I hear about is Russian Reds taking over Hungary and Yugoslavia or putting elected officials on trial in Czechoslovakia or Reds attacking Nationalists in China. We just got rid of Hitler, and now the Communists are coming up to pinch hit!"

Jessica frowned, hesitating before saying, "That's not anything to give you sweet dreams, but what really scares me about this business is branding anyone who sticks up for the working man or civil rights as a Red. That HUAC is a powerful group, and they're not particular about basing their accusations on solid evidence. You saw what happened with the Hollywood Ten. I have some acquaintances who've been put under pressure—James has been seeing some monkey business, as well, in academia—"

"No kidding? Has anyone gone after him? Are *you* on anybody's radar, Jess?" Liz asked, her concern shifting from herself to her sister.

Jessica smiled wanly, "So far, no. But it's bad luck to count my chickens before they hatch. At least for the moment, I'm in the clear—that I know of. Let's hope I'm just too small a potato to attract anybody's notice."

"But surely with James's record with the secret service—and his connections?"

Jessica shook her head, explaining, "You'd think so, but did you see in today's paper about that guy, Leon Josephson? He was working against Hitler before it was *de rigueur*. Now he's in jail for refusing to testify."

"That's a cheery thought," Liz frowned. "I guess ghosts and broken romances *are* small potatoes in comparison."

Jessica wasn't sure if she was relieved that her sister wasn't beating herself up anymore or annoyed with herself for creating more gloom.

They hit another bump, leading Liz to remark, "I thought they cleared away all the tree limbs. They kept us cooling our heels long enough two stops back to get 'em all."

Jess shook her head. Their 6:38 train would deliver them to Portsmouth later than the original 7:38 scheduled, due to the wind knocking branches across the tracks. She'd gotten in a quick call to warn them at Carlyle house that they should pick Liz and her up at Portsmouth Station at a later time.

"At least it's only a dark and *windy* night," Jess kidded, "not a rainy one. You have to admit, Liz, the trip hasn't been all bad. Remember how spectacular the scenery was coming through Massachusetts? And didn't we have a lovely lunch and shopping spree after the meeting where the lawyers settled your deal selling out your business?"

"Wasn't that a lovely check Wilson, Payne, and Greene handed me to deposit?" Liz added, sporting a smile of the Cheshire-Cat variety.

"So, you really don't mind selling, Liz?"

"I don't mind this little nest egg and the opportunity they gave me for freelance designing. No more business decisions, no more customers and buyers and suppliers to schmooze and cajole and steamroller. Just the fun end—designing clothes. All the creative work with none of the financial and mental headaches. How can a gal complain?"

Jess nodded, considering: *Also, no more competition between your work and your guy's. Maybe time to start a family, but still with a creative outlet and financial security. Could Liz be much closer to saying "yes" to Leo McLaughlan than she was letting on or even realized?*

So, Jessica kept her mouth shut and let nature take its course. Well, she might offer one or two gentle nudges in the right direction. *Good grief! Have Liz and I switched places? No, Liz didn't nudge. She shoved!*

"What are you smiling at?"

Elizabeth's wary question brought Jess back to reality.

"Me? Oh, nothing. I was just thinking about the fun we can have on the island," she innocently answered.

"On the haunted island," Liz corrected.

"It's not the island; it's the mansion that's haunted," Jessica pleasantly corrected. "If it *really* is. I mean, that's the story that drew Scott and the sponsor's stand-in to do a remote broadcast on an actual unsolved murder and haunting. They think it will rescue us in the ratings. Those game shows and Jimmy Durante are killing us. Scott insisted on keeping the story hush/hush, so it would be fresh for us when we read the script. All I know is that the ghost of a young woman allegedly wanders somewhere in the house, maybe after being murdered. They never found her body."

"Then how do they know she *was* murdered? She could be living the high life in Florida," Liz countered.

Jessica shrugged and laughed, "If that's the case, let's hope she doesn't hear the show and sue us off the air! Anyway, maybe you can use some of your hoodoo to dig out the truth."

"Oh, is that why you asked me along?" Liz asked skeptically. "You know I'm no medium. I just get my feelings . . ."

"You can tell us what 'feeling' you get about the place. Who knows? Maybe Scott will draw on your expertise and send you into the writers' room. You might earn your keep."

"Smart guy," Liz retorted. "So, they don't have a script? You don't know how they'll be using this haunting?"

"I'll tell you, Liz; it's quite the mystery. All I know is that Scott and the sponsor want the place's 'atmosphere'. I can't imagine they're expecting the ghost to make an actual appearance. It probably violates union rules. Nobody wants to give AFRA something to go on the warpath about."

"Well," Liz speculated. "I think I see now why your Prince Charming found the need to do his research long distance these two weeks. I remember one of Mr. Crawford's bugaboos is ghosts. The last vacation spot he'd opt for would sport a headless murder victim wandering the halls of a creepy old mansion on a deserted island—not even for his lovely bride."

Jessica chuckled, "Oh, Liz, when did I say anything about the lady's lack of a noggin? And the island is just across a causeway from Portsmouth. We're hardly stopping off in Transylvania."

"Okay, but if Boris Karloff or Judith Anderson answers the front door, don't say I didn't warn you."

"I hear Boris Karloff is quite a sweet and gentle man, Liz."

"And what about Judith Anderson?"

"I'll have to get back to you on that one," Jess promised.

"What's James's thing about ghosts, anyway? I mean, does he dive under the bed at Halloween? He did make it through some Val Lewton movies without turning green."

Jessica shook her head. "I don't know. It's something he won't get into. I know his phobia about horses came from seeing a friend trampled as a child, but Blue helped him overcome that. This thing with the supernatural, it's weird. He acts skeptical, but he also gets kind of jumpy over anything too eerie.

"I suspect his skepticism might actually be a kind of denial; I can't say for certain. But the guy's been through so much, I don't want to probe. If he wants to tell me, he will. We just try to joke about it. Anyway, he planned his trip before my project materialized—so to speak."

"Maybe he'll meet Casper, which will solve all his problems," Liz kidded. "You know, like the way his experience with that Blue Warrior changed his mind about horses."

"Right, sure thing," Jess quipped, but she kept to herself exactly how Blue Warrior had cured her husband. The F.B.I. had impressed on both her and James that the story needed to stay under wraps while they tried to discover who had been backing an undercover fifth columnist.

Those thoughts were interrupted by the conductor coming through their car, calling, "Last stop! Portsmouth Station!"

For the first time, Jessica noticed the lights of the city drawing closer. *How long had they been in view?* She glanced behind herself to note the few other passengers pulling together their bundles and what-have-yous in anticipation of debarking. It was a darned good thing she and her sister had shipped their trunks on ahead. Now all they had to gather were their purses and Liz's shopping from Boston.

"Great," Elizabeth purred, balancing three packages in her lap. "I can't wait to get off this bucking bronco and into whatever fancy car they send for us. If this guy's a manufacturing mogul, he must have at least an Oldsmobile. Maybe even a caddy! Those things are like riding in a cloud, I hear."

Jess made a little embarrassed grimace as she was putting on her cap and had to explain, "Um, about the car, Liz. I'm afraid you might be a bit disappointed. Mr. Carlyle, apparently, has taken his fancy car out of town, and the station wagon has been having problems with the butterfly in the carburetor . . ."

"Which means?" Liz lowered.

Hat secured, Jess dropped her hands to the large black pocketbook in her lap and answered as blithely as she could in the face of her sister's irritation, "Which means they're sending a cab—or they sent a cab. I hope he didn't have to wait too long, even though I told them the train was running . . ." a glance at her watch ". . . Good Grief! More than ninety minutes behind schedule now!"

Liz uttered a mildly disgusted sigh but allowed, "Well, it couldn't be any worse than traveling over *these* rough seas." She thought before adding, "Say, when did you learn about carburetors and dragonflies?"

"Butterfly," Jessica corrected. "But don't be too impressed. I just know that carburetors have them—and that you sometimes need to manually flutter them to get a car started. I learned helping James start our second-hand car. Don't go signing me up for a job at Chevrolet."

"Just as long as you don't have to perform surgery on the cab. I'm ready for a nice cozy bed—with working springs."

As if responding with a resentful parting shot, the train jerked to a halt at Portsmouth Station.

The conductor was announcing the stop, waking passengers, briefly answering a question or two, as he moved through their carriage then on to the next one. The sisters quickly gathered their things before moving down the aisle to the exit. On the car's steps, Jess paused to take in and smile at the quaint little station in the glow of tall street lamps: no raised platform; a small and old-fashioned wooden building painted New England red, with windows, a main doorway, and benches facing the tracks. On the bench at the far left of the building, a slender old man snoozed, satchel in his lap. Jessica hoped he wouldn't miss whomever he was waiting for—or hadn't slept through his train arrival. Only one or two people waited to board; none seemed to notice the old gent. A poke from behind let Jessica know that her sister was in no mood for her woolgathering. At least they were the last off their car, so she wasn't holding everyone up—just the most impatient one!

The train station and the tracks being level with each other made it easier to step off and move toward the building. The return trip of their train was the last one out of the station until morning. No need to keep the station open this late when the train was running so far behind schedule and when one could purchase a ticket on board. So, the station was dark inside.

Standing in the unseasonably warm October night, Jessica was hardly aware of departing passengers moving off, around the station, to the headlights of waiting taxis or their own cars or opting to walk home through the lovely evening. Instead, she relished the delicious wind streaming around her, rattling papers tacked to the station bulletin board, swaying and creaking tree limbs, and toying with rogue strands of dark hair about her face. She deeply inhaled the salty tang from Portsmouth harbor and luxuriated in her freedom from the dim, back-torturing train.

"Drat it all!" sliced into Jessica's delight.

"Liz? What?"

"I left a package on my seat! Wait here! I'll be right back!" her sister replied, piling her bundles into Jessica's arms and bounding back aboard before Jess could do more than gape.

Jess rolled her eyes. For a moment, she couldn't swear that she would have minded if the train had rolled back to Boston with Liz still on board.

She turned away from the train, once more surveying the area around her. The old guy in casual clothes was still catching Z's. Now, the other passengers seemed to have found their way off—and, uneasily, she realized there were no more headlights to be seen around the station. Sure, the lights of the city, but where was their taxi? The darkness of Portsmouth Station felt disquieting. How come the cabbie hadn't shown up to meet them?

"Got it!" called Liz from behind, giving Jess a violent start.

"Hey, watch it, kiddo," Elizabeth warned. "You nearly dropped my packages. Let me take those, butterfingers."

"Next time, do you think you could manage to tell me you're here without giving me a heart attack?" Jessica growled.

As she spoke, the train was rolling out, and Jessica vaguely realized that the conductor had earlier called, "All aboard!"

"Oh, don't get your ears in an uproar," Elizabeth returned smoothly. Now glancing around, she questioned, "So, where's our ride? There aren't any taxis in sight, and I don't see anybody but Rip Van Winkle over there."

Jess shot her sister a sharp look for her crack but only said, "I don't know. Scott promised he'd send someone to wait for us. I hope we didn't run so late that the cabbie left."

"Hmm," Elizabeth conjectured, "the taxi could be on the other side of the building, waiting for us. He probably has his lights off to conserve the battery. I've been enough of a crab for the day. You take the packages and sit down over there." Liz indicated the unoccupied bench. "I'll take a gander over the other side of the station."

Jess had settled on the bench, Elizabeth's packages and her own bag beside her. This evening was not turning out how she'd planned: tree limbs on the tracks, a missing taxi. How was James doing about now? It would have been nice to lean against him on this beautiful, if somewhat annoying, autumn eve. Maybe he was wishing something similar. She was sure he'd love this island. They might have been city kids most of their lives, but she could still feel how delicious it had been for them to roam the woods upstate and in the Berkshires, to delight in beaches on the Connecticut side of the Sound . . .

"You might as well wipe that dreamy look off your face, sister dear," Liz's voice crashed her reverie. "We're out here all alone, except for Rip over there."

"What?" Jess sat up, alarmed. "There's no cab? Nothing?"

"There's an old flivver, but no one in it," her sister grumbled, sitting down. "Are you sure your chum Scott got his dates right? He does know we're arriving *tonight*? He told the driver *tonight*?"

Before Jess could answer, the old gent causally piped up, "Oh, your taxi was here all rightie. Only left an hour ago."

Both women started, bewildered, with Jessica finally questioning, "Who are you? How do you know any of this?"

They paid more attention to the man, now, taking in his lean face; his thatch of white hair combed across his head, just slightly askew from the wind; his eyes, blue and as languorous as his New England speech patterns: "I guess I'll answer your second question first. Be easier. Your ride was here earlier with me. We were chewin' the fat, and he told me how he was supposed to pick you two up. Then the station master came out with a message—there was an emergency. He had to take somebody to the hospital on the mainland. So he left."

"He left us in the lurch," Elizabeth grumped.

"Naw, not really," the old guy opined, pulling a cabbie's cap out of his satchel. "See, I'm the other driver on the island. He asked me to take you gals where you're goin'."

"Why didn't you tell us when we got off the train?" questioned an exasperated Jessica.

"Hadn't finished my nap," he replied matter-of-factly. "You weren't going anywhere."

"Of course," Liz ironically concurred with a wave of her hand.

"We-ell, guess we might as well shove off," their chauffeur decided, getting up and approaching the sisters. "I'm parked on the other side of the station."

Elizabeth froze and ventured with trepidation, "The flivver?"

"'Course. Ole Bessie's been travelin' the island since Hector was a pup. She practically knows the way, herself," he answered, drawing even with Jess and Liz.

"Are her springs and shocks in the same graduating class as Hector?" Liz queried.

The cabbie ignored her and said, "Well, I 'spect we best get goin'. Follow me."

"Wait," Jessica began. "Do you think you could help us with these bundles?"

He eyed Elizabeth's packages sourly, then shook his head to reply, "Nope. 'Fraid not. Got a bad back."

"Must be Bessie's springs," Liz muttered.

"Eh?"

"Nothing," Jessica smiled back quickly, anxious to avoid losing their one shot at not having to try to dig up a ride in a strange town.

"Sorry, ladies," he added. "It's the plumbago."

"Don't you mean lumbago?" Jess suggested.

"Nope. Plumbago. I was helping Mrs. Blake move her plumbago in a big pot. So, this warm weather ain't gonna last forever. Ready?"

"Lead on, Mr. . . . ?" Jess urged,

"Jones. Nat'an Jones." He looked Liz square in the eye to add, "Not Rip."

Mr. Jones calmly headed around the building without pausing to see if the two women followed.

"You kind of asked for that one," Jessica teased her sister as they followed Jones.

"Oh, put a lid on it," Liz shot back softly but no less irritably. "Some vacation!"

Chapter Two
Same Night

So, they were in the backseat of Ole Bessie, with Liz's packages piled on her lap. Nathan Jones had warned Elizabeth that he couldn't park them in the seat next to him because, if they hit a bump, everything could go flying out the window that no longer rolled up on that side. Good thing he had a garage for rainy weather, he had added. From the musty atmosphere inside the old car, Jess decided it must have been an old garage that needed quite an airing. Of course, the car's springs creaked with age at every dip in the parking lot—and Jones was pretty good at hitting most of them. Liz, having decided that even this ambulatory torture device was better than hoofing it at this time of night, opted not to antagonize their driver any further. For the moment. She had no such compunction about telegraphing her opinion to Jessica with a burning glare.

Jess could have been grumping, herself. However, she kept her blue devils under control by turning from her sister's evil eye to check out the scenery—as much as she could make out in the darkness. Meanwhile, Mr. Jones seemed to have lapsed into silence. She hoped he wasn't relying on Ole Bessie's sense of direction to recommence his snooze. *Well, there was no place left to go this evening but up, right?*

They skirted the edge of Portsmouth: small businesses, some bars, working-class neighborhoods. Not much going on at this hour. Now they were moving past some larger houses with more spacious grounds as they circled out of town, though not along the ocean. The salt air couldn't quite defeat the cab's mustiness. Jess sneezed.

"God bless you," came out of her sister and Jones simultaneously.

"Great minds think alike," the driver drawled.

"Must be it," Elizabeth concurred, not entirely without sarcasm.

That was remarkably restrained for Liz, Jess concluded. Nevertheless, it seemed wisest to take charge of the conversation before either her sister or her driver could move things in a hostile direction.

"Thank you both. Say, Mr. Jones, you seem to know the ins and outs of this area pretty well, zig-zagging us through Portsmouth. You must have lived around here all your life."

"Pretty much. Born and bred on the island, I was. Spend most of my time here. Get most of my business here. They like to have someone to run them into town or take them from one island to t'other—them as don't have a bike or a wagon or a boat."

"Not many people drive?" Jess inquired.

"Waal, more and more with the young folks, people have been gettin' off the island. Lots of woods, not so many roads good for automobiles. But, like I say, the young folks these days get bored, want to see the city—then, during the war, people were headin' to the city to work—mostly young folks, again. The island is an old island; been settled since 1623 by Capt'n Sidney Birdsong, you know. Farmin' and fishin' was mostly good enough for folks for years, but things have changed over time, 'specially since the war."

"So, it's not overdeveloped now? It's nice where we're staying, at Carlyle House?" Jessica asked, particularly hoping Mr. Jones would say something about their destination to soothe Elizabeth's silent brooding.

"Oh, Carlyle House? Sure. That Philip Carlyle's family knew what it was doing, building that mansion on Saul's Point—no, that's wrong. The Hayward place is on Saul's Point. Carlyle's is on Piscataqua Point! That and the Saunders' place. If I took you to Saul's Point, we'd be clear on t'other side of the island! An' the Haywards turned their mansion over to the Coast Guard for housing during the war. I don't think those fellas would be too happy to find two strange civilians on their doorstep, even if you *are* a couple of lookers."

"Thanks, I think," came Elizabeth's voice from beside Jessica. *Well, her interjection had been kind of good-natured,* Jess thought hopefully.

However, after all the evening's SNAFUs, she was not so hopeful about their driver's sense of direction and questioned, "You *are* sure which house is where, Mr. Jones?"

"No doubt in my head," he happily replied. "There's three big mansions, three old families with big money on the island: the Haywards, the oldest, at Piscataqua Point; the Saunders, next oldest, and the youngest, relatively speaking, the Carlyles on Saul Point."

"Wait a minute," Jessica challenged. "Didn't you say it the other way around before?"

"What? So, I did. It was right the first time. You caught me there, girlie," he chuckled.

Jessica felt Liz's hand on her arm as her sister cracked softly, "Not to worry, Jess. Remember, Ole Bessie here knows her way."

Nathan Jones surprised them both, not just with his hypersonic hearing but with his guffaw: "You got that right, sister! You know, I think I like you. You might put on a sour puss, but that p & v in you makes me bust out laughin'!"

"I'll be happy to entertain you even more," Liz quipped, oddly both annoyed and pleased with the back-handed compliment.

They slowed down, entering an enclave of twisting, narrow streets lined with capes, cottages, and bungalows. The ocean's rush was now much more audible, and the sea (more gale than) breeze overpowered the cab's mustiness. Harbor lights sparkled to their right, while on the left a few of the cottages softly spilled light into the street.

"We're comin' up on the causeway now," Jones informed them. "'Fraid the one we can't take, the one closest to the Haywards . . ."

"Carlyles," Jessica corrected uneasily.

"Yup. You got me there," Jones shook his head. "Anyway, the other causeway is closer to Piscataqua, but there's no road that connects it to the Carlyles'. You have to drive plumb across the island. I didn't want you to think I was takin' you 'round Robin Hood's barn to jack up my fare. That's just the way the island's laid out. Guess the first Carlyles, back in the late '50s, and the Saunders, sometime earlier, liked the isolation. They could of built themselves a fancy place in Portsmouth—that's where their businesses were—but nope. They tucked themselves away in a nice secluded spot across Piscataqua Bay where they could see the mainland, be seen (Carlyles anyway), by the mainland, but put a nice little bay full of water between them and the city."

They had turned onto the causeway, a two-lane, paved road that ran into darkness above the waters toward glimmering lights on a smallish island.

"That's not Birdsong Island, is it?" Jessica conjectured skeptically, noting the size.

"Nah, that's Chevril Island. It's halfway there. Nice little yacht club there, but I don't use it," he chuckled.

The wind rattled the old car, slowing her headway.

"Not exclusive enough for you?" Elizabeth quipped.

Enjoying Liz's crack and unperturbed by the less-than-gentle zephyr assaulting Bessie, he returned, "Nope, can't stand the riff-raff. Even the Carlyles and the Saunders wouldn't join. Like I said, they like to be exclusive. Old Jameson Carlyle wouldn't even use local craftsmen or architects from Portsmouth when he first put up the place. Sent all the way to Boston to have his house planned out and built. 'Course, I can't say they'll have their way forever. Since the war, there's been a lot of talk for change in that department. Young people want more roads. Folks from the city want to move in and have more space—which means more houses, more roads, more trees cut down. Big controversy on how to keep the island. Stay old-fashioned and traditional or build it up and make more money. There's been real estate guys comin' in, checkin' out property. Seein' who's willin' to sell and for how much."

They passed onto Chevril Island, the surrounding trees cutting down the force of the wind. Jessica observed sourly, "Money usually wins."

"Maybe, maybe," Jones opined. "We'll see. The families with big money own a lot of land on the isle, and they have a lot of clout as to what goes. Then again, sometimes old money don't last forever. Anyway, that's one controversy. You're t'other."

"Me?" escaped Jessica as they returned to the causeway with its rattling wind.

"What did we do?" Elizabeth chimed in, just short of affronted.

"I don't even know these people," Jessica protested. "What gives?"

"They know you. Well, your show anyways." Birdsong Island came more clearly into view as Jones continued, "Some folks don't take kindly to your party stirring up a scandal they've been trying to bury."

Liz pointed out smartly, "Well, they haven't been doing a very good job in the burial department if the lady's ghost is still roaming around."

"Hey, I'm in t'other camp," Jones assured the sisters. "Maybe it will bring more tourists to the island."

"More people for you and Bessie to ferry out here?" Liz queried, but she had a concerned eye on her sister, who was trying to understand the resentment against her.

"Sure," Jones agreed, "An' for the people runnin' businesses. More customers. We could make this place a regular tourist stop for people who like to give themselves the heebie-jeebies. That haunted mansion ain't the only spooky stuff we have goin' on. We got the Stone Throwin' Demon from 1682—even brought in that witch hunter Mather guy! Then there's the Hound from Hel . . . Hades, too."

"Sounds as if this place has enough material for a bunch of episodes on your show, Jessica," Liz tried to kid away her sister's consternation.

Jessica, however, had a bee in her bonnet, protesting to Jones, "But why would people blame our program for stirring up a scandal? It was twenty years ago, and Mr. Carlyle contacted our program about doing the show. If he's not upset, why should anyone else be?"

"It's a small village," Jones shrugged, taking his hands off the wheel and alarming the sisters as his action put a little too much zig in his zag. "They got nothing better to do, some of 'em. You should hear them get going over whether the demon threw boulders or just stones. Or whether the Hound is a Doberman or a Great Dane—most votes have been going to the Doberman, what with the war."

"That's patriotic," Jessica commented wryly, somewhat appeased.

"Anybody vote for a Dachshund?" Liz playfully added.

"Your sister just kills me," Jones told Jessica, shaking his head.

Now they were on Birdsong Island, showing Jess exactly how small the community was. At first, they passed some small docks and homes. Moving toward the village, they could make out old cottages, most dark, but some with lights that seemed to proclaim: "No blackout! War's over!"

Jess thought she might have spied the white clapboard of a city hall and a small commercial district, the wind whistling around the buildings. She could still hear and smell the ocean. Abruptly, the road curved them into dark woods, the headlights' weak twin beams forcing them to go even slower. Overhead, the wind now sounded like a hurried rush of water through the branches. At least the two-way road was paved.

Elizabeth broke the silence with, "Jess, I wouldn't worry about too many people resenting you. I don't think many people here stay up late enough to listen to your program."

Jessica smiled quietly at her sister's attempt to buck her up. Maybe she was taking too much to heart. She wished that Scott, their director/producer, had told her more about how the locals felt towards their program's broadcasting on national radio a story so close to home. *Did Scott even know what was gossiped in the town? Of course, Nathan Jones could be exaggerating, even teasing her. It didn't sound as if there was much else to do for fun on the island.*

What was *the full story about this woman supposedly murdered and now haunting Carlyle House? A scary legend on par with such horrors as some infernal canine and a demon who thought it was pitcher Dizzy Dean?* She was about to see if she could pump some answers from Jones, when he slammed on the brakes and muttered, "Where is that dagnabbit turn off, now?"

Before her sister could verbally let Jones have it, Jess distracted her with, "Liz, did he just say 'dagnabbit'? Does anyone actually say that word outside of a Warner Brothers cartoon?"

Elizabeth quirked a smile, repositioned her discombobulated packages, then answered *sotto voce*, "Okay, riding with Barney Oldfield is still better than having to hoof it in these shoes to God knows where."

"Barney" was busy cogitating whether he'd overshot his turn-off in the dark. Maybe being born and bred here hadn't rendered him quite the expert navigator he'd claimed to be. He surprised, maybe unnerved, the two sisters by hopping out of Ole Bessie and pacing down the road into the windy darkness to check for the turn-off.

"Is this where the Devil Daxie leaps out and drags him off?" Elizabeth inquired.

"Liz, I promise once we get to the mansion, we'll kick back and laugh—"

"You want to add some chocolate sprinkles to that banana oil, sis?"

"It's right ahead!"

The sisters nearly jumped at Jones's exclamation. He, however, was oblivious to their reaction, popping back into the car and releasing the parking brake. They rolled on, with their cabbie opining, "Yep, they sure could use more lights on this island—that's one for the folks who want to build—tax revenue brings lights and better roads!"

The car slowed as they moved onto a gravel lane to their right, Jones explaining, "Sorry we can't stay on the main road, but it don't run out to the big houses, 'cept for at Saul's Point. Coast Guard fixed that one up. It's gonna take us some extra time to get there, what with the gravel and dirt roads, but Bessie will do it!"

"If we have to get out and push?" Jessica inquired wearily.

"If *you* have to get out and push," corrected Nathan Jones.

"Oh right, the plumbago," Elizabeth concluded.

As they drove along, Jones pointed out that on a warm sunny day the sparse houses along the road gave you a pretty journey. The trees surrounding the road cooled you from the brilliant coastal sun, while delighting you with gorgeous autumn colors mixed with the dark green of pines. Maybe Jones wasn't quite so poetic. That was Jessica's creative translation.

Unfortunately, this wasn't a sunny, warm day. It was shadowy and windy, with black, towering trees closing 'round the gravel lane like hostile sentinels. The interlinking branches above might have prevented the winds from assaulting Ole Bessie and her occupants, but those limbs couldn't stop creaking and groaning torturously. Jess could only comfort herself that at least no perturbed imp was tossing boulder beanballs at them.

Jones brought the car to a stop, this time without nearly projecting either Minton sister into the front seat. Peering over the wheel into the path illuminated by his anemic headlights, he strained to find a cut-off to the left, muttering, "Waaal looks like this is the shortcut."

"I like the sound of that last word," Elizabeth piped up. "The shorter this ride, the better. Drive on, pal."

"Just want to be sure it's the right one. There's one takes you to the Carlyle place and t'other to the Saunders'. You sure you wouldn't want to end up *there*."

Jessica was about to ask what was so bad about the Saunders' digs when an eerie howl reverberated through the night from the woods on the right.

"AROOOOOO!"

The sisters slid together so hard they collided, some of Elizabeth's packages tumbling to the floor. "Heh, heh," Jones chuckled. "Maybe you two aren't gonna be so smart-alecky about the Hound of Hades."

Jess moved away from her sister and replied with *some* dignity, "Don't be ridiculous. I'm sure it's just some farmer's dog, probably chasing a raccoon."

"Maybe a bear," Elizabeth added.

Jess shot Liz a skeptical look to challenge, "You think a *bear* in the woods is more reassuring?"

"At least he's not from hell," Elizabeth snapped back.

Jones shook his head, "You two are a caution!"

"Fine. Just cautiously take us down the shortcut," Elizabeth insisted.

Under her breath, Jessica snorted, "A bear? Honestly? How'd he get here? Borrow an outboard motor?"

"What a caution," Jones repeated, laughing to himself as he turned the car down a narrower and bumpier road. However, a howl just as harrowing as the first, and maybe even a little closer, silenced everybody as Bessie crawled deeper into the woods.

Chapter Three
Same Night

It seemed like forever, but it was less than ten minutes before Ole Bessie came into a clearing and pulled to a stop before an impressive building, the night hiding its colors.

"Yep, they must be expectin' you, leavin' the lights on an' all," Jones surmised, nodding at the two globes pendant on scrolled, wrought-iron hangers on either side of the great front door. But no light escaped from drawn-curtained windows on either side of the entrance or on any of the floors.

Jessica frowned, then questioned thoughtfully, "Are you sure this is the right place?"

"Like I said, they left the lights on for you, didn't they? Where else would you be, anyway? That road only has one destination. All out—after you pay up."

"Pay up?" Jessica demanded. "Didn't they already pay at Carlyle House when they sent out the cab?"

Jones answered matter-of-factly: "Might have paid Zack, but he didn't pay me. They'll have to get their dough back from him. I need my fare now. I don't do this for fun."

"No one was on this ride for fun," Elizabeth groused.

Jess distracted Jones with, "Fine, but would you at least help my sister with her packages."

"Lumbago," he reminded her, wincing.

"It won't hurt you to just hold the door for her," Jess pointed out before smiling, "*After* you do, you'll get your money."

"Mmm, back's feeling a mite better now," came his causal response before he slid out to hold the door for Elizabeth.

A few moments later, Jessica and her sister stood directly before the front door under the soft, eerie glow of the overhead lanterns. Jones's car was being swallowed by the woods enveloping that torture trap of a road.

Jessica hesitated, staring after him. She turned back to Elizabeth with an uneasy, "I wish he'd waited till we got inside."

"We could probably still catch Old Bessie if we walked fast. Anyway, we're here. Let's knock on the door and get in. I'm dying for a nice feather bed."

Jessica looked back at her sister, voicing her concern, "It just looks different from Scott's description. I can't hear the ocean, either. We're supposed to be near the water."

"Don't be ridic, kiddo," Liz countered, shifting the packages in her arms. "Who can hear anything over that wind? I'm just glad we're not hearing that Devil Dog."

"Hound of Hades."

"Whatever. Let's just get inside, so we can hit the hay. I'm surprised your whole crew hasn't flung open the door and dragged us in already."

"Funny, isn't it?" Jessica pondered, her eyes momentarily taking in the beautiful, if worn, carving on the rich oak door. A less worn space before her on that door revealed where a sizeable knocker had resided. Victim of a wartime scrap drive? Whatever the case, Jess got down to business and pressed the bell.

No response.

Jess and Liz looked at each other, waiting.

"I see you're a big deal on your show," Elizabeth coolly observed. "Do you think everyone's cozy back in the Baxter Building studio, having a good chuckle over sending us out here on a wild goose chase?"

Jessica's baleful glance at Liz would have done her cat Dusty proud. Then she shifted to peek at the windows on either side of the doorway, finally remarking, "I can't see any lights through all those curtains. I know it's late, but I'd expect at least Scott to be waiting up for us."

"Well, then," Liz shoved the packages into Jessica's arms and proceeded to give the bell a punishing. "It's time to wake him up—and everyone else."

"No, wait, Liz . . ."

"Wait yourself, little sister." Liz kept at the bell. "You're just too hanged polite sometimes. If you won't stand up for yourself, I will . . ."

The door slowly creaked inward. The sound, made creepier by the harrying wind accompaniment, made Elizabeth drop her hand and both sisters scooch together.

An old man stood before them, slightly shorter than the 5'7" Liz, his thinned hair, its brownish hue faded by age, was pomaded and parted severely down the middle. His features sere and sunken, his eyes cold, all passion seemed to have dried up and blown away long ago. The glow of the gas lamp he held could not soften those features. Clearly dressed as a butler, he was the most formidably unwelcoming butler either Minton sister had ever met, to put it mildly. They were flummoxed into silence.

Yet, through that formidable front, Jessica could have sworn his eyes flickered over her visage with . . . alarm? Fear? Resentment? All three? Unexpectedly, his cold, sepulchral voice demanded, "What is the meaning of this brouhaha?"

"Are you kidding me?" Elizabeth spluttered. "After we came all this way?"

An uneasy possibility that had been nagging Jessica solidified almost into certainty, and she questioned, "Please, aren't you expecting us?"

"We expect no one here," the butler stated with finality—and closed the door.

"Hey! What the hey!" Liz spluttered. Turning to Jessica, she demanded, "Did you get a load of that guy?! What gives here? Are your friends trying to play some kind of a gag on us? Well, I'm not laughing!"

"I think Ole Bessie doesn't know the lay of the land as well as our pal Jones claimed. He dropped us at the wrong house," Jessica concluded. "Remember how he got confused about the turn-off?"

"Boy, am I steamed!" Liz fumed.

"I don't think he was *planning* to take us for a buggy ride—"

"A buggy would have been faster *and* more comfortable," Elizabeth cut her off.

"*Anyway*," Jessica reclaimed the lead. "He probably wasn't intentionally trying to pull the wool over our eyes. What would it get him? He's just an old guy who's long on gossip and short on memory."

"That explanation is all fine and dandy," Liz groused, "but it doesn't get us to the right place or even tell us where we *are*."

22

"I can take a good guess," Jessica responded. "Remember, he mentioned a Saunders place was the other mansion on Pisca . . . Pissag . . . this point."

"You really think I was paying attention to anything that old codger was saying? For the love of Mike, he used the word 'dagnabbit'!"

Jess didn't argue. In fact, she was more than a little relieved by her sister's memory lapse: maybe Liz wouldn't remember that old Jones had let slip that the Saunders' home turf was the last place they wanted to go. She wasn't about to give her agitated sister one more reason to hit the roof.

Instead, Jessica advised, "Well, Liz, just take a deep breath and calm down. What with Nazi fifth columnists and murderers, we've been in tighter spots."

Somewhere in the dark, twisted woods a howl echoed.

"Arooooooo!"

"Hell Hounds outweigh Nazis! Even Alanna Tewkesbury!" burst from Liz, and she threw herself into a frenzied hammering on the solid door, when she wasn't jabbing the bell.

"Elizabeth Minton, get a hold—"

The door swung inward, nearly sending Liz sprawling inside, except that the Arctic stare of that butler froze her.

His words rasped out like November leaves across a grave: "Cease this immediately. This is a private home. There is no place for your kind here. Leave this property, or I will be forced to call the police."

"Fine," Elizabeth glared back, recovering herself. "Maybe *they* will give us a lift to where we're supposed to be." With the Hell Hound temporarily quiescent, her natural resistance to being pushed around had rebounded.

"No, please," Jessica cut in, shoving the packages back into her sister's grasp. The man hesitated, staring at her face, then caught himself. However, before he could shut Jess out, she gave him further pause with her sincere, "Look, sir, I'm sorry that there's been some kind of mix-up. It wasn't our intention to disturb you, but we are in a jam now. That Jones taxi driver dropped us here by accident, so we're stuck. We don't know exactly how far we are from our actual destination—or even how to get there. If you could just let us come in to use your phone to call Carlyle House . . ."

The minute the name of the other mansion escaped her lips, Jess saw a heavy curtain descend over the butler's watery eyes. He stated, "We have no working telephone."

The door started to swing against their faces, only to be halted by a young woman's voice not far within calling, "Danvers, stop. What's the commotion? Who is it? Is it something to do with my father . . . ?"

She came to the door and halted. She blinked at the sight of the two of them, a beautiful young woman, her soft, white dress gleaming in the lamplight, a white hair band holding back from a soft widow's peak long curls of dark hair. Her face was narrow and delicate, somehow emphasizing the extra white of her eyes that caught the gleam of lamplight in contrast to her dark pupils. Her eyes were not so much sad as having seen too much of life. Those eyes took in both sisters with surprise, lingering with consternation on Jessica. They only lingered a moment; nevertheless, her reaction gave Jessica an uneasy turn.

However, the young woman's words explained her reaction and perhaps the butler's as well, though not in a way that reassured Jess much.

"You're people from that radio program." She spoke with a naturally girlish voice, though her words were no less disapproving. "It seems you have some nerve to come *here*."

Jessica and Elizabeth exchanged speculative glances, Jess thinking: *Great, we got plopped on the doorstep of one of those families who resents the show's stirring up old scandals.* Before her sister's hair-trigger temper could plunge them deeper into trouble, Jessica spoke up, "I'm Jessica Minton, and this is my sister, Elizabeth. Our being here is really not a matter of nerve. As I told your butler, Nathan Jones dropped us here accidentally. We had no intention of bothering you. My sister has had a terrible day and temporarily lost her mind. She's truly sorry. Aren't you, Elizabeth?"

A gentle kick in the ankle persuaded a reluctant Elizabeth Minton to nod her agreement. Her glance, noticeable only to Jessica, signaled that she would fix her later. Nevertheless, fiery-tempered as Liz was wont to be, she also knew which side her bread was buttered on. She was *not* about to become Devil-Dog Kennel Ration.

The girl seemed to hesitate, so Jessica pressed tactfully, "All we want is to come in long enough to make a phone call for a ride to our actual destination. We're sorry if we've inconvenienced you. If there were any other way, we'd take it. We could even wait out here after we make our call . . ."

"With the Hell Hound?!" Liz blurted.

"No," the young woman decided. "That would be unreasonable. I can see that you two mean us no harm."

"But, Miss Jamie," the butler uneasily insisted, "it's not proper for anyone from that program to be here. And your father! What about your father!?"

"Father isn't home," the young woman stated. "We'll put the two ladies in the drawing room, should he return while they're here." She looked back to Jessica and Liz to explain, "The telephone is out of order. That's one reason my father is out." She hesitated, thinking about . . . ? She finished, "Danvers will drive you to the Carlyle Mansion. Please come in while he gets the car."

Jessica and Liz entered and passed into a long, dimly lamp-lit foyer— a rich rug beneath their feet and heavy dark furniture surrounding them. Directly ahead, a staircase was shadowed against the far wall. To their left, the young woman threw open the doors for them into the drawing room.

The room wasn't as shadowy as the foyer, for, oddly enough on this warm evening, a fire was going in the beautifully manteled hearth to their right. A wingback chair sat by the right of the fireplace, a cup and a pot of tea, along with a book, on a little table beside it. Before them, beyond a sturdy modern couch, rose three long windows topped with stained glass that rattled under the October winds. Jess was surprised to see her sister suddenly shiver. Come to think of it, the room *was* a little chill, despite the hearth and the unseasonable weather.

"You may have a seat in here," quietly instructed their hostess, distracting Jess from her sister's odd reaction. "Perhaps not by the fire on such a warm night. I always feel a chill in here . . ." She seemed to reflect on that a moment before catching herself to suggest to Elizabeth, "You will likely prefer to set your packages on this table by the door."

"Yes, of course. Thank You," Liz replied.

Am I going nuts or is Elizabeth avoiding looking at that woman? Jess puzzled. *Never mind, just make like a nice guest.* "We really can't thank you enough for rescuing us. I don't know what we would have done if you hadn't."

Giving her head a quick shake, their hostess replied, "I can see none of this is your fault. But please stay here while I get the car ready for Danvers to bring you away. Let me remind you, no matter who or what you hear, do not open these doors. I can't have my father disturbed by seeing you. I'll come back and let you know when all is ready."

Before either sister could voice a question, the young woman in gleaming white had glided backward and out of the room, closing the double doors before her. For a sec, Liz stared after their hostess, a queer expression once more troubling her. Before Jessica could ask what gave, Elizabeth startled her by abruptly coming to life with, "Can you beat that?! Why's she so determined to hide us from dear old Dad? What's she afraid he's going to do? Shoot us?"

"Do you really want to find out—the hard way?" Jessica cracked, taking a load off her feet on the couch, spreading out her dark chiffon skirt. "I don't want to think about anything but resting these little tootsies—until Danvers pulls up in his chariot."

Per their hostess's instructions, Elizabeth finished depositing her packages on the table, then turned back to question, "Jessica, doesn't this place give you the shivers? No? Maybe it's just the cool reception." She sat down in the wingback chair with a mildly interested glance at the tea, adding, "What's the story with these people?"

All mock innocence, Jessica offered, "They don't like strangers pounding on their door in the middle of the night?"

"That doesn't explain why they've locked us in here."

"Liz, I don't think she locked—"

"Maybe not, but why's she so afraid that her father will see us when he comes back from wherever?" Liz insisted.

Jessica rested her elbow on the arm of the couch, her cheek propped against her hand, thinking. The flickering firelight actually made Liz look sinister. She shook her head to clear the creeping uneasiness her sister's suggestion brought, then tried to laugh, "Oh, Liz, come off it! You're being absurd. You'd think we were in the middle of one of my program's episodes."

"That's kind of what your buddy, Scott, had planned, isn't it?"

26

"What's that supposed to mean?" Jessica puzzled.

Before Liz could reply, the doors opened just enough to re-admit the young woman.

"Are you both ready?" she asked quickly.

From her chair, facing Jessica, not their hostess, Liz briefly closed her eyes with relief.

On her feet, Jess promised, "We'll be no more trouble to you. I can't thank you enough, Miss . . ." She reached for a name less familiar than Jamie, ". . . Saunders? Saunders, is it?"

Liz slowly got up, tiredly looking down.

The young woman regarded both sisters peculiarly. A funny smile played on her lips as she queried, "You two really don't know where you are, do you?"

Jess and Liz exchanged glances. Jessica spoke for them, "I guessed from something the cabbie said that this is the Saunders residence—and that your family wouldn't welcome us. He didn't say why. Whatever the case, I'm very grateful that you're giving us a helping hand."

"And did old Jones say why he thought you might not be welcome?" the young woman asked slowly.

"No. I assumed that you were amongst the people who thought the idea of a radio program about, um, a ghost at the Carlyle place was in bad taste," Jessica awkwardly explained.

Liz was surprisingly quiet, but maybe not so surprisingly. She was not the kind of gal who liked to miss anything that promised to sound juicy. That was what Jessica initially thought, except her sister actually seemed to be watching those shadows surrounding the girl.

"Yes, a question of taste." Their hostess's words jerked Jessica from her thoughts. Jess found herself moved as Jamie Saunders' words came slowly, even a little sadly. "You might say that. It's not a tale my family relishes being broadcast in any form. But I'm afraid you wouldn't understand."

"I'm sorry," was all Jessica could say, "Miss Saunders."

"No, not Miss Saunders. Blasko," she quietly corrected. "Saunders was my mother's maiden name. I'm Jamie Blasko."

She faced Jessica as if expecting her to recognize the significance of this correction. Jess didn't, feeling as if she's missed the boat and was sinking fast. Turning to her sister, Jess saw that Liz was just as lost.

"Ah, very well," the girl responded quickly, perceiving the genuine lack of recognition in her two "guests." "Danvers is here, and you must leave before my father returns. He's not ready to see . . . Anyway, I can hear the car outside."

She turned and led them through the foyer, back to the front door, explaining, "My father took the best car across to the city since he could not use the telephone. I'm afraid you'll have to make do with our service vehicle."

"If it was manufactured after the first Great War, I'm happy," Elizabeth asserted.

Jess was amazed that her sister hadn't tried to pump this Jamie Blasko about her identity, about what her father wasn't ready for. Jess was darned intrigued, herself. Did this family have some connection to their program's story? Still, it wouldn't pay to offend anyone who could get them away from here and into a nice, soft bed. Apparently, as much as it killed her, Liz had the same idea. Her sister said no more than to offer apologies and thanks to this Miss Blasko, who efficiently spirited them both into the back seat of a Studebaker station wagon, behind a taciturn Danvers. They so quickly sped away, Elizabeth hadn't even the chance to cry, "Don't spare the horses!"

Yet Elizabeth's uneasy, lingering glance over her shoulder as they pulled away hinted to Jessica that her sister had something on her mind other than a soft, welcoming bed. Well, it could all wait until morning, if a good night's sleep didn't bury the question in the back of her brain.

Chapter Four
October 16th, Thursday Morning

Morning sunlight glowed red through Jessica Minton's sleepy, closed eyelids. Drifting away, she stretched her legs all the way down to her toes, careful not to disturb a sleeping cat. *Wait! Dusty was back in the New York apartment, reigning over Lois Wong.* Instinctively, Jessica's hand shot out for James. *No, he wasn't there, either.* A momentary twinge. Neither husband nor cat snuggled near in this delicious bed. But she was still so sleepy that the firm comfort of this Queen bed made her forget her loss and soothed her back toward dreamland.

As she drowsed, memories of last night drifted and collided in Jessica's head. The cavernous foyer of Carlyle House was rendered vague by its shadows and her exhaustion. Scott and Gerry had been off searching for them once the car was returned to roadworthiness. The housekeeper had greeted them and seen them to their rooms. Not exactly Gale Sondergaard or Judith Anderson—much younger. Jess seemed to have a vague impression of her being fashionably dressed in periwinkle blue. Had the woman raised an eyebrow when they'd related their awkward stop at the Saunders' place? She certainly hadn't explained the inhabitants' less-than-welcoming attitude toward the radio show. Jessica had some sort of impression of—what was the housekeeper's name? Oh yes, Jeanne Rivers—of Jeanne Rivers being far too efficient getting the Minton sisters settled in to be concerned with anything as frivolous as town gossip. Whatever the case, Jess resolved her main interest would be to give Scott Zimkiewicz the dickens for not warning them about local resentments.

Anyway, time to wake up and see if the room was as delightful as she fuzzily remembered from stumbling through her bedtime ablutions and into the ice-blue nightgown that had been unpacked and laid out across the bed. Better yet, time to take a gander out those nearly ceiling-to-window-seat windows extending almost entirely across the wall to her right: the source of the ruddy light peeping under her still closed lids.

Jessica opened her eyes and turned her head to see a lovely, soft-blue sky wisped with pristine white clouds. From her position in bed, that was all she could see. It was still far more than she'd made out last night when she'd been unable to resist the temptation, exhausted as she'd been, to draw back the curtains on an impenetrable darkness. The night's wind had rattled the panes, not in a frightening way, but sinking her into a dream of wildly romantic freedom—like a night at Wuthering Heights or on the moors, but with central heating and no melodramatic nut cases.

Sitting up and stretching, Jess gave her room a once over, just to clarify her fuzzy impressions of the night before. Her spacious bed faced a maple paneled wall with an ornate, though not rococo, fireplace of russet marble carved with mythic pastoral figures and plants. Crystal candelabras, tastefully framed small artwork, and a clock resided on the mantel. She squinted to read the ornate timepiece across the room: 9:30. Hmm, somehow, she'd expected to sleep much later after the day she and Liz had had. Her stomach rumbled. Apparently, it was late enough as far as an empty tummy was concerned. Nevertheless, Jessica took her time surveying the room, indulging herself in a luxurious setting she could never afford, herself.

To the right of the fireplace, close to the angle where the walls joined, was a door to a walk-in closet. The clothing and accessories sent on ahead had all been unpacked to reside in state there, as Jeanne had informed her. The wall across the room to the left held two doors. The one furthest right led to the outer corridor and the other to a private powder room with a large wardrobe next to it. One of her favorite parts of the suite was the spacious area between Jess and that wall: a sitting area with a loveseat, chairs, and a low table—perfect for entertaining a guest or for solitary reading. It would be fun to invite Liz, fellow player Maura Robinson, and writer Beverly McDuff in for a pot of tea or a carafe of coffee.

Throwing back the covers, Jessica slipped her feet into a pair of slippers. Her fawn crêpe dressing gown with its *faux* fur collar was laid out carefully on a chair near her bed. Quickly, Jess put on and belted the dressing gown, grateful for the thoughtful care of Carlyle House's workers. Even with all this luxurious living, what drew Jessica like a magnet was that row of windows spanning at least half the wall, sunlight glittering through their somewhat wavy panes. In just a moment, she crossed to the windows and pulled back the curtains a tad more. Though the lawn extending beneath her was tawny from drought, its hue only added to the autumn glory of soft orange and flaming leaves beautifully complementing the crisp blue sky. This was the fall she loved to drink in, that took her breath away.

A little wooden footbridge curved over a cleft of indeterminate depth, crossing the small Peron River running into the estuary bay, the bay beyond the view of her window. A few seagulls wheeled across the pure blue, challenging it and each other, sometimes fiercely.

Jessica's eyes followed a brown-grey juvenile, who dipped wildly toward the bridge, then down into the cleft. Her shining eyes shifted past the bridge and down a well-traveled path into the cool of the woods. No Universal horror film of twisted trees here. Instead, something brilliantly beautiful without the garishness sometimes marring Technicolor. *Darn it all that James was missing this. A walk into those woods would be sheer delight to share with him. Maybe a Wordsworth-based quip from him? Certainly not the Coleridge-strange of last night. Still, the dark beauty of the eerie had its pleasures: Coleridge, Debussy, and Val Lewton could be wonderfully haunting.*

An awkward but demanding knock on her door jerked Jessica from her thoughts. She turned, hands on hips to face the door, then laughed on hearing a familiar voice: "Hey! Up and at 'em, kiddo! This thing's heavy. I'm not exactly Charles Atlas, you know."

"Coming, Liz!"

Across the room in a snap, Jess opened the door on her smartly turned-out sister: flowing cocoa-colored slacks and matching jacket that opened in the front in two graceful drapes over a white jewel-neck blouse; dark hair in elegant pompadour bangs and bun. In her hands, Liz hefted a tray laden with a silver coffee urn, two china cups and saucers, plates, cutlery rolled in linen napkins, pots of jam and honey, and a napkin-covered serving dish. The scent was so heavenly that Jessica's tummy rumbled a reiteration of its earlier demand.

"I come bearing eats," Elizabeth announced with a knowing grin.

"Well, come right in," Jessica invited with a sweep of her arm, her sister sailing through before words and gesture were completed.

As Elizabeth set up the repast on the low table, Jessica rubbed her hands together. Scurrying over, she declared, "You are a lifesaver, Liz! I'm starving! How did you know?"

Liz paused from pouring the coffee to remind her sister, "You ought to know by now that when I get a feeling about something, I'm always on the money. So sit. Enjoy."

Jessica smiled as her sister settled on the loveseat. Taking the chair, Jess poked at the basket of fresh-baked croissants before admitting, "Liz, I could eat a horse!"

"No Seabiscuit sausage, I'm afraid," her sister replied before removing the cover from the plate, "but *these* links and eggs are pretty nifty."

Giving her sister a smile, Jess started to dig in but paused to ask, "How about you, Liz? I don't see another plate. You already ate?"

"Oh, ages ago," Elizabeth dismissed the questions. "I had a dandy repast in the kitchen with the girls."

"The girls?" Jess paused, only briefly, over a flaky bit of croissant.

"Sure. In the kitchen. The gals who do all the work around here," Elizabeth matter-of-factly explained as she treated her coffee to cream and sugar.

"That's awfully proletarian of you," Jess observed curiously. "Don't the Carlyles mind? I mean, I don't have a problem; but it's kind of irregular, isn't it, in a big house like this?"

"It isn't if you want to get the skinny on what gives with the resentments of the Saunders and Blaskos and Carlyles."

Jessica wryly observed, "I bet they could have used you in the Secret Service."

"Mmm, you can get cute about my investigative skills, Jess, but I know you're as curious as I was about the reception we got from Jamie Blasko and her pet ghoul."

"I have to admit, I wish that Scott hadn't dropped us in the middle of the town feuds and scandals," Jessica allowed. "Maybe if I'd been more in the know, I could have said or done something to win over that Jamie, or at least put her mind at ease."

"I doubt it. Jamie Blasko's mother was Felicia, the ghost gal you're going to be playing on the air. That's why there's no love lost between the families."

Jessica's coffee cup froze halfway to her mouth. All she managed was, "Wha? What?"

"You heard me, kiddo. Her mother was the murder victim or a gal who did a disappearing act. Your pal Scott and his writers are broadcasting the worst moment of that poor kid's life."

Jessica put down her cup, saying, "Good Grief, Elizabeth. It's a wonder she didn't throw us out on our ear, ears. She actually gave us transportation here. In her shoes, I'd have tossed us to the Demon Dog."

"Hound of Hades," her sister corrected.

"*Now* you get it right," Jess shook her head. "Oh, I feel like such a heel."

"Take it easy, kid. You thought everyone involved was either out of the picture or had agreed to digging up—so to speak—the story," Liz tried to comfort her. "That's how it sounded to me, what you told me about your director's description of the situation."

Jess sighed, reflecting, "Come to think of it, Scott really didn't say much definite. Just that there was a haunted house here on this island and that the family was excited to do our show. I wonder, does Scott know the whole story? He must, to have come out here and talked things over with the Carlyle family. It's just not like him to be so ratings crazy that he'd be this insensitive. It's the fault of our sponsor's brother-in-law, the one who's taken charge of the business while Mr. Wellstone is recovering from his heart attack. This guy will do anything to drive up the ratings and make a quick buck."

Jessica broke from her conjectures to refocus on her sister, "Elizabeth, is there anything else I should know before I put my other foot in a hornet's nest?"

Liz Minton shrugged, answering, "I wish I knew. That Jeanne Rivers rode in on her broomstick, and the girls clammed up tighter than a fifty-cent shoe in the pouring rain."

Jess smiled weakly at the metaphor but countered her sister's assessment of the housekeeper: "Liz, I don't remember anything of the hooked nose, peaked hat, and demonic cackle about Miss Rivers. In fact, she seemed rather youngish and smart in that periwinkle dress."

"It's all in the eyes," Elizabeth pronounced knowingly. "Those girls scattered like chickens when a hawk decides to pay a call—even Lu, her second-in-command."

Jess was impressed that her sister had not only pumped the help for intel, but had sussed out the pecking order amongst them. That was her sister, all right! She only commented, tongue in cheek, "Imagine, a housekeeper not wanting the help to sit around gossiping about their employers with the guests. So, what did Miss Rivers say to *you*?"

Her sister shrugged, "Oh, all very tactful. Suggested I might better enjoy a walk on the grounds since the weather was so nice—or maybe I might want to see if my sister needed me."

"How evil! Playing the guilt card on top of the consideration one. You were outfoxed, Elizabeth. I think that's why you're calling her witchy," Jessica chuckled.

"Hey, at least I got part of the lowdown," Liz countered. "It takes an early fox to con this chicken out of her worm."

Jess started to comment but stopped. Maybe it was best to let mangled metaphors rest in peace. *Oh Gosh! I'm doing it now, too!*

"Liz, all machinations aside, Miss Rivers might have been on to something when she suggested taking a walk and enjoying the grounds." Jessica was on her feet, urging her sibling to follow her, "C'mere and take a peek out these windows."

The sisters paused at the window seat that extended beneath the wall of glass. Yet, what nabbed their attention wasn't the glorious fall beauty.

"Say, Jess, isn't that your colleague Gerry Davis out there?" Liz queried. "And he's talking to some girl. That's an odd shadow by her . . . oh no, it must be one of the darned swooping gulls. Sure, but who is she . . . oh. For the love of Mike, it's, yes, it's . . ."

"Jamie Blasko," Jessica finished, surprised, even puzzled.

"Hmph, what's she doing in enemy territory?" Elizabeth's long finger contemplatively tapped her cheek.

"It kind of looks as if she's here for Gerry," Jess extrapolated, "the way they're talking. But I can't imagine what she'd want to say to him, considering why he's here and all . . . It doesn't look as if she's just arrived, though, to me."

"I wish we could see their faces, but they're too far away," Elizabeth sighed. "I'd love to know what they're saying."

"It's probably none of our business," Jess playfully chided. "But if she's friendly with Gerry, then maybe—"

"Look," Liz cut in. "Gerry's holding one of my packages. I thought I was short one, but I was too tired to count right last night."

"You must have left it in her drawing room or the car," Jess surmised. "It certainly was really kind of her to bring it over after all—"

"There's more to it than that, I'll bet you," Liz speculated. Then she turned to her sister and ordered, "Okay, slip into your walking duds, and we'll go out there for my package. I think it's the gold bag I bought. Don't stand there gawking. Snap to it!"

"I don't feel all that comfortable running into her, with what I know now, Liz," Jessica protested. "Let's wait until she leaves. Besides, I don't want to butt in on them."

Elizabeth was about to fume, when they both saw Jamie Blasko turn on her heel from Gerry and head for the bridge. Gerry, who had an artificial leg thanks to the Germans at Anzio, hobbled after her, aided by his cane. He caught up at the bridge, a hand on the young woman's elbow detaining her. There was a moment of hesitation before Jamie freed her arm, though not as abruptly as she might have.

"This is better than *John's Other Wife*," Liz remarked.

"Never mind that," Jessica ordered, steering her sister away from the window and Gerry Davis's anxious moment.

Liz, however, had other ideas, suddenly marching her sister toward the powder room with, "Fine, just clean up and throw on something walkable so we can go out and get my package. Missy Blasko is gone, so you've got no more excuse to hide in here."

"What about Gerry?" Jessica protested. "I don't want to run into him after an emotional scene. He may be embarrassed."

"He'll be fine by the time you get dressed," Elizabeth pronounced, giving her sister a shove into the powder room after she'd opened its door with her free hand. "You're the one who's been boasting about autumn walks here. Now's your chance to put your money where your mouth is. So, shake a leg."

Peeking back around the door, Jessica inquired sweetly, "Liz, are you sure Miss Rivers suggested you take a walk—or was it a hike? I think there's a short pier somewhere around the corner of the house."

"Why you! Get in there and make it snappy!" Liz commanded, but she was grinning.

Chapter Five

Jessica and Elizabeth moved rapidly across the gallery to the stairs leading into a foyer far less foreboding than last night's shrouding shadows had suggested. The place seemed downright cheery now: light wood paneling; polished antique furniture; and a runner on the stairs in a tasteful mélange of greens, blues, gold, and salmon Victorian swirls.

Jessica Minton was a woman on a mission, hands in the pocket of her soft-orange, linen blazer with black line checks complementing her black blouse and linen trousers. This mission irritated the dickens out of her sister, as it slowed down *her* mission of package retrieval.

"You don't have to call James right now," Elizabeth insisted. "Sure you told him you'd phone this morning, but you don't have to check in this minute."

They were fairly bouncing down the carpeted stairs as Jessica set her sister straight, "We agreed I'd call him at ten. He's waiting by the house phone in the faculty digs." A glance at her watch, the one James had given her, then, "Yikes! It's almost ten now, and I have no idea where the phone is! He'll be wondering if he doesn't hear from me."

"Fiddlesticks! What does he think could have happened?"

"Liz, if I tell him everything that *did* go wrong, I won't be off the line until Christmas," Jessica deadpanned as they reached the foyer floor.

Almost directly across from the front entrance, the drawing room doors unexpectedly opened, admitting a tall woman in her late twenties/early thirties into the foyer. Her medium-length, honey-brown hair was pulled back from her face more elegantly than severely, and she appeared surprisingly stylish in a shirt-wait dress, black with white pinstripes. The professional appearance, in addition to the take-charge expression on her face, clearly signaled she was high on the totem pole of employees in Carlyle House.

"Good morning, Miss Rivers," Jessica pleasantly greeted her. Perhaps she expressed a little extra congeniality to make up for her sister's earlier attitude toward the woman for just doing her job. "Do you remember, last night, I told you that I needed to make a phone call to my husband this morning at ten? Unfortunately, I have no idea where to find the phone. Would you help me?"

"Certainly, Miss Minton," Jeanne Rivers smoothly answered. "I was beginning to debate whether I should wake you. You and your sister had such a difficult evening, I hated to disturb you—although your sister seemed to have gotten up with the birds and gone exploring."

Jess put a tight hold on Liz's arm before her sister could make an unwise rejoinder, justifiable or not. Jess didn't have time to referee; she needed to make her call.

Now Jeanne Rivers was explaining, "Right over here. Under the stairs is the telephone alcove."

Jess loved the old-style, closet-sized alcove with its plush built-in seat and papered walls of turquoise peacocks on a cream background. At least the phone sitting on its shelf was the modern kettle design.

Jeanne Rivers smiled, "I know, quaint. But you are in a Victorian house, and this was the latest thing in the 1890s. At least Mr. Carlyle replaced the crank phone years back. So, take a seat."

As Jessica slid in, she glimpsed Liz giving her an impatient eyeball. Nevertheless, she'd promised James this call, and she so wanted to hear his wry English accent.

"Here," the housekeeper instructed. "Just dial 'O,' and Ida, the island's operator on Thursdays, will pick up so you can give her your number. She'll put through your long-distance call."

Jessica cocked her head and queried as she lifted the receiver, "Is this the only phone in the house?"

"Heavens no," Jeanne dryly smiled. "I have a line for house business in the kitchen. Mr. Carlyle has his own private line in his study."

Jess nodded and the lines of communication were eventually fostered by the operator all the way to Ballard College.

James picked up partway through the first ring. He did have to get through Ida, first, but when he succeeded, Jessica teased, "You must have been sitting on that phone. That would have been an interesting, if uncomfortable, sight!"

"Pretty clever, aren't you?" he teased back.

Jess knew she was smiling like a teenager—and that her husband was, too.

James was speaking again, "So, everything all right at your end? You finally got in and all settled?"

Jess hesitated. No sense in telling him right now how much of a dog's dinner their evening had been. Darned if she weren't starting to talk like him more and more!

"Eventually. There was a mix-up on taxis, but we finally got in all right and fell into the most deliciously comfortable beds."

"Lucky you. I've slept in nicer fields and forests than the bundle of stones they call a bed in this faculty housing," James cracked.

"I'm sorry about that. I do wish you could be here."

"In the bed?" The voice was all innocence but not innocent enough to keep Ida, who hadn't yet gotten off the line, from snorting.

"James!" Jessica chided, though impishly. "We are not alone." She paused, genuine feeling now, "I really miss you."

"Me, too." His tone was quiet, sincere. Then, "But we've had worse separations, love. I think we'll pull through."

"If you finish your work sooner than expected, you could join me," she proposed hopefully. "You'd love it here."

"I'll try to put a rush on it."

She could picture his gentle smile, and she tried not to feel too guilty about not mentioning Felicia's ghost. She'd just steer him clear of Saunders House and Jamie Blasko.

"I guess we're running up a fortune in long-distance charges. I'd better let you go," Jessica reluctantly said.

"Right then. If you give me the number there, I'll call you same time next week. Agreed?"

"You got it, mister!" Jess promised cheerily, but hating to let James go.

Simultaneously, they both said, "Write?"

"You bet," Jessica promised, her husband concurring. The Carlyle number, printed on a round card in the center of the dial, was given, goodbyes exchanged, and Jessica was slowly replacing the receiver. As she sank back in her seat, she briefly flicked something moist from the corner of her eye.

Glancing outside, she expected to see her sister busting a gasket to get her package. Instead, Liz looked quietly sympathetic. *My sister is a good kid.*

Clapping her hands on her knees, Jess got up and said as she exited the alcove, "Okay, Liz, let's go get your bundle from Gerry."

"If he's still out there!" But Liz was only pretending impatience.

"Yes, I saw him from the French doors," Jeanne Rivers informed them. "In fact, it will be quicker for you to exit by them, right through the drawing room, over there."

Briefly, Jessica wondered if Jeanne had seen Jamie out there, too—and was the girl welcome? But Jess only had a moment for that thought before Elizabeth snatched her by the arm to hustle her through the drawing room and out the French doors onto a stone-flagged terrace.

For a moment, the wind died away, allowing Jessica's long dark hair to rest about her shoulders. While Elizabeth scanned for Gerry and her package, Jess strolled over to one of the urns along the balustrade and examined its carvings of the fantastical creatures amongst sea shells and waves or lush greenery. *Beautiful! And how about this deft blending of peach and orchid pansies or creamy marigolds and purple asters arranged in the elaborate urns. At least one of the big families on this island appeared not to have fallen on hard times.* She looked back at the house itself. It rose three stories high, not including the attic, all gothic angles and decorations. Only gargoyles were missing. A one-story extension reached from the front of the main building into the drive. After a spacing of several feet, a line of windows, shades pulled, flanked almost half the addition's length. Buttresses of granite blocks edged the left end of the wall facing her and the point where the one-story extension attached to the building.

"Whew, these are some neat digs," Jessica concluded. "I wonder if the other side has a one-floor extension, too. A design ought to balance."

"Of course it does," Liz answered. "That side is the kitchen and," here she crinkled her nose and upper lip, "Miss Rivers' lair, er, room."

Elizabeth's tone suddenly brightened when her scan of the green prompted a happy, "Oh, there's Gerry! On that bench, near the edge."

Liz gave Jessica's sleeve a quick pluck, then was off through the gap in the balustrade. Jessica paused to spot Gerry, his back to them, sitting forward on a wrought iron bench overlooking the cliff above the estuary. She followed her sister, but slowly, in no hurry to disturb Gerry too soon after his and Jamie Blasko's disagreement. He'd come here earlier, with Scott and the crew, for one reason or another. So, he'd have had time to meet the young woman, but what about the opportunity? Well, she'd better hustle after her sister to make sure that in the process of getting her package Liz didn't poke her nose where she shouldn't.

The sun felt decisively warm on her head. The scent of the estuary beyond the lawn was fresh and slightly tangy as Jessica caught Liz and then trotted past her to call, "Gerry! Beautiful morning, isn't it?"

Gerry Davis turned and waved a greeting. Jess could see that he was genuinely glad to see the sisters, but not before something troubled in his eyes swiftly disappeared into his smile.

Coming up along Gerry's left, for a moment, Jessica's eye was caught by the cliff of about twenty feet above a whitish beach. Not exactly the cliffs of Cornwall, but enough height to break a bone or two if you took an unexpected Brody off it. Well-kept wooden steps with a rail provided far less hazardous access to the beach below.

"So, you two finally made it here," Gerry grinned. "I thought Scott and I would have to rouse a posse to find you." He turned to Elizabeth on his right to finish, "How the devil did you end up at Saunders' place? We came back when Scott checked in with Rivers, and she told us you'd arrived. At that point, I was so beat, I just turned in. I thought Scott was going to have kittens after he found out where you'd been. He really wants to see you this morning."

Jessica sat down next to Gerry and warned, "I don't think he does. Just wait until I get my hands on Mr. Z! I don't know how wise you are to the people involved in this Carlyle ghost story, but there was some kind of mix-up on cabs that really put Liz and me on the spot!"

"You can say that again!" Liz pronounced, proprietarily eyeing the package at Gerry's feet.

"Once is enough," Jessica asserted. "Anyway, apparently, Scott's taxi got called away on an emergency, and the fellow the cabbie got to replace him was an old guy who mixed up his creepy mansions."

"Just our luck, we landed on a two-haunted-house island," Liz added her two cents.

Jess finished, "We got dropped off in the lap of the daughter of our murdered ghost. Can you beat that? The poor girl! I feel terrible. She must be some kind of saint, not to throwing us out on our tuffets."

"Jamie's a good kid," Gerry quietly concurred, looking out to the estuary's silver-blue swells with their white manes.

Jess shared a glance with her sister, whose look urged her to proceed. Beginning carefully, Jessica ventured, "Gerry, you sound as if you know her. But you've been here less than a week."

Gerry turned his dark eyes on Jessica to point out wryly, "Sometimes, it doesn't take that long. A chance meeting on walks in the woods, along the beach . . ."

"You sound sweet on her," Liz conjectured thoughtfully, concern for her package pushed to the background.

"Do I?" He glanced back at Elizabeth with a faint smile. "That would be nuts, wouldn't it? All things considered."

"You mean your being part of the radio program that's dragging her mother's murder into the public eye?" Jess posited. "And, of course, you do live three states away."

"Don't forget that you hardly know each other, too," Elizabeth added from Gerry's other side.

Gerry shook his head, looking from one sister to the other, almost laughing, "What? Are the two of you ganging up on me?"

"Yes," Jessica smiled kindly. "We both think you're a swell guy; we both don't want you to rush into a brick wall. You don't know this girl, and I could see in the brief time I met her that she's carrying a lot inside her."

"Something dark and painful," Elizabeth quietly added.

That gave Jessica pause. She'd only meant that the young woman had seemed troubled, as she well might be by their program stirring up old hurts. Yet Liz seemed to have caught onto something deeper.

Gerry distracted Jessica by calmly but determinedly disagreeing, "Maybe, since life's handed her a raw deal, she could use a helping hand from someone who's caught his own share of bad breaks but managed to come out okay."

His eyes lingered briefly on his artificial leg.

Jessica put a hand on her friend's arm and said, "You know you're one hell of a guy. Any girl would be darned lucky to get you."

41

"Then why am I still single?" Gerry smiled, but Jess caught a twinge of something else in his eyes. His glance fell on the package, and Gerry changed the subject: "Oh, can you beat that? We've been beating our gums about Jamie and why she came, but the reason completely slipped my mind." He reached down to lift up the bundle and say, "You left this in the house or the car. I forget which she said."

"Thanks!" Liz replied, snatching the package with an avidity that seemed to make up for her distraction by Gerry's love life.

"I'd count my fingers if I were you," Jessica dryly suggested.

Gerry returned, "I have quick reflexes."

"Wise guys," Liz pretended to grumble.

The three became quiet, taking in the soft blue of the sky; the warmth of the October morning; and, across the waters, the brilliant oranges flamed with crimson or the soft greens melting into the yellow of the trees. The pleasure of the experience gave Jessica time to work up the nerve to probe further: "Gerry, I don't want to do anything wrong here, but what do you know about Scott's program? What is the whole lowdown on the scandal or ghost story or whatever you want to call it? What am I getting into here?"

Gerry shook his head, "I'm just about as much in the dark as you. Beyond telling me it's her mother's story we're playing with, the whole deal has been off-limits with Jamie. Scott? He's playing it close to the vest. Wants to keep the 'surprise' fresh, though I think that's more from pressure by the sponsor's brother-in-law. All I know is that this lady may have been murdered. And Scott's kept me away from the village, so there wouldn't be much chance for me to hear gossip."

Liz helpfully offered, "You should try hanging around the kitchen."

"Walter Winchell has nothing on my sister," Jessica observed with a shake of her head.

"I'll keep that in mind," Gerry promised, less than seriously. He added, "To be honest, I haven't wanted to probe into Jamie's past more than she wanted to tell me."

"The script arriving on Monday will put the kibosh on that plan," Jessica pointed out.

Gerry nodded, folding his arms, and agreed, "I guess you're right. I'll just have to cross that bridge when I come to it." He shook his head. "I guess it is all pretty hopeless. How could she see me as anything but trouble while I'm involved in the show? She must despise me. You should have seen how angry she was at me before you came out. By the way, please don't mention to Scott I've been seeing her. He'll probably make a big stink, say I'm going to learn too much too soon. I can see him trying to put a stop to everything, not that there's all that much to put a stop to."

"I don't know about that," Elizabeth opined, sitting down next to Gerry.

"How's that?" Gerry puzzled.

"It seems to me," Liz disagreed, "that Miss Blasko could easily have sent that pickle-puss butler to deliver my package. She didn't have to come herself. And if she really has no interest in you, why does she keep bumping into you? It also seems to me that she would have told you where the dog died as soon as she found out who you were. Made an end of things then and there. But she still bumps into you, right?"

"Say," Gerry began, hopefully, "You have something there, Elizabeth."

Liz shrugged, "What, I'm not sure. But there's something going on, to my mind. Where it will go . . . ?"

"Be careful," Jessica cautioned the hopeful Gerry. "I don't mean to be the one to throw cold water—"

"I know, Jess." Gerry put a hand over hers. "I'll go slow. I'm not exactly set to be the next Jesse Owens with this leg."

Jessica laughed, and Gerry was up, saying, "Thanks, you two. Ah well, I've had enough fresh air for now. See you at lunch. Oh, should I tell Scott to come out here to see you?"

"You can tell Scott to—"

Liz slid over and put a hand over Jessica's mouth, answering, "I'm sure we'll bump into Mr. Zimkiewicz sooner or later. I think my sister and I will take a little stroll in the woods."

"Sure," Gerry grinned. "There's an easy path through the trees once you cross the bridge. It leads to a nifty clearing with a pond. Rivers clued me in to it when I first arrived." He thought a sec, then proposed, "Say, how about I take in your bundle, Liz, and have it delivered to your room?"

"Sounds like a swell idea," Liz concurred.

"Okay. See you gals later."

With her sister's hand still covering her mouth, Jessica nodded and waved her fingers at Gerry as he moved off with an alacrity that would have surprised anyone unfamiliar with his dexterity on an artificial limb and cane.

Jessica removed her sister's hand and charged, "What the hey?! What's the deal with the hand over my mouth? You were just as steamed as I was with Scott."

"Sure. I just love doing that to you."

Jessica gave her sister a greatly threatening fish eye but relented when Liz added, "Besides, it cracked Gerry up. You got to admit the guy deserves a chuckle."

"Especially at *my* expense?"

Elizabeth shrugged "innocently."

"Oh, all right," Jessica relented. "C'mon. There's a bosky dell waiting to be explored, Daniella Boone."

Chapter Six

The clearing around the stream-fed pool was not nifty. Dreamy, romantic, otherworldly, but far more imagination-inspiring than "nifty." That was Jessica Minton's conclusion as she sat on the curved stone bench positioned on a flat slate-colored slab lipping the pool. The good-sized pond was kept clear and alive by that stream rushing from a cleft in a towering boulder to her right, then racing off through a break in the enormous glacier-strewn rocks that encircled the clearing, creating its seclusion. Chickadees and Titmice scolded in rough voices from the surrounding forest. Occasionally, a chipmunk poked out a head or half his torso from the gaps in the rocks surrounding the pond.

Clearly visible beneath the pool's waters were the rocks on its bottom and fish darting among the roots of water lilies or hiding beneath their flat, green, cleft leaves. More than one dragonfly zig-zagged over the water, flashing brilliant green or scarlet or creamy blue. A "melodious plot/ of beechen green, and shadows numberless." That thought surged melancholy through her. James was stuck amidst dusty stacks of letters and books, beloved writings but no comparison to this dreamy autumn idyll.

Jessica's glance drifted to a narrow passage between two enormous, New England-grey and moss-painted boulders providing entry to this Algernon Blackwood slice of fairy. A carved Green Man, more friendly than leering, seemed merged into one of the stones by delicately flaky grey-green lichen. To Jess, the natural setting had been embraced, not civilized, by human imagination. The pointers to this lovely enclave had brought home that perception: painted ceramic tiles that trees had grown into, with one affixed to the other side of an entrance boulder.

There was a flash of red and a Cardinal's clucking in the lemony leaves of trees behind and above Jess. Her eyes shifted back across the pond, rimmed by grey boulders with cushions of kelly moss, to the trees beyond.

Some leaves still held their summer color, creating a soft ambiance. *Mmm hmm, this sure seems like a bosky dell.*

But Jessica's eyes now rested on her sister, who had thrown caution to the winds concerning her duds by leaning against an elm, thinking. *Trying to make up her mind about Leo McLaughlan? Just as much haunted by the romance of this setting as me? Something was eating Elizabeth. She hadn't said a word in minutes. Well, Liz might like to talk but she was not one to be coerced into spilling. But going indirect might work.*

"I can see why Gerry and Jamie Blasko might have been romantically inspired if they met up here," Jessica mused.

"What?" Liz blinked, coming out of her thoughts. "What's that?"

"You *are* out in left field," Jessica laughed. "Heck, are you even in the ballpark?"

Liz narrowed her eyes and returned, "Don't get smart. What were you saying, anyway? About Gerry? Romance?"

Leaning against the leg she'd propped on the bench, Jess answered, "I was saying how romantic, idyllic, this place is."

"I do keep expecting Bambi and Thumper to wander in," Liz quipped.

"Anyway," Jess continued, "I can't say as I blame Gerry for having his senses, maybe not snowed, but clouded by meeting a damsel in distress here. How could he help but go dreaming, especially a romantic guy like Gerry? How could anybody not think about *l'amour* here?"

Liz surprised Jessica by not biting on that lead-in to talk about her own romance. Instead, she asked, "Jess, do you think I was too encouraging to Gerry about this Jamie?"

Liz's unexpected response left Jessica fumbling, "I, I don't know. I don't think so. You didn't exactly look up a priest and throw orange blossoms at Gerry."

Liz looked away, pensively folding one arm to prop the other as she rested her chin in the ell of her thumb and forefinger. Something was bothering Elizabeth out of all proportion to the situation.

Jessica pressed, "Gerry is a big boy. He's a wounded veteran and everything. Don't you think he can handle a little disappointment in the romance department? If it even comes to that."

Even as she spoke, Jessica wasn't certain she entirely believed her own words. She didn't like to see her friends hurt, especially Gerry, a romantic with a big heart. Hadn't he already had more pain than he deserved? She finally continued, "I know he and Jamie aren't exactly next-door neighbors, but they might be able to make things work. I mean, marriages have survived the separation of this war." She was on the verge of adding, "Look at James and me," but knew that comparison wouldn't particularly appeal to her sister—although Liz's opinion of James had improved, somewhat, over the years.

"That's not exactly what I'm thinking about," Liz revealed, looking down.

"Of course," Jess realized. "Gerry's involved in a radio show about her mother's death. I'd call that a romance killer. Still, it didn't stop her from seeing him. Maybe Gerry could help her overcome her past. Maybe they could help each other. Isn't that what Gerry said before?"

Liz sighed, slowly circling the pond toward Jessica, kicking aside the scattering of fallen leaves, starting when *she* startled a frog into splashing into the pond. Jessica grinned. However, her humor faded when Liz looked at her, concerned, and resumed, "I think Gerry has bitten off more than he can chew."

Perplexed, Jess responded, "I don't get you. She's not exactly a barracuda in Max Factor like our old pal Mrs. Tewkesbury."

"No," Elizabeth agreed, standing over her sister. "Not in herself."

"Then in whom? Oh, wait, Liz, are you talking about dear old Dad? The fellow she was afraid would see us? Parents can be a problem. Still, our Gerry's a charmer."

"The kid's father is a problem Gerry could probably handle, eventually," Liz hesitated, "but he's not the parent I'm worried about."

"Liz, a person's only got two parents, and her mother is dead . . ." Jessica stared at her sister, shocked by her realization. Finally, she managed, "You aren't saying . . . Wait, before, why did you say two haunted houses . . . ? Are you telling me you saw . . . ?"

Elizabeth sat down beside Jess to explain, "I didn't see anyone, exactly. It was more of a feeling when we were in the Saunders house, around her, screwy as that sounds. But you know when I get my feeling . . ."

Jessica nodded, recalling how Liz's feelings had tipped them both to trouble in the past. But this claim was fantastic!

Elizabeth went on, "Don't you remember, we both felt that peculiar chill around Jamie at the house, even though it was so warm last night? *She* even said that she always felt a chill there."

Jess started to argue that the house was probably just damp, but Liz continued, "I definitely saw, maybe sensed, a shadow around her. Last night, I tried to dismiss it as bad lighting. This morning . . ."

"This morning?!"

"This morning, from the window, I told myself it was the shadow of a gull, but, Jessica, if I'm on the level with myself, there *was* no gull."

Jessica gave Liz a long, hard look. Her big sister was dead serious. Turning back to the pond, Jess concluded, "Darned good thing James couldn't come! Yikes!" Then she faced her sister to puzzle, "Then what the dickens are we doing at Carlyle House if the Saunders place is haunted? Are both of them?"

Elizabeth shrugged, "You got me. I haven't had any sense of something 'off' in Carlyle House—yet. Aside from how afraid the help is of Rivers."

"If labor/management problems were the same as spook infestations, the A F of L would be calling on exorcists not arbitrators," Jess quipped. "You know, if anyone else heard this conversation, he'd classify us as Grade-A screwballs."

"I know," Liz agreed. "That's why we can't really tell anyone, even your director. That's why I don't like this thing between Gerry and Jamie Blasko. It's not as if I can warn him and expect him to take me seriously."

"It'd be a lot for him to swallow." Jessica sighed before adding, "Poor Gerry. Most guys have to worry about their mother-in-law being a witch— not a spook!"

"I don't know that she *is* hostile," Liz ventured. "I just sense something sort of 'haunting' the girl."

"Well, cheer up, Liz. It might not even pan out between them. We'll just have to keep an eye out for trouble and be ready with a sympathetic ear—or Ouija Board."

"Never a dull moment when the Minton sisters get together!" Liz tried to lighten the mood.

Jessica smiled ruefully, reflecting on the truth of those words, evidenced by their having been mixed up in espionage, extortion, blackmail, and murder over the past four years.

Abruptly, the crunch of stones and dead leaves leading into the clearing drew their nervous eyes.

A thirty-ish man, quite tall. So tall he had to duck as he emerged into the clearing. His hair was wavy wheat-brown, with one unruly dash of silver blended into the front over his left eye. The nose ought to have been a bit too large, but the longish square jaw, dark brows, and those deep brown eyes, both mischievous and kind, brought it all together in pleasing harmony. The sports jacket, shirt unbuttoned at the neck, and dark trousers added casual charm.

"Ah, do I see Rosalind and Celia lazing in the Forest of Arden?" he teased.

Jessica was on her feet, eyes sparking as she warned, "Scott Zimkiewicz! Rosalind may have disabused Orlando about the 'very patterns of love.' This Rosalind would love to subject you to the very pattern of a good, swift kick in the pants!"

"Atta girl!" Liz grinned, not bothering to get up.

"Wait a minute! Just what did I do that was so terrible?" Jessica's director kiddingly protested, one hand extended and the other protectively pressed to his chest.

"What did you do?" Jessica demanded, arms akimbo. "How about you left us at the mercy of a cab driver, who probably tootled Noah over to the ark, in the most uncomfortable vehicle since Marie Antoinette took a tumbrel ride to get her head done."

"I couldn't help that," Scott reasoned, coming forward to chance putting his hands on his accuser's shoulders. "You know the Carlyle car had problems. I sent a taxi for you, a reliable one. You, yourself, told Rivers last night that there was a mix-up between the cab drivers. You can't blame me for something I didn't even know about, kid."

Jess shrugged off Scott's hands, persisting, "I'm not done. Liz and I were dropped blind into the lap of the poor girl whose family tragedy I'm going to be turning into 50 minutes of listening entertainment, plus ten minutes from the sponsor. I had no idea that the family was still around to suffer through reliving that tragedy. Do you have any idea of how embarrassed, how guilty I feel? How resentful, how pained that poor girl must feel having me shoved in her face? No wonder Jamie Blasko was worried that her father might see me."

Scott raised a reassuring hand to calm Jessica, "Now you can hold on right there, worrying about the family. I can tell you that Vitus Blasko had no trouble signing a release with our lawyers."

"So you bought him off?" Jess concluded skeptically. Still, she relented enough to say more calmly, "Scott, this isn't like you. You've never gone around hurting people, even for a good story, let alone to make a quick buck. Is this Ungerpreck's bright idea?"

"I'm still a pretty swell guy," Scott tried to kid Jessica out of her indignation. "I'm telling you, no one is being shamed or hurt. Blasko was relieved to get some financial security for his daughter's future. He was even hoping we might shed some light on what actually happened to his wife—give him and his daughter closure."

"Shed some light?" Jessica puzzled. "How? You're no Sherlock Holmes. You and the writers *create* mysteries. You don't solve them."

Scott Zimkiewicz raised an impish eyebrow and tempted, "That's where Bev and I intend to surprise you."

"When?" Jessica pressed. "You claimed you wanted to keep us in the dark over the details so we'd come to the Felicia story fresh, but this is ridiculous. When do we get to see the script? Three minutes before air time? I want some answers."

"And you shall have them," Scott promised confidently. "Tomorrow night at dinner."

Jessica skeptically pressed, "Tomorrow night? Why *then*? Maura and Guy will be here this afternoon. Why not sit us all down today?"

"We-ell, you'll see at dinner-tomorrow night. It will all make sense then."

Jessica's brow creased with trying to decide what to think. Finally, she turned to her sister and asked, "Liz, don't you have anything to add? You were pretty steamed, too."

"You're doing just fine, kid," Liz smiled. "I'm enjoying the show."

"You know," Scott observed wryly, "for someone who's getting a New Hampshire-woods vacation on my tab, you're not helping me much."

Elizabeth arched a brow and replied, "Scott, you're forgetting that I was on the same not-so-merry-go-round as Jess last night. Nope, you're on your own, Ace."

Scott sighed, though not really perturbed. Turning to Jess, he asked with a grin, "Have I ever steered you wrong?"

It was a straight line waiting to be called as one, but Jessica had worked with Scott long enough to know that, though he might be unconventional, he truly was a right guy. She looked to Liz, but her sister shrugged, leaving the final decision up to her.

"You're sure that we aren't hurting the Blaskos?" Jess began tentatively.

"Scout's honor," Scott promised, holding up his hand in pledge formation.

"Okay," Jessica allowed. "I'll give you the benefit of the doubt—until tomorrow night."

Liz warned Scott, "This better be one heck of a dinner."

"No doubt about it," Scott promised with the assurance of a man who had something he knew would WOW!

Then he changed the subject, "So, what say we go back to the house. Maura and Guy should be arriving soon, and I understand there'll be a dandy spread for a buffet lunch."

"I never say no to a good feed," Jess allowed with enthusiasm.

Elizabeth sprang to her feet, grinning, "I guess they're really putting on the dog for us."

That was when a canine howl penetrated their idyllic enclave. It was broad daylight in a drowsy green-gold dell, but all three exchanged leery, unsettled looks.

"No card-carrying Hell Hound would come out in the middle of the day," Jess tried to joke. "The local wouldn't permit it."

"You heard about that legend already?" Scott asked, trying not to survey their environs. "I guess this island is chock full of things that go bump any time of day."

Jessica gave her sister a quiet glance, wondering if Elizabeth would tell Scott about the ghostly Felicia's connection to Jamie. Liz briefly lowered her lids. A definite "no." Instead, Elizabeth said, "I'd like to be chock full of that tasty spread. Let's go!"

There was another howl, no more reassuring for sounding more distant.

"Yep, lunch sounds grand," Scott agreed. "Ladies, let's go."

They didn't dash through the cleft, but they certainly didn't dawdle.

Chapter Seven
Friday, October 17th

The foyer of Carlyle House was bright, almost amber with late afternoon sun, as Jessica Minton came down the staircase. Wearing black and white spectator pumps definitely slowed a girl down on stairs like these if she didn't want to take a flyer. Jess was a little tuckered out, too. The temperature had soared over eighty degrees, peculiar weather for October. So, since *The Wellstone Mystery Hour* had been pre-empted by a sporting event this evening, Jess and Maura had been free to join Liz on the beach below the house. Jeanne Rivers had even procured them bathing suits and caps. Fortunate, because who would have thought to pack that kind of gear for the middle of October? Jess was glad she'd paid at least enough attention to the recent weather to pack this lovely fitted, black linen dress with a sweetheart neckline surrounded by a broad, white-lace collar. It was a favorite number, having seen her through some interesting times.

Reaching the bottom step with a swirl of her full skirt, Jessica paused. Her hand rested on the carved post that concluded the ornate rail on either side of the stairs. *Where to go now?* She was alone because she was early. Unlike the others, she was too restless for a quick catnap or staying in her room to kill time before dinner. Liz had been too preoccupied with rescuing her hair from an afternoon of wind and sun to join her.

What was James up to now? When she was still in New York, he'd said the food at the dining hall was so gruesome it made him long for days of hard bread and turnips in occupied France. Jessica supposed she could have teased him that Carlyle House boasted gourmet comestibles, but she knew she'd enjoy them even more if he were here to share them. Nevertheless, she was not planning to starve herself with regret.

Jessica turned her attention to the drawing room. The late autumn sunlight streaming through the French doors softened the already appealing colors of the room's rug, paneling, and curtains. Maybe she could find a book or newspaper to while away the time in one of the plush chairs. That warm breeze gently swaying the curtains was absolutely delicious. *Better not nod off once you sit down!* There was a kind of Algernon Blackwood dreaminess in the mellowing late afternoon.

Thank goodness Edgar Ungerpreck was nowhere to be seen! Likely off on one of the phones wheeling and dealing. The last thing she wanted was to have this magical autumn afternoon despoiled by his once more harping on how much everyone owed him for what he paid them—and the occasional leer he liked to bestow on the women of the show when he thought he could get away with it. Fortunately, Scott usually ran interference, on top of producing, directing, and writing. If Mr. Wellstone didn't return soon, she might lose her job, and maybe everybody else's, by finally knocking that big donkey Ungerpreck back on his assets. So many people would have been saved so much angst, if Mr. Wellstone's wife had not been so distraught at her husband's illness that she'd allowed her overbearing brother to manage her controlling interest.

Chasing such unpleasantness from her thoughts, Jessica wandered over to the impressive fireplace on the far right. The hearth was tall but not big enough for a girl to walk into—well, why would she? Anyway, the mantel was a tad above her eye level, fine polished marble, with some statuary and candelabra at either end. What particularly drew Jessica's attention was the array of framed photographs, daguerreotypes, and tintypes in between.

Looks as if the family only goes back to the 1850s, less than 100 years. Ha! The upstarts! Jess smiled to herself. *Hmm, there's a fairly good representation up to the 1920s or '30s.*

The most recent pictures were of a thirtyish woman with a strong jaw but kind eyes, an Ethel Barrymore sort, and a serious young man, twenties perhaps, a thatch of thick dark hair, a strong jaw, sharp nose, and piercing dark eyes. The photos seemed to date from around the '20s. Jessica started to reach for the young man's photo, struck by the intensity of those dark eyes but caught herself. *A proper guest doesn't go poking around people's belonging—at least when they weren't suspected of being Nazis or felons.*

No, the Carlyles just lived in a haunted house, haunted by one of their neighbors. Wasn't that odd, even for a haunting? Shouldn't this Felicia be ghosting her own house? Though, according to Elizabeth, this ghostess was doing that, too. Busy beaver, she.

The word "murder" had been dropped in connection with Felicia's mysterious disappearance. *A murder by someone in this house? That would explain her haunting it. Unless she had a special connection to someone here.*

Jessica's eyes returned to those two more recent photos. *Scott had talked about a Philip Carlyle but never mentioned a woman. The clothing and hair of this lady were contemporaneous with the man's. Well,* he was *likely Philip Carlyle. Did that make the lady his wife? Felicia even? No, Felicia was someone else's wife. Her picture wouldn't be here.*

Another perusal of the lady then back to the young man led Jessica to pick up on the family resemblance. *Of course, a sister. They hadn't seen anything of Philip Carlyle because he'd been tied up with his business in Portsmouth, but there was no reason not to have seen her or even heard anything about her. Unless she'd moved away to avoid the scandal, or had she joined Felicia in the great beyond, too shy or aloof to come back and visit?* A look at the woman's kind eyes and Jessica concluded, *No, not aloof.*

It did strike Jessica as odd that, though earlier generations of portraiture included images of children, there were none of the last generation as kiddos.

"You're early, Miss Minton."

The voice of Jeanne Rivers from the doorway drew Jess from her musings to face the housekeeper as she walked into the room, still stylish in a color-block dress of grey and black, her hair elegantly swept up into a pompadour.

"Oh, Miss Rivers, I'm afraid you're right," Jessica pleasantly greeted the other woman. "I thought I might kill some time down here. This room is beautiful."

Jeanne smiled back, her glance shifting to the other side of the spacious room where a sideboard and various paintings adorned the wall, before returning to Jessica. "There are some valuable early Hudson River School paintings on the wall behind me, a Durand and a Church. The first Mr. Carlyle loved artistic beauty. You may not know it, but this mantel is made of precious Carrara marble from Italy and fashioned by the mason Leonardo Manzi. Many of our hearths, including the one in your room, were created by him, as well as the urns on the balustrade."

"I imagine the carvings leading to the clearing and that wonderful green man and bench were also designed by him," Jessica conjectured.

Rivers hesitated a fraction of a second before answering, "Well, no, I'm afraid not. They were done much later, by a lesser talent."

"Oh, well, Liz and I found them beautiful just the same. You know so much about this estate; I imagine you've been here some time," Jessica pleasantly made conversation. "Did you grow up on Birdsong Island?"

"I grew up in this house," Rivers answered. "My mother was housekeeper for some time. I moved away, trying to find my fortune several years back. But, as the song says, 'you'll find your castle in Spain . . . back in your own backyard.'"

"This is quite a castle!" Jessica agreed, spreading her hands.

"Though it's not exactly mine," Jeanne dryly pointed out. "I only work here."

"And your work is what keeps everything running so perfectly," Jessica assured her.

"I try. Plus, I have a promising assistant in Lu Brown," Jeanne allowed. "However, it won't run so smoothly if I don't get back to supervise dinner arrangements. Before I go, is there anything I can get you to keep you amused until the others come down? Perhaps you'd like to listen to the radio?" She nodded at a console against the wall, not far from the French doors.

"Actually, I somehow managed to leave the book I'd been reading at home. It's such a lovely evening that I'd love to sit down with a good read."

"Ah," Jeanne replied knowingly, raising a finger. "Follow me. I think I can help you."

"Okay," Jessica responded, cocking her head curiously.

She followed the housekeeper into the foyer, where Jeanne turned right and down a short corridor, ending in a blank wall. Before they reached that wall, were two doors almost opposite each other. Jeanne threw open the door on the left onto a wonderfully stocked library: floor-to-ceiling bookcases, all fully packed, circled the room. Facing them was a bow window with a cushioned window seat inviting a reader to enjoy the fading warmth of sunlight. As she followed Jeanne Rivers into the room, Jessica noted a fine mahogany desk and a comfortable leather chair to her right. A painting of a beautiful array of wildflowers circling a striking yellow rose was on the wall behind the desk.

Smiling at Jessica's interest in the painting, the housekeeper revealed, "Our founding Mr. Carlyle not only loved art but had a bit of a talent, himself. Not that he let it interfere with his making a successful, enduring manufacturing concern—hard-headed Yankee that he was."

"It's nice to be a Renaissance man," Jessica noted amiably.

"Anyway, Mr. Philip Carlyle may not be an artist, but he is extremely well-read in so many areas," Jeanne explained. "Do you think you could find something to interest you in here?"

Jessica almost gasped, laughing, "Don't you know it!" However, she caught herself and protested, "This is Mr. Carlyle's private library. I wouldn't want to overstep."

"You are Mr. Carlyle's guest," Jeanne assured her. "I've never known him to short-shrift hospitality. I think he'd be delighted if you found something that you loved to read in here. He's a man with a literary inclination—and he'd love to finally have someone else in this house to share it with him. He doesn't get much chance with all the demands of the family business."

"Are you sure?" Jessica hesitated, not really wanting to hesitate.

"Absolutely! Find something that interests you. Even take it back to your room if you like. Just, when you're done, give it to me. I know how to put it back where it belongs. Mr. Carlyle trained me well."

"If you insist!" Jessica grinned.

"I do. I'll leave this door open so you can hear when the others come down. Now, I've got to go. Mr. Carlyle will be back from his business trip soon, so I have to make a final check that everything's in order for tonight's dinner."

Jessica thanked the other woman profusely and was then alone with a room full of books. *Oh, Heaven! Wouldn't it be nifty to settle down with a good read on that lamb of a window seat? Dusty certainly would have loved to share it!*

Looking at the wall next to the door, Jess scanned the backs of the volumes: economics, engineering, business histories, government codes. Behind the desk: more of the same. *Nope! Don't want to snooze past dinner hour!*

Jessica turned and crossed to the bookcases on her left. *Ah! An overwhelming riches of literature!*

Through the window, her eyes were caught by a dance of saffron leaves across the drive, powered by that uncharacteristically warm wind. She smiled at the lemony wall of swamp maple and elm and birch massed against the edge of that driveway, their colors softly goldening thanks to the sinking sun. *"A season of mellow fruitfulness,"* indeed.

Taking the plunge, Jess zeroed in, first, on the section devoted to poetry, then on John Keats. A volume of Keats in hand, Jess smiled as she checked the index to open on "Ode to Autumn." Moving to the window seat, just about to sit down, she paused. Jessica Minton had the darnedest sensation she was no longer alone. Abruptly, she turned to the doorway and discovered her instinct was on the money.

The man who stood there wore a well-tailored, black, three-piece suit, conservative, except for that scarlet tie and gracefully folded pocket handkerchief. He was neither tall nor short, standing about 5'6" or 5'7", of medium build.

Jessica recognized the face under that thatch of thick, dark hair that glinted with threads of chestnut in the setting sun. Yes. The same sharp nose, broad forehead, strong jawline, mordant black eyes, all in the picture on the mantel. Now, though, the face was a bit fuller, some strands of silver were barely noticeable in the dark hair, and a sharp crease from too much thinking cut between his eyebrows. And those eyes. His features were under control, but so many thoughts, feelings chased through his dark eyes: surprise, uneasiness, uncertainty, regret . . .

Even with Rivers' earlier reassurance, Jessica was so unsettled by his scrutiny that she stammered, "Oh, Mr. Carlyle? I hope you don't mind. Miss Rivers assured me it would be fine for me to come in and pick out a book . . ." (She hastily held up the volume.) ". . . to read. I hope I haven't overstepped . . ."

Darn that Catholic guilt! Do I sound like a complete *idiot?*

Stepping forward, Philip Carlyle's suddenly cheery tone and smile assured Jess she sounded fine: "Of course, you're perfectly welcome to enjoy my library, such as it is. Miss Rivers was entirely correct to point you in here. I want my guests to feel at home."

He'd crossed to join Jessica by the window. She liked his voice: roughness wrapped in velvet. "I can't imagine you'd pick one of those dusty, dry tomes on business by my desk. Let me guess what you may have selected." He glanced out at the golden evening, then raised a brow and posited, "Something *apropos* to the present ambiance, I'll conjecture. Something to celebrate a 'season of mists and mellow fruitfulness'? Of 'soft-lifted winnowing wind'?"

Jessica blinked, then laughed, "Good grief! You must be psychic!" She gave him a playfully skeptical look and challenged, "Okay, come clean? How did you know?"

Her companion smiled, tapped the volume in her hand, and admitted, "Keats is a favorite of mine. So this book is a special friend. Every fall, 'To Autumn,' 'To a Nightingale,' and 'To Melancholy' are my companions, here, on this window seat. So, no, I'm not psychic. No black magic involved— though such abilities might come in handy in this house."

Tilting her head thoughtfully, Jessica surprised herself with her bold question, "Have *you* seen this ghost?"

He almost seemed startled, and Jess wanted to kick herself for being forward.

However, Philip Carlyle quickly recovered to smile, "Now, what self-respecting ghost would waste her time on a practical businessman who studied electrical engineering? Tell me, now, Miss Minton, are you trying to pump me for information? That's not according to the rules your director and sponsor laid out, is it? You'll have to wait until after dinner, when all is made clear."

His last statement was in a tone of mock mystery, so Jessica shrugged and kidded, "Can't blame a girl for trying, can you?"

"You are aware of what curiosity did to the cat?" he returned with mock sagacity.

"And you must be aware of what brought her back," Jessica returned with equal good humor.

He bowed his head in partial acquiescence, adding, "Unfortunately for your rebuttal, I've signed an agreement to remain silent. So, I'm afraid you will have to be patient for your information."

Jess smiled. She couldn't really crab about not getting the jump on Scott's big reveal. Instead, turning her attention to the "bloom of barred clouds" and "the maturing sun" goldening the world beyond the window, she observed, "How can a girl complain when she has such a magnificent view in front of her? Keats so hit the nail on the head, capturing the season's ambiance. I love the autumn: the colors, the air. For some people, it's sad, like an ending; but to me, it's this wonderous transition—like a slipstream between worlds. It seems as if the past haunts you in a sweetly melancholy way, while the future opens up fabulous, mysterious possibilities."

Well, that certainly made her sound a silly, dreamy sort! Maybe not to James, who shared much of her soul in his own. But, this man, she hardly knew. *Darn that Johnny Keats and his inspirational negative capabilities!*

Jessica shook her head, embarrassed at her mystical ramblings in front of a stranger, finally saying, "I'm afraid I must sound a little whacky to you. A flighty actress!"

"Not at all," was his quiet response. "I know what you mean. I'm not all business and engineering, though my connections are not the sort who'd understand those feelings."

Jessica looked at Philip Carlyle, surprised and relieved. He smiled sympathetically, then invited, "Come with me. I have something to show you that I think you'll enjoy."

Her puzzled hesitation prompted Carlyle to tease, "Don't worry. No ghosts. I promise. Remember, I'm legally forbidden to clue you in that way."

Jessica relaxed and took Philip Carlyle's offered arm, allowing him to guide her out of the library and across the short corridor to a set of pocket doors. He removed his arm to push the doors back into their slots then admit Jessica into an L-shaped room. The space was suffused with an amber-gold sunset gleaming off the surrounding forest and pouring in through tall windows covering the wall before them, as well as on the wall to their left.

The goldish light softened the dark wood of the grand piano before those windows on their left. It tinted the wainscoting and papered walls, glowing back from what was normally a white ceiling, as well as from furniture set up for an audience of guests to be seated opposite the doors.

Jess loved the trees' embrace of the room, giving it a definite pastoral feel. She finally breathed, "This is absolutely wonderful. Whoever designed this house truly loved nature."

"My grandfather could have settled in Portsmouth, where the factory and the business offices are. There are many stately homes there," Philip Carlyle explained. "However, he wanted to escape the grind of the city. He wanted an enclave where he and his family could never lose touch with what was beautiful and uplifting in nature. In various rooms, you may have seen the Hudson River School paintings he collected. And he loved his Keats, Wordsworth, Bryant, and Thoreau—at least for their love of nature, not for any caveats some of them had with capitalism. He was a bit more pragmatic than Henry David on how his success in business paid for his escape into nature here."

Jessica walked over to the piano. Her gaze shifted from it to the autumn sunset that had turned amber the leaves, only a little earlier suffused by yellow. Above the trees, the silver-to-slate clouds, rosy edged across the bottom, barred the now turquoise sky. She turned to Carlyle, who had joined her, to observe, "You've kept it all up so beautifully since your grandfather's time. That Romantic love of nature must be hereditary."

"In some of us," he replied, then changed the subject: "You seem interested in the piano. Do you play?"

"I can outplay any six-year-old in the house," Jessica answered mischievously. "Unless the six-year-old is Arthur Rubinstein."

"But you love music, I'll wager!"

"Oh, yes, and my husband plays several instruments. I love it when he plays for me," Jess smiled as dreamily as any newlywed of one to forty years of marriage. "Sometimes, we even sing together. I can actually carry a tune, and not just in a paper bag."

"Ah, then perhaps I might add to the autumnal mood by bringing all the arts into play, so to speak."

Sitting at the piano, his back to the window, Philip Carlyle instructed, "Stand there, if you will, Miss Minton. Yes, on my left. Would you be kind enough to turn the pages and continue to enjoy our deepening twilight?"

"You've got a deal!"

"Ah." He was looking at the music already in place. "Quite the appropriate piece."

Noting the title and composer, Jessica agreed with quiet delight, "'Les Trois Gymnopédies.' One of my favorites. You are so right! It's perfect:

dreamy, a touch sad, but not at all depressing. Perfect complement to the Keats. Please, do play. I'd love to hear you."

"I can assure you that I can outplay any eight-year-old, even an eight-year-old Arthur Rubinstein," he solemnly returned, solemn but for the glint in his eyes.

And then he launched into the graceful, melancholy dreaminess of the Satie, moving Jessica's spirit gently through the twilight. It was such a sweet melancholy drift, she almost forgot to turn the page. *Would that James were sharing the moment.*

"Say, I was wondering where you two kids had run off to."

Scott Zimkiewicz's usually pleasing affability jerked them both back to reality almost as much as his Salvador Dali nightmare of a tie in greens, rust, and chartreuse. The kind of tie Lon Chaney, Jr. always felt compelled to wear in his *Inner Sanctum* movies.

Philip Carlyle's last awkward, startled chord still reverberated jarringly in Jessica's head, perhaps strengthened by its contrast with Scott's pleasant smile. Carlyle's expression had soured, the October-twilight idyll ruined for him; but he swiftly composed his features.

Unaware, or just ignoring, the disquiet he'd created, Scott teased, "And so what were you two sneaking off for?"

"We're bowling," Jess quipped, entering into Scott's humor. "What does it look like we're up to, Scott?"

Her friend regarded Jess with playful suspicion, then turned to Carlyle to "caution," "Philip, I hope Jessica here wasn't trying to pump you for the lowdown on this evening's surprise reveal."

"She spun her whiles deftly, but nary a bean was spilled," Philip reassured Scott.

Melodramatically, Jessica clenched her fist and told them, "Drat! You gents have foiled my plans! I guess I'll just have to be patient. You're lucky it's not my sister down here. She could crack a Red spy faster than Assault could put away a pack of racehorses."

"Not knowing anything about horse racing, I'll assume that's remarkably fast," Philip remarked dryly.

"You don't say," Scott speculated. "So that's why I've heard Rivers has been on her toes to keep Liz from giving the servants a successful third degree."

"Jeanne Rivers is nothing if not on her toes—all the time," Philip Carlyle replied. He glanced at his watch and changed the subject, "I see that it's time to adjourn to the drawing room for aperitifs. A host ought to be on hand to greet his guests."

"That's why I'm here," Scott beamed. "I know it's Rivers' job to come get you, but I thought I'd save her those toes she's on a little travel time. Shall we?"

He proffered an arm to Jessica, while Philip Carlyle took her other, and the three proceeded from the room. However, Jessica teased Scott, "I just bet you were only thinking of Jeanne Rivers' tootsies." Turning to Philip, she pointed out, "More like he didn't trust us not to SNAFU his clever little plot."

"Scott underestimates my ability to keep a secret," Philip smiled as they moved down the corridor.

Scott corrected, "More like you underestimate the ability of a Minton gal to ferret one out."

"Ferret, huh?" Jess retorted as they approached the drawing room. "At least you could have compared me to something cute and expensive, like a mink!"

Chapter Eight
Same Evening

The dining room decor was purely Victorian: dark wood wainscoting, plush wine-colored papering, and lighted candles encased in golden sconces and pendant with crystals interspersed along the walls. As they enjoyed their dinner, an elaborate chandelier now wired for electricity added a soft overhead glow. Behind Jessica, the line of windows, mullioned and topped with geometric shapes in stained glass, admitted only darkness, an evening in which the moon was only a sliver now sinking below the trees.

The long table was imposing mahogany, like the chairs and the enormous sideboard that covered the entire wall to Jessica's right, backing the drawing room. A large centerpiece seemed to split her end of the table from the one where the sponsor sat near Philip Carlyle, actor Guy Robinson, and the technicians. Guy's wife Maura was next to him, but this side of the centerpiece. Scott had wisely planned seating arrangements with Jeanne to separate the gals from the obnoxious Ungerpreck.

Across the room, to Jess's left, was another sideboard, smaller and marble-topped. Next to it, by the wall with the windows, a door led into the kitchen. A young woman, pertly uniformed as a server, stood at attention. Jeanne Rivers, on the other side of this sideboard, was eagle-eyed in her supervision.

Jessica took a quick glance at the young server, who swiftly averted her eyes. This was the third time that sensation of an uneasy stare from the girl had inspired Jess to glance in her direction. *What gave?*

Something in the girl's tense demeanor said she had more on her mind than worrying if Jessica's vegetables were sufficiently seasoned. *Do I have a tag sticking out of my dress?* Come to think of it, at least one of the other household help had given a definite start when running into her. Probably it had something to do with their broadcast, but why did they all seem to focus on *her*? She hadn't caught any such reactions to the other guests.

"What's with the furrowed brow, kiddo?" Elizabeth queried from her immediate right.

Jess turned to her sister. Liz had somehow mastered her wind-blown hair into a tidy victory roll over her forehead and scraped off ocean water and sand to encase herself in a flattering satin dress of egg-shell top, a roll of material looping an "L" on her right side, and a high-waisted, taupe skirt. When a girl designed for her own dress company, she never had to worry about looking sleek and lovely.

"It's the darnedest thing, Liz, but I keep getting the sense that people in this house have a kind of, ah, I don't know, *reaction* to me," Jessica struggled to explain. "They keep looking at me funny."

Across from them, Gerry kidded, "They must recognize you from your radio appearances."

"Smart guy," Jessica grinned. "But maybe they saw a picture of me in *The Radio Guide* or *Radio Mirror*. That's possible. Should I be handing out autographs?"

"I'd wait to be asked," Liz dryly advised. "And don't hold your breath waiting."

"I'm wounded," Gerry protested, hand over heart. "No one's staring at me, let alone asking for my autograph."

"You're not as pretty as she is," cracked Beverly McDuff, the auburn-tressed writer in a cool-green linen suit beside him.

Gerry made an expressive gesture of surrender as Jessica said, "Thank you, Bev. We gals have to stick together." Turning to Scott, just this side of the centerpiece, Jess asked, "Is that it, Scott? My pulchritude turns everyone's head?"

"What are you asking me for?" Scott volleyed good-naturedly.

"Doesn't the director know everything?" Jess queried with mock sweetness.

"Maybe not *everything*," Scott returned with a definite hint that he knew *something* she didn't. He took a sip of his wine.

"Oh brother," Bev rolled her eyes. "Modesty doesn't become you, Scottie boy. Or maybe you should display some of that commodity at the next writers meeting."

"From the gleam in Scott's eyes, I can see that he has something up his sleeve he's not telling us," Gerry observed.

"All will be unfolded in good time," Scott promised. Turning his attention to his plate, he changed the subject. "Mmm, I do love salmon!"

Surveying the length of the table and their separation from Ungerpreck and the other diners, Jessica pointed out, "I think there's something fishy about the seating arrangements. Shouldn't you, as director, be down in North Dakota at the other end of the table with our beloved Mr. U. and our host?"

Scott devilishly raised his eyebrows, sliced himself a nice bit of salmon, and explained, "Indeed, I should, but after battling with the 'gentleman' temporarily in charge, nonstop, for two days to keep some quality in our show, I feel perfectly justified in having asked Miss Rivers to give me a seat with a little breathing space."

The chuckles penetrated through the enormous centerpiece to the other end of the table, and Ungerpreck fastened a suspicious look on Scott. The director smiled and explained, "Just a funny story about corrupt Republicans. I know you don't want to hear it, E.U. You know us artistic types."

Glares promised vengeance later from the entrapped Guy and the technicians as Edmund Ungerpreck resumed whatever folderol he'd been spouting.

Maura warned Scott, *sotto voce*, "You may be joining our ghost as a murder victim if Guy has any say. But thanks for rescuing me from having to sit near Ungerpreck—and for saving Guy from losing his job if he had to defend my honor."

"I'm doing the best I can under the circumstances," Scott acknowledged.

Maura now opted to steer the conversation to a less fraught topic: "*Did you and Bev discover for certain that this Felicia Blasko was murdered?*"

Jess noted Gerry's eyes spark with interest. *Of course, he wants to understand Jamie's past.*

"That's an interesting question," Scott granted, misreading Gerry's interest as mere curiosity. "And I may have something of an answer after dinner. I hope all of you can wait that long."

"Fine," Bev interjected. "Just make sure that you don't distract *me* from anything chocolate. Now pass the butter and tell me more about where we'll be doing our writing and what you want in those promotion spots Jess and Gerry are recording tomorrow."

Scott, Bev, and Gerry became caught up in discussing the promos, moving onto some technical issues of recording here. So, Jessica drifted out of the conversation, especially when she caught a subtle, for Liz anyway, poke in the ribs.

"Ow!" Jessica griped under her breath. A sharp glance at Liz, and her sister observed quietly, "The help aren't the only ones around here who can't keep their eyes off you."

In an equally quiet voice, slowly buttering her bread, Jessica questioned, "What are you getting at, Elizabeth?"

"I'm getting at the fact that our host keeps peeping down here at you, especially when you're not looking," Liz answered, a finger tapping her cheek as she faced Jessica.

"What?" Jess halted her roll buttering, but before she could automatically try to peer around the centerpiece at Philip Carlyle, Liz leaned forward to block her, warning in low tones, "Don't draw his attention. What were the two of you up to before we all came down?"

"Up to?" Jess rolled her eyes. "Are you kidding me? All we did was talk about the glorious fall weather, Keats's poetry, and then he took me to the music room to play some Satie for me. Oh, I kind of see your point. But Liz, the guy scarcely knows me."

"That makes it even more likely. No, all kidding aside, I think he's kind of sweet on you. Be careful."

Jessica started to pursue her sister's unexpected warning, only to be diverted by Bev's announcement, "Last night, when I went for a walk at twilight, I heard the craziest howling. Jess, Liz, did you hear it when you drove in?"

Scott answered for them, "That's the famous Devil Dog or Hound of Hell. Or maybe it's the Pooch from Poughkeepsie."

"Poughkeepsie's not hellish," Bev protested.

"I've played there, Bev," Gerry assured her. "Scott knows what he's talking about."

Despite her discomfort with Liz's remarks about Philip Carlyle, Jess couldn't help smiling at Gerry's quip, and soon the continued humor distracted her from Liz's warning.

"I told you this was the perfect setting for performing our broadcasts. What more could you ask for? You've got your ghostly lady, a demonic dog—and a stone-throwing devil," Scott insisted.

"I'll tell you what's missing," Gerry interjected with mock indignation. "No vampires! No fun without at least one vampire."

"Bloody well said," Jessica applauded.

"If you're looking for a bloodsucker . . ." Bev cut in with a voice too low to carry beyond their group, her eyes indicating Ungerpreck.

"Now, Bev," Scott wagged a finger. "Don't bite the hand that feeds you."

"Leave that to the Hell Hound," Liz advised.

So, the dinner proceeded pleasantly enough. The food was superb. The candlelight and soft glow from the chandelier created a dreamy, almost otherworldly ambiance. Still, Jessica felt for anyone trapped with the bloviating Edmund Ungerpreck. Did it help that Scott made one or two trips to the other end of the table to "take the heat off them," as he put it? She didn't expect that Philip Carlyle was exactly having a ball. Should Scott repay his hospitality this way?

Did she want to think much on Philip Carlyle after what her sister had warned? Liz had to be nuts! Her wedding ring and talk of James clearly marked her as out of bounds. Well, yes, she wasn't a kid. She knew that to some people those considerations were more an incentive than a STOP! Sign. Still, Carlyle hadn't exactly come off as a playboy type, to her mind.

She noticed that Scott had returned to the other end of the table, talking briefly to the folks there before moving away to discuss something with Jeanne Rivers. The housekeeper nodded, then crossed to the servant by the door and sent her into the kitchen. Scott turned back to Jess's end of the table, bestowing a knowing wink to those there, lingering unaccountably over Jessica, before he sauntered to the head of the table.

"I wonder just what Scott has cooking in that devious little mind of his," Jessica suspiciously mused aloud.

"Whatever it is, I know it has to do with you," Liz added.

Gerry and Bev gave Liz quizzical looks, with Gerry saying, "What makes you two say that? Isn't he just doing penance to the people we actually like, suffering at the other end of the table?"

"You didn't get a load of his look at my sister," Liz started to explain, interrupted as two of the servants were now clearing away the hefty centerpiece.

"There goes our cover," Bev muttered.

"Maybe Scott thinks it's time we all bear the burden of Mr. Ungerpreck's reminders that we'd better snap to it, earning our keep from him," Jess commented, only loud enough for her near companions.

Bev warned, "I'd be careful if I were you, Jess. Scott's a little devil."

"He must have something pretty nefarious planned for you," Gerry chimed in.

"Will you guys knock it off," Jessica protested, pretty much joking. "You make me feel as if I just won first prize in a contest to be a human sacrifice."

Bev's eyes sparkled with inspiration, and she exclaimed, "Say! What an idea for the show! I don't think that's been done before. I'll have to talk this over with Scott. Maybe we could call it 'The Raffle.'"

"Don't you dare!" Jess lowered. "He's got enough bright ideas as it is!"

Jessica looked down the table at Scott, who was consulting with their host. Philip Carlyle nodded and, in turn, beckoned one of the male servants waiting at attention. Before Jess could observe further, Scott spoke.

"Gang, could I have your attention, please?" With his trademark mischievous-boy grin, he continued, all heads now turned to him, "I know I've been keeping you on tenterhooks about the story we're going to broadcast on the phantom of this mansion. Well, your curiosity is about to be satisfied."

"Uh, oh," Gerry cracked.

Scott ignored Gerry, continuing, "I know you've been going a little nuts, waiting to get the whole story and not being allowed to even go into town. All so I could bring you to our tale unbiased by local prejudices and factions concerning the events and the people involved . . ."

"Scott," Gerry interrupted, "The Chorus does a shorter introduction to *Henry V*. Cut to the chase."

"I intend to do just that, smart guy," Scott replied, gesturing toward the double doors leading to the corridor. "I think this will knock your socks off."

Nothing happened.

Liz remarked out of the corner of her mouth, "I hope you guys do a heck of a lot better with cues on your broadcasts."

Both the sound man and the engineer shot Elizabeth the dirtiest of looks. Jessica was trying to suppress a chuckle when the doors abruptly opened to reveal a servant wheeling in an easel holding a large, vertically rectangular object covered with a cloth.

"Here at last!" Gerry pronounced merrily.

Scott acknowledged, "Cute, very cute, Gerry. However, you'll be whistling another tune in a minute." Scott nodded to the servant, and the man deftly whipped away the covering to reveal the portrait of a woman, announcing, "I give you Felicia Blasko!"

She wasn't tall, though she was slender, in a long dress of Edwardian style. Her long dark hair was swept gently off her face and captured in a chignon at the back of her head. She turned, poised, with one hand raised: To question? To warn? To halt?

It was the face, though, that brought their gasps, especially Jessica Minton's. She faced an almost dead ringer for herself.

Maura Robinson put their shock into words, her dark eyes enormous with disbelief, "Why it's the image of . . ."

"Joan Bennett," Liz nodded decisively.

Jessica was on the point of giving her sister a verbal dope slap, but on reflection, cocked her head and allowed, "Come to think of it . . ."

"Don't be ridiculous!" Ungerpreck charged in. "Why would *my* show care about some gal who looked like Joan Bennett? Use your eyes!"

There was a subtle bristling all around at Ungerpreck's appropriation of *their* program. However, Jessica was particularly struck by the exchange of looks between Scott and Philip. The latter seemed especially annoyed by the conversational detour.

Scott, striving to recapture the moment of his big reveal, tried to nudge Elizabeth in the right direction, "Don't you see a striking resemblance to someone 'closer to you'?"

Liz laughed, "Oh, of course: Hedy Lamarr?"

"Elizabeth," Scott continued to prompt, "take a look at your sister and ask her what she thinks."

Liz turned to Jess and hopefully conjectured, "Ruth Hussey?"

Scott raised his hands in surrender as the rest of the table, except Philip and Jessica, burst into laughter. Jess wasn't sure what Philip was thinking, but she knew she wasn't exactly thrilled at now understanding the reason behind all the stares and double takes. Not thrilled? No, more like unnerved.

All the while, Liz was looking around the table, annoyed at being the reason for such amusement, finally blurting, "What?!"

Gerry Davis suggested, with tongue-in-cheek patience, "Elizabeth, take a good look at that painting and then turn to your left and take a good, long look at the person next to you. Notice any similarities?"

Elizabeth wrinkled her forehead, followed Gerry's instructions, then burst out, "Oh!"

"Light dawns on Marblehead," Philip remarked coolly, drawing Liz's trademark narrow-eyed stare and a lowered estimation in Jessica's eyes.

"What a shocker!" Ungerpreck enthused. "Think of all the publicity we'll get for the show! Shocks and thrills, that's what the public loves! We'll put Durante's ratings in the toilet with this! Think of all the revenue this gimmick will generate for my company when ratings shoot through the roof! You just can't make this stuff up."

But Jessica wasn't exactly listening to Ungerpreck. Her mind whirred through possibilities until, in a Eureka moment, she declared, "Can't you? Make it up? How do we know that Scott isn't pulling some kind of a gag? He could easily have had this painting made from copying a photo of me."

"So what?" snorted Ungerpeck. "People eat this stuff up all the time. They don't care if something's true or not. Just if it gets them het up. All I care is if it gets the suckers het up enough to listen to the show and buy my products."

But Jessica wasn't really listening to Ungerpeck, though she sensed the hostility percolating around the table for his crass view of their program and its audience, so different from the attitude of his brother-in-law. No, she was relieved that she could explain away the disconcertion of seeing herself bodied forth in the form of another born before her lifetime. Scott could be quite the card!

Except the calm, firm voice of Philip Carlyle robbed her of that satisfaction.

"You know Scott did not play a trick on you because *I* can assure you all that this portrait has been in my possession since 1927. You know because it has been in this house, hanging in the foyer for these past twenty years, seen by innumerable people of all walks of life. It would, indeed, be a neat trick if I could afford to squander the time and money to bribe all of them to run a confidence game on all of you. And think about people's reactions to seeing you, Miss Minton."

"If you think about it," Scott added, "the fact that your sister ticked through three actresses who strongly look like both you and the woman in the portrait proves that a powerful resemblance between unrelated people is possible."

"She named everyone but Margaret Lockwood and Vivien Leigh," Bev added.

Pointing her finger, Liz vigorously nodded her agreement.

Jessica sucked in her breath, releasing it slowly, replying grudgingly. "Flattered as I am that my sister and the rest of you group me with such a gorgeous bevy of gals, I still need some convincing. It's all pretty far-fetched."

Her eyes flitted uneasily to the portrait, then back to Scott.

He nodded, answering, "Believe me, Jessica, the whole deal floored me when Mr. Carlyle first contacted me. His housekeeper had seen your picture in *Radio Mirror*, brought it to his attention, then he managed to persuade Bev and me to take a trip out here, see the portrait, and investigate the whole story. We *were* convinced."

Jessica was still skeptical, and her face showed it. Her survey of the table revealed a mixed bag of reactions. Most important, her lodestar Liz was staring inscrutably at the painting, one finger intently tapping her cheek.

Finally, Jessica said, "I may not be from Missouri, but you'll still have to convince me."

There were a few mumbles of agreement; but, undaunted, Scott pressed on cheerily, "That's exactly what we intend to do. Philip, it's your family story. Give them the full low down."

Philip Carlyle nodded, then said to Jessica, "Miss Minton, one reason I can attest to the authenticity of this portrait is that I watched it being painted by my brother."

Recalling the family photos on the mantel, Jessica carefully observed, "I saw no brother in the drawing room photos—only you and your sister."

"There's a good reason for that," Philip admitted slowly. "I'm afraid Bill was what the British call 'a bit of a bad hat'—much more than 'a bit,' truth be told. If you'll listen to our history, intertwined with that of the Blaskos, you'll understand why, as well as why Felicia is said to haunt our home. May I proceed?"

"We're all ears," Liz pronounced.

"This ought to be good," Gerry added.

Jess shot her friend a quick glance. His return look telegraphed his desire to get to the bottom of Jamie's tragedy. She returned her attention to Philip Carlyle and nodded, "Please, continue."

"Felicia Blasko does bear a striking likeness to Miss Minton," he began. "Except for the eyes. There's a sadness, even trepidation, not in Miss Minton's."

"Trepidation?" Elizabeth queried.

"As I continue my story, you will understand," Carlyle explained. His gaze went to the painting and he said, "It wasn't always so. When Felicia Saunders was a child and young woman, she had a lightness, a joy of life." He paused to reflect before continuing, "That changed when she returned here, a married woman and mother. Her parents had sent her away to school in Boston, where she studied the sciences, unusual for a woman. The year she was graduated, apparently, mutual friends introduced her to the up-and-coming Hungarian scientist Dr. Vitus Blasko. I can well imagine how her vivacity charmed the serious scientist. Things went well enough, at first. He was attached to M.I.T., doing tremendously successful research work in electronics. He might have been devoted to his lab, but he was nearby, and so were friends."

The velvet-coated roughness of Philip's voice as he related this tale of what would prove to be tragedy lulled the company of extroverts, skeptics, and wise guys into attentive quiet. The actress in Jessica led her to decide that Philip Carlyle's delivery and striking tones would have made him perfect for the radio—except that hint of the personal in his voice disturbed you with the suspicion you were listening to something not meant for your ears.

"A major lab in Princeton, New Jersey was so impressed with his work that they poached him from Cambridge. He refused to miss the opportunity to work with great minds at labs that offered him an even larger scope to pursue his work. But he told Felicia that she and their daughter shouldn't accompany him. He'd be married to his lab for some time; she'd be bored and lonely; the child would be uprooted. She should stay in Cambridge with her friends and keep Jamie in school there. He'd come back on some weekends, as his work allowed."

Carlyle paused. Guy, of the handsome, almost cherubic face and curly black hair, supplied, "My guess is that work *didn't* allow."

"Precisely," Philip affirmed.

Liz voiced everyone's thoughts: "Okay. We get the sad, but where does the trepidation come in?"

"Here, on Birdsong Island," Philip replied, with a gaze so direct even Liz shifted under it. Taking in everyone, Philip Carlyle continued, "She returned with her daughter rather than stay in Cambridge. Her mother was ill; her father had died shortly after her marriage. That was the kind of person she was, to come back and nurse her mother, return to her childhood roots and friends to raise her child."

"Was she friends with your family?" Jessica asked, pondering the connection between Philip and Felicia—and what it implied for her.

"She was good friends with my late sister, Gladys. I was younger and trying to work my way up in my father's business. Later, when he died, although Gladys inherited control as my elder, I actually had the responsibility of running things. I scarcely had time to be involved in feminine affairs."

"Then how do you know so much, to tell us all this?" Elizabeth puzzled thoughtfully.

"My sister, Gladys, filled me in when she asked me to help Felicia by secretly offering Dr. Blasko a place as an engineer in our business, to keep the family together. I was glad to do it. Obviously, I wasn't in Felicia's confidence, as was my sister, but I could see she was unhappy, the child missed having a father. I trusted my sister's judgment, in most things."

Now Gerry was speaking: "My guess, from your tone, is that Dr. Blasko didn't accept your offer."

Philip didn't quite snort when he answered, but his disapproval of Blasko was palpable: "Indeed, he did not. The man gave me some nonsense about our business not being directly related to his field and worse, to him, too profit-oriented and backwater to allow him to pursue his research to its true limits. The very arrogance of the man! Worse, his family never even came into the question with him. Fate, no, his own ill-calculated decisions cost him both."

"Good gracious!" gasped Maura. "You're not telling us that she killed herself in despair? That's why she haunts . . . well, why would she haunt *your* home? Unless she killed herself here."

Philip forcefully shook his head and set the record straight, "Felicia Saunders was far too noble a woman to kill herself, especially if it meant leaving behind her child. No, she nursed her mother till the woman died, raised her daughter, and locked away her anger and bitterness, but relied on my sister, an older woman, for strength and solace."

"At least she had your home and the people in it for comfort," Maura pointed out. "Maybe she haunts here because she wants to be where she was loved."

Liz whispered to Jess, "Then why did I get the sense of her hanging around the other place?"

Before Jess could think any of this through, Philip continued, flickering candlelight shadowing the lines of age and sadness in his features, "She would have been better off never to have come here. Yes, Gladys was a Godsend, while I was too busy trying to improve Father's business to be much of an influence. But there was my brother Bill at home, always at home."

"The 'bit of a bad hat' brother who doesn't rate even a boyhood picture on the mantel," Jessica surmised.

Philip focused on her; the coldness in his eyes shivered right through her when he repeated his favorite confirmation, "Precisely."

"Just how bad of a hat?" Elizabeth questioned.

Contempt for the mysterious Bill imbued Philip's answer: "A ne'er do well of the first rank. Fancied himself an artist—he did have talent. You can see from the portrait and some tiles and carvings at the forest glen."

Jess gave an inward "ah, ha," remembering how Jeanne Rivers had sidestepped naming the sylvan artist they'd discussed earlier. This black sheep was on *everyone's* blacklist.

"I imagine Bill fancied himself the second coming of Grandfather, artist and businessman, but he lacked Grandfather's discipline, sense of responsibility. Unfortunately, my parents and Gladys indulged him, sending him to study art in Paris—where he wasted his time and their money on . . . well, the less said, the better. When Gladys took over at my father's death, she continued to indulge him. Unfortunately for Felicia, he considered her perfect prey. He even was low enough to try to get to her through her daughter, Jamie. However, Felicia saw right through him. He thought he could seduce her by persuading her to let him do her portrait. Gladys didn't see through it at all. She thought they were just great friends, that they might even help each other. Felicia's portrait would give him a sense of artistic purpose, while Bill's friendship would keep Felicia from being too lonely.

"I hardly had time to come home from the factory, but I could see that my brother had more than friendly designs. I tried to warn Felicia, but she wouldn't believe me any more than Gladys would."

"Was anything said to Dr. Blasko?" Gerry had the nerve to ask.

Philip looked sharply at Gerry, considered, then replied, "I didn't feel I was in a position to do so. It would be like carrying tales out of school. I did my best to talk to Felicia, to Gladys. No good. So, they found out how right I was in a terrible way. Would that I had been wrong.

"It all came to a head the night of November First, 1927," Philip slowly continued. "I was away into the late hours of the night at the factory. When I made it home, the house was quiet; so I went directly to bed. The next day, Gladys, alarmed, woke me, saying she'd overslept and found Jamie alone in the room she shared with her mother when they stayed over, with Blasko gone for so long."

"Alone?" Jess queried. "Where was Felicia? How . . . why would she leave without her daughter?"

Scott unexpectedly cut in, "Those are the $64.00 questions." Multiple glares at his interruption prompted his, "Er, sorry. Philip, go on."

Philip did: "It wasn't until that morning that I heard about the previous evening's events and came to realize exactly how dreadful the situation was.

"Apparently, the reason Felicia had brought Jamie over was not a happy one. Her husband, on a rare visit back, must have let slip turning down the opportunity to move back here for a job. That would have been the final straw for her. The papers later reported they'd had a dreadful row. She left him and came here for refuge—don't ask me why she didn't make *him* leave. Perhaps she needed the solace of my sister. At any rate, Gladys related to me that Blasko later came to our house demanding her return, making all kinds of irrational threats, especially after Bill, doing likely the only decent thing in his life, physically threw him out. The man even cast vicious aspersions about Felicia and Bill—understandable in Bill's case but certainly not in Felicia's. Gladys was so upset that she doused herself with a sedative after finally getting Felicia and Jamie settled for the night."

"And your brother, Bill?" Maura prompted.

"This is where it gets interesting," Philip answered.

"I think it's pretty interesting already," Elizabeth interjected.

Philip ignored Liz, proceeding, "We never saw Bill or Felicia again. Blood had ineffectively been cleaned up on the floor of Bill's studio in the fourth-floor attic. Yet neither Bill nor Felicia was ever found."

It was a moment before Gerry breathed, "Poor Jamie. What happened with her?"

Philip snorted, in a highbrow manner of snorting, before replying, "Suddenly, her father developed a sense of family responsibility. He took her home to Saunders House to raise her. Of course, he might have been motivated by losing his precious position in Princeton, the investigation tying him up here too long and his powers of concentration now broken."

"Investigation, you say?" Maura queried. "What did the police discover, decide?"

Philip shrugged. "What could they decide. No bodies? No definite evidence of exactly what happened? Did Bill kill Felicia for rejecting him and flee? Did they run off together? Did Blasko kill them both, or just one, with the other running away in fear? No one knows. But these ghostly sightings suggest to me that Felicia Saunders Blasko *is* dead. Neither my sister nor I would believe she'd abandon her daughter."

"Mr. Carlyle, what do you think happened?" Jessica questioned. This was a mystery she wanted solved, for how could she help but identify with one of the victims?

Philip turned to Jessica, and his answer chilled them all. "I believe Felicia was murdered. My late sister wouldn't dream of casting guilt on dear Bill, but I would. Nevertheless, I won't let Vitus Blasko off the hook. He's an arrogant man. I'd seen his temper once or twice, myself. My sister told me he was a veritable demon when he came to the house. So, one of those two must have murdered Felicia, but which, I honestly don't know."

"And that, kids," pronounced Scott, "is our story for the next two broadcasts. Pretty gripping, huh?"

"What story?!" Liz countered. "You don't know who did it."

"My thoughts exactly," groused Bev, the writer responsible for working with Scott to turn this unfinished tale into a broadcast.

"Simply this," Scott shot back gleefully. "For next week's program, you and I will hammer out a script based on the story our host related. The following week, we'll reveal the truth."

"Almost all the people are dead," Liz pointed out. "How do you plan to do that? Hold a séance?"

Scott broke into an oddly surprised grin and responded, "Bingo! Elizabeth Minton, you must be psychic!"

Murmurs of "You've got to be kidding!" "What are you, nuts?" "You're pulling my leg!" "Is this a gag?" filled the room, until Elizabeth held up a hand and challenged, "All right. Hold it right there. Look, even believers say that a séance is hit or miss. You don't just whip out a Ouija board and say, 'Calling Central. Patch me through to the ghost of someone specific,' and 'presto!' you've got a direct line. Even if you get something, it might take a lot longer than the length of your broadcast."

"That's why we're not doing it live!" Edmund Ungerpreck smugly insisted, annoyed at having to listen to other people this long. "Scottie says we'll record the séance we do on October Thirtieth then edit it using the studio's new tape machine. We'll do a combination live and transcription broadcast the next night, Halloween! Get it?!"

"And you expect us to be able to call up the spirits of the dead?" Gerry commented scornfully.

The Mintons shared an uneasy look, thinking about Liz's sightings around Jamie. Still, Jessica knew her sister did not see herself as having a direct line to the afterlife.

Scott was explaining: "Take it easy, Gerry. I checked out the medium we've called in, Madame Wanda. She's local and has a good reputation. She actually helped the Portsmouth police with a few cases of theft, recovering goods."

Jessica voiced different concerns to their host, "Mr. Carlyle, this is all pretty hot stuff about your family and the Blaskos. It seems much more painful, even damaging, than I'd expected. Even your own family can come off badly with your brother's involvement. Are you sure you really want to do this?"

"I want to know the truth. I want to know whether my family name can be cleared or whether we can treat William with the opprobrium I think he deserves. I want to know what kind of man my brother truly was. On the other hand, I don't want to see Vitus Blasko get away with murder if he's guilty. Most of all, I want Felicia to be laid to rest. That's what my sister Gladys would have wanted, too."

"And what about Jamie Blasko?" Gerry insisted. "What does she want? How will opening this wound affect her?"

Scott responded, "Gerry, you seem awfully worried about some girl you don't really know. Anyway, she and her father have been amply compensated for allowing us to explore the story. They both seemed just as eager as our host to see the truth come out."

"Well," Elizabeth pointed out, "either Mr. Carlyle or the Blaskos are bound to be a little disappointed since it sounds as if one of these families is hiding a murderer."

"If the truth is out there, I can face it no matter what it is," Philip asserted.

"Can the Blaskos?" Gerry muttered.

"You know," Guy added his two cents, "you're all getting het up over evidence from a source that would have a devil of a time standing up in court."

"Evidence from a séance obviously would not hold up," Philip agreed. "However, it might unnerve someone into making a slip or jog someone else's memory, or even give us a suggestion that we might bring to the

Chief of Police for investigation. He's a relatively new man, retired from the force in New York. He has more knowledge about investigations than the bumpkin we had here twenty years ago. I can't say he'd mind a feather in his cap for solving an old mystery."

While all the others were chattering about the evening's revelations, Liz leaned over and whispered to Jessica, "I don't like this. A séance is just the place where someone gets bumped off to cover another crime."

"Then we don't have to worry," Jess whispered back. "It'll be Scott who gets bumped off for the crime of nutcase-exploitation radio."

Jess just wished she felt as humorous as her words. Sharing a likeness with a woman murdered in the flare of anger didn't exactly give a girl sweet dreams—especially when there was the danger of stirring up a deadly past.

Chapter Nine
Saturday, October 18th, 1947

Dressed in a long jacket of light fawn wool, dark trousers, and a creamy light orange blouse, her hair in a French roll, Jessica moved rapidly toward the music room where she was scheduled to record promos. Maybe the day promised to be warm, but right now her outfit was perfect for the morning. Coming to a stop before the doors, Jess had to steady herself just a little. Maybe she shouldn't have rushed quite so much. She and Liz had shared *some* confab in her room on the evening's revelations. No conclusions had been reached on who really had done what to whom, but plenty of concern had been expressed over Gerry getting mixed up with a girl with Jamie's history. All that had pretty much put the kibosh on Jess getting her fair share of forty-winks.

Jessica pushed aside the doors but was given brief pause by the changes wrought in the music room. To create an adequate stand-in for a broadcast studio, the golden world of late autumn was banished. Now, heavy curtains were pulled across both sets of windows, not to block the light but to mute intrusive sounds during recording.

Of course, the room wasn't in complete darkness. An overhead chandelier illuminated adequately, abetted by electric wall sconces and table lamps. Still, the room possessed a gloominess quite different from Jessica's earlier experience here. Foley's portable sound table, the dictograph, and the engineer's control board were arranged near the piano. Most of the furniture had been moved out of the way, with a row of standing mikes taking center stage. Scott was reviewing notes on a clipboard with Chet at the engineer's table. Soundman Vic Foley was nearby, checking some of his equipment. Bev sat, bored, at the piano.

Oh, right, Scott is having her play musical cues since we have no organist or orchestra. He's not about to use recorded music and bring the wrath of Petrillo and AFM down on our heads! Lucky for us, Bev had started out as a studio musician and still had her union card.

"Hiya, girl with a ghost's face!" Bev teasingly greeted her.

Jess narrowed her eyes, kidding back, "Don't get smart, or I'll haunt you with a kick in the pants some dark and stormy night."

Scott glanced up and smiled, then finished his discussion with Chet before coming to Jess to say, "Here's our star. All ready to do some emoting to lure in the audience?"

Waving a hand around the room, Jessica replied, "You certainly created the right atmosphere. Gloomy as all get out, and cold, even if the sunshine is pushing up the mercury outside."

Despite her humor, an involuntary shiver took Jess.

"Say, you don't have to get *that much* into the mood," Scott remarked, surprised at her shiver.

"Aren't you cold?" Jess queried, pulling her jacket a bit tighter.

In long sleeves but no jacket, Scott shook his head, replying, "Not really." He gave Jess a mischievous look to say, "Maybe old Felicia is keeping tabs on you, so you play her right."

"I wouldn't be surprised," Jess replied. "After the night I just had in bed."

Scott cocked his head and raised a brow, querying, "Do I even want to know what *that* means?"

"It means I had bad dreams about our heroine. That's it," Jess returned, shooting Scott a look as sarcastic as her crack.

Bev sounded an ominous chord on the piano and interjected, "Who can blame you? I'd hate to have everyone comparing me to some gal searching for her murderer's exposure. Watch out she doesn't try to possess you to get her full allotment of life." Another ominous chord.

"Thank you, Bev," Jessica responded dryly. "I don't know which I 'appreciate' more: your 'sympathy' or your sound effects."

Soundman Vic kidded, "Hey, I'm the one who does sound effects," squeezing a car horn for a comical "Ah-U-Ga!"

With a Groucho Marx eye wiggle, Bev added, "A little other-worldly possession might make things more exciting for James."

"No one is more exciting for James than me," Jess quipped airily before adding with a malevolent gleam, "But if Felicia does take possession, probably the first thing she'll do is fix the little red wagon of whatever smart alecks mocked her—or at least I can always *claim* it was she."

Vic feigned horror, and Bev accorded Jessica victory with a playful coda.

"Okay," Scott cut in, though not harshly. "Are you kids done fooling around? We do have work to do. Gerry already made his recordings. I have to get Jess's on disc so we can run them into Portsmouth for the messenger to rush to New York. And don't forget, Bev, you and I need to do additional research in town for our story if we want to get a decent script for Tuesday."

"Fine, Scott," Jess teased. "But in the time you spent yakking, we could have recorded half the spots."

Bev played "tick-tock, tick-tock, tick-tock."

"All right. You girls got me. Now, let's get to work."

Scott brought Jessica the script for the spots: two where she sounded mysteriously alluring and two where she was all innocent victim—both designed to tantalize audiences with the promise of something terrifying, mainly because it was true! Coming into her own as she went to work, Jessica nailed each reading with one take, abetted by Bev's eerie piano tinklings.

The piano sounded different from Philip Carlyle's Satie, yet both haunted her. What *did* she think about Philip after hearing his story? How did the way he saw Felicia affect his understanding of her?

"Earth calling Jessica Minton." Scott snapped his fingers before her. "What gives with you? I don't like that frown on your face. Are you okay?"

Jessica admitted, "This connection between me and Felicia Blasko is disturbing, Scott. People look at me and see someone else. It gives me the willies. I had such dreams last night."

Genuinely concerned, Scott frowned before saying, "Jessica, honestly, it's only a show. The resemblance is just a coincidence. Don't take it so personally. You're a professional."

"Of course I am, Scott," Jessica replied. "But the more I think about this story, the more I think playing with the past is not such a hot idea. What if you hit too close to home for the real murderer? He may still be around. I can't imagine he'd take too kindly to your poking around, exposing him."

"Or *her*," Scott corrected Jess with a smile.

"The only two females around back then were Gladys and Jamie. Since one is dead and the other was only a kid at the time, I think it's safe to say 'him,'" Jessica replied.

"She's got you there," Vic agreed.

"Thanks to the peanut gallery," Scott nodded to Vic. Turning back to Jessica, he continued, "No one's going to take our show seriously enough to commit another murder. It's only entertainment, and most of the participants seem to want the truth to come out."

"But, Scott," Jessica argued. "I could see last night this is all more than entertainment to Philip Carlyle, and you told me pretty much the same about the Blaskos."

"Both families seem perfectly willing for the truth to come out," Scott countered.

"But someone we don't know about might not be so cooperative," Jessica warned.

Scott shook his head, "I don't believe that. Anyway, I'm sorry, but we're committed. I can't change our plans now. We either go on or there goes the program. Ungerpreck made that crystal clear to me. Don't expect anyone to let you go to the head of the breadline if he pulls the plug on us. Until his brother-in-law is back on his feet, E.U. has complete authority over us, like it or not."

Jessica frowned, unable to come up with a good counterargument. Maybe the case *was* so old that even if Scott turned something up, no one would be around to kick about it. Maybe those bad dreams haunting her last night had just put her in a morbid mood. Maybe Scott might actually bring the two families peace, after all. What wasn't a maybe was that she hadn't the clout to control the show's content. Ultimately, they were all at the mercy of their regular sponsor's sensation-loving, greedy substitute.

Scott put an arm around Jess's shoulder, walking her to the door while saying, "Look, I'll try not to overly sensationalize this story, despite E.U. I promise I'll be careful about treading on toes. Anyway, did it ever occur to you that we might come up with something that would help these families close the book on the mystery?"

They reached the doors, which Scott pushed back into their pockets.

Reluctantly, Jess allowed, "The thought crossed my mind." She looked into Scott's eyes intently and worried, "It's just that none of our scripts ever made me feel like this before. I feel, well, haunted."

Scott smiled, grasping Jessica by the shoulders and sympathizing, "Poor kid, I guess my melodramatic reveal in the atmosphere of this big old house was a little too much for a sensitive gal like you. No wonder you had nightmares. That Philip Carlyle can tell a tale like nobody's business! He could be an announcer with that extraordinary voice. Anyway, I guess I have been stoking everyone's imagination pretty intensely."

"I'm not that sensitive, Scott. I have a strong imagination, but I'm not exactly a hysteric—and Liz has been antsy about this place, too."

"Sure, sure," Scott replied. "But you've had a lot of stress ever since the two of you hopped on the Streamliner from the city. To tell you the truth, I've been dodging shadows, myself, in this place. I'm looking forward to hitting Portsmouth this afternoon with Bev. If there were room in the auto, I'd say you and Liz should come with and take a day to see the sights, such as they are. But, hey, when Bev and I went into the village for some research at the historical society, we saw some shops and places to eat. There's a green, and, I think, even a boardwalk. So, dig up, um, find your sister and see if you two can take your minds off things."

"You don't think the villagers will chase me through town with pitchforks and flaming torches to try and exorcise me?"

"I think you're pretty safe," Scott laughed. " Most of the villagers I've met seem more interested in making a living than living in the past. Now, I've got to get my materials together and go. Okay?"

Jess nodded and left Scott. Walking down the corridor to the drawing room, she pondered whether he had been right about her imagination getting the better of her. Yet Scott didn't know what her sister had sensed in connection with Jamie. Still, that was connected to Jamie, not her—unless Felicia had transferred her interest from Jamie, trying to get her story through.

What had Liz seen or sensed? Maybe there was more in heaven or earth, yadida-yadida-yadida. That still didn't mean Elizabeth had experienced Felicia's presence. Even Liz wasn't sure.

It would have been nice to call James and talk this out—and say what? She was afraid of a ghost? Of murder? Or just that she was acting in a program that was giving her the creeps big time? The last thing she wanted was to talk hauntings with him. He'd listen, but it would haunt *him* in a particularly tender spot. Even if it were all for nothing, he'd worry that she was worried. No, she wasn't about to disrupt his enjoyment doing research. She was a big girl who would not give in to some moody heebie-jeebies.

She could talk to Elizabeth, though. The sound of classical music coming from the drawing room as she approached reminded her that Liz had said last night she'd probably be downstairs by 10:30.

And there was Liz, wearing beige slacks and a blouse with teal and yellow stripes, sitting on the couch by the fireplace, reading. The cherry-wood radio console behind Liz, next to the French doors, entertained with the dashing joy of Holst's "Jupiter." Plump gourds, purple grapes deliciously bursting their skins, and boundingly joyous harvest-home celebrants came to Jessica's mind's eye. This *Music and Memories* broadcast inspired her to take Scott's advice and blow away some of the gothic cobwebs with a trip to Birdsong Island village.

Elizabeth looked up and greeted Jess, "All done with your radio spots? Free now? What new adventure awaits?"

Sitting on the settee across the low, marble-topped table from Liz, Jess began, "Scott suggested we get away from the gloom of last night's tale by paying a visit to the island's village. He made it sound lovely and quaint. What do you say?"

"You mean he's released us from solitary confinement? I thought your director wanted to keep his cast uncontaminated."

"Actually, he and I were talking about that last night over dessert and coffee," Jess explained, "when you and Maura were chatting. Scott seems to think we've been 'fortified' by getting our tale straight from the horse's mouth, aka Philip Carlyle. We now have a standard for measuring any gossip."

"Hmm," Liz reflected. "Of course, Carlyle might be a kind of witness to the events, but I suspect he has an axe or two to grind of his own. I just can't figure out exactly whose neck he's aiming for. Clearly, he resents Blasko for his treatment of Felicia, but maybe more for dragging his family into a scandal."

"Not to mention driving down his real estate value with this pesky ghost business," Jessica smiled.

"There's that," Liz agreed before going on. "There's also no love lost between him and his phantom brother. Did you notice there's no sign of this Bill among the family pictures on the mantel over there? Not even an embarrassing baby picture? I'll bet those two were at odds long before the Felicia scandal."

"I did notice that about the pictures," Jessica concurred. After a glance back toward the foyer, she cautioned with a lowering gesture with her hands, "Maybe we had better be more discreet with these kinds of conjectures. You never know who might be strolling by. I don't want to so offend the master of the house that he throws the kit and kaboodle of us out on our collective ears. More than once, Scott has let me know how much is riding on the success of these broadcasts."

Elizabeth arched an eyebrow but opted to change the subject: "So, Scott thinks the village is quaint and that we might enjoy a visit? Well, if there are any antique or specialty shops, I will never turn down an opportunity to go shopping."

"That's right," Jessica responded with mock innocence. "It's been two whole days since you spent money."

"Smart guy!" her sister shot back, not without affection. "Anyway, you could definitely use a change of scenery. I was a little concerned about how unsettled you were by that painting and Philip Carlyle's tale, not to mention all that ghost talk over dessert and coffee. Did you get any rest last night? You look a little peaked now."

Jessica hesitated. Still, this was Liz: one person with whom she could always come clean. She plunged ahead, "I'm afraid my slumbers were not so hot. I had the weirdest, not dreams exactly, more like half-dreams. I kept being haunted, oops, bad word choice, troubled by voices of people arguing, calling for help. A woman, different men. Then I'd suddenly wake up, and it would all be still, except for the wind rattling the windows. It was so black outside. No moon."

An uneasy silence seemed to envelop the two sisters, until Elizabeth snapped shut her book and decided, "That sinks it! I'm getting you out of Castle Dracula *now*. Scott is right: quaint is just the ticket for curing that overactive imagination of yours—mine, too! Let's see if we can't get someone to drive us into the village in that lovely Oldsmobile I've heard our Mr. Carlyle favors."

Happy to shove aside dark and dreamy memories, Jessica slipped into her sister's good humor to point out, "No dice on the Olds, Liz. Mr. Carlyle's driver is running him, Scott, and Bev into Portsmouth with that car. It's roomy; but, unless you're willing to sit on someone's lap, there's no space for us."

"I doubt Leo or James would be too pleased with that arrangement," Liz concluded. "So I guess if we want to go, we'll have to hoof it?"

"Not to worry, big sister, there's still the station wagon, not nearly as elegant, but—"

"But it's already in town," Liz apprised Jess. "Earlier, I was in the kitchen getting an apple, when I heard Gerry hitching a ride into the village with Rivers' second in command, Lu something."

Disappointed, Jessica shrugged, "So, there go our plans to get into the village. Darn, I was looking forward to it."

Jess hadn't even finished speaking when Jeanne Rivers entered from the foyer. Seeming surprised to see the sisters, the woman paused before acknowledging Jessica's friendly, "Oh, Miss Rivers, good morning. I see we gave you as much of a start as you gave us."

Sedately elegant in a wine, two-piece dress, Rivers smiled, responding, "A housekeeper's inspections are never done. But I think I heard you talking about trying to find means to get into the village today?"

"You did," Jessica smiled wanly. "Scott Zimkiewicz suggested we'd enjoy a little change of scenery, not that the scenery around here isn't beautiful and impressive."

"Impressive, yes," Jeanne agreed. "Sometimes a little *op*pressive, if you're not used to isolation. After hearing the family ghost story last night, you might need a break. I'm surprised you didn't have nightmares last evening. There are times it gets to me, and I was born on this island."

Jeanne Rivers' playfully conspiratorial tone would have drawn an admission from Jess that she'd hit the nail on the head about bad dreams, except Elizabeth glided into the conversation with: "Did last night's show give you nightmares?"

Jeanne shrugged, explaining, "I grew up on the island. I've heard this story and a dozen variations, including poor Felicia being carried off by the Hound of Hades. You might say I'm almost immune. However, I must admit that last night, Mr. Carlyle was in especially good form."

Jessica tilted her head, querying, "Good form? You make it sound as if he were putting on a show. Are you telling me he's playing all of us?"

Jeanne hastily backtracked, "No, no, not at all. He really does want to know what happened. He'd be more than happy if your program could clear the family of scandal or help him understand what happened with his brother, what happened that night. He's a scientist. You know, those kinds of people always have to understand why. A mystery irritates him."

"He certainly seemed to enjoy making the whole deal sound mysterious last night," Elizabeth observed.

"I didn't say he had no sense of humor—or imagination," Jeanne answered pleasantly.

"Definitely quite the imagination," Jess mused, remembering Carlyle's love of Keats, Satie, and the saffron, autumn evening.

"Yes?" Jeanne prompted curiously.

Jess shook her head, "That's it. Nothing more." She laughed. "I know he likes poetry."

"Tell me, Miss Rivers," Liz casually changed the subject. "Do you believe there's a ghost? Have you ever seen or experienced anything?"

Jeanne laughed outright, "Who me? Maybe the autumn and winter glooms occasionally give me the heebie-jeebies, but, no, I've never seen anything. The help, visitors, supposedly Miss Gladys did, and then, they say the Blaskos . . . well, those are all rumors. Who knows—but never mind all that. You two would like to get into the village and shake off the glooms. I think I have just the solution. Can you both ride a bicycle?"

"Not the same one simultaneously," Liz quipped, "but, yes, we ride."

"Then how about this? We have several bicycles that I or one of the girls takes into the village for errands. I can't drive, and neither can most of the others. The bikes are in good shape, and Mr. Carlyle had a path made for us about a mile or so through the woods. It will take you right to the main road about a half mile out of town. It's lovely this time of year, and the path has been packed down firmly, so the ride is smooth. Today is so beautiful that I think you'll find it a delight. I don't know how fast you ladies ride, but I can't imagine it would take you more than fifteen minutes. What do you say?"

Jessica smiled broadly, "I think some exercise is just the ticket! Now, Liz, aren't you glad you and Leo joined James and me for those bike rides in Central Park?"

"I guess I could stand to work off some of last night's dinner," Liz allowed.

"And both of your desserts!" Jess teased. "I hope you gave your compliments to the cook."

"She did," Jeanne Rivers pointed out dryly. "In the kitchen. This morning." Before Liz could retort, the housekeeper turned to Jessica and asked, "So shall I set the two of you up with the bicycles? Follow me through the kitchen. We keep the bikes in the mud room.

"Oh, you will have a lovely time in the village. There is a nice cafe and some lovely antique shops. I can only afford to window shop, but even that can be fun."

Shopping talk distracted Elizabeth from verbally evening the score with Jeanne. After leading the sisters to the kitchen, the housekeeper gave them more specific directions before setting them up with their two-wheeled steeds. Moments later, Jess and Liz were traveling across the drive between the mansion and the garage and onto a well-traveled path that opened under a cathedral arch of autumn-tinted forest.

Chapter Ten

When they entered the forest-enclosed path, the way was wide enough to ride abreast. Liz quipped, "It's not as fast as those horses you ride, but it's a lot easier on a lady's derrière!"

"You never did quite get the hang of posting," Jess laughed.

"The only thing this gal likes to post are letters. Oh, that reminds me: I better drop Leo a line when we get back. If I'd known we were going into town, I'd have dashed something off this morning to mail at the local post office."

Jess glanced at her watch, careful to maintain her balance, before observing, "The post office is likely to have closed by the time we get there. It is Saturday. I'm sure Jeanne Rivers could have the letter run into town on Monday. Or you could pedal in yourself. If I didn't have a script meeting, I'd go with you."

"You're probably just afraid of running into the Hell Hound."

"I don't hear anything more threatening than a few chipping chipmunks or chattering squirrels here," Jess laughed, right before the narrowing path required them to move into single file.

Liz called, "I'd rather take my chances with that Devil Dog. Squirrels are too devious for me."

Jessica chuckled, coming alive, refreshed by the rushing water sound of wind in the treetops, as well as by the startling fall colors. The hard-packed dirt led them down a tunnel of soft yellow/green light. Glacier-strewn boulders rose grey and craggy through the trees. Nothing ominous. Just homey with the rich scent of leaves, earth, and forest. Sometimes, they'd pass a brook paralleling the path and bubbling over rocks and fallen branches. Occasionally, splashes of scarlet and maroon vines were wending up the trees: poison ivy! How could anything so beautiful leave you feeling so miserable? Chickadees scolded and Titmice hawed displeasure at their passage. Glancing up revealed brilliant blue sky piercing through the waving bright canopy.

Jeanne Rivers had accurately timed their progress. Less than fifteen minutes later, the trail widened. Green firs interspersed the yellows and soft oranges of maples and elms. The sisters glided to a stop as the trail opened onto the main road, the two-lane paved affair running the island's length. Directly across from them, separating them from the bay, was—

"A cemetery," Elizabeth pronounced. "How cheery. Little Miss Rivers didn't mention that landmark."

"The mood we were in before, she probably thought it would scare us off. You know, though, it's pretty—so serene, peaceful."

"Yeah, I imagine once you're dead, you give up being much of a party animal—although on this island . . ."

"Wise guy," Jessica teased. "Anyway, it's nice, in a plain, simple fashion. I don't see any elaborate statuary. I bet it's the town cemetery for plain-dealing New Englanders."

"Nothing like we two fancy-pants New Yorkers," Liz teased. "Still, I wouldn't imagine families like the Saunders and Carlyles who built those ultra mansions would settle for plain stone markers."

"Probably, they have their own separate cemetery, with all the requisite weeping women, wings of Horus, family statues, and towering angels. Still, this is sweet and peaceful. On the bay, fringed by forest, it would be nice to visit." Seeing her sister's frown, Jessica added with a smile, "But not today. Today, let's quote the inimitable Three Stooges and 'go places and eat things.'"

"And buy things, too," her sister sagely added.

"Sounds great!" Jessica agreed and, after checking both ways for traffic, led her sister off to the left toward town.

Ironically, this part of the route was both easier and a bit more trying. The paved road made traveling smoother, with little traffic to bother them. However, a breeze off the ocean kept switching between hitting them sideways or head-on—the bane of any cyclist. And, then, they hit a hill that forced the sisters to stand up in the saddle to pedal furiously. Fortunately, what went up also came down. Liz ceased grumbling as they flew downhill. Sitting back, Liz extended her legs straight out, off the pedals, and glided ahead.

"Show off!" Jessica laughed, the blues of last night's dinner and dreams left somewhere back at the top of the hill behind them.

The scenery was a delight, too. The forest gave way more and more to houses: capes or colonials or an eccentric ad hoc mixture, usually gleaming white in the brilliant October sun or bearing unpainted, weather-browned or grayed wooden shingles. Many places sported front gardens of sunny mums, creamy orange or yellow marigolds, or splashes of purple and magenta flowers. Jess especially loved the gardens bordered with sun-whitened shells. Marking the upcoming holiday, jack o'lanterns mischievously, or malevolently, resided on many porch steps. Sometimes a woman out front gardening or a child playing would pause, look up, and offer a friendly wave—which neither Jess nor Liz failed to return.

The nearer the two cyclists drew to the village, the closer the houses sat, with paved or gravel narrow lanes leading into pleasant warrens of side neighborhoods. Jess tried to catch sight of the turn-off Nathan Jones had taken, but they were moving too fast, and she now had to watch for traffic. On a Saturday morning, adults were busy with errands, while kids were making up for fun lost when imprisoned all week in school.

The road curved to the left just as they glided by a smallish but still stately brick building. It even had a turret with a peaked, verdigris-copper roof. The large sign out front, easier to read than the relief lettering over the door, proclaimed (in plain, dignified New England script) Birdsong Island Library and Historical Society. *Ah*, Jess thought, *that's where Scott and Bev had done some research.*

They glided around the bend and into Birdsong village proper, passing a one-truck volunteer fire station. Sidewalks commenced here, so Jess and Liz slowed and kept close to the side of the road to avoid the leisurely flow of traffic, while watching out for pedestrians. Now, across the street was a small police station, a recent building, but still likely pre-war.

Elizabeth signaled Jess to pull over, then suggested, "Let's walk the bikes from here. We can check out the town better at a stroll." They stopped under a maple, while people bustled about their business, too busy for more than a casual glance at the strangers. Liz continued, "If we can just find a place to tie up our steeds."

"Before they wander off?" Jess quipped. "It's a shame you can't train bikes to ground hitch."

Liz shook her head, adding, "Or to resist if someone tries to walk off—sorry, ride off—with them."

"You've been living in the big, bad city too long, my girl," Jessica kidded. "This is 'trust-your-neighbor-because-everybody-knows-everybody-else' New England. Small town values."

"If it were that idyllic, they wouldn't need that police station," Elizabeth returned. "And your Scott wouldn't have a mystery for his program. Though, if you ask me, the more I think about it, this Felicia's fate is nothing more mysterious than sipping Bacardis in Cuba with the brother for twenty years. Nice work if you can get it."

"Wait a minute, Liz," Jessica countered. "What about the presence you saw . . . sensed?"

"I said it was *a* presence, not necessarily Felicia's. If it were really she, wouldn't she have dropped a clue to someone about who done her in? Maybe it's Great Aunt Minnie, for all I know," Liz dismissed the question.

"Gosh," Jessica frowned. "Bacardis, huh? That wouldn't make for much of a finale on the show." But determined not to waste a lovely day on uncertain worries, Jessica asserted, "Oh heck! Enough of Felicia and the whole creepy crew. We're here to take a break from all that. Say, look over there." She pointed to a storefront a few buildings down. "That looks like an antique shop, with a little alley next to it where we could park our bikes. What do you say?"

"I say all reet!" Liz replied, merrily sliding one hand across the other like a hep kitten. "I've got some Lincolns and Hamiltons begging to be liberated. But, first, I'm taking off this jacket. I'm practically boiling now. *This* is October?"

Jess agreed, removing her own jacket, but warned, "Don't knock it, sis. Wait until it starts to sno . . ."

"Shh! S-N-O-W is a four-letter word! Especially up here."

A few minutes later, Jess and Liz opened the antique-shop door to the tinkling of an overhead bell. A sixtyish woman smiled at them from behind a counter to their right, then went back to chatting with another lady of similar age.

Jess wasn't sure, but the eyes of the woman behind the counter seemed to linger on them. *Swell! Was someone else pegging me as a dead ringer for the island's number-one mystery gal?*

To forestall an uncomfortable situation, Jess ducked aside her sister and tried to guide Liz to the further end of the large, packed room.

"What's got into you, Jessica?" she protested. From the corner of her eye, Jess caught the ladies giving them a second look at Liz's words.

Thinking fast, Jess replied, "Sorry, Liz. I thought I saw a tea service you might like down at the far end of the store. Let me take you down there—"

"Great! I've been looking for something like that. Lead the way, kiddo," Elizabeth loudly pronounced.

Wasting no time, Jess moved her sister deeper into the store. However, now she had to actually find a tea service to satisfy her incentive to Liz. *Well, there was something not too far off on the shelf ahead, though maybe not far enough away to distance them from the two ladies' attention.*

Even as they stopped before the tea service in question, Jess was disquieted to still hear the two women talking swiftly, furtively.

"Jess," Elizabeth cut into her thoughts, "didn't you hear what I just said? I asked you why you thought I'd be interested in this service? You know it's not my style—and the color's all wrong for my apartment. What's with the pale face, kiddo? Are you all right? Did you get overheated? Maybe the proprietress could get you a glass of water."

"No," Jessica returned in almost a whisper, but with finality. Her voice even softer, while making sure her back was to the two women, she insisted, "Liz, I think coming in here wasn't such a hot idea, after all. I think—"

"Huh? Why not? You love antique stores. Are you sure you didn't get overheated?"

"No, I'm fine, but those women," Jessica whispered. "I think they may have picked up on my unfortunate resemblance. Maybe we should take a powder."

"Too late."

"What?"

"Brace yourself, sis. They're coming over, now."

Jessica turned with trepidation, steeling herself on perceiving both ladies carefully approaching, exchanging nervous (or were those wary?) looks.

"Excuse us," began the proprietress.

"Yes?" Liz answered. A touch protectively?

"I hope you don't mind us coming over here and asking," added the second woman. "But you look *so* much like her; we just *had* to find out."

"Yes," Jessica managed, trying to sound nonchalant, even congenial. Her resemblance must be quite unnerving because they were now both concentrating on Liz and not her.

"The resemblance is uncanny," the proprietress said to Elizabeth. "Are you Rosalind Russell?"

Jessica blinked, then giggled at her own silliness.

The two ladies exchanged embarrassed looks, so Elizabeth stepped in, pointing out, "No, no. She's much older, you know."

"Not *much*," corrected Jessica with a barely suppressed grin.

"I told you it couldn't be her, Martha," the proprietress chided her companion. "What in tarnation would Rosalind Russell be doing on Birdsong Island, big Hollywood star and all that."

"It is a lovely vacation spot," Jessica supported "Martha." "Lots of people come to the New Hampshire and Maine coasts to get away."

The proprietress carefully appraised Jessica before saying thoughtfully, "We've never seen you two around here before. That what you're doing, taking a vacation?"

Jess hesitated. They'd just gotten off the stove, but would mentioning their connection to the radio program plop them smack into the frying pan? Nathan Jones had warned them that a lot of people weren't crazy about their stirring up old scandals.

For good or ill, the proprietress's friend took the problem out of Jessica's hands with, "They must be with that lot out to the Carlyle Mansion, the bunch that's doing the radio program about that murder, Annette."

Jessica and Elizabeth waited for Annette's response, which left them still hanging when it came as a laconic, "Is that so?"

Girl Scout Jessica couldn't lie and wasn't about to chicken out, either, answering: "Yes, that's so. I'm Jessica Minton, the lead actress on the Wellstone Mystery Hour. This is my sister Elizabeth, who's not a performer."

"Well then," decided Martha, "The littler one is a kind of celebrity, being on radio and all. Not as good as Rosalind Russell, but it's something to make the day."

"Guess you're right, Martha," Annette nodded. She looked at Jessica and queried kindly, "You wouldn't mind if I didn't ask for an autograph, would you, dearie? Things are kind of crowded around here as it is."

"I think I'll survive," Jessica impishly smiled. "Besides, you have to save some space for when the real Rosalind Russell shows up."

Annette gave Jessica a warm laugh, then commented, putting a hand on Jessica's arm, "Bless you, kiddo. I'll have to give your show a listen sometime. Maybe even for the story I heard you folks are doing about the island."

"Do you ladies know much about the story?" Jessica asked.

The older woman laughed again and revealed, "Dearie, everybody over thirty knows that story. Trouble is, just about every one of them knows a different version. Those that really know are all dead."

"Except for Philip Carlyle and Vitus Blasko," Elizabeth suggested.

The other women again exchanged knowing looks. It was Annette, again, who spoke: "Philip Carlyle knows mainly how his machines work, and Vitus Blasko—I'll bet if he does know anything, it's in his best interest to keep it to himself."

"So you think he's guilty of whatever happened to Felicia?" Jessica questioned. "What about the brother?"

This time, Martha smiled knowingly to reply, "That's a good question. I think that no-good Bill Carlyle was up to something. He had quite the reputation, and that Dr. Blasko, he was so upset when his wife disappeared."

"Because he probably did her in," Annette disagreed assuredly.

"My money's still on Bacardis for two in Cuba," Liz added.

The two women gave Elizabeth quizzical looks, so Jessica explained, "My sister thinks the whole thing's a put-up by the missing couple to hide that they took off together."

"She has a point," Martha noted to her friend. Turning back to the sisters, she continued, "But it's not as fun as the little running argument Annette and I have going on the real story. Maybe your director will settle the question."

"I wonder which way, with you guiding his research over at the Historical Society?" Annette queried with a twinkle. She added for the sisters' benefit: "Martha is in charge of records there."

"I saw the library, bicycling in," Jessica replied. "It's beautiful. You must enjoy working there."

"Not so much when winter sets in and the heat conks out," Martha answered, "but it is a gracious lady of a building. You must come by sometime. I'll give you a tour, if you like. I imagine Philip Carlyle has almost as many books as the library does. But if you're looking, I can guide you to some background on the scandal."

"That sounds interesting," Jessica replied.

"I think my sister has gotten herself immersed enough in this story for now," Liz interjected. "The poor kid had nightmares last night."

"Liz, you don't have to tell everyone everything," Jessica prickled.

"Well," Annette began, "I've always found one of the best ways to take my mind off my troubles is to do some shopping, and we do have some lovely things here."

"Good idea!" Elizabeth concurred.

"We'll leave you to browse," Annette smiled.

Chapter Eleven

Twenty minutes later, the Minton sisters stepped cheerily out into the October sunshine, each carrying a treasure of her own: Liz, jade earrings, and Jessica, a golden spray of rhinestone stars. A brigade of roller-skating kids sent them leaping into the street, laughing, though most of the other affected pedestrians reacted with far less humor, including one threat to call Chief Winslow or Winston on them.

Not a worry for the Minton gals, on their way to lunch in a café down the street recommended by their new friends, Martha and Annette. The antique-shop ladies had promised the sisters would find the best cup of Keemun tea in town there. Even on this balmy day, that desire for tea marked Jess and Liz as true New Englanders. Entering the café, they found it ordinary looking, as the older women had predicted. With any luck, their predictions about the comestibles and the tea would be equally solid. Anyway, Jess had faith, even if her sister viewed the place with skepticism. Since it was around lunchtime, the restaurant was pretty crowded, so Jess hoped their "in" with Annette and Martha might procure them one of the few tables open.

Jess and Liz approached the hostess's station, where a fortyish, not quite plump woman with long, curly blonde hair was busily checking over some papers. Before her sister could get bossy, Jessica caught the preoccupied woman's attention with, "Hello there, Mrs. Brunelle. Martha and Annette at Risdon's Antiques sent us over. They told us that if we were looking for a premium pot of Keemun tea, Brunelle's was the place. I hope you can squeeze us in. We've had a long bike ride through the woods, so we could certainly stand some sustenance."

Being called by name by two people she'd never met, Mrs. Brunelle cocked her head and wrinkled her brow before responding, "You say Annette and Martha sent you over? Strangers, aren't you?"

"Yes, we are," Jess answered, she hoped winningly. Maybe they didn't have as much of an "in" as she'd thought. Nevertheless, she pushed on,

"We were over there shopping and had a lovely chat with them both. A couple of cards, but nice ones. When my sister mentioned we'd give an arm and a leg for a good cup of tea and lunch, they sent us straight to you. Told us to ask for the special Keemun."

Mrs. Brunelle brightened. "That's Martha and Annette, all rightie. You two must be okay for them to tell you about the special blend." She hesitated, studying the sisters' faces before adding, "I know you're definitely not islanders, but there's something familiar about you . . ."

"Oh, I know," Liz waved her hands. "Everyone mistakes me for Rosalind Russell."

"No, not you." A nod at Jessica. "Her. I know I've seen you somewhere."

Jess tensed. *Maybe I ought to start wearing a sandwich board proclaiming: "I am NOT Felicia Blasko!"*

Mrs. Brunelle snapped her fingers. "Oh, sure! You're the lead actress on *The Wellstone Mystery Hour*. I saw your picture in *Radio Mirror* and one of that handsome young man who was here this morning. I love your show. Scares the living daylights out of me. Good gracious, you people are the cat's meow!"

"Thank you!" Jessica brightened, an appreciative glow infusing her voice. "Glad we can scare you—I think!"

"That's my kid sister," Elizabeth teased. "Just don't give her a swelled head. I have to live with her."

Recognizing sibling banter, Mrs. Brunelle smiled at Liz, "I think you're probably very proud of your sister." Then she shifted to business: "Anyway, you two do look famished. Follow me. We have a nice table open by the window."

With that, the woman picked up two laminated menus and led the sisters over, explaining with a wink, "I only have tables for four right now, but better two extra seats than not enough."

Sitting down, Jess and Liz thanked their hostess, smiling their appreciation.

"Oh, that's no never mind. Anyway, if I run short, I may have to send some strangers over to join you. I'll put in that order for tea and have Frances come take the rest of your order." She started off, but stopped and turned to Jessica to ask, "Seeing that I am a fan of your program, I don't suppose you could give me any inside scoops on that show you're doing about the Carlyle Ghost."

Jessica shot her sister a quick, uncertain glance before answering, "To be honest, Mrs. Brunelle, I haven't even seen the script yet, myself! I'm not sure where our writers are going with it. But," here Jess hesitated, "tell me. Is there a lot of resentment on the island about our dredging up the story?"

"Well," the other woman considered, "most folks here are too busy trying to make a living, pay their bills, and raise their kids to worry about some rich folks' troubles. To tell the truth, those that take an interest find it kind of entertaining, even satisfying, to see those upper-crust families get a comeuppance, especially since Mr. Carlyle runs a business off the island but don't employ many folks from here."

"So, my sister doesn't need to worry about being burnt in effigy for playing Felicia Blasko over the airwaves?" Liz quipped.

Facing Jessica, Mrs. Brunelle reassured her, "Oh, don't worry a thing about that, honey. People are more up in arms about the developers trying to buy up property cheap now that there's a building boom on. The old money and the folks with vacation places, they're all on the warpath against selling out to split up the land and build housing. Young people, though, they want to break up the land and sell so they can get out to see the world or just make some money."

"In other words, unless my sister wants to invest in tract housing, she's safe from the flaming torch and pitchfork crowd?" Elizabeth concluded, tongue in cheek.

Mrs. Brunelle laughed, "I guess you could put it that way. Now, I'll give you girls time to decide what you want." The attractive woman turned to go but paused. With a playful look, she said to Jessica, "And if you can let me know the skinny on your program . . ."

"I'll let you know whatever I can without getting fired," Jess promised with a wink. "My director is very hush-hush. All I can tell you is that he's got a big surprise of some sort planned."

Mrs. Brunelle winked back and left the Mintons.

Elizabeth queried, "Feeling better now that you're not about to cause Armageddon with your role? No one even cares."

"That's not encouraging ratings-wise," Jess snorted, but not seriously. She *was* serious when adding, "Besides, it wasn't the islanders in general who concerned me—just the families involved."

"Scott did tell you they were all on board. You heard Philip Carlyle say so last night."

"I didn't hear any Blaskos chime in," Jessica contradicted. "Besides, lately, under all this pressure from Ungerpreck, I don't think Scott's been entirely on the level. I think Scott may have stretched the truth to justify his ends."

"For example?"

"I'm not sure. As I said, I haven't heard the Blaskos' views. Jamie Blasko didn't exactly roll out the welcome mat for us."

"She didn't throw us to the Hound of Hades, either," Liz reasonably countered.

"I guess you're right," Jessica agreed, none too enthusiastically. "But, speaking of Miss Blasko, I'm still surprised you seem to have changed your tune about her being haunted by her mother—all your talk about Felicia lamming off to the tropics with the other Carlyle brother. Which is it?"

"Okay, then maybe it's Great Aunt Minnie doing the haunting, for all I know. Or maybe Felicia took off to become some kind of voodoo Queen, sending bad juju back home."

"Oh, that last one's plausible," Jessica deadpanned.

Liz was about to quip back when a tapping on the window next to her and Jessica interrupted. Both of them faced the cherubic countenance of Gerry Davis, the wind playing with his hair. Jessica broke into a big smile and motioned Gerry to join them. With a pleased bob of his head, Gerry started for the door with his uneven but quick stride.

It was but a few moments before Jess's colleague was heading for their table, kidding, "Fancy meeting you two here."

"Right," Liz remarked, "there are so many hotspots to choose from around here."

Gerry smiled at Liz's crack, then pulled out his chair and inquired, "So, are you ladies having a nice day? The weather is pretty darned swell for October."

"Liz went shopping. She's never blue when she's doing that," Jessica teased. Seeing Gerry looking for a place to rest his cane, she took it from him and leaned it against the wall beside her.

Gerry smiled a "thanks" before turning to Elizabeth with, "I wouldn't think a New York sophisticate would find much to her liking in a one-horse town like this."

"Gerry," Liz purred, "I could find a buy and make a honey of a deal on a life raft."

"She could, too," Jess concurred.

"Hey, as long as your trip was a success. But, say, how did you two get in? I rode in on the milk run. Did Master Philip give you a spin in the luxury sedan?"

"I wish," Liz grumped. "No, we came in the old-fashioned way, by bicycle. Let me tell you, my seat padding is *not* what it used to be."

Jessica teased, "I suppose we could have called a cab—like the one that took us round Robin Hood's Barn and still left us at the wrong place."

The young waitress, Frances, arrived with three glasses of water bunched in her hands as Liz snorted, "Puh-leeze! Even with my springs sprung and on only two wheels, I could still get here faster and with less bother than I could with that old goat and his even older jalopy."

Frances perked up and couldn't keep from interjecting, "You got stuck riding with Nathan Jones? Heaven help you! At least you won't have to worry about that happening again. He blew out of town a day or so ago. Came into a big bundle of cash. I think he won a lottery or something."

"Maybe he made a bundle at Rockingham Park, where you did that presentation last summer," Liz kidded Jessica.

"It's October, Liz. The Rock is closed. The horses are running at 'Gansett now," Jessica corrected matter-of-factly.

"It's like having Damon Runyon for a sister," Liz deadpanned.

"An odd image," Gerry decided. "Odd, but interesting."

Frances was lost by this detour in the conversation. Since Jessica could have chowed down on a small pachyderm at this point, she put things back on track: "Enough with the smart talk. I don't know about you, Gerry, but Liz and I need to refuel. Frances, we've got some high-priority orders for you."

Their orders given, and Frances on her way to place them, Gerry put his palms on the table and addressed Jessica, "So, Jess, it looks as if this trip into town has returned you to your chipper self. You'd been looking off-kilter since Scott sprang that doppelgänger portrait on you, and Philip Carlyle reeled out his tale of mystery. I barely heard a squeak out of you all through dessert."

"She was too busy eating," Elizabeth coolly noted.

Jess realized that her sister was trying to kid away any returning uneasiness, but she wasn't about to chicken out on facing facts.

"To tell the truth, Gerry, the resemblance did give me a start. However, I don't let anything come between me and my cherries jubilee. Seriously, though, it does give me a queer feeling to know that people may be looking at me and thinking about a murdered woman."

"Unless she's alive and well . . ." Liz began.

". . . and sipping Bacardis in Cuba. I know," Jess finished.

Gerry regarded the sisters with confusion, finally saying, "I don't follow."

"Elizabeth questions whether Felicia was a victim of foul play, to sound clichéd. She wonders if the lady and that black-sheep brother didn't just take a powder for parts unknown together." *The less said about Liz's earlier conjectures that a spirit haunted Jamie, the better.*

Jess was a little surprised to see Gerry sit back and do some tall thinking. *Had Jamie told him something about her family that lent credence to or that undercut Liz's theory?*

Though Jessica was too polite to put that question into words, Elizabeth was not: "You've been pretty buddy-buddy with the kid, Gerry. What's her take on the story?"

"Elizabeth!" Jessica chided. "Don't ask Gerry to betray a confidence."

Gerry surprised Jessica by shrugging and saying, "No, that's all right. Fair question, all things considered." He took a sip of water, then finished, "As far as betraying a confidence . . . I can't reveal what I don't know."

"So, she's said nothing about what she thinks happened to her mother?" Liz pressed. "About what she believes concerning her father's or Bill Carlyle's involvement?"

"All I know is that she came back from living off the island to nurse her Dad when he got sick recently. So, she couldn't believe he was any kind of a murderer. Beyond that, I don't know anything. Don't forget, I've known her less than a week," Gerry pointed out.

"But you've fallen for her already," Elizabeth observed. Turning to Jessica, she insisted, "And don't you give me that disapproving look. You agree with me, and you're just as concerned about Gerry."

As he spoke, Gerry put a hand over Jessica's, mitigating the glare with which she was searing her sister, "You're a good kid, Jessica. I know your heart's in the right place—your sister's, too. I do understand that Liz is just trying to put your mind at ease, and I suspect she's even trying to protect me. But I'm a big boy. Fought in a war and everything. Take it easy—and don't let that resemblance thing get to you. Remember, according to your sister, the portrait looks like half the silver screen's brunette sophisticates—on two continents. The only one who didn't get thrown into the mix was Rosalind Russell."

"I got that this morning," Elizabeth informed him.

Gerry gave Liz a visual once-over, then compressed his lips decisively to pronounce, "I can see that, except, isn't Rosalind a little older?"

Elizabeth gave Jess a knowing nod, who just shook her head and smiled, relaxing a *bit* now. Jessica wanted to say more, but Frances returned with a mug of coffee for Gerry. So, she waited, marshaling her thoughts into words. After Gerry thanked the waitress and the friends were alone again, Jess felt free to speak: "Well, guys, I *know* I'm not some kind of reincarnation of Felicia, especially since I was alive when she died. That's not what still isn't sitting right with me. It's, as I said before, how are the Carlyles and Blaskos looking at me?"

Gerry teasingly assured her, "I don't think anyone's planning to do you in out of fear he didn't get it right the first time."

"That's not really what I mean, Gerry," Jess corrected her friend, "but thanks for raising *that* possibility. It's so awkward trying to interact with people when I know that my face is evoking painful memories and emotions. I'd hate to open old wounds."

Liz tried to make Jess feel better by saying, "Remember, Scott said that the families want the past opened up. Instead of beating up on yourself, look at it as you're helping clear the debris of the past so they can find the truth and heal. Maybe someone will get peace."

Jess wondered if her sister was also referring to Jamie Blasko's dark cloud.

Liz pressed on, "Philip Carlyle actually sounded darned eager to get to the bottom of things, even if it meant airing his family's dirty laundry. Your show might even help him clear his brother."

"He didn't sound all that concerned about his brother's reputation," Jessica disagreed. "In fact, from the way he told his story, I don't know whom he dislikes more: his brother or Blasko. I almost think he wouldn't mind finding a way to make them both take the rap."

"The only one who came off at all positive was the innocent victim, Felicia," Liz speculated, a little too much irony in her tone.

"What's that supposed to mean?" Jessica questioned, noting Gerry tense a bit at her sister's indirect criticism of the object of his affection's mom.

Gerry spoke his objections: "Jamie may never have directly told me what she thinks happened that night, whom she blames, but I can tell you in no uncertain terms whom she does not blame. She reveres her mother."

"Settle down, you two," Liz dismissed them. "I'm not bad-mouthing Felicia. My focus is on Philip Carlyle. I think he's not at all as neutral on Felicia as he would like us to think. It certainly explains why he's so hostile to both men involved in the disappearance. Unrequited feelings can lead not just to idealization but obsession. That's why I think Jessica should be careful of him. He might see her as a second chance, which could have miserable consequences all around."

"Oh, ho," Gerry replied, folding his arms before him. To Jess, he queried, "And what do you say to that, Miss Jessica?"

Annoyed, Jess asserted, "I say that my sister likes to exaggerate. See this little gold band, third finger, left hand? He knows I'm married."

"It sounded as if you two had quite a little *tête à tête* before dinner last night: Keats, Satie, autumn splendor, and all," Elizabeth returned knowingly. "I saw a glance or two in your direction by our friend during dinner."

"Oh, for Pete's sake," Jessica insisted. "We didn't say two words to each other after dinner. In fact, when I did notice, Mr. Carlyle seemed very engaged with Scott, Vic, and Chet over some technical questions. Honestly, Gerry, did you get the same impression as my sister?"

Gerry shrugged and disagreed, "Sorry, gals, I can't attest to either of your views. After Carlyle's recitation of the Blasko story, I was thinking about Jamie. That set me considering point of view. Bev and I were discussing how an eyewitness might not be so reliable when he's already got a stake in the story. So I began to wonder if digging on my own at the local library and historical society might help me ensure that Scott doesn't slant the script in favor of the family hosting us and against the Blaskos. Maybe I can protect Jamie or even come across some info to help her learn the truth."

Jessica cautioned, "I hate to say this, Gerry, but what you discover might have the opposite effect. The truth isn't automatically what we want to hear."

"True," Gerry allowed. "However, if I give her even an unpalatable truth, I think I could cushion the blow, help her accept it."

"Or she might want to shoot the messenger," Elizabeth quietly warned.

"At least I'll go down in a noble cause," Gerry responded ruefully. "That's the least I can do for her. Sometimes when you come out of a war, it's enough to know you saved something or someone from being destroyed."

"You're a good scout, Mr. Davis," Jess smiled, putting her hand on Gerry's arm.

"You can say that again," Liz affirmed.

"But don't," Gerry kidded, breaking the sentimental mood. "Let's all agree I'm a prince among men and leave it at that. Unfortunately, I'm not a very effective prince. One reason I came into the village was to do some of that research in the historical society, but it closed early today. Now, I'll have to find time before Scott and Bev get too deep into the script."

The sisters exchanged smiles, with Jess promising, "You're in luck, Gerry, my boy! One of the ladies who recommended this restaurant is the curator. She gave me her card with a number to call for an appointment to come in sometime."

"Ain't serendipity grand?" Gerry beamed.

Their orders arrived and the three proceeded to have themselves a merry lunch. Liz ended up pronouncing, "Gerry, I do believe a record has been set. My kid sister has gone nearly two whole hours without mentioning James."

"Smart guy," Jess shot back, then impishly added, "But you don't know what I've been thinking. Hmm, maybe I'd better write my guy when we get back."

"Ah, newlyweds!" Gerry kidded.

"Not so new!" Jessica corrected. "We had our second anniversary earlier this month."

Gerry started to tease Jessica, but catching sight of something by the door, his expression flashed from radiant to worried. Jess had to turn around to see, though she had a good idea of the source of his rollercoaster of expressions. *Yup*, just as she'd suspected.

In a cream-colored dress stood Jamie Blasko just inside the entrance. She caught sight of their threesome at the table and tensed. Yet her eyes lingered on Gerry. Before she could turn away, he waved and beckoned her to join them. She hesitated—but abruptly left.

"Mrs. Brunelle is not going to like your effect on her customers, Gerry," Elizabeth remarked.

Gerry gave Liz a disapproving look, then signaled Jess to hand him his cane. As she complied, the anxious young man was pulling bills from his wallet, saying, "This should cover my lunch. There's something very wrong with Jamie. I've never seen her react like that."

"Maybe it's *me*," Jessica proposed slowly. "You know, the resemblance."

"I'll go after her, see what I can do to help," Gerry explained. He was heading for the door before Jessica could offer either sympathy or warning.

"He's got it *bad*," Liz pronounced.

"And that ain't good," Jessica finished the song lyric. "Oh, Liz, she's going to break his heart. I just know it. I don't mean she's a *femme fatale*, but she's got way too much emotional baggage for this to end well."

"Enough baggage to open a luggage shop," Elizabeth sourly noted. Jess didn't smile at the quip, so Liz apologized, "Sorry, you know I can't resist a straight line. Honestly, Jessica, you've got to remember that he's a big boy. He's got to live his own life without us mother-henning him. He's already survived worse than a broken heart, if it even comes to that."

"I know," Jessica agreed, "It's just that he's such a good guy. I want to see him as happy as James and I."

"There you go. I knew you couldn't make it the whole two hours without speaking his name—reverently. I'm surprised you left out Dusty."

"I wonder if she's eating right for Lois," Jessica mused, slipping into a grin as Liz rolled her eyes.

"Never mind her," Liz said. "*I* want to be eating right. Excuse me while I flag the waitress down for a slice of pie. I'll need all the energy I can muster to pedal up some of those hills on the way back."

Chapter Twelve
Sunday, October 19th

Just returned from Mass, Jessica strolled into the drawing room, bright with sunshine and a warm October breeze rolling through the open French doors. She was looking spiffy in her black redingote over a cream blouse and soft-rust-colored skirt, matching the shade of her coachman's hat, trimmed with a black veil tied beneath her chin. Liz, now upstairs writing Leo, had earlier decided that getting away from this manse of dark secrets, putting on the dog a little, not to mention spending some quiet time with the Almighty, was just the ticket for her and Jess. She'd been right. A priest, whose sermon spoke about the power of hope and forgiveness opening up all kinds of possibilities in a shattered world, combined with the friendly greetings of Annette and Martha, had relaxed the taut atmosphere created the night before by Gerry and Scott locking horns over the séance.

At first, it had been so pleasant after church, chatting with the two older women in the October morning about something other than ghosts from tragedies past. Then someone remarked on the sky having turned duller, gauzy grey with smoke, and the conversation turned to those forest fires seething in Maine, threatening whole towns. Martha was worried about a cousin living near Kennebunk Village. Before Jess knew it, Annette mentioned that she and Martha had to zip off to see to a friend who had been too under the weather to attend today's service. *Now, why had Annette and Martha both looked at me, then exchanged knowing smiles? Must be that their pal was another fan of our program.*

Switching on the radio confronted Jessica with more news of the wildfires. The governor of Maine had canceled the hunting season. *Which was tougher on the animals, the hunters or the fire?* Then the announcer gave her reason to smile by citing the areas where the blazes seemed to be coming under control. *Yay! That should take a load off Martha's mind!* She turned the dial until the bouncing joy of Debussy's "Fêtes" whirled about her until—.

"There you are!" Gerry Davis came through the open French doors. "I've been looking all over for you."

"Liz and I went to church, Gerry. Thought we'd put in a good word for you heathens with the Almighty—though I guess we Minton girls do come up a good deal short of saintly," Jessica kidded. Her levity faded, however, when she got a good look at his expression.

"This is serious, Jess," he stated quietly. A quick look at the doors opening into the foyer prompted Gerry to cross the room, close them, and return, saying, "We need to talk."

"Gerry, what's wrong? Are you still stewing over last night's argument with Scott?"

Instead of answering Jessica's question, he instructed, "Get the French doors, will you?"

"Ye-yeah, sure," Jessica answered, hesitating in puzzlement before complying. The doors closed, Jessica turned back to her friend with, "Gerry, you're worrying me. What's wrong?"

Gerry fastened Jessica with keen eyes and questioned, "Can you still get us in to check the historical society records?"

"Uh, sure, I imagine so," Jess answered slowly.

"Good. Could you arrange something for today?"

"Today? Sunday?" Jessica blurted. "Are you kidding?"

"No. Not at all," Gerry replied firmly.

"Gosh, Gerry, I hate to let you down, but the answer is 'no.' The whole place is closed, and Martha Royle mentioned today that she'd be visiting a sick friend," Jessica explained.

"Did you set up a later date for us?"

"No. There were more pressing things to talk about, and I also didn't want to ask a favor so soon. Gerry, what's the big rush? Has this anything to do with your flare-up with Scott. What's eating you?"

"What's eating me is what this whole setup is doing to Jamie," Gerry intensely replied. "When I caught up to her after I left you, she told me she doesn't think she can bear having all the old memories of that time dredged up. Worse, she's afraid of how it will affect her father."

"Wait, Scott said that her father *wants* to know," Jessica carefully disagreed.

"'Scott says, Scott says,'" Gerry bitterly repeated. "Scott wants a hit show. He's changed a hell of a lot from when we started the program under Mr. Wellstone. Ungerpreck has changed Scott's priorities."

"Are you saying that Vitus Blasko actually *doesn't* want to know? He wants things to remain buried? Is that what Jamie told you?"

"Not exactly." Indicating the couch by the hearth, Gerry offered, "Please sit down, Jess. I need to get this off my chest. I've been walking and thinking, waiting to talk with you."

Jessica took a seat and said, "Well, Gerry, I think you better explain exactly what you *do* mean. I hate to see you all tied up in knots, but I can't help if I don't have the full story."

"Okay, okay, it's like this." Gerry looked down to pull his thoughts together before continuing. "When I caught up to Jamie, tried to talk to her, she said she couldn't face me or any of us, knowing what might be coming in the broadcast. But she isn't just afraid for herself. It's mostly about her father because she believes he doesn't know what he's letting himself in for. She worries that he hopes to be cleared; but if Scott comes up with a script that doesn't do that, it could push him over the edge, even kill him. Yes, Scott and Bev have been doing research, but they're still relying on something as flimsy, no, phony, as a séance to settle the question."

"Oh," was all Jess could say. She certainly did not want Vitus Blasko's life on her conscience. Her idea slowly formulating, Jess proposed, "Why couldn't we persuade Scott to slant the blame towards Bill Carlyle? It can't hurt him: he's dead. And Philip Carlyle clearly despises him as a black sheep. He pretty much said so at dinner."

"Despises him enough to intentionally 'blacken the family name' with a murder accusation?" Gerry returned skeptically. "Would Scott really chance offending our host?"

"Then there's the wild card of the medium," Jessica pondered.

"Do you honestly think this medium will come up with a result that Scott doesn't want?"

Jessica blinked. Of course! Why hadn't she been thinking of Scott's medium as a phony? Because of her sister's experiences? Yet, even Liz had been skeptical of this medium.

Gerry speculated, "If we can do our own research, we can tell if Scott is cooking the story. We'll have ammunition to force him to give Blasko a square deal. And maybe we can get the lowdown on this Madame Wanda."

"Well," Jessica considered, "I could also see if Elizabeth's beau, he's a police detective, could get some info on her, as well. But that might take time. And, Gerry, there's another catch you haven't thought of. What if our own research points the finger at Blasko?"

Her friend looked away before admitting, "I know, but I have to take that chance if it means I *might* be able to help Jamie."

The drawing room doors opened unexpectedly, and Scott Zimkiewicz cheerily waltzed in, saying, "I've been looking for you kids."

Seeing fire in Gerry's eyes, Jessica was prepared to duck, except Scott knocked both her and Gerry for a loop with, "Gerry, I owe you an apology for last night. You had valid questions, but I let you get my goat because I was so danged tired from working all day."

Somewhat mollified, Gerry replied carefully, "I'm glad you see my point of view, Scott, although you're a bit vague on precisely what you agree with and what you're going to do to make sure the Blaskos—"

"And the Carlyles," Jess politically added.

"Yeah, the Carlyles, get a fair shake. I'll be honest. I intend to do a little digging of my own," Gerry revealed, diplomatically leaving Jessica out of it.

"Fair enough," Scott agreed. "I think you'll find that Bev and I will play square, no flim-flamming the facts."

"So, what about this medium business?" Gerry pressed. "You're not going to base your final conclusion on some hocus-pocus baloney."

"I was thinking about that all last night," Scott replied. "I can understand your skepticism. But I didn't just fall off the turnip truck, myself, Gerry. I've researched this gal; I've even met her. I think she's the real deal."

"*I've* never met her, so you can understand that I'm not impressed. As far as I'm concerned, she's just some dame working a pitch as old as the hills," Gerry responded coolly.

"Well, chum," Scott affably came back, "I think I can alleviate some of your doubts. In fact, that's exactly what I intend to do tomorrow night. I've invited Madame Wanda to join us for dessert and coffee to answer everyone's questions. You can see for yourself she's not making a monkey out of any of us. And when you do your own research on the case, check out some of the local paper's stories about her. Fair enough?"

Gerry gave Scott a long, pensive look, then warned, though without hostility, "Don't do any crabbin' if I put her through the wringer."

"Hey, if you can find a hitch, I'll be grateful," Scott assured him. "Anyway, it's all just entertainment, right?"

Gerry hoisted himself to his feet, looked Scott square in the eye, and warned, "That's just it, Scott. To Jamie Blasko and her father, it's *not* entertainment. You represented this to them as a chance to reveal the truth about a terrible point in their lives. Do you have any idea what you may do to them?"

Scott responded seriously, "I've no intention of hurting anyone, Gerry. Wait and see."

"Yeah, well, we all know what paves the road to hell," Gerry quietly returned before he pressed out of the room on his cane.

Scott glanced after Gerry before turning back to Jessica and remarking, "That was a real barrel of laughs."

"Well, Scott," Jessica reasoned, "Gerry has a point. This is not a fictional story. Real people are affected, maybe even hurt, by how it ends. Think about it."

"Hmm, did you think about that Gerry is only worried about how it ends for the Blaskos? He couldn't care less about Philip Carlyle and his family," Scott answered calmly. "He's nuts about that girl, and it's clouding his thinking."

"How did you know . . . I . . . what makes you say that?" Jess inwardly kicked herself for that flub.

Scott gave her a knowing half-smile before answering, "Even if it weren't so obvious, you don't think there's more than one little bird gossiping in this house? The woods have eyes and the walls have ears around here. On top of that, Jeanne Rivers let me know she was worried Gerry might talk me into giving her boss a bum deal."

"She ought to mind her own business," Jessica grumbled, maybe now understanding a little of Elizabeth's feelings about the housekeeper.

"I guess she sees her employer's well-being as her business. Company loyalty—which I could stand some of, myself," Scott ruefully pointed out.

Jessica shifted uncomfortably, just a little, at Scott's reference to her private *tête à tête* with Gerry. She could understand how Scott might see it as undermining him. That hadn't been her intention, but what had Gerry just said about good intentions?

Seeming to read her thoughts, Scott explained, sitting beside her, "Look, Jess, I'm not going to fault you for helping Gerry keep us on our toes. Just don't fight me. *I'm* fighting like a bastar . . . doing the best I can to keep our show on the air. I'm not a guy usually into gimmicks, but Ungerpreck's going to pull the plug on us if I don't get our ratings up. No one wants that."

"No," Jess agreed but added, "Tell me the truth, Scott. Do you honestly believe this Madame Wanda is the real McCoy? Even if she is, do you think she can deliver on demand?"

"That, my friend Jessica, is why we're not broadcasting the séance live. Thanks to that nifty newfangled tape machine the station invested in, we have a whole day to edit whatever she gives us into a recording. Let's just hope Madame Wanda comes up with something worth editing."

"It sounds as if the problem might shift from the families worrying about what comes out to your worrying whether *anything* comes out."

"How can such a sweet kid be so good at giving a guy nightmares, Jessica Minton?"

Chapter Thirteen
Monday, October 20th

It got dark so early in October. Seven o'clock could be downright gloomy in the candlelit corridors. That's why the overhead Victorian globe seemed to glow so brilliantly over Jessica Minton in the rococo telephone alcove. Her midnight-blue, quilted Chinese jacket with its tiny embroidered soft pink and blue flowers, like the dark blouse and skirt, gleamed under that illumination. So different from the shadows of the foyer outside.

Jessica reached for the receiver, yet hesitated. James wasn't expecting her call. She might not catch him. But she wanted so much to hear his easy British accents after the last few days. Gerry had resisted all of Scott's friendly overtures since yesterday's "chat." Ungerpreck had been on everybody's backs to make sure they realized how important these two episodes' success was to the program's future. Liz had even delivered a bit of a jolt by immediately shutting down Jess's suggestion they ask Leo for help checking out this Madame Wanda's *bona fides*. Her sister had pointed out that he had way too heavy a caseload for her to burden him any further. Jess couldn't argue with that. She hadn't had the heart, or was it the nerve, to tell Gerry. *And what had Gerry thought about the packets Scott had prepared for them for tonight's shindig with the medium?* The info was interesting, but Jess was still not entirely convinced.

Nevertheless, she was not planning to bother James with any of this. He had his own work to do, work he was enjoying. She wasn't about to throw a monkey wrench into it over a bunch of problems that were *her* responsibility to deal with. Hearing his voice would just take the edge off.

Jess dialed the operator and gave the number at the faculty residence hall, pleased that the nosy Ida wasn't on shift tonight. Waiting for her call to go through, Jess reflected, *Thank goodness Scott had found a place in the budget to cover my long-distance calls. Philip Carlyle might be a generous host, but expecting him to foot the bill for an actress's lonely heart would be a little nervy. Yeah, Scott is a good egg. Just all that struggling to get out from under Edmund Ungerpreck's thumb and still keep the show afloat was causing such trouble.*

"Hello, love! Flushed out any spooks lately?" James's voice came over the wire.

"Hello there, mister. I was afraid I wouldn't catch you."

"No, I just had a peculiar feeling I might hear from you tonight, so I didn't stray far from the phone."

Every single one of her heart's cockles warmed at his easy voice. Jessica returned his good humor: "So, how's tricks down in your neck of the woods? Having any trouble living without me?"

"Oh, I'm getting by. We had the loveliest lumps pretending to be mashed potatoes; and the roast, I believe, was lately something you bet on at Belmont Park."

"James," Jess feigned indignation, "you know how I feel about dead-horse jokes, especially a horse I bet on."

"Sorry, love. Forgot myself. Roughing it here and all."

"I think you've had it rougher," Jessica kidded. "Anyway, how is the work coming? Found something you can use in your research? You must be done cataloguing by now."

"Done cataloguing, and now I'm zeroing in on which letters I'll want to work with. You'd like some of the things I've discovered. We'll have to talk more about it when I get back."

"Will that be soon?" Jess asked hopefully.

"I'd like it to be," James said gently. "It won't be soon enough. I can say that much."

"I know. Same here."

A moment of silence spoke volumes more than all their words so far.

Then James broke the quiet: "What about you, Mrs. Crawford? How are all your ghosts and goblins and long-leggedy beasties? Anything gone bump in the night, yet?"

Caught off-guard, Jessica's reply was less than smooth, "Oh, it's an old house with lots of, um, character. And the people . . . Well, the house is beautiful and our host gracious . . ."

"Jessica?" his voice was curious. "What's wrong?"

Realizing that she'd better, she wanted to, come clean with James, Jess explained, "It's nothing to worry about, really. It's just that the whole story around this Felicia Blasko is so tragic. I've only started to see how her disappearance affects both families, especially the husband and daughter. They're going to expect answers from Scott that I don't see he can provide. I don't want to be a part of hurting these people. I wish I could get out of this whole deal."

"But you can't?"

"I suppose I could break my contract, sink the show, and be blackballed; but I don't think that's the smartest plan," she dryly replied.

"Well, I'd be happy to let you stay home to curl up on a couch with Dusty to eat bonbons, but you wouldn't be happy, and then Dusty and I would both be in the stew. I know it sounds like a bit of a dog's dinner, but you can't blame yourself for something that's not your fault."

"You're right," Jessica agreed. "Sorry. I wanted to make this a nice, cheery call for you, and here I am crying on your shoulder. I'll pin my hair back up now."

"And a nice mop of brunette curls it is," James assured her. She could almost see that twinkle in his eyes. "Anyway, it's all part of the job description. Tell you what: maybe I can put some of this work on hold and make a trip up there—"

"No, no," Jess insisted, as much as she wanted to say, "Yes! Yes!" She continued, "You've planned this research for some time. You need it to keep your position. I'm not going to be a dog in the manger and put the kibosh on all your work. If you *really* finish up ahead of time, fine. I will greet you, sir, with bells on!"

"Could be a bit chilly this time of year, not that I'd mind."

"And the rest of my clothes, too, smart guy!" she kidded back, again glad that Ida wasn't her operator. Jessica added, "Anyway, don't worry; I'm going to be fine. Sometimes things get to me more because I miss you and Dusty." She hesitated before adding, "I've been blathering about myself. How about you? Sleeping all right?"

Vicious memories of the war had haunted James after his return, but he had been doing better this past year—though there still were restless nights and patches of time when he seemed almost out of reach.

"Yeah, actually, yeah," he answered honestly. "I'm busy, and I got in some pick-up football, soccer, games that knock me out for the night. If you can believe it, I actually met someone down here whom I knew during my time under Occupation. We understand where each other has been. It's made a difference. Don't worry. Honestly."

"It's part of the job description," she echoed his earlier reassurance. "And, for some crazy reason, I love you."

"I rather had that impression, Mrs. Crawford," his voice was quietly playful and tender. "Love you, too." Then, more assertively, "And stop trying to carry everybody's burdens on your shoulders. Believe me, Dusty and I are more than enough for you—especially with that sister of yours around."

About to wisecrack back, Jessica suddenly became aware of someone right outside the alcove. Instead, she said, "Hold on, James," glancing up to recognize Jeanne Rivers standing there expectantly.

"They're waiting for you in the drawing room, Miss Minton. Madame Wanda will be here soon," the housekeeper informed her.

"Oh, thank you, Jeanne. I'll be right there. I'm just finishing," Jessica answered.

The other woman nodded, leaving Jess to wrap up her call.

"Hello? Sorry, James. Dessert calls—and Madame Wanda," she laughed.

"Who's this Madame Wanda?" he asked curiously.

"Oh, didn't I tell you? Scott's planning a séance to help uncover the fate of Felicia Blasko. Was it foul play or, as Liz suspects, an escape to the Caribbean for tropical drinks and sandy beaches? Scott invited her tonight to face everyone's questions and prove she's legit. We'll see."

"If you're trying to raise the dead, maybe I'll wait until afterward to come and visit, especially since you seem to be feeling better now."

"Well, I better get going before the housekeeper comes back to retrieve me. Love you, wise guy. Write me. I'll call you again same time next week."

"You, too, love. And if you need someone, talk to your sister. She's a right gal—just don't tell her I said so."

They both chuckled, and the call was over. Despite missing James already, Jessica was still enveloped by the warmth of the love she and her husband shared. As she exited the alcove and headed toward the drawing room, the shadows no longer seemed gloomy but soft, almost dreamy. Like the soft darkness in "Ode on Melancholy." Good. Their chat had mostly resolved her anxieties without her having to complicate things by mentioning the weird resemblance she shared with Felicia. It was just a silly coincidence, anyway. She was sure.

The drawing room was almost brilliant in comparison to the foyer. Overhead chandeliers and lamps around the room poured out illumination. The furniture had been rearranged to create a V spreading away from the fireplace. The wingback chair was now situated where that V opened. *Putting Madame Wanda on display or giving Philip Carlyle a magisterial place?*

Jess noticed that despite the aura of excitement at the evening's impending visit, there was also a sense of relief in the air. Not at all surprising since Edmund Ungerpreck had been called back to New York for some important business with the board of directors of his brother-in-law's company. Of course, he'd puffed that they couldn't get along without his advice. She could just imagine the hash the big bloviator would have made of Scott's attempts to soothe troubled waters in his ranks tonight.

Now, Jessica turned her attention to the seating by the hearth, mostly because her sister beckoned, elegant in a full-skirted black voile dress belted in patent leather. In fact, Elizabeth had put that full skirt to good use, spreading it over the rest of the settee to save a space for Jess.

With a nod in response, Jess swiftly crossed to Liz, mumbling a quick "excuse me" as she passed Bev McDuff. She just missed banging a shin on the coffee table that separated Liz from the couch across from them, where Maura, Guy, and Gerry sat. Elizabeth rolled her eyes at the narrow escape of Jess's shin. Gerry did not set her at ease, for unlike Maura and Guy, he seemed too darkly preoccupied to greet her. *Not a great sign.*

"Hey, kiddo, break out of dreamland and take a seat," Liz caught her attention, flipping her skirt away to clear Jess a space.

"Hmm. That 'new length' does come in handy for practical matters," Jess playfully observed. "Even if it does obscure the fact a girl might have nice gams."

"That sounds like something Leo might say, or that fella of yours— speaking of whom, how did the call to Gentleman James Crawford go?" her sister queried.

Jessica beamed, "Swell, actually, Liz. That guy can always drive off my worries without making me feel like a dope for having them in the first place."

"What did he say about the portrait, your resemblance to Felicia?" Elizabeth asked curiously.

"Well," Jessica hesitated, but finished more boldly, "I never got to it. It just seemed too weird, too complicated to talk about over the phone. What I'm really happy about is that James might finish early and come join us."

Elizabeth leaned over, speaking softly so only Jess could hear: "I guess you didn't tell him about the 'presence' I sensed around Jamie? I can't imagine he'd be burning up the road to get to a place where the ghost was more than a legend."

Jessica shot a quick glance at Gerry. *No, he'd heard nothing.* Turning back to her sister, she said, "You forgot to mention the Hound of Hades howling after us all over the island. Anyway, I thought you were following the Bacardi theory? I didn't catch you blabbing to anyone else about what you thought you sensed."

"Oh, I don't have to," Elizabeth returned sarcastically. "We have a *bona fide* medium for that."

Bev McDuff startled them with a preoccupied growl at the notes she'd been assiduously working on in her lap. Suddenly aware of her near neighbors' attention, Bev explained, "Rewrites! I wish Scott hadn't wasted time on tonight's dog and pony show. We've got to hammer this script into shape for tomorrow!"

"Oh? You have the script almost done?" Maura queried from across the coffee table, "You wouldn't mind giving us a little peek, now, would you, Bev?"

"Or maybe you could accidentally on purpose drop it on the floor over here?" her husband added.

"Maybe I could just accidentally on purpose chop off my head and save Scott the effort—because that's what he'll do to me if I let anything slip before he's ready to deliver it to you. Nope, no one sees anything until we hand you the pages tomorrow afternoon. We still haven't worked out all the details. This is a tough one, and Scott wants to get everything as right as he can."

Jessica noted Gerry listening tensely to the conversation. He seemed on the verge of jumping in, but he held back. *Biding his time?*

"So, gang," Maura's voice interrupted Jess's thoughts. "What do you think this Madame Wanda is like?"

"Probably 5'2", weighs 300 pounds, with scraggly hair, a gypsy skirt, and fingernails down to her knees," Guy chuckled.

Gerry spoke up now, questioning Bev thoughtfully, "Have you met her?"

Bev gave him a half-smile and replied, "I have."

"Do you think she's on the level?" Gerry persisted with a calm that impressed Jessica, knowing his emotional entanglement in the issue.

"I don't know if I think any of them are entirely legit, although I think some believe they are. I just hope her séance gives us something to hang a story on. Scott's taking a big gamble here. You have no idea the pressure he's under to keep the show going. You may think you do; but, take my word for it, you don't. That Edmund Ungerpreck is a so-and-so from way back and . . ." Bev caught herself. It didn't pay to impugn the guy signing your paycheck too vociferously, even among friends. She finished, "Anyway, I'll be happy when Mr. Wellstone is back on his feet and in charge. I'd be even happier if they moved at least Durante to a different time slot."

"Amen to that," Guy took up Bev's cue to change the subject.

Gerry sent Jessica a knowing look, then got up and wandered over to the French doors, where a heavy second layer of curtains were in place to quiet rattling from the wind.

Bev returned to writing while Maura and Guy chatted about plans for dinner in Portsmouth tomorrow night. Elizabeth turned to Jessica and observed, "I see you've still got that just-got-off-the-Amechi-with-James afterglow."

Tongue-in-cheek, Jess replied with a wave of her hand, "Our love is like shining armor inviolate."

"Good thing, cupcake," Liz whispered, tilting her head towards the other side of the room, "because here comes your boyfriend. I bet you didn't tell Mr. Crawford you have a not-so-secret admirer."

Jessica followed her sister's gaze to note Philip Carlyle approach, looking natty in a fawn-colored suit and black tie with striking blue diagonal stripes, a welcoming smile lighting his features.

"Elizabeth, really," Jessica chided, "don't be absurd."

"I hope you're all comfortable here," he affably greeted the crew by the fireplace. There were friendly responses all around, with a peremptory grump from Bev as she continued writing.

After Liz's words, Jess felt more than a little uncomfortable when Philip Carlyle focused on her and said, "Oh, Miss Minton, I see that you never received your coffee. I'll remedy that immediately, if you like."

"It does smell tempting," Jessica replied, "especially after all that colored hot water we drank during the war."

"Cream and sugar?" he thoughtfully inquired.

"Why yes, that would be fine," Jessica answered, a little embarrassed by all the attention. She was even more so after Elizabeth surreptitiously elbowed her in the ribs when Carlyle turned away to signal Jeanne Rivers to bring over the coffee.

"Some of us get quite the service," Liz noted pleasantly.

"Not a t'all," Philip smiled at her. "But your sister was absent when everyone else was served. Ah, and by the way, Miss Minton, I trust you had a happy conversation with your husband."

Philip's mentioning James made Jess answer brightly, "Thank you, Mr. Carlyle. It was lovely. He's such a good guy."

"It's a pity he couldn't join you, but I understand he's doing research on a newly discovered cache of letters of John Keats. I've been quite impressed with his scholarship on our favorite poet. He just keeps adding to his golden reputation. At any rate, I'm sure he would have enjoyed our conversation in the study the other evening—and I'm willing to wager he'd have enjoyed the Satie in the 'golden autumn sunset' of the music room."

"I bet it would have been a treat," came from Elizabeth.

Jess wished Philip would turn away so she could forcefully implant her elbow in her sister's side. *No dice.* So, instead, she asked him, "How did you know about my husband's academic reputation? I can't imagine that you'd have read anything he's written."

"Can't you? I'll let you in on a little secret: if I hadn't had to take responsibility for keeping our family's concern afloat, I would have loved to have devoted myself to literature. I could easily have seen myself in ivy-covered halls, digging into the depths of poets from the nineteenth century, loving the exhilaration of challenging ideas. But my older sister had no head for business, even though she was nominally in charge. Thus, it all fell on my shoulders. Bill never had a head for anything, even his art."

The bitterness edging Philip's last words touched Jessica, but all she could say was, "I should think you'd need more of a heart than a head for painting."

Philip was rueful in answering, "I doubt Bill had much of that, either. I'm sure Felicia would have been able to testify to that."

"And yet her portrait shows not just talent but feeling," Liz pointed out.

Philip studied Elizabeth shrewdly before allowing, "So it does, Miss Minton. However, Felicia could draw that out of people, even Bill. Unfortunately, I doubt there was enough heart in him to prevent him from . . ."

His voice had trailed off, so Elizabeth took up the thread with the forthright, "So, you think *he* is guilty?"

"Elizabeth!" Jessica chided, highly displeased by her sister's bluntness.

Carlyle faced Elizabeth straight on to answer, "I believe my brother is a guilty person—of what, I'm not sure. I'd like to find out."

"You don't believe that Vitus Blasko is responsible for what happened to Felicia?" The question came from Gerry Davis.

Philip turned to Gerry and replied, "I think both of them are responsible for making her dreadfully unhappy, for putting her in jeopardy. As for exactly how and why she disappeared—I don't know."

"She wouldn't abandon her daughter," Gerry contended.

Philip cocked his head thoughtfully before agreeing, "No, she would not—but how would you know that?"

Maybe it's not such a bright idea to reveal your strong connection right now, Gerry. At least, that was Jessica's gut feeling. So, she seized on serendipity to change the subject: "Oh, here's Jeanne with my coffee. Doesn't it smell grand? Mr. Carlyle, do you have a special bean in your larder? Liz, how does it taste?"

"Special," her sister dryly answered.

Philip Carlyle stepped back to allow his housekeeper through with a tray carrying bone-china cup and saucer; spoon; and silver creamer, sugar bowl, and small coffee pot. She placed the tray on the coffee table before pouring the caffeinated treasure. Carlyle, then, dismissed her.

As the housekeeper left, Jessica looked over the tray and almost laughed "All this? Just for me?"

"This must be star treatment," Elizabeth quipped, barely raising an I-told-you-so eyebrow at her sister.

"I wish I could say 'yes,'" Philip admitted. "However, I realize that Madame Wanda will be arriving shortly, which means that, unlike the rest of us, your sister won't have time to leave her seat for additional coffee, should she desire it."

"Stay in our seats?" Guy joked. "Is she going to give us a sample séance? Horns and ectoplasm and furniture flying through the air?"

"Not this furniture, I should hope," Philip responded wryly. "They're valuable antiques. But no, as I understand it, she will talk to you about herself and answer your questions."

The doorbell resounded through the house's lower floor.

"That must be Madame Wanda," Philip decided. Turning to the other side of the room, he nodded to Jeanne to answer the door. Facing his guests again, he said, "If you'll excuse me, your director and I will greet her in the foyer before bringing her to meet you."

With a nod, he left them.

"And now, ladies and gentlemen," Liz pronounced, "on with the show."

Chapter Fourteen
Same Night

She came in, linked arm in arm with Scott and Philip.

"Well, you were right about one thing, Guy," Jessica remarked. "She is about 5'2"."

That 5'2" was nicely curved in all the right places, shone off in a nip-waisted, shiny green satin jacket, its peplum over an equally satiny black skirt that led your eyes down to a pair of gams that would have made Betty Grable green with envy.

She looked to be in her mid-twenties, but it was hard to gauge with those cherub cheeks; startlingly mischievous green eyes; and clear, square forehead. Her soft brown hair was gently pulled back under a cap of black velvet shot with bands of gold. The makeup was perfect!

Scott presented her: "Everyone, this is Madame Wanda." Then he introduced her to members of the show, individually.

Peeling off her black gauntlet gloves, a black clutch tucked under one arm, Madame Wanda took them all in with a perky smile and the greeting, "Evening, folks. I understand you'd like to chat with me about my *bona fides*. Fine with me. I've got nothing to hide."

Liz muttered to Jess, "Not in a get-up that tight."

The bright green eyes zeroed in on Elizabeth and she asked, "Like the outfit? It's one of my faves."

Scott headed off any rejoinder from Elizabeth with, "Madame Wanda, thank you so much for coming. Please, take a seat over here, in this chair."

"Hmm," she commented, noting that the majestic seat provided her was the focus of everyone's view. "Not putting me on the spot much, Scott, are you?"

"You won't be on the spot if you're on the level," Gerry coolly told her.

Frowning, Scott reproved, "Gerry, you could try to be more gracious. Madame Wanda didn't have to give up her evening to drive over from Portsmouth."

"Never mind, Scott. I don't have a problem with a little skepticism. It's healthy." Turning to Gerry with a wink, she added, "And you, fella, should live to be one hundred."

Gerry didn't respond, so she shrugged, put a hand over Scott's as he stood by her chair, and told him in an easy voice, "Scott, you can knock off the 'Madame Wanda' business. That was my stage name. Wanda is just fine."

"Stage name," Gerry repeated almost accusingly. Jess cringed as he continued, "It's all just entertainment for you. We will base a story that could shape people's lives on entertainment."

Wanda targeted Gerry with her green eyes to return confidently, "Don't act so affronted, Mr. Davis. Certainly don't act as if you've uncovered a significant secret. It's all in the information Scott put together for you. Yes, I was a hotel and nightclub entertainer in Florida. Quite successful, too. I used my abilities to amuse people. That's no crime, and you can see I have no criminal record."

Jessica looked at her sister, wanting to share the thought that not having a criminal record wasn't the same as never doing anything criminal. It might even mean that you were an exceptionally good crook for never getting caught. Liz, however, was too focused on Wanda, as the woman smiled with charm but not submission at Gerry's cool stare. *What did Liz perceive in the gal with the sparkling green eyes?*

"I see there is another skeptic here," Wanda said, snapping her head around and staring, for a moment, Jessica thought, at herself. *No, Madame Wanda was locking eyes with Elizabeth.*

Scott gulped, "Say, that's something! You sensed that without anyone saying a word."

"No, you, goose," Wanda laughed. "I saw her out of the corner of my eye," a nod toward Elizabeth, "raising a skeptical eyebrow at me." This to Liz, "But you aren't one of the actors, are you?"

"No, I'm not," Elizabeth replied smoothly. "Though I'm sure you don't need psychic powers to deduce that. Scott or Philip Carlyle could have filled you in beforehand."

Scott shrugged and said, "Well, that is true, but Madame, er, Wanda never said she was drawing on any hoodoo just now."

"'Hoodoo,' Scott?" Wanda almost chuckled. "Is that the scientific term for what I do? Maybe you'd better not try to help me."

While Wanda was teasing Scott, Philip, who had come to stand behind Jessica, quietly commented, "Good one for your sister."

Jessica smiled back, thinking, *How nice of him to appreciate Liz. Exactly what did he think of this Wanda gal? Had he been involved in bringing her into the scheme?*

"I have a question," Jessica spoke, determined to get some answers to her undecided thoughts. "How did you get drawn into all this? Scott never told us who brought you in. Anyway, why would you give up the glamour of performing in clubs in what most people would consider vacation spots for cold New England winters?—this bizarrely warm October aside. What brought you *here*?"

"That's actually three questions," Wanda responded with a twinkle. She beamed her charm, but Jessica wasn't charmed, shooting back, "Fine. But you haven't answered any of them."

She felt a reassuring pat on her shoulder from Philip Carlyle. *Maybe he hadn't been too thrilled by the woman's involvement.*

Wanda abruptly went serious to reply, "Intelligent questions. They deserve answers. Sorry for being so flip. I'm a little on edge, performing like this. All right. Why did I quit show biz? Yes, it was good money, an exciting life, but I couldn't help the guilt. Here I had these gifts, and I was making money off them. It didn't feel right: not like when I would use my sight to help people. I wanted to do more of that."

Wanda surprised Jessica by looking at Elizabeth as if seeking confirmation of something. Liz just folded her arms in front of her and said, "But you haven't answered all my sister's questions. Why *here*? New Hampshire?"

Jessica added, "And who brought you to *this* house?"

Wanda hesitated but finally explained, "If you're completely a skeptic, you won't buy my answer." She looked at Elizabeth a moment, then continued, "I had a feeling I should settle in Portsmouth. So I did. I got a job managing a bookstore. When people sometimes need my 'talents,' I help them out. You can read about it in the local testimonials."

"From people we don't know," Gerry countered.

"I have to stop you there," Scott corrected. "Bev and I checked out some of them. They seemed legit."

"Through a private detective?" Gerry pushed.

"Well, no. Bev and I—"

Gerry snorted and shook his head, but Wanda took over: "Mr. Carlyle isn't in that batch, but he can attest, can't you, Mr. Carlyle?"

Jess swiveled her head as her eyes, like everyone else's, fastened on Philip Carlyle.

Carlyle was acutely uncomfortable, finally saying, "Miss O'Malley, you had promised—"

"*O'Malley?* Wanda *O'Malley?*" Gerry chuckled. "*That's* your name?"

"Hardly mysterious or alluring," she allowed. Then she returned to Philip and said, "Will you tell them, or shall I?"

He actually glared across the room at her, and Jessica couldn't help but feel for his embarrassment.

"You must excuse Mr. Carlyle," Wanda began. "A level-headed guy, man of business and science, yet it must absolutely kill him to admit he'd experienced something neither science can dismiss nor dollars buy off. Not even his chivalrous qualities will prevent him from letting a lady's character be impugned if it would damage his proud image of himself. Well, folks, here's the low-down."

The Minton sisters exchanged quizzical looks, Jessica knowing her sister was just as surprised as her that Philip Carlyle was letting Wanda get away with her audacity. Even Scott appeared a little panicked. Jess wished she had the nerve to look at Philip. Did she hold back out of sympathetic embarrassment or trepidation at the prospect of seeing a normally restrained man blow his top?

Surprisingly, Carlyle didn't make a move to silence Wanda. Jess noticed the tension in Jeanne Rivers from across the room. Wanda went on.

"I decided to take a drive one lovely summer day and ended up here, on the island. I'd heard the stories about demons and ghosts, so it's not so mysterious that I came here. I was in the café and overheard one of the help from the mansion talking about a presence in the house, one even haunting the master . . ."

Jessica did turn, now, to Philip Carlyle and insisted, "You told me that you never saw . . ."

He dipped his head at Jessica's reminder of his earlier humorous dismissal of her question on the subject. Though now that she thought about it, Jess realized he hadn't actually said he'd not *experienced* Felicia's presence, just that he'd never *seen* any manifestations.

"He was too embarrassed, I'm sure, Miss Minton," Wanda explained, reading her accurately. "At any rate, I felt a bolt of enlightenment when I heard the story. Just like in the past, I knew what I had to do. I came directly to this house, much more than serendipitously. You see, when I was admitted, he and Miss Rivers were discussing their talks with Scott. They were trying to figure out how to satisfy Scott's suggestion that it would be just grand if there was a medium on board to contact the ghost and perhaps even solve the mystery. The waves of the universe harmonized. I was attuned, and we all came together."

Gerry began a slow, deliberate clap, returning them all to reality. He pronounced, "Bravo, Miss O'Malley. Splendid performance. Scott, you should sign her up for our show."

"I'm sorry, Mr. Davis," Philip responded reluctantly. "As much as I wish I could, I can't dispute what she says. Miss Rivers can confirm."

All eyes on her, the housekeeper tightened her lips and nodded, not looking happy to do so.

"So," Gerry reasoned, "might we also conclude that it was less a psychic 'feeling' that inspired your appearance on this doorstep than a shrewd calculation of what you could parley some superstitious servant's blabbing into? I wish I'd had that kind of feeling the day I lost my leg in Italy."

"Okay, Gerry," Scott jumped in amongst the others' gasps at the young man's bitter sarcasm.

However, Wanda cut off Scott with her words to Gerry, "It's terrible what happened to you, but not everyone has the gift. It's not fair, but I didn't make the rules. Those of us who have it must use it to help others, no matter what people think of us. Right, Elizabeth Minton?"

Jessica looked swiftly from Wanda to her sister. *How did she know about Elizabeth's own special talent?*

"I don't follow you," Elizabeth replied smoothly, though Jessica knew she did, indeed. Her sister, however, was not about to step into a trap.

"You get these feelings, too," Wanda said simply. "I can recognize it in you. People with our gift often can."

"Funny," Liz easily returned, "I don't get the same feeling about you."

Wanda smiled, "It's not all that surprising. I've honed my abilities for years—and some people just aren't as gifted as others."

Jessica put a hand on her sister's arm to keep her from hurling anything heavier than an insult, but Liz just smiled. If she were riled, she wasn't going to give this dame any satisfaction.

Wanda went on, "But I think, like me, you've sensed something—a kind of presence around here. I'm right, aren't I? Like me, you've sensed a disturbed spirit abroad who wants to tell us something. To have the truth revealed."

Clever play, lady, trying to butter up Liz into supporting you. Now, what's your move, Sis? Jess considered.

Liz made her move, cool and honest, as far as her words went: "If you're asking me if I've seen Felicia Blasko floating around this house, the answer is 'no.'"

"I didn't say it was Felicia," Wanda replied levelly. "Someone else disappeared that night. No one really knows to whom the blood belonged."

"Good Lord!" gasped Philip. "Are you talking about my brother?"

Wanda shrugged and answered, "No one really knows, yet. That's what I'm here for."

"Wait, wait a minute," Scott cut in, his and Bev's whole laboriously created script going up in the flame of this new suggestion. "How come, then, the sightings have been of a woman, not a man."

Wanda explained patiently, "Spirits aren't physical beings. To 'see' them, our brains have to translate that essence into something familiar, what we expect. The standard story has been that the ghost must be Felicia. So, people's brains translate what they perceive into what they expect to see. And many people don't see anything. They only sense something. Just ask Mr. Carlyle."

Scott looked sharply at Philip; Jess joined the others in following suit. Slowly Philip nodded but argued, "I refuse to believe my brother is still here. He cursed us enough in life. If he were here, I'd call in a priest to exorcise this house."

"Or you could let him speak and find release—if it is he," Wanda suggested.

Jessica turned to Elizabeth, her eyes questioning: *why would Bill Carlyle's ghost be attached to Jamie?* Liz frowned her answer. She wasn't buying.

Everyone's attention was caught by Gerry Davis's fiercely controlled voice: "Wait. If the blood is Carlyle's, then what happened to Felicia? If *he's* dead, is she also? If she isn't, are you implying Felicia killed Carlyle?"

Wanda spread her hands, responding, "I'm not implying anything. I only want you to realize that there are all sorts of possibilities people haven't fully considered. Maybe it was a double suicide."

"How comforting to her daughter and husband," Gerry sarcastically shot back. "And I suppose both bodies spontaneously evaporated?"

Philip Carlyle came forward, next to Jessica's seat, and spoke solemnly, "Rest assured, Mr. Davis, that Felicia Blasko was neither a killer nor one who would destroy herself. She was an unhappy woman, undeservedly so; however, she would never take her life and certainly would not leave her daughter all at sea."

At the probability that they would not have to rewrite all night, Scott and Bev looked much relieved. However, Jessica found herself even more concerned about Philip and Gerry, whose anxieties had a far less self-centered basis.

Gerry was concentrating on Madame Wanda. So Jessica turned and gave Philip a comforting smile before leaning forward to pour herself more coffee. After this long day, and longer night, she was too much in need of caffeine.

Scott was talking—had been for a second or so. Something about Wanda's explaining the way her performance worked.

"It's simple," Wanda commenced. "I need to put my mind and soul in a receptive state, clear away the cobwebs of false cynicism and doubt. That heightens my receptivity to the essences of a higher plane."

"How do you do that?" questioned Maura, seriously interested.

"I usually use a few shots of scotch," Gerry quipped.

Wanda laughed, then explained, "Frankly, alcohol and other drugs merely cloud the mind, dull my spirit—basically make everything fuzzy. No, I rely on hypnosis to put my conscious mind to sleep and let my spirit open to the universe of which we're a part. I used to work with a partner in the act."

"And who's your partner, now?" Gerry asked suspiciously.

"Me, myself, and I," Wanda answered brightly. To her audience's confused or distrusting expressions, she explained, "My partner was pretty sore and left me when I ended our profitable act to help clients *pro bono*. So, I learned self-hypnosis. I hypnotize myself to say a specific phrase after a specific time limit, which automatically brings me out. It's worked like a charm so far."

"How do we know that you're really under?" Gerry persisted.

Nodding toward Gerry, Wanda told Scott, "He's a clever one."

"Bev and I did our research," Scott explained. "Trust me."

"A wise man once told me to trust no one," Gerry returned, unconvinced.

An uneasy silence fell over the group. Pensively, Jess took another sip of coffee, wondering who would say what next. Fortunately, Guy good-naturedly spoke up: "You know, as far as I'm concerned, it doesn't matter if she's hoaxing us or not. It's only a radio show. No one believes it's real. Like her club act, it's just a performance."

"Except for the Blaskos and the Carlyles," Gerry disagreed. "They're looking for actual answers. Is it fair to get their hopes up or smash their lives for the entertainment of a thrill-hungry audience or to fill Ungerpreck's wallet?"

"Mr. Davis," Philip said carefully. "I appreciate your sentiments; but, to me, it's worth any chance to know what happened. I think Vitus Blasko feels the same. We want justice for Felicia. We want her peace. I want my house at peace."

"Then I'm done here," Gerry decided, pushing himself to his feet, braced by his cane.

Things broke up after that, awkwardly, but definitely. Maura and Guy went for more coffee. Scott and Philip saw Wanda to her auto, while Bev scurried off to work on the script in quiet, if not peace. That left Jessica alone with her sister.

"Well, Swami Elizabeth, what do you make of all this?" Jessica covered a yawn before elaborating, "I'm surprised Philip Carlyle lied, sort of, about seeing or sensing Felicia. *Do* you believe Madame Wanda?"

"I don't know what to think about her, except she's a real pro—at what, I'm not sure. Leo told me how fake spiritualists can be darned clever and thorough about digging up background on their marks to sound insightful. She certainly seems to have played your pal Philip like a violin."

"He's not my 'pal,'" Jessica grumped through another tired yawn.

"Your own personal silver urn of coffee? None of us got super service like that," Elizabeth teased.

"Don't be a wise guy," Jessica cracked. Still, maybe Liz was onto something. Maybe she'd better not get too chummy with their host. Jess then changed the subject to something that genuinely interested her: "What do you think about Wanda's conjecture that *Bill's* actually doing the haunting? That's downright alarming if everything Philip says about him is true. Yet, the presence you described didn't sound dangerous. Why would Bill follow Jamie around, anyway?"

"You've got something there," Elizabeth agreed. "There's no real connection between them—that we know of. Philip said his brother only buttered up the kid to get to her mother. Besides, what I sensed might have been dark, but it was more sad than threatening. Something's screwy here; I just can't fit all the pieces together." To Jessica's third yawn, Liz mocked, "I'm not keeping you up, am I?"

"Uh, sorry, Liz. I am *so* tired. Coffee can do that to me, believe it or not, especially after a long day. Anyway, back to Felicia. To my mind, 'sad' and 'lost' are the perfect words for her: alienated from her husband, taken from her child, likely murdered. I wish the poor woman would find peace."

"I just hope that Madame Wanda isn't a fraud who will hurt the living," Elizabeth sighed. "Worse, she could be the real thing and reveal secrets that the living can't deal with."

"Mmm. Everybody's searching for the truth, but there's no guarantee the truth they find is the one they're looking for," Jessica sadly concluded. Another yawn, then: "I wonder what questions James would have tossed at her? He's pretty good at seeing through people."

"I was wondering how long it would take you to finagle Mr. Crawford into the conversation. C'mon, let's hit the hay. You look beat."

Chapter Fifteen
Tuesday, October 21st

Jessica Minton stood before the hearth in the Carlyle drawing room, hands clasped behind her back. The sun streaming through the open French doors brought out the chestnut in the long, dark hair curling down to her shoulders. The day had cooled down. So, Jessica had opted for her fawn blazer over a soft-orange blouse and dark brown trousers for her venture to the historical society/library with Gerry earlier today. Gerry was in his room, brooding over their research and Scott's news about the script. She restlessly desired a walk, but was there time to get back and change for dinner?

However, taking a walk wasn't what was really on her mind. It was the day's research: not what she'd found as much as what she hadn't. Little in the way of ammunition to protect Jamie, Gerry's main goal. It wasn't as if they'd come across *nothing*, just nothing earth-shattering. Well, it was interesting that Bill Carlyle had briefly studied electrical engineering before chucking it to pursue art, such as he did. Also interesting, though Jessica doubted relevant, was a tidbit that Martha Royle had mentioned about Jeanne Rivers. It made Jessica wonder if Jeanne knew way more about Felicia's life in this house than she had let on to the radio crew. Of course, she could have filled in Scott, but maybe he already knew. Well, if Jeanne did know more, maybe she could help Jess really get inside the mind of Felicia, to do justice playing her.

Jessica's thoughts returned to photos she'd see today, especially a wedding portrait in the old paper clippings of Felicia Saunders and Dr. Vitus Blasko. The two looked happy in their own ways: Felicia, excited, in love; Vitus, a little stiff but almost surprised with quiet happiness. So what had gone haywire? Why hadn't she stayed happy? Why hadn't his seeds of happiness bloomed? The work? Devotion to science? Such sad choices for them both.

"Miss Minton."

Startled, Jessica turned sharply to the source of that address: Jeanne Rivers entering through the drawing-room doors.

Rivers laughed gently to Jessica, "Oh, sorry. I didn't mean to give you a turn. I only wanted to deliver a message."

Jessica smiled slightly, then walked over to Jeanne, even as the other woman continued, "Your director wanted to get ahold of you about the script. He was truly concerned and asked me to send you to him the minute I saw you."

"Have no fear," Jessica explained lightly. "Scott nabbed Gerry and me as we came through the front doors a little while ago. He just wanted to warn us that he and Bev had hit some snags, so we wouldn't get the script until after dinner. Nice bedtime reading, don't you think?"

"Lovely," Jeanne agreed with an ironic expression.

No need to tell Jeanne how Gerry had nearly hit the roof over the added delay.

"So," Jeanne said conversationally, "how was your trip to town? Did you find what you were looking for? Anything interesting?"

How nice of her to ask, Jess decided before answering, "Interesting? Yes and no. Nothing that we haven't heard before, really. Still, looking at photos of Felicia, I couldn't help seeing into her a little more deeply and feeling for her. But it's hard to know someone you've never met. That must have been an impediment for Scott, so I imagine he must have asked you about her."

"Me? About Felicia Blasko?" The housekeeper seemed genuinely surprised.

"Well, Martha Royle said today that you lived here as a child with your mother when all the tragic events occurred. That surprised me; you didn't mention it when you told me before about growing up here."

Jeanne Rivers stiffened for a moment, and Jess immediately regretted her words. Quickly, she tried to smooth things over: "I'm sorry, Miss Rivers. I didn't realize it was a sore spot. Please forgive me. Sometimes I get so wrapped up in trying to do my job thoroughly, I just blunder—"

"No, no," the other woman cut her off, trying to reassure Jessica. "It was so long ago, part of another life. I'm afraid I was so young I can scarcely remember that time. Anyway, I sometimes feel that people think I came into this job because of my mother, rather than on my own abilities. So, I don't like to bring her up. That's all."

"How could they think that?" Jessica protested. "You have this house running like clockwork! You've more than proved yourself."

"Yes, well, I think I told you that I'd left town as a young woman with the attitude I had bigger fish to fry in the world outside this island. Instead, the world fried me, but good. People in small towns have a high capacity for remembering and a low one for forgiving. Mr. Carlyle took a chance on me, so I was determined not to let him down," Jeanne explained.

"Your mother must be very proud of you, carrying on the family tradition so beautifully," Jessica reassured the other woman.

For a fraction of a second, Jeanne seemed to debate how to reply, finally saying, "My mother talks more to Martha Royle and Annette Risdon than to me. It's just as well. I'm glad she has those friends. Her memory's not what it used to be, but she remembers how I left. The less said, the better."

Feeling rather like a heel, Jessica apologized, "Again, I'm sorry I poked my nose where it didn't belong. I didn't mean to bring up anything unsettling."

Jeanne replied kindly, "No need to apologize, Miss Minton. I know your intentions weren't bad. No terrible scandals revealed. Anyway, I like where I am now. I'm proud to keep things humming here. At least now, I understand that my mother was not the schmo I thought she was before I left, for being proud of her work. So, what will you be up to until it's time to dress for dinner?"

"Ha!" Jess laughed, happy to return to pleasant ground. "That's the $64.00 question. I'm too restless to sit and read, but I'm not sure I have time for a walk. It would be nice to stroll somewhere new, though."

"You've come to the right person," Jeanne assured her. "I know just the walk for you."

"Yes?"

"Yes. It's right up your alley," Jeanne explained. "I'd been thinking about how you were saying you liked the quaint cemetery by the sea, but you'd really love to stroll through something with unique monuments. There is just such a place, not too far away, through the woods. You could get there, walk around, and get back in time for this evening."

"Really? That sounds great!"

"Really. It's where the island's best families and the wealthier professionals have been buried since the 1860s. Let me tell you, these people love their monuments. There are quite some striking statues. There's also a hill with a stone bench that gives you a lovely view of the bay."

"That sounds wonderful," Jessica enthused. "It's so nice of you to think of me."

Jeanne proceeded to give Jessica directions to a path through the trees, joking that no Hound of Hades or Stone-throwing Demon had been known to howl or pitch rocks in that actual neck of the woods.

Those directions didn't lead directly into the cemetery but brought Jessica out onto the shoulder of the main road, so she could approach the graveyard through the main gates. The cemetery was bounded by a stone wall, topped with an elegant, black iron-railing, only a few patches of rust eating through the paint. The gates were something else: tall, ornate, held on each side with gothic pillars topped by copper angels, robes flowing as if in flight and trumpets erect to announce the coming Resurrection. Except, one angel couldn't go full celestial Harry James: its instrument had been snapped just beyond its gripping hand. At least no verdigris had transformed them. Though the main gates were closed, a small, pedestrian side gate opened inward for visitors.

Before entering, Jessica had to pause and survey what lay beyond the gates. The stretch of an acre or so rolled gently up a hill. It should have been green, but several months of drought had reduced the lawn to parched tawniness. Predominating from the hilltop was a beautiful mausoleum of white stone, square but with a copper roof and Corinthian front columns. Saunders? Carlyle? Another family? The stone bench that Jeanne had mentioned resided nearby. To the left of that bench was a stone angel with a sword facing the mausoleum. Even in profile, he must have scared off invaders by sea.

A gravel path ran centrally toward the hill, then split. On the right, it wound up the rise and passed among an impressive array of statuary. On the left, the path extended along the bottom of the hill into the woods through a break in the stone wall. The forest surrounding the cemetery provided gorgeous walls of saffron, apricot, green-going-chartreuse, and slashes of scarlet.

Passing through the side gate, Jessica was almost immediately impressed with a large stone topped by a carved open book, apt monument for two partners in publishing and their families. And there was so much more to see, with the weeping women, heads bowed and robes flowing; the angels rising heavenward, sometimes guiding a child or young woman; the graceful urns soaring atop gothic cathedral supports or classical columns; the weather-dissolved lambs marking children whom wealth and power could not protect from mortality. Mockingbirds flitted from atop gravestones to chatter at her. Robins bobbed amongst the grasses, with the occasional rabbit suddenly coming into focus, initially camouflaged as its color blended with the crisped grass. The cemetery was well mown, though grey-green or rusty lichens ate into some of the stones.

A glance to her right, and Jessica gasped at a bald eagle surveying his domain from high in a saffron tree. As if annoyed by her intrusion, the enormous bird launched itself from the tree and glided toward the ocean. Even knowing he was just as likely to feast on road kill as dive bomb his prey in the sound, Jessica smiled with respect for the bird that had taken off into the wide blue yonder.

Unfortunately, though, that yonder still might be wide, it wasn't nearly as blue as when she and Elizabeth had first arrived at Carlyle House. Its graying wasn't from anything as revivifying as storm clouds but from the huge chunk of Maine being devoured by fire. There were even blazes in Rochester, New Hampshire, about forty miles northwest. Jess had almost wanted to cancel her and Gerry's appointment when Martha Royle had told them stories about the furious, inexorable blazes roaring through entire towns. However, that was not what Gerry wanted, and she hated to let him down. It wasn't as if canceling would end the fires.

Not for the first time, Jess decided it was a darned good thing that James wasn't here. Sure as shootin', he'd be volunteering to go fight the fires. She'd prayed to get him back safe and sound from a world war, so there were no two ways about risking him to a war with those hellish flames!

What's wrong with me? This should be a quiet, relaxing stroll. Look at all this beauty: nature and art combined. Like a miniature Mt. Auburn in Cambridge, the granddaddy of all the rustic cemeteries. People used to come to these places for family picnics in the 1800s. James would certainly love it here: the cemetery's delicious melancholy of Keats, rather than the gruesomeness of Monk Lewis, was exactly his cup of tea.

Jess laughed a little at the monument she now came up on: a stone cut into a high-backed chair with arms carved as happy Golden Retrievers. Next to it was a tallish, flat stone embellished with the relief of a smiling bulldog seeming to emerge from the monument. Clearly, the dog lovers' section. *Dusty would not approve!*

Nearing the top, Jessica noticed the path below on the left curved through a gap in the stone wall into the duskiness of the woods. A quick glance at her watch revealed there was insufficient time for that side trip, so she proceeded up the hill, happily realizing her choice was the right one. Under the protection of the age-grayed angel, Jessica took in the wonderful scene below. The Piscataqua River, broad as a bay, stretched slate blue beneath her. Splotches of islands sprang up between her and a mainland that sported trees flaming or golden and white houses tinged pale blue in the late afternoon light.

Standing here, facing away from the fires, smoke clouded the sky much less, especially as the winds had shifted. Although the sun had started its descent, Jessica calculated she still had time to enjoy the scent of the salt air, though not untainted by that of burning wood. Nevertheless, she enjoyed feeling as if she might spread her arms and join the eagle. God, she loved the autumn! To some people, it was a season of decay; but fall gave her a sense of being on the verge of something new, unknown, wonderful.

Jessica sat down on the stone bench, leaning into its back, carved, with "leaf-fring'd shape[s] . . . of deities or mortals, or of both." Above, Gulls wheeled, dived, and powered skyward again. The sights around her seemed to release all her worries about hurting or letting down anyone. Jess closed her eyes. *Mmm.* James could be right here beside her, an arm around her. He wouldn't have to worry about his responsibility to make his trip pay off or about the dark memories of his past. They wouldn't even have to talk. It would just be heaven, lulled by the rush of waters below.

"Pardon me, Miss?" came a voice with rhythmic accents.

Jessica's eyes fluttered open. The light was amber gold on the waters, gilding the houses, the sky—and this man before her. Drowsily, she focused on him, her brow furrowing as his features registered familiarity: the rounded face with a strong jaw-line, the round cleft in his chin, the dark and incisive eyes, the black hair slicked back under a dark hat. She knew that face, but younger, with fewer careworn lines and eyes far less sad. Where? Keats's question, "Do I wake or do I dream?" floated through her sleepy consciousness.

In a flash, two disturbing thoughts swept her: she'd dozed off into nearly sunset, and this tall, spare man in dark trousers, suede and corduroy jacket over a white shirt, and dark tie was Vitus Blasko. Jess opened her mouth; yet the possibility of what he might think of her, feel, facing the woman so deeply resembling his wife, confounded her with embarrassment, anxiety, guilt.

He must have read that inchoate jumble in her face, for the man put forward a calming hand and reassured Jessica, "Please, Miss Minton. I did not intend to frighten you. I should not have startled you, but I do need to speak to you. So I could not let this moment slip by. Please forgive me."

The rhythm of his accent was strangely soothing, while the kindness in his dark, troubled eyes drew Jessica in. There was none of the pride and almost imperiousness she'd seen in the wedding photo, heard about in Philip's tales. He had changed. She couldn't help feeling touched. Finally, Jessica managed, "I . . . yes . . . we can talk, but about what?"

"The radio program."

"Oh," Jess uttered faintly, thinking about how their broadcasts would affect him and his daughter.

He read her anxiety immediately and surprised Jessica by gently, urgently assuring her, "No, I'm not here to criticize you. I am not upset. But it is important that I talk to you. May I?"

His words put Jessica somewhat more at ease; and, all things considered, listening to the man was the least she could do.

"Yes, please, go on," she said, mustering grace. "I don't know how I can be any help to you. Maybe if you explain . . ."

Her words trailed off, but he nodded acknowledgment. At least he could see her heart was in the right place.

As if feeling he had to justify his presence, he began, "I come here often at this time of day. It makes me feel closer to her."

Jess wanted to concur, "Of course she would be buried in her family crypt," but caught herself. Who knew where or if Felicia was buried? *How poignant that even this tenuous link Blasko held was illusory.*

Even as those thoughts crossed her mind, Vitus Blasko continued, "It's especially fortuitous I came upon you before I go north to help fight the blazes."

Jessica tensed. *Does my likeness to his lost wife make this meeting so important Blasko?*

Blasko must have read that thought in her face, for he reassured Jessica, "No, don't think like that. You do resemble her, but there is more to a human being than appearance. I can see in your face that you are a kind and sensitive person, but you are not Felicia. I lost her a long time ago, even before that night. Life does not give second chances. What I want to talk to you about concerns my daughter, for no one knows whom the flames in the north may claim. If I end up paying for my past in the blazes, then I want to be sure Jamie is not left alone and lost."

Jessica started to speak, but to say what? How could she help Jamie and Gerry? Was Vitus Blasko for or against their relationship? Finally, she said, "I'd like to help you, Dr. Blasko. I've met Jamie, and I can see she's a troubled young woman. But I don't know what I can do for her. What are you asking of me?"

Niggling at Jessica's mind were the questions: *What* did *Blasko think he would absolve in the flaming woods: neglecting his wife or something much more sinister?*

He nodded pensively before answering, "I have not been very clear. Of course, you are confused. I spoke badly. This unexpected opportunity overwhelms me with all I want to say. Please be patient with a man who has been alone with his thoughts for too long."

The last words touched Jessica deeply, for it reminded her of James's broodings over his part in a brutal war. But James had her; whom did Vitus Blasko have to help him exorcise his guilt? Jamie? Was dragging his child into that morass a further burden of guilt for him?

He confirmed her speculations: "I've brought too much pain to my child. I drove away her mother, perhaps to her death. I brooded, angry and guilty, afterward, until my daughter left me for school and never looked back—until my past ruined her life."

Jessica shot Blasko a startled, puzzled look at his troubled admission.

He explained, "Jamie had moved to Chicago to work in a university. She met a fine young man from a good family. They were engaged, until the family found out about our dark story. That was it. They threw her over. She hated me for that."

"Hated you?" Jessica repeated, surprised. "She certainly doesn't seem to hate you now. She seems downright protective. Why would she live with you and look out for you if she hated you?"

He smiled sadly but a little proudly when answering, "That must be Felicia in her. Some time back, I became seriously ill. I didn't want her to know. I'd wanted no longer to plague her. But Danvers thought differently. He found her and persuaded her to come back, care for me; and, as I recovered, we seemed to find a bond. Perhaps not one of deep, spoken sentiments, but I think she may have forgiven me, a little. She might have seen a proud man humbled and felt pity. And it was not easy to show how I felt. I have little right to expect that any sentiment from me might be treated with regard. Still, I have tried to make life easier and more secure for her here. I've even given her the opportunity to travel at times. Always, though, I feel a cloud over her, a darkness or a bitterness. I don't want her to become like me."

"So, how would I help?" Jessica asked quietly, moved by Blasko's inability to connect with his child because of his past wrongs. *Hmm, did Gerry know about the broken engagement?*

"I know that she has been drawing close to a young man in your company," Blasko replied.

"How?"

"One must be exceedingly skillful to keep a secret on an island this small. Servants see all and share all. Danvers keeps me apprised."

Jessica wrinkled her forehead. *Was Blasko's interest in Jamie the concern of a loving or of a controlling father?*

He pressed on. "I want to know what kind of man this fellow is. If I don't come back, is he the sort who might care for my child, give her happiness and peace at last? Or would he just bring her more heartache? I dread leaving her alone to that."

Guided by her respect for Gerry, Jessica answered, "Gerry's the kind of guy who literally sacrificed a part of himself for his country. He's not limping because he had a couple of bone spurs. You can bank on him."

"I, too, came through a war," Blasko revealed knowingly. "I know that combat does not wound only the good."

"Well, that may be, Dr. Blasko, but Gerry thinks the world of your daughter. You couldn't ask for a better catch for her. To be honest, I've been worried Jamie might break his heart," Jessica defended her friend.

"Then I see we both have high opinions of those we care about," Blasko nodded. "Perhaps we are prejudiced, but I think our views of these two should reassure us both. However, considering what happened to Jamie's engagement, I wonder if your friend can be relied upon, no matter what comes out of your director's research or the séance."

"What comes out?" Jessica repeated uneasily. "What do you think will come out?" Before she could stop herself, she added, "What are you afraid of?"

The worst Vitus Blasko has to fear is being revealed as his wife and Bill Carlyle's murderer. Jessica curled her hands in tension as she saw that realization flash through his features. And there was anger in that face, now tinged red as the sun sank deeper and painted the sky magenta into pink. *God, why can't I keep my big trap shut! What is he going to do?*

But his expression lapsed into such sadness that Jessica wanted to kick herself for her melodramatic fear in the face of his suffering.

He said tiredly but bluntly, "I loved my wife. I failed her as a husband, but I loved her. Do you believe that I could have harmed her?"

Seeing his pain and regret but no viciousness, after hearing him bare his heart these past minutes, Jessica could honestly say to Blasko, "No, I don't see a murderer."

Still, Jessica didn't add that she could only speak about the man who stood before her now, not what he might have been twenty years ago.

Fortunately, Vitus Blasko either didn't perceive her thoughts or chose not to acknowledge them. He quietly said, "Thank you."

"You don't have to thank me for speaking the truth," Jessica stated, still not sure how she felt about being alone with him. James would probably want to give her the dickens for not finding a way to take a powder, pronto!

"There is something more," Vitus began slowly.

Jess gave him a quizzical, "Yes?"

"The script your director and his colleague are fashioning, then the séance, I agreed to allow the story to be told, partly to assure some financial security for my daughter, but mainly in hope of finding out what happened. Do you think the truth will come out?"

Jessica raised her hands in resignation, answering, "I'm sorry, Dr. Blasko, but *I* haven't even seen the script yet. I won't until later this evening. I don't know *what* Scott and Bev have come up with. Gerry has been pushing them to find info to protect Jamie. I hope that eases your mind a bit. But this is a radio show, not a criminal investigation. Please don't hang your hat on it. I see the same problem for Philip Carlyle."

Vitus looked down, thinking, then faced Jessica to state, "You think I am a fool to hope for some peace from this."

Jessica's heart went out to him. She wanted to offer some comfort to this man who made mistakes, paid dearly for them, and continued to pay. Still, instinct put some check on her compassion. She said, "Dr. Blasko, I'm only an actress. I have no control here. I might be able to make a point if I think the script is unfair or doesn't work, but I haven't much power. I have a question for you, though. Are you saying that you think Bill Carlyle is responsible for what happened? Are you hoping he'll be proven guilty?"

Blasko sighed, flummoxed on how to answer her.

Odd. Shouldn't he have been railing against Carlyle all along, the only other suspect? Was Bill a perpetrator or a victim?

At last, Blasko said, "Bill Carlyle was no good. Even his brother despised him. He had a reputation . . . Never mind that. I'd like to blame him, but I have no proof. His disappearance plagues me. And it haunts me that Felicia might have . . . No, she would never voluntarily have left Jamie. Yes, you're right. It's part of my doubts, about myself as well. I'm sure you've heard the story about my demanding in a fury that Felicia return with me that night. When I failed, I went home and, for the first time in my life, drank myself unconscious. So, yes, I want to blame Bill Carlyle.

"Nevertheless, if I'm honest, I must admit I cannot account for the rest of the evening. If I push too hard for Carlyle's guilt, the family could push back on my blank hours. I don't believe I could ever have hurt Felicia, but Lord knows how Jamie would react."

Jess was on her feet, questioning, frustrated, "Then why in heaven's name did you let this can of worms be reopened if you knew the answer might go that way?"

"I'm not a wealthy man. Developers have been pressuring me to sell, but I promised my wife's family I would always maintain their estate for future generations. It seemed the least I could do after I so terribly betrayed my promise to cherish their daughter. Your people offered me enough to let me keep the estate intact for Jamie and to honor the wishes of my wife's family. And I want the reassurance that I am innocent, for my peace of mind and for Jamie's sake. The truth must come out."

The pain in his eyes silenced Jessica from warning that the truth that came out could very well drive him deeper into hell and wound his daughter worse than ever. There was no use in her voicing that possibility when it was too late to stop this avalanche.

He spoke again, "I think I've sensed Felicia's spirit: here, in the grove that devil Bill Carlyle created, by the cliff, and in the window of the room where she used to stay at Carlyle House. I abandoned her for my research, and then my love of research abandoned me when I lost her forever."

"Wait a minute," Jessica questioned, brushing her wind-played hair away from her face. "You've been haunting the Carlyle property?"

Blasko sighed, admitting "A fool, aren't I? Believe me; I'm careful. They don't know. But I need to be where I feel her spirit. I drove her from her own home in life. Now, in death, I haunt the haunter."

Jess genuinely felt for this man, knowing what it was to be separated from the person you love. Though at least she had the comfort of a deep and shared love with James binding them across the miles. Yet, she also saw that Blasko's devotion danced with obsession, threaded with disturbing guilt. She had nothing more to offer him.

And what had happened in those hours that he couldn't account for? Jamie was right to worry about how the truth could wound him. Even if he were innocent of the worst crime, he would still have to relive how he had thrown away his marriage and family for nothing. Yes, she felt for the man; but, as she'd warned him, she had no power to undo the juggernaut he'd put in motion by agreeing to let the show proceed.

The world around them had turned purple-blue, with the sun only a pink glow over the horizon, which Jessica only now really noticed. A frantic glance at her watch, and she blurted, "Good grief! I've got to get back!"

Blasko abruptly escaped his brooding to question, "Do you have a flashlight?"

Jess shook her head anxiously, replying, "No. I never expected to stay this late. And I came through those dark woods. This road, could I find my way back along it?"

Now, Blasko shook his head, warning, "There's no direct route. It's much too long. And there are no lights. We haven't much traffic, but you'd still be taking a risk in the dark. No, you should come with me."

"You?" Jessica responded hesitantly.

"You're afraid?" he queried, a bit sadly. Even a little affronted?

"No, no," Jessica protested, not entirely honest.

Blasko only said, "Look down there, to the gates. Danvers has the auto waiting to drive me north. We can take you to the bottom of the Carlyle drive. I don't think I would be so welcome bringing you to the door. Please, I cannot let you chance harm in the dark woods."

From not very deep in those woods, a hound howled mournfully. Blasko added with a smile, somehow both ironic and mysterious, "Of course you would want to avoid the Hound of Hades."

"Of course," Jessica agreed dryly. Well, Danvers would be there, and she didn't really fear Vitus Blasko, right? "Yes, thank you. I do appreciate your kindness. I wouldn't want to worry anyone in the house, either, by coming in dreadfully late."

Jessica and Blasko moved quietly down the curving path. After this encounter, tonight's script could only prove anti-climactic.

Chapter Sixteen
Later that Evening

Jessica leaned back against the wall of her room's window seat. The windows themselves rattled from time to time under punishment of the wind in the night beyond. She still hadn't slipped out of her evening wear, the blue-verging-on-purple, silk-velvet dress with splashes of powder blue and pink flowers at her V-neck. It might have been late, but she had to get cracking on Scott and Bev's script. As much as she wanted to read, her eyes drooped in the soft lamp-light. She would have been deep into it, but Elizabeth had marched into the room with her right after dinner, determined to discover what had put that gleam of excitement and uncertainty into her eyes. Her dusk encounter was not something she was willing to share with the rest of the crew, not yet, anyway. So, Jess had challenged Liz's patience to the breaking point by making her wait.

Wanly, Jessica smiled as her eyes drifted wearily to the coffee service on the low table across the room. Scott had arranged for all the actors to have a supply of caffeine after dinner so they could go directly to work reading—and keep going all night if necessary. However, Elizabeth, waiting like a vulture to pounce on a new and juicy tidbit of news, had prevented Jess from following Scott's instructions.

Elizabeth's reaction to Jess's newfound "friend" in the purpling twilight of the cemetery had certainly packed a wallop. "Get out of town!" and "Are you out of your mind? Chumming around with that guy alone, in the dark?!" were the mildest words she let fly. Even harder to tamp down had been Liz's barrage of questions: "What did he say? What was he like? How did he take your resemblance to Felicia?" It left Jessica breathless just hearing Liz, never mind trying to answer her.

Only when Liz had paused to tank up on some of the premium-blend coffee had Jessica a chance to reply. Her response all came down to saying she felt awfully sorry for the guy. No, he hadn't gone all "Tomb of Ligeia" on her, as Liz had put it. To her mind, Blasko was a man grieving the past wrongs he had done and worrying about his daughter's future.

Initially, Elizabeth seemed mollified, but she'd taken Jessica by surprise with: "So, do you think he could have killed his wife, maybe even Bill Carlyle?"

Those were questions requiring deep thought before Jessica could honestly reply, "Not the man I met tonight, but twenty years ago, with a hole in his memory . . . ?"

Now, though, Jess looked out at the half-moon riding above the trees. It was red with the glow of fires devastating Maine, driving people and creatures onto the beaches, into the water. A prayer for Vitus Blasko's safety, for the safety of so many, slipped into her thoughts. Whatever he might have done, he was trying to do good now.

Liz's anger with Jeanne for sending Jessica where she could run into the man flitted to mind. But really, with all the housekeeper had on her plate, it hardly seemed likely she was up on Blasko's social calendar. Liz was probably still sore about having been ejected from the kitchen.

Never mind all that. Scott would be more than a little sore at *her* if she didn't get cracking on this script for their roundtable discussion tomorrow morning. Kicking off her shoes and tucking her feet under herself, Jess resolved: *Put all that sympathy in cold storage and concentrate on your job, kiddo!* She yawned. *Maybe I should have drunk that whole pot of coffee instead of sharing it with Elizabeth. At least, I drank most of it. Onto the script!*

Black velvet. Folds of soft, black velvet enwrapped her—at first. Then came the voices, faint, now flaring, shifting her peace into flickers of bright fear as the words became more distinct. A woman's voice, a man's, the man's again—or was it a different man? Names: Bill, Felicia, Gladys, Vitus—even Jamie—danced into perception, then away. Some names invoked trepidation, but the words those names seemed to speak were never quite distinct. Yet clarifying them felt so vital.

The swaths of velvet cleared, if cleared were an accurate description. Gas lamps gave a soft illumination that muted the colors she expected. She was in a corridor now, one much like that outside her room. Her room and yet not hers.

What was she holding in her arms? A bouquet of roses tied with a blue velvet ribbon. *Fresh roses? In October? How?* Yet she vaguely knew why; a part of her did, anyway. A part? Yes, because it felt as if someone else struggled to be heard inside her. But which one was she? Jessica Minton! And yet, not. The other part denied Jessica and urged her on—with those roses. The part that wasn't Jessica knew where and why. It struggled to push through Jessica and direct her. Jessica Minton was stubborn, though, and held on more tightly to who she was. Still, Jess was curious, curious and cagey. She knew the Other would not let go until she delivered the roses, so Jessica played along, for now.

Without ceding control, Jess allowed the Other to guide her down to the corridor's end. The light olive folds of her long dressing gown, its brocade trim down to her feet, rustled in graceful drapes. The long sleeves ended in capacious brocaded openings. She'd packed a ton of clothes for this trip, but this outfit had never taken up residence in *her* closet.

It's mine! The Other flared, almost crushing Jessica with a flood of determination to bring those roses into the room, *her* room—the Other's room—except, who was the Other?

The door was before them both. Her hand reached knowingly into the dressing gown's pocket for a key to that door. The Other was strong, strong in her need to place these roses in the room, as if doing so could somehow avert disaster.

Jessica and the Other stood in the room, though Jess couldn't remember opening the door or entering. She was just . . . now here. An uncanny familiarity swept over Jess, even comfort? As if she were back where she belonged. She or the Other?

The room was large, its walls papered in a design popular at the time—which time, though? The windows were shuttered in front of her, but she knew they looked out upon the same gorgeous scene as did her room below. The other identity resisted, but Jess fought for the concept of the second-floor room being her own. Jessica Minton would not be suppressed.

The furnishings were tasteful and elegant: a bed to her right with built-in headboard picturing a painted pastoral scene and a child's bed next . . . no, it was gone, as if a memory hastily erased. Why? Oh, Jamie, where was

Jamie? How could she be protected from this dreadful mess created by adults so selfish and foolish and angry? Like children themselves. Her daughter must be spared the influence of their stupid mistakes, but already she could see mistrust and resentment eating into Jamie's heart.

Forcing her body to turn left, a command echoed in her head: "Look at the mantel. Look at the mantel."

Just a hearth with a mirror above its mantel. Lovely, but Jess could see nothing significant about it, aside from the fact that it was probably directly above the fireplace in her own room. *Yes, my own room!* Jessica insisted over the Other's protest.

Wait. There was something else to see on the mantel: two beautifully shaped candleholders, heavy, glass-petaled tulip shapes with large pools of candle wax inside, their wicks flickering. Crystal pendants dangled from the petals. The waiting vase was in the center, under the mirror. *The mirror.* Her reflection. Her face, white, framed by dark hair waving, longer than usual, far past her shoulders. Didn't she usually wear it up, like in the portrait? Shouldn't it be up as it was in my portrait?

No! That is Felicia's portrait! I am Jessica Minton!

Jess threw the flowers to the floor, driving the O ther to plead, *No, it's a peace offering. Send me and him peace. We need it! You must!*

Two shapes, dark and shadowy, seemed to hover behind her in the mirror's reflection. She whirled and grabbed for one of them—and now she was alone with the Other. Then, sounds of footsteps in the corridor outside paralyzed them both. The approaching tread was heavy, angry, deliberate. A man's. Both she and the Other were filled with dreadful anticipation. The Other seemed to remember what was coming, while Jess's own imagination began to fill in the gaps.

She backed away, toward the windows. The tread stopped outside the door. *Was that a man's voice? Yes, but it was distorted.* She couldn't tell if he spoke in the rhythmic accents of Blasko or with Bill's voice. Well, she had no idea how the lost Carlyle sounded. The Other didn't help her. Panic flamed through them both, for the doorknob turned. They shot a glance to the child's bed again, next to the master bed. Empty! Thank God! She was sleeping with Auntie Gladys tonight!

Relief was short-lived because Felicia knew what was coming, flooding Jessica with an inchoate memory of horror and death.

"James!" Jessica shouted. But he wasn't there. No, but the memory of how he had taught her to defend herself back in San Francisco raced to mind. She started to position herself behind the door, but the Other, inside, tried to hold her back, protesting, "I can't do that!"

"I can!" Jessica insisted aloud.

Except a voice that penetrated from the other side of the door seemed to make her head reel with Felicia's terror. The words were fuzzy, but the anger and hostility were crystal clear. Jess shook her head free enough of Felicia's frightened grip to realize she had lost her place for surprise by the door. She was next to the mantel—the mantel and those noggin-cracking candle holders. She wasn't Felicia. She would not go down without taking some hide off her assailant! Jess turned to reach for her weapon—without warning the black velvet curtains descended upon her, even as she raged, "No!"

Jess's eyes abruptly flew open. Still wearing her silk-velvet dress, she was tucked onto the window seat. The script had fallen onto the floor. Sunlight streamed through the glass, deliciously warming. And now she realized someone was knocking on her door, calling her name.

"Just a minute!" Jessica responded, glancing at her wristwatch, only to utter, "Good Grief! Nine o'clock!"

That realization really woke her up.

Jess picked up the script, tossed it on the window seat, then hurried to the door. All the while, her mind was racing: *Jeepers crow! The meeting's in a half-hour, and I haven't even washed and dressed, never mind had breakfast! Thank heavens, I finished reading before I nodded off. Maybe not so fortunate, considering that doozy of a nightmare!*

Opening her door, Jess was met by Jeanne River's surprise at seeing her still in last night's attire. However, the discreet housekeeper only said, "I'm sorry to disturb you. Mr. Zimkiewicz was worried you might miss the meeting when he didn't see you even after breakfast. He asked for someone to check on you. I didn't have a girl free, so I came myself."

"I guess I overslept," Jessica smiled sheepishly. "You wouldn't believe the honey of a nightmare I had! I guess between reading the script right before bed and running into Dr. Blasko in the cemetery . . ."

Jeanne's eyes widened, alerting the still sleepy Jessica to what she'd let slip—and she'd been so careful yesterday not to tell anyone but Liz.

"You saw Vitus Blasko yesterday?" Jeanne blurted. "In the cemetery?"

"Well, yes, by the Saunders' Mausoleum," Jess admitted.

"I'm so sorry," Jeanne apologized. "Had I known he'd be there, I'd never have sent you. How could I have known, though? It's not as if she were buried there. Oh, forgive me; that was tactless. I don't know what I'm saying. I feel so bad. I hope he didn't do anything to upset you."

"No, no," Jess tried to soothe Jeanne. "It's not your fault. And, actually, I found him more sad and lonely than anything. Did you know he went off to help fight fires in Maine?"

"No, I didn't," said Jeanne carefully. "How, ah, noble. Perhaps, he's trying to make up for past, well, errors."

Jessica studied Jeanne. Clearly, this woman had no liking for Vitus Blasko. Maybe it was the lingering effects of the dream, maybe it was her uncertainty about the man she'd met in the cemetery, maybe it was concern for what Gerry might be getting himself into—maybe all three. Whatever the case, Jess was emboldened to ask, "Jeanne, you don't like the man, do you? Why?"

Jeanne took a deep breath, then tossed her professional reticence to the wind: "Because the whole family has brought the Carlyles nothing but grief. Well, maybe not the child, but the parents! My mother couldn't keep me from seeing the pain and trouble Miss Gladys went through, caught in the middle of their troubles—and poor Mr. Philip, having to pick up the pieces afterward and save the family name."

This was a far different take on Jeanne's life amidst the Carlyle/Blasko tragedy than she'd given Jessica yesterday. Interestingly, she'd mentioned the effects on every Carlyle but Bill.

Jeanne didn't have to be Madame Wanda to read that thought in Jessica's expression and added, "Even Bill, yes. He was the black sheep, all right. Probably, if it hadn't been this, it'd have been some other way he'd have brought us down. But it was through Felicia and her husband, so it's those two I resent the most."

"Well," Jess surmised, "that certainly lays it on the line. I'm just sorry that there's been so much misery here."

"Do you think that script will make things any better?" Jeanne asked intently.

Jessica inhaled. Scott would have her head if she gave away anything before the broadcast. But Jeanne had opened up to her more than she ought to have. Did she owe the woman more? Did she like keeping her head on her shoulders?

Jess compromised, "I don't know if any script could set things right for everyone. Helping you could hurt Jamie and vice versa. Anyway, I'm sorry, but I have to snap it up and get ready; or after Scott gets through with me for being late, there'll be another ghost around here!"

"All right, then," Jeanne replied neutrally. "I'll clear away the coffee things. I guess both you Minton sisters had rough nights."

"Oh?" Jessica queried, pausing at the bath's door.

"Sure," Jeanne answered as she gathered the tray. "She's not up, either. The girls in the kitchen were getting antsy for another gossip."

Lingering as long as she dared in the doorway, Jess laughed, "Just wave the sales section of the paper under her door. She'll be out in a jiffy."

Jeanne smiled as she headed into the corridor. Disappearing into the bathroom, Jessica, her mind returning to work mode, wondered how Gerry had taken that script. It would be interesting, to say the least.

Chapter Seventeen
Wednesday, October 22nd

The skirt of Jessica's silk wine-colored dress, sprigged with light green, pink, and blue, swirled gracefully as she descended the main staircase. She traveled remarkably quickly, considering that her bizarre dream had left her a bit groggy. Too bad she hadn't had time to check in with Liz about her bad night, but there hadn't even been time for breakfast! There could be no missing Scott's 9:30-sharp meeting!

Striding past the drawing room, Jessica forced away the cobwebs cluttering her brain. There was work to do—and something emphatic to tell Scott Zimkiewicz about this script. As she approached the music room, voices drifted to her through the open doorway. *Gosh*, she really could stand a nice cuppa right now. *No time, though!*

The room was bright, for the sound-muffling curtains were drawn back with no broadcasting or recording going on. A table had been set up by the windows across from the doorway, cast and crew gathered there. Scott looked up at Jessica and teased, "So, our leading lady makes her grand entrance at last."

"Your leading lady is right on time," Jessica insisted, tapping her watch. "And I have a thing or two to say to you about the script." Jess glanced at Gerry, then back to her director. "You guys did a great job. Wouldn't you say, Gerry, that Scott and Bev gave everyone involved a fair shake?"

Gerry Davis nodded, admitting, "I was afraid Blasko would get railroaded, but you were square with him, Scott. You played out just the facts, nicely dramatic, of course. How you'll wrap up with that séance, though, still concerns me."

Jess nodded as she took her seat, partially agreeing, "If this story has to be told, you tried to be as sensitive as you could. You two did a grand job setting up the background for the confrontation with Vitus over his wife's coming here. It's not exactly flattering, but it's not a hatchet job. He doesn't come off as a monster. I like the touch of pain you allow him, without sanitizing him. It sounds like him."

"Hold on. Back that up," Scott insisted, surprised. "How do you know what an island recluse sounds like?"

Gerry looked downright startled.

Well, it was bound to get out sooner or later, especially after your slip to Jeanne. Anyway, that meeting might lend authority to any criticism you have.

"Yesterday, before dinner," Jessica answered calmly, "I ran into Dr. Blasko in the cemetery in the woods. We talked for a bit. He impressed me as a decent fellow, but a troubled one."

"You never said anything," Gerry began, but Scott took over with, "I don't suppose he made a full confession?"

"Not at all, Scott," Jessica set him straight. "He is concerned about the program, but he didn't seem afraid you'd 'expose' him. He did confirm what you've been saying, that he wants this program to continue." A quick glance at Gerry for that. He only frowned. *Thinking of Jamie, of course.* "He's hoping this will bring some kind of release to his daughter, reveal his innocence."

"So, he puts the blame on Bill Carlyle," Scott speculated.

"He didn't exactly say that," Jessica disagreed. "However, if the two of them are the main suspects, and he's not volunteering a confession . . ."

"Did he positively clear himself?" Scott pressed. "There is the matter of him blacking out after returning home."

"How did you know that?" Gerry questioned, his tone indicating that what surprised him wasn't the information but someone else knowing it.

Scott replied to Gerry, "Bev and I did quite a bit of research. That includes talking to servants and going over old police reports. Chief Winston wasn't crazy about letting us dig through them, but he let us. I might ask how *you* knew, Gerry, but I don't really need to—the island grapevine and all."

Gerry frowned, ready to retort, except Jessica's stomach startled them all by rumbling out her hunger.

"Lions and tigers and bears, oh my!" teased Guy, provoking laughter that broke the tension.

Jessica mumbled, "Excuse me. I missed breakfast."

"And your tummy won't let *you* forget!" Guy added.

Reverting to his characteristic good-guy nature, Scott requested, "Chet, I know it's not in your contract, but would you mind grabbing something out of the kitchen for Jess? I'd send her back, but right now we're discussing only the acting end of the script. So I need her more than I need you."

Chet, an affable guy, agreed with a promise not to rat out Scott to his union. Now, everyone else returned to the script.

For Gerry and Jamie's sake, Jessica was happy that Madame Wanda's insinuation that Felicia might have murdered Bill and skipped town had been scotched. Felicia had not at all been portrayed as some kind of *femme fatale,* nor Blasko as an outright villain. No, they were two lonely and confused people made miserable by their inability to communicate with each other. More insightfully, the script conveyed their love for their child, despite the misfire of their own relationship. *Probably old Ungerpreck wouldn't be thrilled that the script wasn't dripping with illicit sensation. Nuts to him!*

Gerry had the task of voicing Bill and Philip to Guy's Blasko (double, even triple duty was the radio actor's forté). She wasn't surprised that Gerry gave Bill's voice notable smugness and irony. So much so, Scott directed him to tone it down, not make Bill Carlyle's guilt a foregone conclusion. *How would that shadow of doubt affect Jamie and her father?* Again, the wildcard of the séance gave her a turn.

Two hours or so later, the session finally broke up, for the actors, anyway. Now Scott was busy working out details with Chet the engineer and Vic the sound man. Afterward, he and Bev would spend today and tomorrow revising, editing, and polishing any problems today's read-through revealed. Friday morning would be a full rehearsal to test drive their improvements.

Gerry had given Jessica the word he wanted to talk with her later, but for now he had slipped away for a previous "appointment." Jess more than suspected that Jamie was about to get a heads-up on the program. Scott might be able to keep the physical script under wraps, but he couldn't exactly put a gag on Gerry. *Best not to give him any ideas, though.* Jessica was delighted, however, to see that as Guy and Maura slipped out, her sister slipped in, attractively casual in a golden-brown, tweed skirt and long-sleeved cream blouse. Her hair, loose and free, curled down to her shoulders.

"Morning, Liz," Jess grinned at her sister. "I guess I'm not the only one around here who was a slug-abed."

"Except, your sister doesn't get paid to be on time," Scott winked. Before Jess could kid back, he became more serious. "As I said earlier, I really want to talk to you about your meeting with Blasko. It'd be a great help to pick your brain about who he really is, how to write him."

"All from a fifteen-minute conversation?" Jessica returned. "Do I look like Sigmund Freud?"

"Your beard is much nicer," Liz supplied, adding, "So, you finally spilled to Scott?"

Feigning surprise, Scott chided Jess, "You gave your sister a heads up before me? I'm the one who needs the straight dope. She's just along for the ride."

"Blood's thicker than greenbacks, bud," Elizabeth quipped.

"I'll remember that come time for contract renewal," Scott returned.

"C'mon, Elizabeth," Jessica jumped in. "I'm getting you out of here before you demote me from starring in a radio program to starring in sweeping up the studio."

Waving so-long to those still at the table, Jessica called over her shoulder as she maneuvered her sister out of the room, "If you need me later, Scott, I'll be around the old manse. Liz and I don't have any plans to go into the village."

Out in the corridor, Jess began, "I guess we were both a couple of sleeping beauties. Too bad our princes weren't around to wake us with a kiss. All I got was a rap on the door from Jeanne Rivers."

"That's a thrill," Liz remarked. "You did have quite a day yesterday: spending hours in the stacks with Gerry, then meeting up with Vitus Blasko."

"Tell me about it," Jess shook her head as they moved down the corridor. "And it didn't end once my head hit the pillow. I had the craziest dream where I was carrying a bouquet of roses to this room. I think it was Felicia's. When I was in there, I had this horrible dread. The worst part was, I felt as if I wasn't alone in my own head! Brrr!"

"Maybe you need a new line of work, kid sister," Liz suggested.

"Damn!"

The word came from Jeanne Rivers. The sisters were halfway past the drawing-room doors when the passion, even pain, in the housekeeper's voice halted them. Both women turned to discover what had set off the woman preoccupied with hurling something furiously, even defensively, into the cold hearth.

Jessica's concern violently shifted to shock as she recognized what Jeanne had cast down. Even as the woman pulled a long match from the ceramic jar on the hearthstone, Jessica left her startled sister behind and strode into the room, declaring, "Stop! Don't destroy it! Where did you get that?"

Jess knocked the match from the flummoxed housekeeper's hand and persisted, shaking inside with disbelief and anxiety, "Where did you get *that* bouquet?"

"Jess!" came Elizabeth's voice from beside her, "What's got into you?"

Jessica held Jeanne Rivers' frightened, yes, frightened, eyes, then reached down and picked up the bouquet of roses tied with the same blue ribbon as in her dream. Staring down at the flowers in her arms, a fearsome sense of confirmation overcame Jessica's disbelief. The same bouquet and yet not. These were roses, all right, secured with a blue ribbon. However, where the flowers of her dream had bloomed a deep and healthy red, these were brown, brittle, ancient.

"You have to tell me where you found these," Jessica reiterated to Jeanne.

Jeanne looked anxiously at Elizabeth. With a hand on Jess's arm, her sister asked quietly, "Jessica, what's wrong?"

Jessica faced Elizabeth, feeling oddly embarrassed and determined at the same time, trying to put the impossible into words. "These are the roses in my dream. The ones I put in the room. It was Felicia's room—and now here they are, but dead and desiccated after one night." She turned back to Jeanne and demanded, keeping her voice level, "What, exactly, is going on here?"

Studying Jessica, Jeanne's face was taut as she considered something unspoken. Finally, the housekeeper questioned, "You *dreamed* you put these flowers in Felicia's room?"

Jessica bit down her anxiety and disorientation at the impossible somehow made possible. She managed to reply calmly, "I know how crazy this sounds, but, yes, I dreamed I went to Felicia's room with a bouquet of roses; only mine were fresh." She paused, puzzling over the change, before continuing, "Were these from Felicia's room? Is that where you found them?"

Jeanne replied slowly, "I didn't find them. One of the girls did this morning when she went up to clean. She delivered them to me just before you came by."

Jessica abruptly insisted, "I want to see Felicia's room, where the flowers were found."

Jeanne shook her head, "I don't think so. Mr. Carlyle doesn't like anyone going in there, except to clean."

"He doesn't have to know," Jessica said simply, surprised at her own audacity. Nevertheless, she wasn't about to let this bizarre coincidence haunt her. "I promise not to break anything. Look, things have been a bit crazy around here, and I think I have a right to know, to put my mind at ease."

Jeanne chewed off a little Max Factor before reluctantly agreeing, "All right. I'll take you there, but no one must know. Is that clear?"

"Completely," Jessica agreed with a calm she didn't feel. "I just want to know."

"Know what?" Elizabeth proposed. "That your astral spirit wanted to make Felicia's room a little homier?"

Jessica returned, "It didn't work very well, if what happened to these flowers is any indication."

The three women left the drawing room.

The corridor was just as in the dream, albeit sunnier from the window at the end of the hallway behind them, where they'd come up the stairs. At least Jessica *thought* it was the same. Yet wasn't it also similar to the floor below? Did that make her feel better or worse? Did she want her dream confirmed or debunked? *The latter, of course! But those roses . . .*

Jeanne led them to the door, pointing out that Mr. Carlyle occupied a suite on this floor. Fortunately, as this was a work day, he was in Portsmouth. Jessica looked at her sister; Liz looked back tensely. Usually, poking her nose where it wasn't supposed to be was one of Liz's pleasant vices, but Jess could read trepidation in Liz's expression at poking into something that might disturb her kid sister.

As Jeanne put her hand on the doorknob and turned it, Jessica commented, "It's not locked? I thought the room was off limits."

The housekeeper coolly responded, "Until you people came, the only ones in this house were Mr. Carlyle, myself, and the servants. They all know better than to come in here, if they want to keep their jobs."

"All of them?" Elizabeth commented. "Except for the joker who left that creepy excuse for a bouquet."

"Yes," Jeanne agreed, pausing. "Probably one of the girls who thought it would be fun to scare poor Minnie—it was her turn to clean today. I can't see any of the male hands sneaking into the house to try something like this, although there is one young man, a mechanic, who's something of a wise—"

"Could you please just open the door," Jessica interrupted, momentarily pleased with herself for not adding "damned" to "door." However, the looks given her by both Liz and Jeanne told her that she'd fallen short of cucumber frigidity.

Then Liz put an arm around Jessica and said, "Sorry for jawing, kid. I gotta admit, I'm as curious as you." To Jeanne, "Open sesame."

Rivers pushed open the door, all the while explaining, "I must say I'm disappointed in Lu Brown. I've been depending on her to keep the others in line when I have to attend to bigger concerns . . ."

Jeanne's words faded from Jessica's consciousness as she squared her shoulders and forced herself to march right in, despite the sharp pricks of anxiety at the room's familiarity. The window across from her, the carpeting, the wallpaper, and even the furniture, all seemed to float back uncertainly from the night before. Yet, now that she thought about it, wasn't the all-around character of the room similar to hers?

Jessica turned to Jeanne, now standing on her right, to ask, "The layout here, it's similar to my room? And I'm directly below this one?"

"Correct on both counts," Jeanne nodded.

"So, what do you think?" Elizabeth asked from Jess's other side.

"I think . . ." Jessica turned to her sister, but her voice trailed off as she now had a more solid view of the hearth—so unlike the one in her room, so like the one in her dream.

Jessica walked slowly, she hoped not shakily, to the smooth, white mantel. There was a vase and the two heavy-glass, tulip-petaled candelabras, though maybe a little dusty. These, however, were clear of any wax or wick. Through her shock, cut the brief thought that Minnie hadn't gotten quite this far in her dusting before coming across the bouquet of death. *Bouquet of death? Oh, for Pete's sake! Would you listen to yourself!* Yet that flutter of humor couldn't quash the growing alienation from reality this scene brought her.

Forcing herself to be calm, Jessica faced her companions and pointed out, "These unique candelabras, they were in my dream, and the vase, too. Except this vase is dry now. How can that be explained?"

Jessica's eyes focused on her sister. But Jeanne popped Jessica's growing balloon of fear with, "They're not so unique. We have a few others in the house, on the main floor. You probably saw them without realizing it. They were sitting in your unconscious and just floated up in your dreams."

"Everybody's a shrink these days," Elizabeth tried to kid away the tension.

Jess gave her sister a look of consternation as she tried to reconcile dream, reality, and conjecture into something she could trust. She certainly didn't want to believe anything supernatural was going on, especially if it meant a murdered woman was getting inside her, animating her! It would be a load off her mind if she could chalk up her nightmare to no more than "a piece of ill-digested cheese" wrapped around overwork, half-forgotten impressions, and recollections of disturbing experiences from the day previous.

"The flowers!" Jessica despaired aloud. "How did I know about the flowers? I mean, yes, you could have some smart alec playing a gag. But if I've never been in this room, how would I know about them? And how could they have withered overnight?"

"I have an explanation," proposed Jeanne. "You might not like it. You might think it diminishes you a little. Maybe you were sleepwalking, and your half-dreaming brain made dead flowers appear fresh."

"Sleepwalking?" Jessica bristled. "I've never done that in my life!"

"That's true," Elizabeth concurred. "I've been her sister for thirty-two years, and I've never known her to sleepwalk."

"How about since she's been married?" Jeanne countered.

"I think my husband would have mentioned it to me," Jessica pointed out.

Jeanne shrugged, noting, "Well, it's an explanation that's certainly less alarming than you were possessed by a disturbed spirit. There's always a first time, and you have been under a lot of stress here."

Liz slowly nodded as she admitted, "Much as Jeanne and I don't see eye to eye very often, I think she has something there."

"Really?" Jessica queried, unsure how relieved she was at the thought of being a sleepwalker. Still, it definitely beat the creepy alternative.

"Sure," Elizabeth continued. "Think about it. You're not quite yourself because you're separated from that husband of yours. You're involved in an emotionally charged story, so you get all worried about the effects on people around you. And yesterday, what a day! You come home from spending the day with Mr. Angst, Gerry Davis, pouring through stacks of stuff on the story, then you go for a walk in a *cemetery*, for the love of Mike, where you run smack dab into Vitus Blasko. He manages to tune you up with his heartbreaking story. So, what do you fall asleep on? A script that lays out the whole eerie, heartbreaking tale! I'd be surprised if your sleep *wasn't* messed up!"

Jessica gave her sister a relieved, embarrassed look and asked, "You honestly think so?"

"I do not buy that you were possessed in your sleep," Elizabeth pronounced.

Jessica carefully questioned, "But what you said about the 'feel' at the Saunders' House . . ."

"I may not have Madame Wanda's super-sized supernatural powers, but I don't consider myself a schlub in that department, either. I don't feel anything in this room," Elizabeth assured her.

Ever the practical skeptic, Jeanne Rivers added, "I don't know about 'feelings,' Madame Wanda's or your sister's. All I know is what makes sense, common sense. So, Jessica, are you satisfied?"

Jessica surveyed the room, familiar and yet not. Strands of Felicia's— or what she thought was Felicia's fear—were tattered cobwebs to her now. Yet those cobwebs had not been entirely swept away. However, she nodded and said, "I guess so. Perhaps I got a little too into the role. Gosh."

"Good. If that's settled, we should leave. As I warned you, Mr. Carlyle does not want people in here. It holds too much tragedy for him," the housekeeper instructed, moving them toward the door.

"Maybe he'd be happier if he just packed up and left the joint," Elizabeth suggested as they exited, "if the place makes him that miserable."

"Sometimes, I wish he would sell off to the developers and move into Portsmouth," Jeanne admitted, closing the door behind them. "But this is his family home, designed and built by his grandfather. When he marries and has a family, he can pass it on. At least he kept it out of Bill Carlyle's greedy hands." Seeming to regret letting her opinion slip, she added, "I'd better get the key and lock up this room until I get to the bottom of who the smart alec is and fire him or her. I have work to get to now, anyway. I'm going to take the servants' stairs, but you both can find your way back by the main staircase; the way we came up."

"Sure, brought my compass," Liz replied confidently.

Jeanne gave Elizabeth a sideways glance, then opened a door to their left, which actually looked as if it led to a closet. Without a word more, she headed down the stairs beyond.

Releasing the heaviest of sighs, Jess leaned against the wall then asked, "Elizabeth, do you think your sister is nuts?"

"Kiddo, please don't give me an opening like that." At Jessica's annoyed expression, Liz put an arm around her sister and reassured her, "I think you're overworked and could probably stand a good nap after last night." Starting them both down the corridor, Elizabeth promised, "I'm going to see to it right now. You conk out in your room while I'll sit in one of those comfy chairs and read."

Jessica smiled, "Afraid I might wander off and get into mischief?"

"As if you need to sleepwalk to do that!"

"At least there's one good thing," Jessica decided. "James isn't here for all this spook business. Bro-other!"

"Actually, it's too bad he isn't here. I bet he could take your mind off things, keep you occupied, if you know what I mean."

"Elizabeth Minton, you are terrible!" Jessica laughed. "Not that I couldn't stand a little distracting by my honey. If you're not careful, you might end up accidentally saying something nice about the boy."

"He does grow on you after a while," Liz allowed. "Something like lichen."

"So, I might say that you've taken a 'lichen' to him?"

Elizabeth halted them at the top of the stairs and pronounced, "You ought to be dope slapped for that God-awful pun. But I'll let it slide. It's no picnic, being possessed by a murder victim."

Jessica smiled at her sister's teasing, even though, deep in her mind, a cobweb faintly vibrated.

Same day, evening

There were days when Elizabeth's big-sister-knows-best routine made Jessica want to puck her one in the kisser. Wednesday, October 22nd, was not one of them. After that nightmare-fraught sleep and then the crash from seeing Felicia's room, it had been sheer heaven to luxuriate in a long restorative nap with big sister casually reading in a nearby chair. Then, there was lunch served in bed, with no pressure on her to save the show or someone else's emotional stability. Liz made darned clear to both Gerry and Scott that any infringement on her kid sister's rest and recovery would put their well-being at risk from her. They backed off.

By dinner, Jessica was back on an even keel, slipping into a black satin number with a bias-cut neckline and doing up her hair in an elegant chignon. The meal had gone rather pleasantly, with Philip Carlyle making thoughtful inquiries about her having been under the weather. Overhearing, Jeanne River's eyes had flashed her a reminder not to plague Carlyle concerning the strangeness in Felicia's room. So, Jess had sidestepped the issue, explaining that the pressures of the show had cost her a good night's rest, but a long afternoon nap left her now in the pink. True, as far as it went, and maybe a fib to protect both Jeanne and Philip wasn't a mortal sin.

There had been one glitch, though, once the topic of the forest fires came up. At first, Jessica found her own concerns put in perspective by news that large swaths of Bar Harbor and nearer resorts like Kennebunk, Kennebunkport, Biddeford, Saco, and Wells had been reduced to ashes— not to mention the devastation of smaller towns further up the coast. Heartbreakingly, so many people had been forced to flee, with less than twenty minutes to pack up, before their homes built with love, often many generations back, were consumed by flames. The conversation prompted Gerry to bring up Jamie's telling him about her father's going to fight the fires, also mentioning Jessica's talk with Vitus Blasko in the cemetery. That information had put a troubled expression on Philip Carlyle's face, though only fleetingly.

Jessica didn't have time to ponder his reaction, for Elizabeth proposed that since Scott didn't seem to need the cast tomorrow (final rehearsal wouldn't be until Friday morning), those who were interested could go to the village to offer the Red Cross their help. Word had come out over the radio and local paper that no hand would be turned away who could load supplies, prepare food, organize donations of clothing and such, or aid refugees seeking out connections on Birdsong Island. Liz's proposal earned her kudos from Scott, who expressed frustration that his responsibilities to the show kept him from pitching in.

After dinner, as the Minton sisters walked toward the dining room doors for coffee in the drawing room, Jess had genuinely perked up at the prospect of doing something concrete for others. That was until Philip Carlyle, lingering at the head of the table ostensibly discussing some business with Jeanne, smoothly moved forward and stopped them. Jeanne stepped back by the sideboard; but, to Jessica's mind, now *she* was lingering, whether Philip realized it or not.

Philip's "I wonder if I might have a word" to Jessica had been followed by a glance at Elizabeth, implying "alone." Liz blithely opted to act oblivious. She even smiled.

Too well-bred to press the point, Carlyle turned to Jessica with, "I hope you won't mind my asking, but how did you happen to be in the cemetery to come across Vitus Blasko? How did you even know about that cemetery?"

Behind Carlyle, Jessica caught Jeanne shoot her a warning look. She didn't want to be dishonest, but she also didn't want to get Jeanne in dutch for accidentally putting her into the situation.

"I was at the historical society earlier that day. They have so much information about the island," Jessica answered, partial truth to the rescue. Still, even for a good cause, fibbing always made her extremely uncomfortable.

His brow puckered. Philip Carlyle was *trying* not to mask how unhappy he was that she had met Blasko. She'd better seize the initiative and keep Philip from asking questions that would plop well-meaning Jeanne in hot water.

"Why do you look displeased by my running into Dr. Blasko? It was a brief meeting, and he just seemed a very sad and lonely man. I can say from our conversation that he's looking for the truth just as much as you are."

From the corner of her eye, Jess thought Jeanne had relaxed a notch as the topic shifted from *her* responsibility for the meeting. The housekeeper left them. But Jess's attention was quickly returned to Philip, who, shaking his head, warned, "You seem very kind-hearted, sympathetic to the lost souls around here. Just be careful. Some people can be adept at putting on a good face so that others don't know what darkness lies within—until it's too late."

"I don't understand." Jessica tilted her head. "Exactly what are you driving at about Dr. Blasko? You think he was trying to snow me into getting Scott to go easy on him?"

Philip Carlyle packed a lot of earnestness into his reply: "Please consider that your resemblance to his wife must be highly unnerving to him. It could well jog memories of past emotions and events that he'd successfully suppressed—memories that might be dangerous for him to recover. You know he claims to have blacked out the night when Felicia disappeared. Even if he's telling the truth, he could have done anything and completely suppressed it in horror at his actions."

Just short of stunned, Jessica glanced over Philip's shoulder at her sister for advice. Liz only shrugged as if to say, "You got me."

"Philip," Jessica questioned, "are you accusing Vitus Blasko of murdering his wife but blocking it from his consciousness? You think he might even have killed your brother? But what's your proof?"

Although Jess didn't really know Blasko, her impression of him and Jamie's care for him argued against his murdering Felicia—though neither factor could entirely refute Philip Carlyle's insinuations.

Philip seemed to back down slightly at Jessica's resistance, answering, "I don't have incontrovertible proof, just my experience with the people involved. I'm only cautioning you about trusting that man too much. Who knows if his going off to fight wildfires isn't some grand gesture to elicit sympathy? I'm not being biased. If my brother were here, I'd be warning you against trusting his dubious charm. But he's not; and his disappearance, as much as Felicia's, speaks volumes about where the guilt lies."

"Yes," Jessica asserted, "it does, although maybe not the text you're suggesting. If I'd committed a murder, I'd have hightailed it out of town so that someone else would be left behind to take the rap. That's an equally valid possibility, wouldn't you agree?"

As soon as the words were out of her mouth, and Liz's eyes had popped, Jessica realized she'd probably put her foot in it. Maybe Philip and Bill hadn't exactly been best pals, but they *were* brothers. Her counterargument had tossed something other than glory on the family escutcheon.

Philip cocked a brow, prompting Jessica to hastily apologize, "That was out of line. I'm sorry. I didn't intend to insult . . ."

Carlyle lifted a calming hand before saying, "I'm afraid what you said is all too true. However, Bill is not here to menace anyone. Blasko is another matter. Even if innocent, he's not a stable man. So, you should be extremely cautious. Perhaps your friend Gerry Davis should also think twice about his involvement with the family. That's all I mean to say. Now, if you will excuse me, I have business to look to in my study."

He was gone before Jessica could say another word. Elizabeth spoke first with a bemused, "Well, whaddayaknow?"

"I know I feel like the back of a shoe," Jessica sighed. "A heel."

"You? I don't think so, kid."

"I do, Liz. The guy thought he was looking out for me, and I shot him down," Jessica guiltily disagreed.

"You don't need his protection," Elizabeth insisted. "That job's already been filled by the biggest pain in the neck this side of the Atlantic. But he's *your* pain in the neck."

"Oh, Liz, I can protect myself. And, frankly, I'd like to protect James from putting his foot into this hornet's nest."

"This *haunted* hornet's nest. Say that three times fast!"

Jess chuckled but wondered, "I have to say I'm a little surprised at Philip. Why's he showing so much more animosity toward the Blaskos *now*? I don't think he's being quite fair to Dr. Blasko. When I met him—"

"The *one time* you met him," Elizabeth pointed out. "Not strong grounds for drawing a healthy conclusion. Take some sisterly advice, Jessica: Philip Carlyle may be on to something. Now, don't get your ears in an uproar—listen. Blasko does not sound all that stable, even if he's not a killer. Though, to be fair, I don't exactly trust Philip Carlyle, either. I think he and Blasko are caught up in a fascination for a gal they both lost twenty years ago, and it would make Carlyle darned happy to think that he'd pinned the blame for her death on Blasko. I also think both of them can't help seeing too much of her in you, so your best bet is to steer as clear of them as possible. Just so they don't see you as an opportunity to replay their old romance with results more to their liking."

"But they both know I'm married," Jessica insisted.

"Whose husband isn't here," Elizabeth amended, "which makes it easier for them to forget the fact and see you as fair game."

"Gee, thanks, Elizabeth. Now, after a day of building me up, you've totally creeped me out! I can just imagine the sweet dreams and lovely peregrinations I'll be making tonight!"

"Not to worry," Elizabeth brightly reassured. "I'll be bunking with you, remember? You start to wander and I'll tackle you like a New York Jet."

"Thanks, I think."

Elizabeth added, "Besides, instead of worrying about yourself, think of all the people we'll be helping tomorrow. Now *there* are folks with problems."

Jessica nodded, "Elizabeth, you said it! I can't imagine what they've been through. I feel like a super-dope."

"Nah," Liz disagreed, "just the regular kind. Anyway, let's hit the drawing room for dessert. Tonight is pumpkin pie, and Scott threatened to go for thirds."

Jess grinned and headed off with her sister. Liz had a talent for putting things in perspective, sometimes a screwy talent, but definitely an effective one. The cobweb barely vibrated now.

Chapter Eighteen
Thursday, October 23rd

Jess, like Elizabeth, had always believed one of the best ways to put your troubles behind you was to help someone else. Today, she had the best therapy ever, lending a hand to the Red Cross at the local high school. Under Annette Risdon's supervision, she worked the assembly line making sandwiches being shipped out to the guys fighting to save Rochester, forty miles away, and for the towns across the Piscataqua River in Maine. Elizabeth had been helping out here as well, until some kind of beef about *slicing* the beef for the sandwiches had Annette transferring her to minding the children in a play area. That was oke with Jess. She still had her friend Maura working beside her, not that either had much time for conversation. Jessica did have a moment to notice an old woman at the far end of the long table where she worked, slicing the freshly baked bread for the sandwiches. In fact, the old lady seemed to take notice of *her*. Nothing too obvious, just a few thoughtful pauses in Jess's direction. Another *Radio Mirror* addict or someone who had known Felicia Blasko? The lady appeared old enough to be the latter. Then again, there was no reason she couldn't be both.

A glance across the auditorium gave Jess a glimpse of Gerry Davis moving in his uneven but rapid gait out the wide doorway. He was helping supervise the distribution and loading of materials—materials that Guy had been assigned to load for transport out to the fires. Jess took a moment to brush back a strand of dark hair with the back of her hand, though most of her locks were secured off her face by a snood and ribbon of the same cadet blue as her slacks and the stripes on her blouse. A glance down the end of the table, revealed that the old woman had been relieved by someone.

Annette Risdon stopped by, catching Jess's attention with, "You girls have been doing a bang-up job for some time now. Why don't you take a break? We can spare you a minute or two."

"Thanks," the titian-haired Maura replied brightly. "I could actually stand a cigarette—I know, outside. I might even catch a glimpse of that swell guy I married."

Jessica smiled, waved her friend off, then reassured Mrs. Risdon, "I'm okay for now. Let me do just a few more—"

"Nonsense. You go rescue that know-it-all sister of yours from those charming little monsters. I think they could do in even her!" Annette Risdon joked.

Jessica looked across the auditorium, not seeming so huge now, packed with people, stacks of food or clothing, and activity. She laughed, "I don't think so. Take a good look at them!"

Liz was leading a bevy of kids in a parade of drumming and singing, paper-hatted just like her followers. Surprisingly, it was the kids who were starting to flag; some had even conked out on the floor. Elizabeth was indefatigable!

Annette chuckled, "Well, I'll be! I never thought a big-city gal like her would have so much endurance."

"Oh, Annette, you don't know my sister. She goes on shopping marathons that make this look like small potatoes. Believe me, no seven-year-old can hold a candle to her stamina."

"Whatever the case," Annette smiled warmly, "we appreciate you people pitching in in an emergency. You don't even come from here, and you're giving us your time. Especially when there's some living on this very island who haven't lifted a finger. Why that Jeanne Rivers, you don't see her working with the folks she grew up with."

Jessica suggested, "Maybe she couldn't get away because Mr. Carlyle needed her."

"There's another one," Annette disapproved. "Laid off a batch of his fellow islanders from the factory last year without a second thought. And when he wanted to spruce up the place for you folks to come, he brought in off-islanders to do the work. Wasn't here himself much during the war, what with business trips. As for today, he probably thinks helpin' out is other people's business. Nothing like his father. Not like Dr. Blasko, either. Fighting the fires isn't beneath *him*—and he's no spring chicken. Even his daughter is here, somewhere. You'd think she'd at least want to see her own mother."

Jessica blurted, "Who, Jamie?"

"Sakes no," Annette clucked, amazed at Jessica's misinterpretation. "No, Jeanne Rivers' mother. She was here, slicing the bread. Maybe Martha took her on break. Before she had the stroke, Edna got Jeanne the interview with Mr. Carlyle for the job when she showed up a little over a year ago. Even after Jeanne blew out of town and never sent her a word for eight years after going to nursing school and getting work in Manchester."

"Wait a sec." Jess put out her hand. "Jeanne studied to be a nurse? I had the impression she left the island under a cloud."

"Don't know where you got that idea," Annette set Jess straight. "The only cloud was the dust she stirred up when she blew town. Though there were some rumors that she lost the hospital job over some funny business, then disappeared. Anyway, she has as little to do with the rest of us as possible, even her mother. She barely checks in, even after Edna had the stroke."

"How is her mother doing now?" Jessica asked.

"Not bad, considering. As I said, she was here, working. Just don't ask her to do any calisthenics. Now, never mind town gossip. You go find that sister of yours and have a real break. Shoo!"

Jessica smiled and walked off, amused at literally being "shooed away." Still, as she crossed the auditorium to Liz, she couldn't help wondering why Jeanne's version of her departure differed so much from Annette's. It was more than a case of differing perspectives. *And why the seeming rift with her mother? Had it anything to do with their being a part of Felicia's story? Is it any of your business?*

By the time Jess reached her sister, Elizabeth had conked out all the toddlers and was now playing peek-a-boo with a yearling.

Coming up behind Liz, Jess inquired, "Which of you two is ahead?"

Elizabeth smoothly turned around and quipped, "It's a draw." To Jessica's grin, while kneeling down to hug the baby, Liz inquired, "So, how did you manage to get off the hook with mean old lady Risdon? Lay the meat in the wrong direction across the bread?"

Jessica laughed, "It looks to me as if old lady Risdon isn't quite so mean. You seem to be having a ball with these kids—and vice versa."

"Well, somebody has to keep them occupied while their mothers are helping out here, and a few of these little guys escaped the fires by the skin of their teeth. Their families lost everything. They need someone to help them blow off steam while their parents try to straighten out things or just collapse for a while. Anyway, it beats the sandwich assembly line."

About to tease Liz for her maternal instincts, Jessica was stopped short by her sister's inexplicably raised eyebrows. The mystery of Liz's surprise was solved by a quiet voice from behind Jess: "Miss Minton, I want to talk to you. It's important, about my father and your program."

Jessica steeled herself before turning to say, "Hello, Jamie. I don't think I can say or do anything to change the broadcast. I can tell you that I believe Scott and Bev have tried to be fair, but it does address everyone's involvement. Maybe it would be best if you kept your father from listening, just in case—"

"No, no, you don't understand," protested Jamie, her features prominent against her long black hair. "I've completely changed my mind."

"You have?" Jessica returned, bewildered. She shot Liz a puzzled look. Liz only shrugged. Jess focused back on Jamie for, "I'm not one to look a gift horse in the mouth . . ."

"Either end is problematic in my book," Elizabeth observed.

"As I was saying . . . what gives, Jamie? I'm glad you're feeling better about the program, but why the sudden sea change?" Jessica carefully explored.

Jamie closed her eyes briefly, as if about to cry, but answered, "My father was sent home from the fires last night. He'd been injured."

"Oh no," Jess commiserated, a hand on Jamie's arm. "Is it serious?"

Jamie shook her head, "No, not too bad—a burned hand. So, he wasn't much help to them with an axe or a shovel. He'll be all right. It might sound funny, but it was the best thing for him."

"Getting burned?" escaped a skeptical Elizabeth.

"No, not exactly. It was working with all those people, putting himself on the line for them," Jamie explained earnestly. "He escaped that wall he'd set up. He became part of a bigger picture. I think that made him stronger. Strong enough to listen to your program, especially from what Gerry told me about the script. I even think facing a replay of his past could help him come to terms with it."

As relieved as Jessica was at Jamie's revelation, she also knew the importance of keeping the story on the q.t. before the broadcast. She explained, "Jamie, I am so glad that things seem to be working out better for your father. However, there's something important that you have to understand. Scott, all of us, have so much riding on these episodes luring in a sizeable audience with suspense. So you mustn't repeat any of what you've heard from Gerry to anyone before the broadcast. Even your father. You never know if a servant would overhear, and you know how news spreads around here. It might not seem important to you, but—"

"I understand," Jamie reassured Jessica. "Gerry impressed all that on me. You can depend on me. I just wanted you to know, and for you to tell Mr. Zimkiewicz that I've lifted all my objections. I'll even make sure we listen. If there's anything I can do to help him, I'll make certain to oblige."

Jessica was silent, trying to process Jamie's turnaround. She was pleased over Vitus's change, as well. Still, doubt lingered. Would *facing his past be the best thing for Vitus Blasko? What would his mind encounter?*

Elizabeth filled in the conversational gap: "So, since you and Gerry Davis are such good pals, why not have him be your conduit to Scott instead of putting my sister in the middle?"

Jamie immediately answered, "It was Gerry's idea. He said he and Mr. Zimkiewicz had been so much at odds lately about his connection to my family that it might sound better coming from someone else, like Jessica."

Jess was about to admit she saw Jamie's logic when Elizabeth questioned, "Don't you think it would be even better if he got it directly from the horse's mouth: you?"

Jamie's expression turned ironic when she answered, "Perhaps, but you're assuming I could make contact with Carlyle House. Miss Rivers wouldn't take my phone call, let alone let me step foot in the house. The Blaskos aren't terribly popular there. I don't imagine any of that would be policy without Philip Carlyle's permission. But you, Jessica, could get word to your director for me."

"Well, I . . ."

"Thank you! I've got to get back to working on the clothing drive. Thank you!"

She was gone.

"What do you make of *that*?" Jess questioned, facing her big sister.

"I make that you should stay out of her business. Let her carry her own water."

"Elizabeth, I'd just be passing on a message," Jessica disagreed. "Wouldn't it be nice to *unruffle* a few feathers? Maybe Jamie has some insights to help Scott better frame the séance."

"'Frame,' huh? Interesting word choice. As in frame Bill Carlyle? Or, at the very least, make sure her family comes off like shining angels?" Elizabeth coolly conjectured.

"Scott's a big boy," Jessica contended. "He can winnow the wheat from the chaff. Anyway, I'm only the messenger."

"And you know what happens to messengers, don't you?"

"They get really big tips?"

Elizabeth snorted.

"C'mon, Liz," Jess coaxed. "I promise I won't get in any deeper than telling Scott that Jamie approves and wants to talk to him. Personally, I thought she sounded sincere."

Elizabeth relented, "I guess I did, too. I just don't want my kid sister caught in the middle. Anyway, if Jeanne Rivers doesn't like her, the kid must be all right."

"You'll never forgive her for bouncing you from the kitchen, will you?"

"No," Elizabeth returned decidedly. "And speaking of bouncing, it looks as if some of the munchkins are reviving. I better go back to wearing them down for their parents. You better get back to the sandwich brigade before General Risdon declares you AWOL."

Jessica gave her sister a hug and started back. She still couldn't see any harm in delivering Jamie's message. Those thoughts were swept away, though, as Jessica noticed Annette flagging her down from the far end of the sandwich table, where she stood beside the older woman who'd earlier seemed interested in Jess.

As Jess approached, Annette called, "Jessica, there's someone here whom I'd like you to meet."

Jessica joined the two, and the seated woman's features were welcoming as she looked Jess over.

"Edna," Annette began, "this is—"

"I know who it is," the woman shook her head. "I'm not so feeble that I can't recognize that face."

Jess gave Annette a quick, nervous look. This gal *was* old enough to remember Felicia.

"I read the *Radio Mirror* like everybody else," the woman added. "This is one of the actresses from the radio program up at Jeanne's house, my old house. Jessica something or other."

"Minton," Jess supplied, more relieved than she wanted to admit at not being mistaken for Felicia. Then she did a mental double take: *"Jeanne's house"? "My old house"? "Edna"? This was Jeanne Rivers' mother, who had been in the thick of the mystery!*

The woman had clearly seen those startled thoughts flash across Jess's features, for she said, "Now calm down, child. Don't worry. I'm not one of those folks who sees Felicia Blasko's face in you. Oh, you look like her, a lot like her. But anyone with half a brain can see you're not her. There's none of that sadness in your eyes. You're a happy child. Life hasn't beaten you down the way it did her."

Annette wryly stated, "I guess I'm behind the times, introducing: Jessica, Edna Rivers; Edna, Jessica Minton."

Jess couldn't speak, thinking of all she wanted to ask Edna Rivers. The lady must have so much knowledge of the woman Jess had to play, but she couldn't treat her as if she were just an encyclopedia to be picked for information. She was a person with a life of her own. With a daughter of her own, a daughter whom, apparently, Jessica saw more of than she did. For the moment, Jessica opted for a polite: "I'm so pleased to meet you, Mrs. Rivers. You must be very proud of your daughter, taking over where you left off at the Carlyle House. She does a beautiful job."

"Does she?" the woman's tone was wistful. "Well, maybe I taught her something, after all. But that's children for you. They move on." Then she bucked up and said, "So you folks are going to solve the mystery of Felicia? Good luck to you! I don't hold truck with that séance nonsense, but your director and his partner picked my head bone dry. Maybe they can pull some threads into more than whole cloth." She chuckled at her pun. "Anyway, I don't remember a lot from that time, since I had the stroke. Who wants to remember *that*?! I have happier memories. My advice to you, dear: hold on to the happiness. No, wait, one more thing. When you play Felicia, play her right. She weren't no saint, but she was a good enough woman, all told. You do her justice, Jessica Minton, but don't turn her into a plaster saint."

Jessica accepted Edna Rivers' charge: "I'll do my best. I hope it's good enough."

Edna smiled, turning to Annette for, "This one's all right." Back to Jess, "Now, we best get back to work. There's a mountain of loaves to slice, and you need to start filling them with some solid food. Our men work up quite an appetite battling that flaming beast."

Chapter Nineteen
Friday, October 24th

A hard day's work helping people gave Jessica a good night's sleep with nary a dream. Well, maybe there was something delicious about a cozy fireside snuggle with James, interrupted by Dusty demanding Polish ham. Certainly nothing of the haunted variety, unless you counted being haunted by a hungry feline. So, Jess woke up Friday morning refreshed and rarin' to rehearse!

That rehearsal went like a dream—a good one! Usually, they had more time, but everything seemed to fall into place. Jessica's creative juices were snap, cracklin', and poppin'—giving Felicia strength and pathos but following Edna Rivers' advice to keep her human. Though Scott had a few pointers, he gave everyone an all-around thumbs up.

There was only one odd little exception to the general good feel of the day. After an early, light dinner, Jeanne Rivers had held Jess back in the dining room. Before Jessica could tell Jeanne about meeting her mother, the housekeeper had thanked Jess profusely for not troubling Philip Carlyle about her sleepwalking or Jeanne's showing her Felicia's room. As Jessica reassured her, the other woman started, asking if Jess had heard something in the pantry, between the dining room and the kitchen. Jess hadn't, but she hadn't been listening. Following Jeanne into that room, she saw—no one.

The other woman had started excusing her jumpiness by explaining how some on the staff so resented her for making them do a solid day's work that they would love to overhear something to get her in Dutch with Mr. Carlyle. That was when Guy had popped his head in with an, "Oh, there you are!" to Jessica. "Scott wants to go over some business with us right now. Don't make the poor guy wait. He's having kittens!"

After giving Jeanne's arm a reassuring squeeze, Jess had taken off with Guy. She'd liked to have been more comforting, but she had a job to do;

and the vision of Scott Zimkiewicz giving birth to baby felines was not something she wanted in her head.

All that Jessica Minton did have in her head for the next several hours was the broadcast. Vaguely, she was aware that Elizabeth, Philip, and Jeanne had taken seats arranged near the windows, their only audience. She'd felt lighter knowing that Edmund Ungerpreck was still in New York with the board of directors of Mr. Wellstone's company.

Now everything—and that meant everything—was out of her conscious mind other than becoming Felicia Blasko and syncing into rhythm with her fellow players; the sound effects Vic integrated into their playing; and Bev's piano underscoring the sorrow, anger, menace, even terror, that they portrayed. Still, Jess always had an eye on Scott, who impossibly managed to monitor the engineer, signal the soundman, and guide their performances.

The commercial breaks they had to play gave them only the briefest respites before they were back to recreating the intertwined tales of Felicia's desertion; Vitus's angry demand for her return; Bill's insistence she flee with him; closing with Felicia's rushing to her room, a door slammed, and the woman's scream.

A silence hung in the air, perfectly timed to unsettle and taunt the audience with questions before Gerry read the closing: "What did happen to Felicia Blasko? To Bill Carlyle? All that was discovered was a blood-stained carpet in Felicia's room. But whose blood? Felicia's? Bill's? Did her husband return as some have speculated? No one saw him, but *could* anyone have? Why *did* Bill Carlyle disappear? Out of guilt, or was he a victim? Of whom? Or did he and Felicia flee together? Still, many doubt she would leave her child. One thing seems certain: Felicia Blasko did not survive. If she had, would her spirit have been sighted so many times, by so many different people, haunting these halls?

"And why would she haunt? Guilt over her failings or a thirst for justice? We, on *The Wellstone Mystery Hour*, plan to help her reveal the truth when we set up a séance with a renowned medium to uncover that truth, to help her voice her plaint to free her. Join us next Friday when we broadcast a transcription of the truth behind Felicia Blasko's mystery. If you dare, hear the barriers between this world and the next broken when we take you into an actual world of mystery. Same time, same network, 9:00 P.M. Eastern Standard Time."

Then Gerry swiftly changed into a smooth, fast-talking announcer: "We now return you to station WSRH from remote broadcast at Birdsong Island, New Hampshire, via our sister station, WDPY in Boston. Stay tuned for the 10:00 p.m. news break, followed by the *Friday Night Fights*."

Scott signaled "cut"; everyone fell out of character, laughing, shaking hands—and the lights promptly failed.

"Uh, oh, maybe Felicia and Bill weren't too pleased," Guy cracked. "Everybody's a critic."

"I think Felicia's telling us thumbs up," Jess disagreed, in an upbeat mood. "She waited until the broadcast was done to black us out."

Jeanne was already up, lighting candles as Scott proposed the more down-to-earth conclusion, "More likely the juice we needed for the transfer broadcast blew a fuse in this old place."

Candle in hand, Philip Carlyle joined them, concurring, "Being more practical and having lived in this house for decades, I believe Scott called it correctly."

"Sorry," Scott said to Philip. "Our engineer thought we had the amperage calculated right."

"But you can't always calculate for a lemon in the fuses or how much power the rest of the citizens on the island decide to use at a given moment," Philip reassured him. "Don't worry. I sent a call to the groundskeeper to take care of things. Just be grateful the fuse held until you signed off."

"I think Jessica had it right," Liz decided, joining them. "The hand of the supernatural held off until the right moment. Looks to me as if Felicia is on your side."

"More importantly," Guy added, "let's hope the *living* radio audience is with us."

Jeanne re-entered, promising coffee and coffee cake in the candlelit dining room, putting a delicious seal on the all-around feeling of success.

Several hours later, after 11:30, their engineer host and his groundskeeper had repaired the faulty circuits. So now, Jessica Minton could sit at the writing desk to finish her letter for James by the light of a desk lamp. Not a word about sleepwalking had been included. *Why should it? It had happened that one night.* Rather, she wanted him to share in the triumph and excitement of that grand performance. Nevertheless, a few "miss yous" made their appearances.

She signed and enclosed her letter in an envelope but paused before licking and sealing it. Had James heard about the dreadful wildfires in the news? Was he worried about her? Maybe she should have written something calming on the topic? No, James would have called her if he were concerned. She sealed the letter: *a nice, chipper message is just the ticket for us both.*

She had a right to feel chipper, too. The celebration after the broadcast had been a treat. In fact, a few folks had opted for something with more zip than coffee. Gerry had seemed a little strained before escorting her and Liz to the feast of triumph; however, he'd perked up in the presence of everyone's conviviality. Probably, he was a little anxious over how Jamie and her father had taken the broadcast. Jess strongly hoped that the girl was right in believing the program would help her father reconcile with the past. Well, at the moment, *she* would *not* entertain any dark thoughts.

Getting up to stretch, a yawn escaped her. Maybe her high was beginning to wear off. After going full throttle, once the adrenaline washed away, you could really crash. Exhaustion was beginning to catch up with her now, and she was *so* comfortable in her one-piece, sky-blue jersey pajamas. Yet her mind refused to relax completely. She reflected that Philip Carlyle had handled the insinuations about his brother with not just good grace but even satisfaction. Well, revenge was a dish best served cold—and Carlyle must have kept a lot of resentment on ice for a long time. Not that the script had outright villainized Bill Carlyle. They'd given him intelligence and charm, while making his darker traits seem an individual's aberration in a fine old family. So, Philip Carlyle could have his cake and eat it, too: the brother, not the family, was undercut.

Was Bill Carlyle as bad as all that?

Jessica sauntered over to the windows to look out onto the court, the green, and the forest beyond. There was a romantic beauty in the soft blue-grey of moonlight and the mysterious darkness of the towers of trees swaying slightly. With no Hound of Hell baying at the moon, those trees seemed dreamy not "Goodman Brown" sinister, even with the haze from the fires.

Another form of illumination now added to the moonglow. The light, barred by the shadow of the window's frame from the room directly above Jessica, created a large, square spotlight. A man moved swiftly across the lawn to stand in that spotlight: tall, trim, dark-haired, wearing a shirt and tie but no jacket. Though the days had been unusually warm, the evenings could be October chill. Yet he stood with barely a shiver in the autumn wind. His hand was bandaged. Vitus Blasko. His gaze was uplifted to the window above hers: Felicia's chamber.

Almost hypnotized, Jessica couldn't take her eyes off the man who only had eyes for the room illuminated above her. *What went through his mind? What did he hope to see in Felicia's room? What did he see there now? Would he be rooted there all night? This didn't look like a man coming to terms with his past in a healthy way.* The intensity of his gaze almost made Jessica expect to see Felicia descend to him on a moonbeam.

Blasko shifted his gaze directly to Jessica, his guilt, longing, even agony hitting her like a wave. He seemed to know her, to be looking deep into her. Jess backed up, away from the window, from Blasko.

Call for help! thundered in Jessica's head. She was shaking at the raw emotions she could still feel assaulting her, though their power gradually fell back like waves returning to sea. She turned her eyes to her door. *Call for help, but from whom? Liz? Scott? Have Jeanne Rivers or Philip Carlyle rally the troops to give that tortured soul the bum's rush off the property—or, worse, arrest him?*

Jessica slowly went to her bed and sat on its edge, weighing her options. She doubted Philip would be terribly merciful to Vitus Blasko. And the poor man looked so anguished. Treating him harshly now wasn't the answer. He wasn't hurting anybody. He didn't look like a man planning to hurt anyone, just someone in pain. He had told her that he sometimes silently wandered this area before with no bad results. But this peregrination had come after hearing their broadcast. Did that make her impersonating Felicia partly the catalyst for his behavior tonight? How could she call out the dogs on Blasko if she was even indirectly responsible for his transgression?

Jessica was on her feet, moving cautiously to the window, having reluctantly decided that one more look at Blasko might help her make up her mind. It unexpectedly did. She relaxed with surprise and relief to see Jamie Blasko with her father in the spotlight of the upper story's window. An arm around her father, the young woman guided him away. Mightily sighing satisfaction, Jess turned off the lamp by her desk and slowly returned to bed. Vitus Blasko was now in good hands; she didn't have to rat him out, even for his own good.

That relief didn't last long, though. Concern for Blasko dissipated, Jess now wondered: *What in Sam Hill was a light doing on in Felicia's room? The room Jeanne had sworn to lock? Who the dickens was up there?!*

Forcing herself to calm down, Jessica reasoned: *Jeanne could be doing some housekeeping duties that the bustle of today's show might have forced her to put off. Philip could have been moved by their retelling of this tragic event to go there and reflect in the privacy and solitude of the late hour. Except neither Philip nor Jeanne would have inspired that rapt fascination, that anguish, in Vitus Blasko had he seen them. Well,* had *he seen them?*

The conundrum gnawed at Jessica. She wanted an answer. A glance at her door, and Jess realized there *was* a way to find out. She could go up to the third floor and enter the room to face its inhabitant. That's what the heroines she played over the airwaves would have done. That was what Barbara Stanwyck did in *Cry Wolf*: clambering over roofs, riding down a dumb waiter, and tearing on horseback through forbidden woods to rip open the curtain of deceit. The prospect of moving through Carlyle House's shadowy corridors, sharp-angled staircases, and into her nightmare room of a haunted past drove Jessica to do what any mystery heroine should do when faced with the terrifying unknown. She jumped into bed and pulled the covers over her head. She could always ask about the room tomorrow, in the daylight.

Chapter Twenty
Later that Night

Jessica didn't conk out right away. However, after the day's exhaustion, even the disturbing image outside on the green didn't stave off sleep. With sleep came another dream. Once again, that black velvet folded around her. Once more, there were voices, a man and a woman. She could distinguish them from each other, but identify them? No.

Her vision cleared, somewhat. This was a new room, an artist's studio. It was night. Stars glimmered through the skylight into the gloom of this place. A tall man, his face shadowed, was talking to her, no, urging her to go—leave Blasko and Felicia's child with Gladys. He said "her" child, but Jessica knew Jamie wasn't hers. He thought she was Felicia, but she knew differently. He couldn't or wouldn't hear her arguing that he had the wrong woman. Yes, they looked alike, especially with her back in this cinched-waist, olive dressing gown. She could feel the belt grabbing her waist, the velvet plush beneath her fingers. Where in Sam Hill were her comfy jersey pajamas?

He roughly took her arm and tried to propel her over to "the portrait no one else knew about but they two." Those were his mysterious words, exactly. She tried to jerk her arm free, warning him her actual husband, James Crawford, would fix his little red wagon if he didn't leave her alone. He didn't hear but threatened her if she didn't go with him. She prepared to take a stance that would allow her to put to use the little jiu-jitsu she knew if he grabbed her again—though something tried to convince her she *couldn't* have that skill. The point became moot as he pulled out a gun and actually said something about no one else having her if he couldn't. Implying they would both die here, together? His eyes drifted anxiously beyond her at the sound of a heavy tread ascending stairs that she somehow knew were beyond the door.

She took advantage of his distraction to hurl a bottle of turpentine she'd spotted—but the velvet fold enveloped her before she could tell if her projectile had connected.

Kicking back the covers, Jessica Minton sat up suddenly. Thank God, this was her room, all right. These were her blue pajamas. Sun streamed through the windows, curtains still undrawn. Her head felt heavy. Strange. Though it seemed as if she'd just escaped her nightmare, she also had a sense she'd been sunk in mindless darkness for some time. Had she taken another midnight stroll? Or had her intense involvement in the radio drama and the vision of Vitus Blasko in the moonlight conspired to give her that bad dream?

Jess shook her head to clear the lingering dullness, then took a gander at the bedside clock. *Eight o'clock. A reasonable time to wake.* The funny thing was that as her head began to clear, rather than anxiety, she felt her Irish bristle. Memory of someone trying to push her around left Jessica determined to push back. Funny, she kind of felt that she'd actually won a round, after a fashion.

The rat-a-tat on her door more strongly forced Jess into the world of the waking. She grinned, recognizing that rapid-fire tattoo.

"Be right there, Liz!"

Slipping into her slippers, Jessica crossed the room, still a little sleep-woozy, to unlock her door and greet her sister, whom she found picking up a small card from the floor.

"What's that, Liz?" Jess inquired, admitting her sister, dressed casually in a striped blouse and slacks.

"Oh, nothing, kid," Elizabeth replied. "I just dropped one of my business cards when I was looking for something in my pocket. So, how are you doing this morning, Sarah Bernhardt? You look a little peaked, happy, but peaked."

Jess closed the door behind her sister and, as she guided Liz to a chair, answered, "Still a bit tuckered out after the show." She hesitated to give away Blasko, even to her sister. After all, Jamie had taken him home with no harm done. Instead, sitting down, Jessica finished, "I did have another crazy dream last night, though."

"Did you?" Elizabeth asked, with a knowing tilt of her head.

"Yes," Jessica answered slowly, wondering at her sister's attitude. "But I think it was just brought on by last night's broadcast. I don't think I wandered off. It took place in a totally different room. Say, Liz, you look as if you know something you're not telling me."

Elizabeth smiled broadly and assured Jessica, "You bet! I know for a fact that you didn't take a somnambulant stroll."

"Really? I suppose you were parked outside my room all night?" Jess posited wryly, but encouraged.

"I didn't have to be," Elizabeth winked. She held up the card Jess had caught her picking up earlier and explained, "See this little beauty? I actually dropped it when I was taking it out of the crack between the door and the jamb. Since your episode, I've been putting it there every night and retrieving it every morning. Not once did I find it on the floor, which I would have if you'd opened the door and gone for a midnight stroll. So, I can give you a clean bill of health."

"You sneak!" Jessica chuckled, relieved her sister had proved her safe from dangerous nocturnal meanders. Her curiosity piqued by Elizabeth's test, Jess asked, "Hey, where did you pick up that little trick?"

"Leo told me he used it on occasion when he wanted to make sure no one was traipsing into a place to mess with evidence. Pretty neat, huh? I bet your James would like to learn it."

"He uses a toothpick. It's thin and small, so it's harder to notice," Jess explained with a smile.

"Well, that's one way to ensure you don't take a peek where he's hidden the Christmas presents," Elizabeth concluded. "We've nabbed ourselves a couple of slick fellas."

"I guess," Jess agreed. "But let's cut the chit-chat. I'm starving. Give me a minute to throw on some clothes, and let's hit the breakfast table."

"Fine, but I have to make it a quick bite. Maura and I are going into town to work with the Red Cross again."

"Oh, Okay. I'll make it snappy so I don't hold you guys up," Jess promised.

On her feet, Elizabeth said, "I, um, talked to Scott about this last night. We both thought that you seemed pretty tuckered out, what with carrying the show so much, not to mention more than a few people's emotional problems. So, you ought to take the day off. We're going in without you. You still look a touch peaked."

"Oh," was Jessica's deflated response. "But don't they need every hand? I should be helping, not sitting around on my—"

"They're still going to need help later in the week. Rest up today, kid, so you can be more help then. Take your sister's advice."

"Maybe even Sunday, after Church?" Jessica proposed.

"Yeah, maybe," Liz agreed with a smile. "If you're willing."

"Of course, I'll be willing," Jessica told her sister emphatically. "Just let me get ready to go down to breakfast."

Moving into the bathroom, Jessica again wondered if she ought to tell Liz about Blasko's visit and the unexpected light from Felicia's room. But could she depend 100% on Elizabeth not letting slip that information? Jess did not want to get Dr. Blasko in trouble. He hadn't really threatened anyone. Maybe Elizabeth would even complain to Philip Carlyle out of unnecessary concern for her. No, unless some good reason came up to spill, Jessica decided to keep her lips zipped. And the light in Felicia's room? Again, both Jeanne and Philip had very good reasons to be there, which were likely none of her business.

Her burnt-orange jersey top warming her on this cooler October morning, her bias-cut gray flannel skirt swirling as she moved, Jess stepped through the French doors and onto the stone terrace. Sitting outside and reading on the stone bench overlooking the bay would be just the ticket. She would lay odds that, after the last news report, smoke was no longer overcasting the October sky's blue nearly as much.

But thoughts of reading and dying fires slipped away as she caught sight of Jeanne Rivers off to the left. Was she mistaken? Had a curl of smoke wafted away from the woman? Seeing Jessica, the housekeeper hastily stubbed out a cigarette in the heavy glass ashtray in her other hand.

Their eyes automatically locked, so it was too late for Jess to pretend she hadn't seen anything.

Jeanne shrugged, then admitted, "I guess you caught me dead to rights, breaking my own rule about no smoking on duty. But I had quite a morning."

"No one ever accused me of being a stoolie," Jess gave her smiling reassurance as she crossed to join Jeanne. "I'm sorry you've had a trying morning. Is there anything I can do?"

Jeanne rested the ashtray carefully on the stone balustrade, answering, "No. You people are not the trouble, really. No, it's one of the servants. All the best ones seem to have left for war work and never come back, except for Lu Brown. I'm afraid I caught one of the temporary girls red-handed stealing after last night's broadcast. I had a feeling when I hired her that I was taking a chance, but I needed the help. Anyway, I fired her."

"I'm surprised Liz didn't say anything to me before she left for town this morning," Jess wondered.

"There was no one to repeat tales to your sister," Jeanne replied firmly. "Out of misplaced discretion, I took the girl outside for a confrontation. The nasty little creature repaid me by saying vicious, even threatening, things to me. Anyway, I didn't want the staff to hear such insubordination, so I made her wait outside for a cab that I called to take her to the village to catch the late bus for Portsmouth."

"Pretty generous of you. Threatening you, you say?" Jessica responded uneasily.

"Oh, nothing physical or violent," Jean clarified. "But she implied that she could make things unpleasant for me or Mr. Carlyle. Lord knows that man has been through enough over the years. I wonder if I shouldn't have had the cab run her all the way into Portsmouth, so she couldn't hang around the village and spread rumors. She's that kind of a girl."

"Wouldn't people on the island be wise to her? After all, you said you had doubts about hiring her in the first place. The Carlyle family must stand for something around here," Jessica offered, even though she recalled Annette's less-than-positive views about Philip.

Jeanne gave Jessica an odd look, and it occurred to her that Annette might not be so alone in her opinion of the present Carlyle family or of

Jeanne Rivers. Owning the murder manse probably didn't exactly create loads of prestige, either.

Before Jess could salvage the situation, her companion spoke: "Whatever the case, the needs of a big house never rest. I'd better get back to work before Mr. Carlyle decides he wants me for something."

"Oh? He's home today?" Jessica asked, surprised. "He's not at the office?"

"*Occasionally*, Mr. Carlyle spends a Saturday at home," Jeanne smiled. "I know it may seem he lives at the office. The man really needs to take a breather, but when he is home, I have to be on my toes. So, if you're willing to keep my indulgence here our little secret . . ."

"Mum's the word," Jessica nodded, miming zipping her lips. This camaraderie suddenly spurred Jessica to ask, "Jeanne, the room above me late last night, I saw a light from it shining onto the lawn. Was that you?"

The other woman's brow furrowed and she responded, "What would I be doing up there at that time of night? Are you sure you actually saw a light? It could have been some kind of optical illusion. Maybe it was one of your peculiar dreams."

"I know a window light when I see it," Jessica retorted, feeling decidedly less camaraderie now. "And I was not asleep at the time. You did say that you would lock up the room in the future, and you are the one with the keys. I'm not about to chalk this up to a ghost. Who else could it be?"

"I'm not the only one," Jeanne replied sharply, then frowned, as if kicking herself for being defensive. To Jessica's questioning expression, the housekeeper hesitated, finally deciding it smarter not to make her answer seem so momentous. "Mr. Carlyle, of course."

"Why would he go up there at that time of night?"

Maybe it was none of her business, but after all she'd been through in this place, Jessica felt entitled to some straight answers. Besides, Jeanne's intimation that she wasn't much of a reliable observer rankled.

Jeanne shrugged, suggesting, "Your show may have jogged some memories. Perhaps he wanted to try and make sense of things. I don't ask too many questions. You shouldn't, either."

Jessica frowned. It hadn't been a slap in the face, but it hadn't exactly been friendly advice. *Was Jeanne hostile to questioning or just defensive of Philip Carlyle? Well, she did work for the guy. He had given her a chance to straighten out and make something of her life.* And perhaps, Jess had to admit, she was a little hypersensitive about what might not have been a challenge to her stability at all.

As if reading Jess's thoughts, Jeanne said, "Look, I don't doubt you did see a light. Likely, Mr. Carlyle was just up there reflecting on the past. I wouldn't give it another thought. It's not as if you saw something really unusual last night."

Jess tried not to give away she *had* seen an unusual visitor in the moonlight. *Blasko had been hurting no one but himself, aching for a past he'd thrown away years ago.* She brushed strands of breeze-tossed hair from her face, concerned that perhaps Philip had seen Vitus Blasko. Probably not, though. *There'd been no sign of a commotion about it this morning. Wouldn't Liz have nosed it out? Still, Jean had been able to keep the thieving servant 'scandal' off her sister's radar.* Those thoughts must have registered on her face, or perhaps she'd taken too long to agree with Jeanne, for the other woman pressed, "Jessica, *did* you see anyone? Anything?"

"Nobody there but us, I mean, this chicken," Jessica joked.

"All right, then," Jeanne concluded. "So, it's a nice day. Going for a stroll in the woods?"

The thought of perambulating through the shade and shadow, alone, gave Jess a shiver. At Jeanne's curious expression, she covered with, "I think it's a little too chilly. No, sitting on the bench over the water, in the warm sun, while I read is just the ticket."

"Smart," Jeanne nodded. "Again, thanks for keeping my smoke break our little secret. And no one else needs to know about Miss Sticky Fingers."

Jessica smiled slightly as the housekeeper picked up the ashtray and hid it behind the folds of her skirt before heading inside. Watching the other woman pass through the French doors, Jessica couldn't help wondering if Jeanne had bought her innocent act. *At least she hadn't challenged it. Exactly how far* would *Jeanne go to protect Philip and the Carlyle home?* On the other hand, how far was Jessica, herself, going to protect the Blaskos? Maybe she'd already put *herself* out on a limb?

Forcing that question aside, Jessica strolled to the bench. Here, Gerry had first told Liz and her about his involvement with Jamie. *Hmm, what would Jamie be up to now? When she'd brought her father home last night, had he been cleansed, freed by the program and his late-night visit? Maybe that was too much Rebecca-of-Sunnybrook-Farm thinking.* She wished they were done with this whole unnerving tale of ghosts and murder and betrayal. *One more week. But there was still that crazy séance to face. How would Vitus Blasko and his daughter get through that? What about Philip Carlyle? If Vitus had haunted the grounds outside Felicia's room, apparently, Philip had been similarly drawn to the room itself. What kind of emotional detritus would be left behind when cast and crew returned to New York?* Jess reflected that though Scott had never been one to put ratings above people, things had gone pretty far awry under the iron hand of their greedy temporary sponsor. Not temporary enough, if you asked her.

The Piscataqua, pungently salty, stretched between her and the mainland. Only a few nights back, she'd sat on another bench overlooking the bay in the flaming sunset and met Vitus Blasko. Compassion surged through her but was tainted by disquiet. She did think that Philip's warning against Blasko had been sincere, but was it based on a true understanding of the other man or a festering resentment over his treatment of Felicia? The wail of gulls and terns was not particularly soothing to her state of mind.

It took Jessica a minute to realize that one of those melancholy calls formed her name—and it didn't emanate from the still somewhat hazy October skies but from the lawn behind her. Jessica swiveled in her seat to recognize Jamie Blasko hurrying across the grass; the closer she came, the clearer the concern on her face. She grasped a white paper tightly.

Jess was on her feet, alarmed at the younger woman's appearance: not the look of a daughter relieved by a father's breakthrough. Dropping her book on the bench, Jessica hustled to reach Jamie. The two met not far from the stone balustrade of the court; Jamie's glance of trepidation at the house compounded Jess's concern.

Before Jess could get out a single word, Jamie questioned, "Have you seen him? Did he come here? Did he talk to you?"

"Your father?" Jessica stammered under the young woman's intensity. "Do you mean about last night?"

Jamie stopped short, taken aback that Jessica knew of her father's nocturnal visit. After a moment, she ventured, "You saw him here last night? Did you tell anyone?"

Trying her best to calm Jamie, Jessica answered, "I did see him. I saw you take him away, as well. I also saw that he wasn't hurting anyone. And, no, I didn't say anything. It would only cause upset all around and for no good reason." Jess paused before adding, "But that's not what you were asking. You were surprised when I said 'last night.'"

Jamie shook her head anxiously, then let spill, "This morning, right after he read this letter. He said he had to see you immediately, to find out if it was true."

Jessica's eyes were on that crumpled missive in Jamie's hand. *He had to see me?*

"That letter in your hand, Jamie, it said something to him about me?" Jess forced her voice to be steady.

Rattling the sheet that she grasped, Jamie burst out, "This letter set him off. He was troubled but calm when I brought him home, but he became so upset by this thing! He exploded, and then he wouldn't explain to me! I'm afraid for him, now. I have to find him before he does something . . . he shouldn't."

Jessica gripped Jamie and gave her a steadying shake, commanding, "Jamie, get ahold of yourself. I can't help you or your father unless you calm down—"

"You don't understand."

"And I won't unless you calm down," Jessica insisted firmly. "Now, from the beginning, what's this about a letter? This it? In your hand?"

Instinctively, Jamie grabbed the page tighter when Jessica touched it. Then she relaxed, as if her brain were just a beat behind registering Jess as her ally.

"Okay," Jessica continued calmly, "let's get to the bottom of this so I can figure out how to help you."

The paper, crumpled by a man's anger and a daughter's anxiety, opened in Jessica's hands. Reading it, she found it was her turn to go all jelly in the knees, though she fought off the sensation for Jamie's sake. The handwriting was rushed and scrawled, clearly not trained by the Palmer School or a nun's ruler.

Dear Mr. Blazco,

You wanta kno what hapened to yor wife? Ask that actris what plays her. she go wanderin round the house at nigh. Goes to yor wife's room. talks in her sleep. I thin the actriss is pozzesest. Your wife tell her stuff. I overheerd. You make her tel you who dun kilt her. Get even with them Carliles or mabee you afeered to know?

A Frend

"Holy cats," Jessica breathed. Her eyes were already scanning the woods for the impending visit of a man desperate to make her tell him the truth about Felicia. But that was crazy! How could he possibly believe she knew anything? She'd only had dreams, and they hadn't told her anything solid. How would the writer even know about her dreams and sleepwalking? The oft-repeated comments on eavesdroppers in the house, on the island, jumped to mind. It took a ton of nerve for Jess to assert self-control rather than to run into the house with a Three Stooges yell of "Nyaaaaah!" Nevertheless, she steadied herself to demand, "Jamie, you're telling me that your father actually believes what's written here?"

Seemingly influenced by Jessica's self-control, Jamie pulled herself enough together to answer, "My father did not take the program the way I'd hoped. Too many memories, guilt, I don't know. He was very controlled during the broadcast, but I could sense what was warring inside him. He went out for a walk, 'to clear his head,' he said." Her eyes transfixed Jessica's as she continued, "Apparently, his walk took him here, so he wasn't as in control as he tried to appear. I was able to bring him back without a struggle, but he was a deeply troubled man last night. I was heartened, at first, this morning. He sat down to breakfast with me, and things were . . . all right . . . not happy but not exactly tense—until Danvers brought in the letter that he'd found addressed to my father, sitting on the receiving table in the foyer, early this morning. It was odd because the regular mail doesn't come until the afternoon. Considering what's inside, it's no surprise there's no return address or post mark."

"That's interesting," Jessica pondered. "I mean that it didn't come with the regular mail, and it's not postmarked. Could it have been put there by anyone in your house? A resentful servant?"

"We treat our servants well, the few we can afford to keep," Jamie replied indignantly. But she paused and reasoned, "However, I take your point: if it didn't come by the postal service, someone had to get into the house to deliver it. I must admit the windows' locks are not the most secure. Locksmiths cost money."

Jessica nodded, an eye still on the woods, just in case Blasko appeared and rushed her as his daughter feared. She was pretty sure she knew what semiliterate might have overheard of her experiences in Carlyle House and had time or inclination to sneak over to the Blasko place to stir up trouble. But why hurt Vitus? Or was he just collateral damage?

However, Jamie's voice shocked away Jessica's reflections: "And where did that crazy story about you being possessed by my mother come from? What spurred that particular fabrication? What basis could it possibly have?"

Jamie's questions hit a nerve, and Jess realized she'd left her poker face somewhere else.

"What!" Jamie breathed. "You're not trying to tell me you think you have been possessed by my mother?!"

"No," Jessica asserted. "I do not in the least think your Mom is the new roommate in my head. However, I did have a few odd dreams—and, apparently, I sleepwalked one night. But I was never under the influence of a spirit! Let me tell you what the real screwy thing is: I only knew of three people for certain who knew about the whole deal. You can bet your bottom dollar neither Liz nor I would pull this cruel kind of a joke on your father."

Jamie temporized, "I thought, maybe for publicity . . ."

"Honestly?!"

"I guess not. Not after you two have been kind to Gerry and me. I do know about your meeting my father in the cemetery, that you were sympathetic to him. So, I'm sorry—but wait, you said there were three. Who's the third?"

"That wouldn't make sense, either," Jessica explained. "What motive would Jeanne Rivers have?"

Jamie narrowed her eyes as she thought aloud, "I visited here quite a bit as a child. I knew her then, somewhat. She was the housekeeper's child. I think she might have resented people who had more than she did. She often got in trouble for roaming the house as if she owned it. But that was all years ago; it had nothing to do with my father. No, Jeanne being guilty doesn't hold water."

Jessica added, "I also genuinely doubt Jeanne would want to do something reckless enough to likely cost her job. Besides, *I* have a hard time picturing her being that, well, mean."

"I think it's the work of someone nursing a grudge against my father," Jamie decided.

Jamie's conclusion brought back a suspicion that had come to Jess earlier in this meeting. She proposed, "A grudge, but maybe not against your father. Maybe someone has it in for Jeanne, and your father is an innocent bystander. See, the other night, Jeanne and I were talking, we believed in private, about my weird experience. Jeanne thought she heard someone in the next room, but she couldn't catch the person. If there was someone who got away, and that person was the same one whom Jeanne told me she fired last night . . ."

"That's a lot of 'ifs.'" Jamie observed somewhat doubtfully.

"Maybe, but at least there's a definite and understandable motive," Jessica countered. "And you did suspect Jeanne as the only other person who knew, right?" Jess cast another uncomfortable glance at the woods before adding, "Maybe we should go inside where there are more people. It's more comfortable."

Jamie's face fell as she sadly concluded, "I've made you afraid of my father. You're thinking he'd hurt you?"

Jess couldn't help asking, "Do you think he would?"

It wasn't especially reassuring that Jamie didn't answer her question immediately, but said vaguely, "Perhaps you'd feel more comfortable if you did go in. I'll keep looking. I'm sure I'll find him, eventually. Perhaps Gerry could help me?"

Jessica frowned, "I'm sorry, Jamie. Gerry went into town to pitch in with the Red Cross."

That disappointing news wasn't why Jamie tensed, though, looking over Jessica's shoulder toward the house.

Jess realized that the French doors had opened and a voice, gravel wrapped in velvet, was saying, "Miss Blasko? Are you all right? You look so troubled? It's not your father, is it?"

Jessica was relieved, even a bit surprised, that Philip's voice was concerned rather than challenging, for she knew how he felt about the family. Apparently, when the chips were down, he was a right guy.

Jamie, however, didn't seem able to see that. She just stood there with a deer-in-the-headlights expression. Indeed, it must have been terrifying to ask this family for help for Vitus Blasko. Nevertheless, Jess realized that something had to be said.

"Philip, someone has played a cruel and disturbing trick on her father. Sent him a poison-pen letter. He left home, distraught, and Jamie is trying to find him before . . ."

"He hurts someone?" Philip finished.

At that response, Jessica really wanted to clock her not-so-right guy, but Jamie verbally beat her to the punch with: "I'm worried he might hurt *himself*, by accident; he's so distracted."

Carefully, Philip responded, "Then perhaps we should call Chief Winston."

"To arrest him!" Jamie was alarmed.

"No, please, Miss Blasko," Carlyle calmed her. "We'll say that your father was agitated by last night's radio broadcast, and they should merely be on the lookout for him to bring him home. We don't even have to mention the letter's upsetting him. The less said about it, the better. Don't you agree, Jessica?"

Jessica knew she'd love to see the nasty little snip who'd set this whole mess in motion caught and punished. However, then Jeanne's letting her into the room despite Philip's injunctions and her own embarrassing midnight rambles could come to light. Indeed, the less said, the better! All that flashed swiftly through her mind, so Jess seemed to respond almost immediately, "Sure, yes."

Jamie nodded and folded the letter, putting it away in her pocket. With that, the three went toward the house, Jessica surprised and decidedly pleased that Philip had put aside his antipathy for Vitus Blasko to help his innocent daughter. A quick glimpse back at the woods reassured her that she needn't fear a sudden confrontation with a man convinced she could connect him to his wife. She felt a sliver of guilt for that relief; after all, it would have delivered Jamie's father to her. Yet, honestly, she couldn't face him knowing that though there were seeds of truth in the letter, they could offer the unsettled man no answers. Nor did she want to admit to Philip Carlyle an experience that might seem to have profaned Felicia's room. And Liz had thought leaving her here would be so much more restful than making sandwiches at the high school.

Chapter Twenty-One
Sunday, October 26th

Sunday morning light streamed into Saints Barnabas and Quentin Church, its brilliance amplified by the white-washed walls and painted pews. A bit on the plain side for a Catholic church, but the carved and painted statues of the Stations of the Cross along the walls, the stained-glass above the plain latticed panes, and the beautifully gothic white altar gave glory to God through human craftsmanship.

Jessica Minton shared a pew with her sister amongst communicants packed in to thank God for the diminishment of the fires. Now blowing smoke away from Birdsong Island, the wind rattled the exterior of the clapboard building. The day was cooler than many previous. So, Jess was glad she'd selected a rust-colored jersey dress with a geometric cut-out pattern in the front. Her hair fell to her shoulders under the brim of her rust, round-crowned hat. Liz was also respectably turned out for Sunday service in a toast jersey dress under a pale-tan, draped coat. Her tall, peaked-crown hat had a brim with an angled dip enabling her surreptitiously to survey the congregation for anything of interest. Looking past Jessica, Elizabeth gave her sister a nudge.

Jess's responding frown was redirected to her left by Liz to see Jamie Blasko slip late into a pew—alone.

Jamie, her girlish features rendered even more childlike by her overwhelming picture hat, as dark as her severe suit, looked back at Jessica with somber expression. She nodded before shifting to face the priest.

Liz whispered Jessica's very own thoughts into her ear, "Does that nod say everything's hunky-dory with dear old Dad? He's safely at home. Or does it say we need to talk? Or just thanks for trying?"

Jess licked her lip, wondering if she shouldn't have told Elizabeth about Jamie's visit yesterday. Still, word was bound to get out to her sister somehow; better that Liz get the straight facts from her.

Anyway, Philip Carlyle had no knowledge of how things had ultimately worked out. Once he'd delivered her to the police station, she had refused to trouble him further and insisted he return home. Anyway, as much as Jessica prayed that Dr. Blasko hadn't taken a Brody off a cliff into the Piscataqua, Jamie had managed to pretty much exhaust her moral support before driving off with Philip. Jamie's being here, not waiting at home by the phone for news, was a good sign. But she was alone, though looking . . .

". . . strained but not wrecked," Elizabeth's whisper completed Jessica's appraisal. "So, he mustn't have done anything tragic."

More than one glare homed in on Liz, not that she quailed.

Some people did *want to hear Father Gerard's sermon.* Jess knew she would, *if Liz could ever shut—*

"What do you think, Jess? The guy's sleeping off a bender at home?"

"No one said he was drinking, just that he was upset," Jessica quietly shot back—and received a glare or two, herself.

"Do you think the police arrested him—or at least picked him up and brought him home? I wonder if he made a spectacle of himself in front of any of the other islanders."

"I have no idea. Now pipe down. You've already racked up about 150,000 years in purgatory for talking so much during mass. You want to shoot for an even 200,000?" Jessica growled *sotto voce.*

"I'm not worried," Elizabeth whispered none too softly. "I've been earning indulgences from my prayer book."

"Oh yeah, now you're down to 149, 999 years and forty days."

Liz settled down for a while and, tempting as it was, Jessica avoided slipping Jamie any more glances. *The poor kid. With any luck, her father hadn't caused her any scandal in the eyes of the islanders. Still, do I want to know the whole story?* The Blaskos had tangled themselves more than enough into her life. Yet, what could she expect after playing the woman around whom their tragedy centered? Nevertheless, she could bear only so much guilt and pain from others. But if Jamie and her father needed help that she *could* give . . . ?

Looking up at the graceful circle of risen Christ in the stained glass above the altar, Jessica ruefully thought, "You know, I could use a little help here."

"For the love of Mike, this service is running forever," Elizabeth grumbled in her ear, an eye on her watch.

"You're just chock full of spirituality," Jessica whispered back. "You have somewhere else to be? It's Sunday. No mail. No packages, even."

Liz raised an eyebrow and advised, "You're not as smart as you think, wise guy."

"250,000 years now—and I'm stuck there with you!"

For the rest of the service, Elizabeth remained annoyingly antsy. The only relief was that coming back from Communion, Jess noticed Jamie Blasko was gone. As concerned as she'd been about the Blaskos, Jessica needed some separation from them, especially if the father seemed to think he could get to his wife through her.

Once the service was over, Liz practically marched her out the door. Jess almost thought Liz would have a conniption when she stopped to talk to Martha, Annette, and Edna Rivers. She'd feared she'd have to hold Liz back at this opportunity to indulge her curiosity about Jeanne by meeting her mother. But, no, her sister almost knocked her for a loop by being polite and patient with the old lady, yet not demonstrating a whit of her usual nosiness. Jess's relief over her sister's newfound circumspection doubled, for Edna Rivers seemed not to be having "one of her good days," as Annette put it, actually lapsing into thinking Jessica was Felicia. Knowing Liz's heart was as tender as her curiosity was capacious, Jess concluded her sister had decided not to take advantage of an old woman's incapacity.

On the ride home, Jessica realized her sister's spirits were rising perceptibly the closer they drew to Carlyle House. *Hmm, Liz is far too chipper with this many years on the purgatorial rock pile ahead of her. There's something up her sleeve, but what? Had Liz slipped some arsenic into Edmund Ungerpreck's Ovaltine, now that he was back on the island? Not enough to kill him, just enough to make him miserable. After all, Liz wouldn't want to get bounced out of purgatory into the Big House of the Afterlife.*

When they finally stepped into the mansion's foyer, Jess noticed the drawing room doors were ajar. Elizabeth was all Cheshire-Cat grin, until she looked around and blurted, her crest falling, "The foyer's empty. I was sure . . . empty."

"What? You were expecting Glenn Miller and the Army Air Force Marching Band?" Jess wryly inquired.

"They'd have to find Major Miller for him to lead the band," came a familiar British-accented voice as the drawing room doors were pushed completely open.

Jessica's knees definitely wobbled with delight, but not for long. She flashed into the arms of a tall, thirtyish man with longish dark hair, a full mustache, and a mischievous glint in his green/brown eyes.

She would have cried, "James!" but she was too busy wrapping her arms around him, being wrapped in his arms, sinking into his passionate kiss.

"Surprise!" cried Liz, only to shrug as she recognized that these two no longer knew she was there. She couldn't help quipping, "Hey, you guys! Come up for air!"

Neither seemed to hear her.

To Jessica, it was so wonderful to be squeezed this tightly and to feel James's hand under her dark hair, massaging her neck.

"Good heavens!"

Jeanne Rivers' exclamation was what it took for Jessica and her husband to pull somewhat apart. For James's arms still warmly encircled Jessica as they turned and faced the housekeeper.

"Umph," Rivers cleared her throat. "We do have young women working here, easily swayed."

"Relax," Elizabeth flapped her hand. "They're married. A little necking is perfectly legal. Anyway, this is kid stuff compared to some of what those girls see at the local Rialto—on and off the screen."

Nevertheless, James was looking a bit sheepish, though still not letting go of his wife. He apologized, yet with a twinkle in his eye, "Oh, ah, sorry about that, Miss. The wife and I aren't usually apart for this long, and, you know, we have been separated for some weeks."

"It seems like months," Jessica added innocently.

"Yes, well, Mr. Crawford," Jeanne said primly. "I've had your bags sent up to Miss Minton's, or I imagine I should say, Mrs. Crawford's room."

"That was kind of you, Jeanne," Jessica offered, trying to offset the bad impression.

The housekeeper appeared somewhat mollified, though she was not exactly regarding James with welcome.

James squeezed Jessica's shoulder and agreed, "Yes, of course, very kind."

Looking up at James, Jess broke the awkward silence that had descended with a double meaning they'd employed before: "Darling, you really should see the *view* from my room—it's just magnificent. I think you'll enjoy it."

James tilted his head, puzzled, until Jess's real meaning dawned on him. He smiled beneath his mustache and agreed, "Oh, yes, the *view*. There's nothing a chap enjoys more than a nice view in the afternoon." James squeezed Jess's shoulder affectionately again and said, "Well, love, lead the way." To Jeanne, "Thank you ever so much for getting me settled." Then he winked at Liz before gesturing that Jessica lead on.

Jess cocked her head at that wink and said, "Wait a minute. There's something fishy here. Why do I think that you two," wagging a finger from her sister to her husband, "were in cahoots to bring off this reunion? Strange as that partnership sounds."

"Probably because when he came out of the drawing-room, I piped up, 'Surprise!' And he just winked at me," Liz returned. "You'd have to be some kind of knucklehead not to add up those clues." She took the couple by the arms and rushed them towards the stairs with, "Now, for the love of Mike, go enjoy that view!"

Neither Jessica nor James had to be told twice.

It was some time later that Jessica and James actually were enjoying the view of the sherbet trees flashed with crimson, catching the late afternoon sun's rays. They were nestled in the window seat, James with his back against the wall and Jess tucked against his chest, his arm around her, his hands twined in hers.

"It is quite lovely out there," he remarked, rather pleased, "You certainly seemed to have nabbed the pick of accommodations."

"Of course, I'm the star," Jess replied airily. "Stick with me, kid, and it will be nothing but champagne and roses."

"This isn't the room of the murder, then?" James queried "innocently."

Jessica sat up and looked back at her husband, blurting, "Good grief! That would be downright ghastly! Don't even joke about it!"

James put his hands up in surrender. "Sorry, love. You know my gallows humor. Didn't mean to put my foot in it."

Jess gave a little shudder and explained, "If you'd been here as long as we have, been as immersed in all this tragedy, you wouldn't even think about cracking wise on that subject. I'd have thought Liz would have briefed you better when you two were cooking up this reunion—this *wonderful* reunion."

James smiled, seeing he was mostly out of the doghouse, then he turned Jessica back to pull her close, his cheek resting on her head. Finally, he said, "I'm just happy that you seem yourself. Your sister had me rather worried when she called and gave me my marching orders over this sleepwalking business."

Again, Jessica sat up and faced her husband. *How worried had Liz and James been? Should I be worried, myself?* She asked carefully, "James, what, exactly, did my sister tell you?"

Recognizing her concern, James tried to make light, "Oh, just that I'd better get up here pronto to rescue my wife from the unwanted attentions of two old geezers."

"Geezers? Who are the old geezers?"

"Your host and the chap whose wife was done in. Blasko, right?"

"You stinker," Jessica half-laughed, feigning indignation. "Philip Carlyle is only in his mid-forties, and Dr. Blasko has barely tipped 50, I think. You know they're both younger than Ronald Colman."

"Ah, is either of them a dead ringer for Ronald Colman?" James teased.

"Hardly, but Philip Carlyle does have admirable taste, and Dr. Blasko—"

"Is a bit loopy? Thinks his wife looks like Joan Bennett?" James finished.

"What? No. Where did you get Joan Bennett?"

"From your sister. It got a little fuzzy. She seemed to be saying his wife looked like Joan Bennett . . . and there was something about Hedy Lamarr and Margaret Lockwood. She lost me around there. It was clear, however, that you needed me—so here I am."

"And I am glad of it," Jess smiled happily. "I feel 100% better with you here." She paused, more serious now. "But there's something I'd better straighten you out on, for you to really understand the problem. Felicia doesn't so much resemble those glamour girls as she does me. Some of the people around here look at me and see her."

James frowned and wondered, "On the level? How do you know?"

"I've seen the portrait. We do look a lot alike. It's a little unnerving."

James's sharp features tensed at her words before he finally conjectured, "And these two fellows, do they frighten you? Have either of them been out of line with you?"

Jessica decidedly shook her head, answering, "Not really. I mean, no one's been fresh. Hmph, that's not a word you'd associate with either man." Jess hesitated. Should she tell James about Vitus's appearance on the lawn two nights ago, or the effect of the poison pen letter on him? *That could make things look worse than they were. Well, maybe the Vitus issue was moot now, since Jamie hadn't seemed wracked with worry this morning.*

"You're taking a long time to answer me, love," James noted, his hooded hazel eyes searching hers, his concern clear.

Jessica shook her head quickly and smiled. "Don't fret that handsome, shaggy head of yours. I think Dr. Blasko is a sad, hurt man, but his daughter has him under control. Besides, I have my *preux chevalier* to protect me, in the unlikely event of a haunted husband storming the castle. I suspect my sister may have exaggerated things, bless her pointed little head."

James regarded Jessica thoughtfully before allowing, "I can't deny that I sometimes think Elizabeth is the Queen of Histrionics. And I'm relieved I needn't regret not retrieving my Colt from our safe on the way here. However," he grew more serious, "there's another part of your sister's news report that has me concerned. I want to know more about this business of nightmares leading to sleepwalking. I've never known you to do that."

Jessica sat back against the window pane. She'd thought she'd buried the dis-ease of the dreams, of that walk, but hearing James's voice, the doubt quietly troubling her set that cobweb vibrating again.

"I, well, there was an odd nightmare about being in a room I'd never seen. Then Jeanne Rivers showed Liz and me the room: identical to the one in my dream. Walking in my sleep seemed the best, most believable reason for how I knew what it looked like. I'd heard that it was above this room, so that must be how I found it," Jess finished, hoping James would reassure her that this non-supernatural explanation made sense.

James did not appear satisfied. He considered before suggesting, "You're sure that you never went in there, or perhaps that Scott hadn't described it in detail for the program?"

Jessica shook her head, "No, none of that. Liz and I thought the pressure of putting on the program, with all the people involved in the tragedy surrounding me, might have tried to work its way out of my unconscious in my sleep." Then Jessica grabbed at one bright point, "But it hasn't happened since. Liz even did this trick with putting a card in the door to see if I'd opened it to 'take a stroll,' and it never fell out. So, proof positive I haven't been meandering in my sleep! I did have another screwy dream, but that was the night after the show, so what do you expect?"

James carefully raised the topic, "Elizabeth told me that you wouldn't see a doctor when she suggested it."

Glancing down at her hands, Jess admitted, "Well, no." Facing her husband, she explained more confidently, "I didn't want to make a big deal. Scott would have been concerned—"

"About you or the show?"

"Both, and I can't say I blame him," Jessica reasonably replied. "All our jobs depend on his keeping this 'special program' going. Frankly, I'd feel like a weak sister, making a big to-do over a flash-in-the-pan anomaly. Don't I seem fine now?"

"You look a little tired," James answered.

"Well, I've been a busy girl this afternoon," Jessica grinned impishly.

"That you have," James agreed with an equally devilish glint as he pulled her close. They held each other quietly, deliciously, for some time before James broke the silence, "I wonder if you wouldn't do me a favor. Tomorrow, we could nip into town for a bit of a look about; and then, perhaps, you could pop into the local doctor's office to have him check you out concerning that sleepwalking business. And, of course, we could find a place for tea."

"I love the way you sandwich in the doctor's visit between shopping and tea. Nice try, mister, but, really, I'm just fine. I've been feeling stronger every day. Now that you're here, I'm on top of the world."

"That's all very flattering, Mrs. Crawford, but I'd feel much better if you'd humor me on this," James said persuasively. "If you are just fine, then fine. You'll feel better, I'll feel better, with a clean bill of health. If anything is wrong, we'll find out how to take care of it. You're too smart not to see the logic."

Jessica thought over James's words and admitted, "I know. You're right, but I don't want the others to know about my little bout. It would worry them too much. So, let's do it on the q.t. Happy now?"

"Hmm," James responded, "what would make me happy would be to ring up Dusty to put on the kettle and to pack you off home over my shoulder."

"You and what battalion of marines?" Jessica challenged, raising her chin in playful defiance.

"Feisty women are my downfall," James shook his head.

"Oh, so who are the other feisty gals in your life?—Oh no!" Her glance had fallen on her watch. "Goodness! It's time to dress for dinner."

"'Dress' for dinner?" James queried skeptically. "Is this the sort of establishment where a gent needs to don a monkey suit to sup?"

"No," Jess returned, getting up. "That's only for the séance next week."

"The . . . what?" James was not quite startled, but his feelings about the supernatural showed.

Unsure whether she felt guilty or impish at unsettling James, Jessica explained quickly, "I guess what I told you earlier slipped your mind. The second episode will be an edited version of the séance, held the night before with a real medium. But, gosh, I'm sorry for joking about something that shakes you up sometimes. You know, you could take the night off in Portsmouth, dodge the whole thing. You were so good to come here when I needed you. How can I ask you to be miserable?"

On his feet with mock bravado, arms akimbo, James asserted, "Enough of that, Mrs. Crawford. If a chap can deal with Nazis, fifth columnists, collaborators, and tinned chipped beef, he can stick by his lady when the hordes of darkness are about."

"I wouldn't exactly call Felicia a horde, dark or otherwise," Jess quipped, hugging James.

But James held her away to add, "But only if I don't have to wear a monkey suit."

"I'll see what I can do about that," Jessica winked. The kiss they shared almost made her forget about dinner.

Chapter Twenty-Two
Later that Evening

Jessica and her husband were ready earlier than they expected, so their knock on Elizabeth's door had her telling them to go on ahead. Rather than loll about the drawing room, Jessica suggested James follow her to the music room to see the set-up for the broadcasts.

It was wonderful to link her arm through his and feel his warmth through the wool of his dark jacket. The grey turtleneck gave him a nattily erudite look, she decided. They crossed the foyer into the short corridor, needing no words, only a quick, shared smile. Her dark brown skirt with its wide leather belt moved gracefully with her as they entered the music room. The light through the windows turned all a gold edging into bronze. As a treat to her husband's musical proclivities, she introduced him to the grand piano, no longer miked up for the show.

A hand on the slight ruffles of her cream, V-neck blouse, Jessica asked, "So, what do you think of all this equipment?"

Surveying the mike set-ups, the soundboard, the transmitter, and the equalizer, James grinned. After a quick glance to make sure there was no one to overhear, he answered, "It's a darned sight more complicated than the transmitters I used in France."

Jessica smiled at her husband's ensuring no one would catch the reference to his war work. *Good thing the walls didn't really have ears.* She continued, "Take a gander over here, at this baby. It has a beautiful sound. We used it for mood music in our broadcast. Philip Carlyle was gracious enough to allow us."

"Did he, now?" James inquired conversationally as they picked their way past equipment to the piano. "It certainly is a nice instrument." He lifted the keyboard cover carefully, observing, "There must be a player in the house for it to be in tune."

"Definitely," Jess concurred. "Philip Carlyle. He has a nice touch on the keys."

"Oh, does he?" James queried with mock suspicion. "Serenaded you? Should a chap be jealous?"

"He did play Satie's 'Les Trois Gymnopédies,' after quoting Keats to me," Jessica teased.

"Well, then, if a fellow uses this piano to flirt with my wife, I have no compunction about flirting with his piano to woo her back," James reasoned with a glint as he took a seat on the bench and studied the keys a moment.

Jessica flicked on the light above the keyboard, returning, "A crack worthy of Elizabeth's cracked logic, but please, pound those horse teeth."

James nodded and from memory slipped into one of Jessica's fairly recent favorites, the dreamy "Stella by Starlight." She smiled her delight and closed her eyes as the early notes drifted dreamily, romantically around them. Except now the dream slipped into chords of the eerie, even macabre, reminding her of the piece's source: *The Uninvited*. The plot and mood of the film flashed disquietingly to mind. The darkened corners of the room seemed to invite the other world through this song from a story of ghosts and possession.

"No, James," escaped her abruptly.

He halted. Quizzical was an understatement for his expression. After a moment, James said, "I thought you loved this piece."

Jessica sighed, "I do, but it has a history that I don't think would make you happy."

"Didn't you say it was from a movie about a fellow having trouble with his potential mother-in-law?"

"Strictly speaking, yes. Except the mother-in-law was dead and possessing his fiancée."

"Maybe something else," James decided.

Jess nodded emphatic agreement, adding, "It just felt like an open invitation for Felicia to glide in. I don't think you'd do very well with that."

James looked at Jessica with a penetration she didn't expect and asked, only half joking, "Are you saying you actually believe this place is haunted?"

Jessica hesitated. She couldn't lie to James; he wouldn't want her to. Was she even sure what she believed? Her answer came slowly, "There have been lots of reports—maybe just servants' imaginings. Still, there were supposed experiences by Philip Carlyle, who's pretty pragmatic. So, I just don't know. There are more things in heaven and earth, and all that jazz."

She was about to add Liz's vague impression, but James was looking a little green around the gills. Maybe it was more important to try and get to the bottom of why these circumstances were getting to a guy who'd run with the Resistance in France. Maybe he needed her help with a haunting that went beyond his war experiences.

"James, you explained to me why you'd had a phobia about horses, but you've never come clean on this thing you have about the supernatural, particularly ghosts. You're smart, adventurous, logical, so why this bugaboo? What's behind it all, honey. Talk to me so I can help."

James gave her a quick, almost nervous smile, but only kidded, "Can't a bloke have a secret or two? Keep a little mystery in the marriage?"

Jessica sighed and replied, "I've had enough mysteries over the past four years for twelve marriages. I only want to make things easier for you, but here I've made you sign on for a week in a place that would give Boris Karloff the willies."

"Don't worry. I can tough it out, especially if the food is good," he teased, himself again. Putting his hand over Jessica's, James changed the subject, "How about 'Stardust'? You love that one, and I doubt Hoagy Carmichael has ever put the hoodoo on anyone."

"Okay, mister," Jessica relented, deciding it best to join in her husband's renewed good spirits. "Make nice with the eighty-eights."

"Love it when you talk swing to me," he kidded, launching into a song special to them.

"Ah, Jessica, you decided to take up my offer to play . . ."

Philip Carlyle's voice trailed off as, coming deeper into the room, he realized that Jessica was not playing.

James ceased and rose, extending a hand to introduce himself: "James Crawford, husband of the lovely Jessica."

Philip briefly glanced at Jess speculatively, then took James's hand as he came around the piano, saying, "Of course, the professor. My housekeeper informed me you had arrived. Something of a surprise, I might add, but a delightful one if it puts such a glow in Jessica's face, I'm sure."

"I'm sure you're sure," James smiled, equally friendly, adding, "I hope I'm no trouble."

"Of course not. I'm delighted that Jessica brought you in to try the piano. I offered that opportunity to my other guests. You have a nice hand, for an amateur," Philip noted.

"You should hear me on clarinet," James returned smoothly.

Jess couldn't help thinking the old licorice stick probably was the last thing Philip would enjoy hearing, other than bagpipes. In fact, she had the distinct impression of horns being lowered, despite all the British and Old-New-England-family grace. Time for a girl to step in.

"James was just playing one of my favorites, 'Stardust.'"

"Ah, of course, popular music," Philip allowed. "As much a favorite as 'Les Trois Gymnopédies'?"

"Oh, this?" James inquired, sitting down and deftly slipping into the Satie.

"You must be rusty. You made a mistake," Philip pleasantly observed.

"I didn't notice," Jessica asserted.

James kept playing, undistracted, though a hint of a smile did flit beneath his mustache at Jessica's defense. And Jessica? Her sympathetic feelings for Philip decidedly diminished after his swipe at her husband.

Abruptly, the mood shifted as Scott and Liz strolled in. Elizabeth, in a black wool jumper and a blouse striped in green, blue, and rust, playfully chided James, "Say, can't you play something with a little more jump and jive, Professor Crawford? These digs are crying for you to chase away the shadows!"

"Not on this lovely instrument," James smiled. "When we get back to the city, I'll serenade you with 'Begin the Beguine.'"

Deciding to move everyone firmly onto cheerier ground, Jessica cracked, "'Donkey Serenade' is more like it."

"Is that any way to treat your sister," Scott teased. Turning to James, he said, "Say, great to see you, James. How's the Keats research going? Any surprising new discoveries?"

Before James could answer, Philip Carlyle was all convincing warmth, going on with his admiration of James's scholarship. Jess was silent. Had she overreacted a moment ago? Perhaps all the intrigue whirling about the two great houses on the island had queered her judgment.

Elizabeth's skeptical appraisal of the three men, and a knowing look at Jess, brought her to the conclusion that dinner ought to prove interesting.

It did, indeed, prove an interesting dinner. Jeanne had switched Jessica's and Elizabeth's seats to put James on Jess's right. Philip was still at the head of the table, and everyone silently thanked God that Ungerpreck was up in his room with an attack of gout.

"So," James began after a sip of wine. "I'm the new chap on the block. Why don't you folks clue me in with more detail on your little tale from the dark side."

"Don't tell us you didn't listen to your wife last week," Scott chided.

"Let's just say that the faculty housing only has one wireless, and no one had the nerve to switch from a local political debate to something they'd consider on the low-brow side."

"Well, I like that," Jessica pretended to fume. "Casting aspersions on *my* art."

"At least he wasn't listening to the competition," Guy interjected.

"Not last week," Scott pointed out. "As much as I hate to admit it, Ungerpreck might be on to something, pushing us to do true-life sensation."

"Don't tell him that," Maura warned.

"No, but honestly," James continued, "what is the whole story. I'm interested."

"I'm surprised your wife hasn't shared much on the subject with you," Philip Carlyle answered amiably, hinting that the two ought to be better attuned to each other.

James ignored the hint, buttering a roll as he explained, "I've gotten bits and pieces, but we've both been so hard at work we've neither of us been able to get together on the story. I'm all ears now."

"Why don't I let Philip tell you," Scott suggested. "He's the only one at the table who can tell the tale from experience."

James nodded at Philip with interest, and Carlyle once more recounted the strained relations between Felicia and Vitus, his brother's perfidy, his family's blind eye to him, and the events as he knew them of the fateful night—down to the only trace of either Bill or Felicia being blood on the floor.

James reflected before querying, "But you'd no way of determining whose blood it was? You didn't say it was tested to match types . . ."

"This is a small town," Philip interrupted. "We didn't have the technology, the capability."

"What about Portsmouth?" James asked. "Surely by 1927, they or the state police could have run the tests."

"Say," Scott pondered. "I wish I'd thought of that before we put together the program last week. I don't know how Bev and I missed it. Juggling too many balls at once, I guess. Maybe we should sign you on, James, as a consultant."

"Sorry," James declined lightly, "academia keeps me too busy. Besides, one dabbler in mystery and the supernatural in the family is enough. Still, it is curious, Mr. Carlyle, that a sharp man like yourself didn't call in the necessary authorities."

Philip did not look happy. He explained, but reluctantly, "I wanted to protect my sister, Gladys. You see, she was so upset by the disappearances or murders, she couldn't bear to see that patch of blood in Felicia's old room. She bleached it out before it could be tested. Yes, my sister tampered with evidence: it took all our family influence to keep local and state police from causing her trouble. But everyone knew Gladys only made a foolish mistake. She cared about both victims so much. Since there were no bodies to prove murder most foul, she was never prosecuted."

"Family influence is useful," James concluded, short-circuiting Philip's resentment with, "if it protects an innocent and well-meaning woman. Still, it is curious that there *were* no bodies. You don't actually know if either or both were murdered. Or who murdered whom."

"I can assure you that Felicia Blasko was incapable of murder," Philip responded decisively.

"Can you?" James pondered. "How can you ever really know that about a person until the moment of truth?"

"I'm sure you wouldn't consider that lovely woman you married capable of killing," Philip answered decidedly.

James gave Jessica a wry smile and inquired, "What do you say about that, love?"

"I say that you'd better never tempt me," she replied, smiling but wondering why James was doing so much digging.

"That goes double for me," Liz added.

The chuckles around the table evidenced that the sisters had broken the tension. Now Scott pointed out, "Anyway, James, Felicia wouldn't be able to haunt us if she hadn't been murdered."

"Ah," James smiled. "That's where your reasoning begs the question. You're basing your argument on the assumption that Felicia could only have died as a murder victim twenty years ago. What if she died much later and returns now out of guilt or because she wants to straighten out your misperception? She may want forgiveness for all the grief she caused by running away or for something else she did that night."

"She wouldn't leave behind her child," Gerry insisted forcefully. "Jamie Blasko is certain of that."

"I fully concur with Gerry Davis," Philip said. "No. I believe that Scott and Beverly are on the right track: either my brother or Blasko killed Felicia and disposed of her. If Blasko is guilty, he could well have finished my brother." To mollify Gerry's reaction to his accusation against Jamie's father, he added, "However, my brother could well be guilty. He could have killed that wonderful woman and disposed of her but lost his nerve to brazen out an investigation and fled."

"So, you'd discovered he'd packed his bags and taken them with him?" James questioned.

"You really should have listened to the broadcast," Philip Carlyle replied cooly, at first. "Yes, he'd packed his bags—even riffled the safe in the study, but he appears only to have left with his coat, his wallet, and, Gladys said, some document (not that she was sure what). I never found anything missing that I knew of. I've even wondered if Vitus Blasko caught him and exacted justice for Felicia's death. It would certainly explain Blasko's guilt and odd behavior if he weren't responsible for what happened to *her*. I can't say that I'd exactly blame Blasko."

Scott suggested, "I guess it could go either way: he took off in a panic with what he had in hand, or someone disposed of his body, coat and wallet and all."

Philip added, "And as far as Felicia's possible guilt, Mr. Crawford, it's hardly probable, just for the fact that my brother was six feet tall, while

Felicia was just about your wife's build. I doubt Jessica, here, could easily kill a man, haul off his remains, and hide them with enough time to flee before I returned."

James gave Jessica an inquiring look, to which she responded, "He's got you there, Ace—but, again, don't put me to the test."

"That's why we're hoping the medium and her séance will clear things up," Scott concluded.

"A medium and her séance," James repeated skeptically. "I don't claim to be Harry Houdini when it comes to debunking such things, but you don't honestly expect to find the answer to all your questions through supernatural mumbo-jumbo."

"She is reliable," Philip Carlyle asserted. "I know."

"How do you know?" James questioned, surprisingly earnest. Jess caught Gerry nodding in sympathy as James continued, "Many of those sorts might not be intentional frauds, but they convince themselves they have spiritual powers when they're just doing a good cold reading, responding to the subtle reactions of their subjects. I know. Growing up back home, I saw spiritualism quite the rage. In fact, my mother got caught up after my last brother died. Pain can leave even the sharpest customer vulnerable."

"James," Jessica said gently, "I never knew that. You never told me."

He put a hand on her arm and tried to lighten the mood with, "Not to worry, Mrs. Crawford. It's all long in the past."

Philip Carlyle seemed to soften at James's candor. Maybe he even empathized, for he opened up to explain everything he'd revealed the night Scott had brought in Wanda. Jessica was surprised at how patiently James listened. Philip had scarcely finished before dinner ended, and they adjourned to the drawing room.

Jess entered the drawing room, arm linked with James's. She could hear her sister somewhere behind her chatting with Gerry. About to take a seat by the fireplace, Jess felt James subtly guide her toward the French doors.

"Where do you two think you're going?" kidded Guy as they passed him and Maura.

"Beautiful moon," James pointed out. "Can't a chap enjoy it on the terrace with his beautiful wife?"

215

"The beautiful wife thinks it's a swell idea," Jessica concurred, happily anticipating a romantic break from the rather morbid table talk.

"I remember when you couldn't wait to get me alone like that," Maura archly reminded her husband.

Guy elaborately checked his watch and said, "Okay, I'm giving you kids twenty minutes, then it's our shift for a little moonlit romance."

The lights from indoors pooled yellow on the flagstones, while the moon illuminated the lawn and dark range of trees beyond. In the crisp air, the waning moon rode a bright, imperfect white medallion, free of the gossamer, black clouds scudding past the stars, and no longer lurid from Maine's fires. Jessica strolled ahead of her husband, so happy to be with him, away from the dark memories lurking in the mansion's shadowed corridors. A chill, though, made Jessica cross her arms and rub her shoulders.

"Ah, I should have anticipated there'd be a nip in the air this time of evening," James said, coming up behind her to place his jacket over her shoulders, then his arms about her waist.

Wonderful! Jess inwardly purred.

They stood like that for a few minutes before James said, "I don't think I particularly endeared myself to your host. Too many awkward questions for his taste."

Jessica gave a ladylike little snort before turning her head to look up at her husband and say, "On such a night as this, you're worried about Philip Carlyle?"

But James replied, dead serious, "I'm thinking about what a fishy setting this whole deal is. To tell the truth, I think Scott's too wrapped up in worrying about his ratings. It's going to create quite a dog's dinner before he's done, with a lot of unstable people pushed past good sense. And your alleged resemblance to this Felicia makes me think that this séance nonsense will land you smack in the middle of the maelstrom. If you are going to stay until the bitter end out of misguided loyalty, I'm going to make damned sure I know exactly what the score is so that I can protect you."

Part of Jessica wanted to protest that she was a big girl and could take care of herself, but she also knew that, by herself, she was in over her head.

Still, she did press James, "So, do you or don't you believe this séance is worth a hill of beans?"

"I think that Scott can edit his experience with the medium to get whatever he wants, or at least make even a flop sound mysterious—less can be more," James replied seriously. "But I can't answer for what this Philip Carlyle will do. I haven't met any of these Blaskos, but I'm not sanguine that either the father or the daughter is all that reasonable, given what I've heard since I came here. And what's the story with your friend Gerry? He seemed suspiciously defensive of Miss Blasko and her family for a chap who's just acting on a radio program."

"I guess you could say he's suspiciously in love with her," Jessica explained. "Neither Elizabeth nor I is all *that* keen on the situation. She's a girl with a lot of troubles, with those parents of hers. There's even a broken engagement in her past because of the scandal. Gerry could do better, to put it mildly."

Their attention was diverted by the French doors opening to bring Elizabeth onto the terrace. Jess wasn't sure, but James seemed as relieved as she was by the identity of their visitor.

"Hey, kids, what's cookin'?" her sister called as she approached, cigarette in hand. Almost upon them, Liz dropped her voice to comment, "James, that was quite a grilling you gave Phil and Scottie in there. Come up with anything useful?"

James quirked a smile and answered, "I found out that you two have signed on with some rather odd ducks. Tell me, whom do you think would rather give me the boot more, Phil or the dragon lady, I mean housekeeper?"

"Jeanne doesn't hate you," Jessica protested. "Where on earth did you get that idea?"

"Oh, she can't stand him," Liz affirmed with a decided nod before taking a draw on her cigarette and then folding her arms.

James, briefly, seemed to give that cigarette a longing look but went on, "Before you two returned, the lady was definitely not happy to let me in the door when I introduced myself. She practically shoved me off into the drawing room."

"So, she had it in for you even before you and Jessica threatened to single-double-whatever-handedly undermine the morals of her entire female staff," Liz concluded. Another draw on the cigarette.

"I'm afraid so," James wryly affirmed.

"Maybe she was just surprised to discover she had an added guest," Jessica disagreed.

James shook his head, "I'm afraid I can tell the difference between surprise and displeasure."

"Maybe she was hoping to save my sister for the master of the house, and you eighty-sixed her plans," Liz proposed.

Tossing her hands up, Jessica cracked, "Scott should hire you two to cook up nefarious plots for our show."

Liz shook her head. "Nope. We're talking about soap opera, not mystery or horror." Turning to James, she asked, "So, what *did* you decide after your dinner inquisition?"

"Hardly an inquisition, Elizabeth," James corrected her easily. "Nevertheless, I need more to go on to keep a proper eye out for Jessica with this lot." Turning back to Jess, he finished, "So that makes me think we'd better go to Portsmouth, not the village, tomorrow."

"Oh, shopping?" Elizabeth inquired hopefully.

"Not exactly," answered Jessica. "James wants me to see a doctor, just for a check-up, after he heard about my bad dreams and my sleepwalking." Jess noted her sister's raised brow at her taking a suggestion from James that she'd rejected from Liz. She added, "I figure if you both have the same advice, maybe I should listen, even if I do feel so much better now."

"But why go all the way into Portsmouth? There's a perfectly good sawbones in town," Liz puzzled. "Vic was telling me he was satisfied with seeing him about an in-grown toenail, not that I couldn't have gone a lifetime without *those* details."

"James and I discussed this while we were changing for dinner," Jessica began. "In a small town tongues wag. A stranger seeing the doctor, especially one of us from the program, would really set off some blabbing. The last thing I need is to draw the attention of the Blaskos or Philip Carlyle to my sleepwalking adventure, lending credence to that poisoned pen letter." She asked James, "That about sum it up, hon?"

"I also want to get into Portsmouth to dash off a wire to my old contact Dick Streeter and ask him to dig up a little intel on this crew: Carlyle, his brother, the dragon lady, the Blaskos, and definitely Madame Wanda. The more I have to go on, the better I can suss out their motives, their level of threat."

"Should I be that afraid of them?" Jessica questioned, a bit taken aback by how seriously James was taking things.

"Look at it as I'm trying to discover if you *don't* need to feel threatened. But I'd trust not one of them," James reassured her, sort of.

Liz eagerly demanded, "Are you planning to do some investigating of that Madame Wanda when you're in Portsmouth? That's where she lives; you'll be right there."

James shook his head, explaining, "I don't want to arouse any suspicions: a stranger poking around, asking questions. No, I think Dick can tell me what I need to know, and with more detail than I could dig up in a short trip." He looked at Jessica and proposed, "Can we get a ride into town, then slip off to catch a bus to the city?"

Jessica thought before explaining, "No, borrowing a car or getting the driver to take us in is a little complicated around here. It can be done, but you've got to float it past too many people, including your 'dragon lady.' No, I have a better idea. No one makes a big deal about borrowing the bicycles. That will get us into town quickly enough, and we don't need to worry if anyone, like the driver, sees us hop the bus for town."

James nodded, "Makes good sense. You're a sharp one, Mrs. Crawford."

"And I can come, too?" Elizabeth eagerly added.

James and Jessica exchanged glances. Jess spoke, "I don't think so, Liz. Too many of us gallivanting off would draw attention. It *would* be helpful if you kept an eye on things here while we're gone."

"It would be useful," James confirmed.

Elizabeth surveyed them skeptically, questioning, "Are you two pulling my leg?"

"The same leg or one a piece?" Jessica deadpanned.

"Wise guy." Liz narrowed her eyes.

James mollified his sister-in-law, "Truthfully, Elizabeth, all three of us traipsing off would look fishier than two reunited 'lovebirds' disappearing for the day. And you do have a definite talent for observation that would be useful."

Jessica decided it would be smarter not to score one off her sister by translating "talent for observation" as "you're a nosy Parker from way back."

Elizabeth mulled James's words through a long draw on her cigarette.

Jessica *definitely* picked up on her husband's envy of Liz's smoking, prompting her to offer, "James, I know you've been trying to quit . . ."

"For two years," Liz observed.

"Talk about the pot calling the kettle names," Jessica cocked her head at her sister's Kent. Turning back to James, she suggested, "If you really want to stay out here and have a smoke, well, it's been a long day—"

An elongated, mournful (even menacing?) howl from the dark, jagged woods cut off Jessica: "Aroooooo!"

James looked about, alert, even startled. Elizabeth observed with not nearly as much *sang froid* as she'd intended, "We haven't heard from that precinct in a while."

"What is it?" James questioned, protectively moving closer to Jessica, standing between the sisters and the woods. "Someone's stray dog?"

"That's one theory," Liz replied. "Another is that it's the Howling Hound of Hell."

The hound, of whatever origin, called again, further off. Jess shivered, even as James tried to lighten the mood with, "Exactly how many supernatural beings have you around here?"

"Oh, I almost forgot the Stone Throwing Demon," Elizabeth added. "Though I can't say anything's flung even so much as a pebble so far."

James looked around before saying, "Maybe it's getting a little too nippy for us to stay out."

"I thought you were such a tough guy," Liz remarked.

"Tough and stupid aren't synonymous, Elizabeth," James returned. "But if you want to remain here in the moonlight to enjoy that canine serenade, infernal or earthly, be our guest."

As if in taunting support of James, the mystery canine released another bay at the moon: "Ar, ar, arooooo!"

"Lord, it's cold out here," Liz announced. "The dragon lady ought to have that hot coffee ready by now!"

Chapter Twenty-Three
Monday, October 27th

Exiting the doctor's office onto the Portsmouth Street, Jessica buttoned up her cadet-blue jacket matching her trousers. Her expression was relaxed. *That exam had gone pretty darned well!* She'd liked the doctor. He'd been a bit gruff, this Dr. Del Forrest, but he'd had such a twinkle in his startling blue eyes that she'd enjoyed his no-nonsense (but still caring) demeanor. She looked up and down the street. *No James, yet.* He'd come with her to the appointment (which they'd been lucky to get at short notice), keeping her company in the waiting room until she'd been called in. As planned, he'd then gone off to find a private place for calling Dick Streeter about getting him the lowdown on the cast of characters in her Birdsong Island adventure.

Then, around the corner, there was James, loping toward her. A smile burst across his face to see her, but his eyes also held concern. Jess set off rapidly to meet him. The two came together and he asked, taking her hands, "You look relieved, I'm glad to see. What did the doctor say?"

Jess smiled mischievously and replied, "He thinks you need a haircut. He saw you with me in the waiting room."

They started down the street, and James noted, "I take it from your smart crack that he gave you a clean bill of health."

"Just about," Jessica assured her husband. "My blood pressure and heart are fine. Temp is normal. He checked my reflexes, peered deep into my eyes with one of those eye-peering instruments, looked me over good, and took some blood for testing, just to be on the safe side. I don't think Blue Warrior got this kind of a workup before a race!"

"His verdict?"

"Just what I've been saying: probably too much stress, seasoned with big dollops of imagination and empathy," Jessica grinned, more pleased than she wanted to admit. Then she checked her watch and said, "Say, it's actually close to the next bus's departure. What about we skip having a cuppa here and just catch this bus. I'm still full from lunch—which I told the nurse to take into account before she weighed me. If we're in the mood when we hit the island, we can stop at Brunelle's."

James agreed, "That sounds smart. I'm so glad to hear you're feeling chipper." They moved toward the station, with James adding, "So, the good doctor thought you were just a victim of stress?"

"Pretty much. Oh, well, he did ask me if I had been taking any sleeping pills for my nerves from the show; and, if I was, not to take any more. Sometimes, he explained, too high a dosage can cause weird reactions. I guess he was thinking along those lines because of my grogginess some mornings," Jess answered matter-of-factly. "But if you don't get enough sleep, how can you help but be groggy?"

"That's not like you," James shook his head. "Well, you weren't, were you, taking pills?"

"Of course not," Jessica harrumphed. "I told Dr. Forrest that my idea of night-time stress relief was a good book, a tender cat, and a handsome husband to snuggle with."

"What did he say?" James laughed.

"That he wished more of his patients followed that prescription!"

"Even if the husband needs a haircut?" James inquired.

"For me, *especially*! I adore you this way!"

"Fortunate for a bloke like me."

"And don't you forget it, buster!" Jess affirmed. She changed the subject, "Enough about me. How did your 'mission' go?"

"Not much of a mission, love," James answered. "I managed to put the call through to Dick. He said he'd see what he could do. Made sure I knew I was asking for a big favor and gave me a hard time for asking for a rush. But he knows they owe me more than one favor. We'll hear back fairly soon. In the meantime, don't worry. I'll have my eye on you—and a pleasant eyeful you are."

"How can a girl argue with that?"

As they neared the bus stop, James decided, "Yes, I fancy it would be nice to have a cuppa in town. I can't say I look forward to going back to that big, broody mansion, nice view and all. And may I suggest that you cut back on that after-dinner coffee? Too much stimulant might have been stirring up your unconscious. That brew is rather strong."

"You know coffee sometimes conks me out, strange as that sounds," Jessica pointed out as the bus pulled up before them.

"Yes, but once you *are* out, the chemicals could be going to work on that hyperactive imagination of yours, Mrs. Crawford," James reasoned as they got in line for the bus.

"You could be on to something, Dr. Crawford," Jessica allowed. "However, right now, I am looking forward to a lovely afternoon cuppa with you at Brunelle's Café. That should leave plenty of time for me to recover before bedtime."

For the bus ride back, James had given Jessica the window. Feeling him snug beside her on the short seat was so nice. James was thinking now, so Jess gave her attention to the Victorian and colonial houses slipping by her window in Portsmouth, their colors heightened by the gold, scarlet, and apricot foliage. Now that the cast wouldn't see a script until after the séance, she had some spare time. This setting would be perfect for leisurely walks. Facing James to share her idea, Jess found him still lost in thought.

"With inflation, how about a dime for your thoughts, Mr. Crawford," she gently teased.

"What? Oh, sorry, love. I was just wondering if Dick could get back to me in time for it to matter. Perhaps I should have tried to do a little snooping of my own on this Madame Wanda. I just didn't think I had enough time."

"Well, James, old boy," Jessica reassured him, "perhaps you won't even need that intel, after all. We're only here until Saturday; then it's back to town. I've got to tell you, I already feel much more at ease since you've been by my side."

James smiled but admitted, "I wish I had more on this Wanda."

"Do you think she's a phony?"

"Does it matter?" James pointed out. "Legitimate or not, if the murderer's still around, he won't want the pot stirred over something he thought he got away with years ago. That's why if you won't let me take you away, I intend never to let you out of my sight while we're still at the Castle of Otranto."

"Mmm, that could be fun," Jess archly decided. The kiss they stole certainly was.

Leaning his head against hers, James seemed so much more relaxed now as he kidded, "So, I wonder what your sister has come up with at the haunted mansion?"

"Knowing Liz, she's probably cracked Philip Carlyle's safe, pumped the entire kitchen staff for everyone's history back to the 1700s, and house-trained the Hound of Hell."

James's grin made Jess glad she'd never told him about Liz's sense of something haunted attached to Jamie. As if her husband needed fuel added to his smoldering anxiety over the supernatural. For the first time, she hoped the upcoming séance turned out to be a bust.

Chapter Twenty-Four
Wednesday Morning, October 29th

It was an absolutely lovely Wednesday morning. Alone in the drawing room, Jessica Minton was waiting for James to return from their room with his wallet retrieved. True to his word about keeping a close eye on her, James had only left Jess because Gerry had been with her. James, however, hadn't anticipated Scott dragging Gerry off to the music room to get his reaction to some ideas for the next broadcast. But since she'd only be alone for a few minutes, she felt safe enough. So, Jessica let her brown and white spectator pumps stroll her over to the radio, her blue blouse hatched with thin dark-brown lines accentuating the brown skirt. Maybe it was even a little nice to have a moment, but just one, to herself. She reached for the dial. Her hand never reached it.

Jessica gasped. The French doors opened and in walked a tall, spare but strong, fortyish stranger with a lantern jaw, a brush of thick auburn hair, and a mustache as full as James's. A man she'd never seen before in her life! When his eyes, speculative eyes, fastened on her, they widened with as much shock as hers.

The man, however, recovered sooner than Jessica. A sardonic smile shaped his features before he spoke: "Of course, I should have known you, with all the publicity. The resemblance is remarkable, I must admit."

"Who in Sam Hill are *you*?" Jessica demanded, her trepidation turning to irritation at his smug mysteriousness.

He seemed a bit surprised until his eyes swept the array of photos on the mantel. A knowing look came to his face, leading him to conclude dryly, "No, of course you wouldn't recognize me since I've been erased from the family tree."

Putting two and two together only took Jess a fraction of a second: "Bill Carlyle! But you're supposed to be dead!"

With a bitter smile, the "resurrected" Carlyle observed ironically, "I believe Mark Twain had relevant words on the subject."

Jessica wasn't amused, cutting to the chase: "*You* know. You can tell us what happened to Felicia."

Jessica's hand flew over her mouth. *What are you saying? If this guy knows what happened to Felicia, it's likely because he did it! And I'm here alone with him?! James, where the dickens are you?!*

He was speaking, "It's not as straightforward as you think, Miss . . . Minton, right? After I heard last week's broadcast, I traveled quite some way for this séance to get some answers."

"*You* need answers? Why? You were there," Jessica uttered, bewildered.

He shrugged slightly to reply, "In a manner of speaking. Apparently, you don't know the entire story."

"Good Lord!"

Philip Carlyle's voice cut the thread between Jessica and the prodigal brother.

Briefly, it crossed Jessica's memory that Philip had decided to stay home to support Scott's preparations for recording the séance. Now, she saw Philip steady himself against the door frame, blazing hatred directly at his brother.

That brother gave him a devilish look that made Jessica forgive Philip's earlier prickliness toward her husband. Moving toward him, she questioned, "Philip, are you all right? Sit down. Do you need some water?"

Carlyle waved her back, then squared his shoulders to demand of his antagonist, "What are you doing here, Bill? I thought you were out of our lives forever."

Bill Carlyle laughed, returning coolly, "What a heartwarming welcome, Philip. No 'Glad you're still alive' or 'Why have you stayed away from us so long?' or 'What happened to you?' Not even this young woman's 'What happened that night?' Nothing has changed with you in twenty years."

"Never mind that," Philip retorted, his anger now icy. "I demand to know why you're here now."

Bill Carlyle smiled, not a friendly expression to Jessica's way of thinking. He asserted, "I'm here for answers."

Curiosity overcame her disquiet at being caught between the warring brothers; Jessica found her voice: "I don't understand. If you were here that night, you must have seen what—"

"No," Bill cut her off, "I left here when Felicia refused to run off with me after that big scene with her husband. I don't know what happened to her."

Shocked, Jessica demanded, "Are you implying that Dr. Blasko must have come back and killed his wife?"

Bill Carlyle shrugged, concluding, "It seems most likely, doesn't it? My hardworking, dedicated brother was away all night at the factory, while dear Gladys and the child slept the evening through in the room below Felicia's. I hardly think it was the housekeeper, Mrs. Rivers, or her brat."

"Jeanne?" Jessica blinked.

Surprised she knew the name, Bill stared at her. He turned to his brother, who stated, "Jeanne Rivers took over for her mother. I'm sure she has fond memories of you, too."

Bill ignored the jibe, only noting, "So, she's come full circle."

Jessica wasn't in the least interested in Bill Carlyle's swipes at Jeanne. Even if Philip inexplicably seemed to hold back, she wanted to get to the truth. Felicia Blasko's life had become too entangled in her own for her not to. She pressed Bill, "If you thought Blasko was guilty, why didn't you come back? Help clear things up, at least."

Bill Carlyle gave Jessica a coolly bitter clarification, "You're that much like Felicia; you actually believe the system is fair. It was my word against everyone else's. Felicia and I had quite a quarrel when I tried to convince her to leave the kid and escape with me. Mrs. Rivers broke it up, and Gladys sent me off to my studio to cool down. The other servants heard it all. I didn't hang around—only long enough, unfortunately, for the others to turn in so that no one saw Felicia alive before I left. Gladys, dear Gladys, never gave away my location that first night. She sent me word that things looked as bad for me as for Blasko and insisted that I keep going to South America. But not without sending me a little something to speed me on my way. Rio turned out to be rather pleasant, for a time."

"And you're only returning *now*?" Jessica pressed. "Didn't your sister tell you that the case was closed because they never found the body? You could have come back ages ago."

"Apparently, Gladys inconvenienced my brother by dying before she could inform him," Philip explained with cold sarcasm. "And wherever he was hiding out in South America didn't carry a special report on the news of southern New Hampshire. How inconsiderate of the Allies and the Axis to monopolize world news. You'll have to forgive me, Bill, if I find it difficult to believe a burning desire to learn the truth about Felicia brought you back after all these years."

"He's not very sentimental, is he?" Bill addressed Jessica. He had a way of initially lilting his words but ending his sentence in a tone that intimated the hardness of his heart. Jess compressed her lips, wondering where Bill Carlyle would go next. She didn't have to wait.

Bill swiveled back to his brother and said, "As always, Philip, you're the hard-headed businessman. No beating around the bush. Fine. I have some hard business for you to face. Gladys may have sent me money to speed me to safety, but she also handed me an even more powerful claim to security. You see, she gave me her revised will, done out of town to prevent anyone's interference. The lawyer was distant enough from Birdsong Island that your lawyers never got wind of it. Unfortunately for you, our dear sister apparently died before she told you, since I can tell by the look on your face it's news to you. But I have the will right here with me, saved for such a day as this."

"I don't believe you," Philip scoffed. "Gladys may have favored you, but I can't believe she'd do anything so foolish."

"Brother, you'd better believe it," Bill smiled wickedly. He gave Jessica chills. "So, you'd better change your tune towards me because Gladys left me all of her stake in the business, her money, and the property. I believe that means I now hold two-thirds, a controlling interest, in everything Carlyle."

Philip went white.

Jessica reached a steadying hand toward him, but Philip waved her away and tightly informed his gloating prodigal brother, "You've always been running some kind of a pitch on people, but this is the lowest. I ought to throw—"

"Throw me out, Phil? I don't think so. Even if I weren't on the level, I'm still a Carlyle, still entitled to my third of the estate, including my old room and studio. I wouldn't try it if I were you. Remember, I don't have to fear being blamed for a murder—not with no corpse these twenty years."

Philip Carlyle's eyes narrowed.

What was he calculating? He was angry, damned angry—but he was even a little afraid?

"If you doubt me," Bill began easily, taking a manila envelope from his inside jacket pocket, "here's a photostat for you to review with your lawyers. I think you'll find it all satisfactory, if not satisfying."

Snapping up the envelope, Phil pulled out the copy for a quick once-over before he looked up and threatened, "Don't think I won't have every scintilla of this fraud torn apart."

"Good," Bill returned, enjoying his brother's anger. "I wouldn't want you to have any doubts. Doubts and questions are terrible things. They come from trusting too much, don't you think? I find proof positive so much more comforting." He added to Jessica, "Don't you agree, Miss Minton?"

Jess started at the unexpected address. She'd been concentrating on being a discerning listener.

"Sorry, didn't mean to unnerve you."

"Yes, you're so concerned about unnerving others," Philip cut his brother. Addressing her, he apologized, "I'm sorry that you were exposed to all this, Jessica. There's no excuse for my brother airing our dirty linen—"

"Is that what I'm doing?" Bill interrupted. "It seems to me there's so much more—"

Now Philip interrupted: "I don't have time to argue with you. I am going directly to my lawyers in Portsmouth and have this 'will' examined. I have far more resources to fight than you."

"Not quite as much as you think, brother dear," Bill smoothly corrected. "My lawyer tells me that since most of your money and property, and of course the business, are all in dispute, we can tie them up until the case is settled. But, go ahead into Portsmouth, have a confab with your attorneys. I'm sure it will be enlightening, if not enjoyable. Meanwhile, I'll get settled in my room. Have Jeanne prepare it. Do you think she still remembers me? She was quite the restless brat back then, always wandering *our* house, turning up unexpectedly in the damnedest places."

Philip made a sound of disgust and strode out of the room. Jessica started to follow, partly out of concern; however, to be honest, she did not want to remain alone with the sardonic Bill Carlyle.

He had other ideas.

Stepping between Jess and the doorway, the tall man insisted, "No, wait. I want to talk to your director, Scott something, right? I'm sure he'll want my input on what happened that night."

"So you can help us find the truth about what happened to Felicia?" Jessica sarcastically replied. "After witnessing you attack your brother, I believe everything he said about you being no good—and then some!"

"Do you?" he queried, a little surprised by Jessica's feistiness, though not at all rattled. "Perhaps you'd like to hear another side of the story."

"Perhaps I wouldn't trust whatever came out of your mouth," Jessica retorted. "Perhaps I should warn Scott to take whatever you say with a few tons of salt."

Bill moved a little closer. Jess moved back, less out of fear than determination to keep this guy out of her face. He said, "My, you may look like Felicia, but you certainly lack her gentle disposition."

"We can all see what 'gentleness' got her," Jessica returned, crossing her arms resolutely in front of her. He might be a big guy, and an even bigger question mark, but she could see he liked to feed on others' fear. She wasn't about to serve herself up. And she just didn't like him.

Bill continued in a sympathetic tone that Jessica was far from buying, "Felicia's husband was never very stable—"

"And you, apparently, have never been considered Mr. On-the-Square by anyone in southern New Hampshire," Jessica shot back, her eye catching something in the foyer that further emboldened her.

He crooked his mouth, too caught up in trying to master Jessica to realize that she'd seen something he hadn't: "Then if I'm not on the level in absolving myself and accusing Blasko, that leaves only one likely suspect in Felicia's fate. Aren't you afraid to be alone with a dangerous man like me?"

"I'm not alone," Jessica pleasantly smiled back.

Bill's brow furrowed until he heard a British-accented voice from the doorway: "Hello, Jessica. Who's the new chap?"

"Oh, Mr. Carlyle," Jessica graciously introduced, knowing her manner was just a hair's breadth short of smug, "you don't know my husband, James Crawford. James, you'll never guess who's not dead, after all!"

Clearly, James had heard enough from the foyer to understand what was happening. He made no double-take when observing, "It seems this island is quite the place for resurrections, between Felicia's ghost and the return of the lost brother."

Bill looked from one to the other, finally giving them both a slow nod, responding, "Indeed, Mr. Crawford, you're right. Though I think you'll grant there's quite a difference between a wraith and a flesh and blood man."

"I wonder which could stir up more trouble?" Jessica pondered "innocently."

Bill again looked from one to the other as James came to stand beside Jess. Finally, the black-sheep brother offered, "Perhaps we'll find out tomorrow night at the séance."

"Came all this way just for the séance?" James inquired pleasantly, though his eyes belied his tone.

"Mr. Carlyle also has business to work out with his brother, sticky business," Jessica added, her tone signaling she was far from Bill's ally.

"It can wait until after tomorrow night," Bill explained. "I think it's time some truths came out about the murder."

"So you have special knowledge?" James questioned. "Did you witness what happened?"

Bill Carlyle ran a hand across his brow, and Jess felt sure he was acting—doing a good job—but trying to pull the wool over their eyes just the same. He replied, "I'm sorry, Mr. Crawford. I just had a dreadful scene over this with my brother. Your wife can attest to that. Now, I've got to find this Scott, the director, and recount all I know to him. I'm not about to go through it all three times. I'm sure your wife can fill you in. I'm sure she'll give you an unbiased account. Now, if one of you will inform me where I can find the man I'm looking for?"

"He's in the music room, where we record," Jessica answered. Knowing that Carlyle's appearance at this late date would likely give Scott a coronary, as much as she hated spending more time with this man, she started to offer, "Maybe I'd better go in first and prepare him. You could follow and wait in the corridor while I—"

James put a hand on her arm and advised, "I think Scott's man enough to handle this on his own. Bev, Chet, and Vic will be there to catch him should he faint, and we were on our way out, love."

"Far be it from me to keep the two of you indoors on such a fine day," Bill said with an affability Jess doubted he felt.

James gave him a nod and smoothly guided Jessica into the foyer. Pausing only long enough for Jess to grab her golden-mustard swing coat by the door, they were soon standing outside.

James noted, "This is all a bit of an eleventh-hour twist. Now do you see why I hate to leave you alone here? Where did Gerry go, anyway? No, never mind. That's really the missing Carlyle brother? What the devil is he doing here? You only need to look at him to see he's as crooked as a dog's hind leg. He didn't do anything to upset you, did he, Jessica?"

Jess answered, amused, "I can't remember when I've ever heard you blurt out so much at once! At least without there being Nazis involved. But don't worry; I'm fine. That stinker did nearly knock the pins out from under poor Philip, though."

To get to the service vehicle that they had arranged to borrow for going into town, the two walked to the rear of the house, but not around the side where the fireworks with Scott were likely exploding now. It *was* a temptation for both not to do a *little* spying on the confrontation between director and long-lost brother. However, Jessica had had about all she could stand of Bill Carlyle, while James was happy to shield her from any more. As they walked, Jessica filled in her husband on everything she'd learned in Bill's confrontation with Phillip. They reached the car, parked outside the garage, and James shook his head when Jessica finished, telling her, "If that doesn't just take the biscuit. I never thought I'd feel sorry for Philip Carlyle, but he has himself quite a nice mess to deal with. Does this Bill have any real answers to offer Scott, let alone the authorities?"

"He seems to want to sell us on Vitus Blasko as Felicia's murderer," Jessica proposed.

James opened the car door for her and asked, "Do you believe him?"

Jessica paused before answering with a query, "You think he's lying, don't you? To be honest, I think he's a bad apple. I don't know that I'd believe *anything* he said."

James nodded, closing the door behind Jessica after she slid in. He said nothing more until he sat behind the wheel: "As much as everyone around here seems more or less nuts in the head, Bill Carlyle strikes me as particularly something of a bad hat. A real dark horse."

Jessica put the question directly to her husband, "Do you think he's Felicia's killer?"

Thinking, James stared directly through the windshield—or windscreen, as he would have it. Finally, he faced his wife and said, "He'd certainly be bold to come back like this if he were guilty. Then again, a chance at controlling all the Carlyle authority and money, that would be quite an inducement."

"Especially if, thanks to our program, he could hang the blame on Vitus Blasko—or at least enough of it to keep himself in the clear."

James gave Jessica a wan smile, reassuring her, "It's not your fault if Scott's grand design gets hijacked. You just do your job, and we'll all get out of here."

Jessica protested, "It's only that all this manipulation, what's happening to innocent people's lives—it's not right. It's not fair."

"No," James agreed, "I don't imagine it is. But I've seen much worse. This is just the way things are. You can only do what you can, and I think you've given some of these people more than they deserve. I'll be damned if I let anyone drag you in deeper. Now, let's get away from this mess and have a nice relaxing holiday in town."

James had the car in gear and was taking them back around the house to the drive when Jessica exclaimed, "Oh my Gosh! Elizabeth! I didn't tell her about Bill dropping in out of the blue! She'll kill me for not cluing her in!"

"That *would* be a problem," James mused. "Between you and your doppelgänger, Felicia, we wouldn't know which spook we were dealing with."

Chapter Twenty-Five
Thursday, October 30th

Jessica Minton peeked out of the powder room and into her suite. It was getting on time for the evening's adventures in the preternatural, so she was antsy. James had already zipped and hooked her into the long, midnight-blue velvet dress, but she was finishing up her *toilette* now. She'd had no intention of smearing this gorgeous outfit with makeup or mussing her hair when she had to wiggle into it. And there was James, staring out into the evening's moonglow.

Jessica popped back to her mirror. Usually a night like this would be just lovely for snuggling up together after an exhilarating walk. Tonight, she'd be snuggling up to a Ouija board, or whatever supernatural aids Madame Wanda favored. *Good grief!* Did she ever owe James big time for sticking with her through all this! Another quick glance. Her handsome guy was still preoccupied with the dark eve outside. Something in his stance said he was dying for a cigarette.

As she finished mascaraing her eyes and putting that stick of soft-red Max Factor to work, Jessica tried to get excited that the worst would be over after tonight. Tomorrow, Scott and Bev would whip up some narrative to, hopefully, make sense, suspenseful sense, out of tonight's endeavor, which the actors would record. Scott and the crew would edit both into a program to be broadcast by transcription during their program's normal time slot that night. Then everyone could pack up and leave on Saturday. By the evening, Dusty would be regaling them with mouse tales—or tails? So, why wasn't she relieved? Why did she feel as if she were only kidding herself? That there was one hell of a chasm between tonight and Saturday home in New York?

It didn't help that James had grown increasingly preoccupied and restless as the hours had passed, drawing them closer to tonight's journey beyond the veil. If only he would come clean with her about why. She felt in her bones that there was more eating at him than concern over her safety. It seemed to her it all went back to his uneasiness with anything supernatural, a little more of which he'd revealed in his talk about his family and spiritualism. But over the past few days, James had stonewalled her when she'd tried to get him to open up more when they were alone. How could she help him if he wouldn't level with her?

Maybe I should turn him over to Liz and let her worm the truth out of him, for his own good. No, that would probably violate the Geneva Conventions. Well, turning on the pizzazz might at least kid away his jumpiness.

"Ready for gorgeous?" Jess called playfully before leaning around the corner to give James a nice view of how the midnight-blue velvet fit in all the right places: from the low, square neckline with its illusion material to a band of velvet around her neck; to the draped short sleeves; to the split tunic that descended below her hips; to the A-line of her skirt brushing the floor.

James's features relaxed into a surprised grin and a, "Rather nice!"

"See, I told you this dress was worth the investment," Jessica teased as she glided over to her husband, hands extended.

"I didn't argue the expenditure—much," James returned, taking Jessica's hands in his. "You do look a treat. What say we skip the evening's festivities and celebrate here, together?"

"No chance, smart guy," Jessica answered. "Scott wouldn't just fire me. First, he'd shoot up here and drag me off by the hair. The show must go on."

Still, her husband's suggestion *did* have definite appeal.

"Don't you think I could defend you?" James feigned wounded pride.

"I think Scott knows a heck of a lot is riding on the success of *both* our remote broadcasts. And I think I don't want to see the whole cast and crew out on the bread line. Anyway, at least you don't have to wear a monkey suit."

"I'm still not clear on why you and the others have to wear formal dress for a *radio* program," James noted skeptically.

"True, as far as it goes, oh husband savant. However, Scott is having publicity shots taken. You know, participants holding hands around the table, then a group shot when the séance is done—before and after shots."

"I see, one with your hair normal, another with everyone coiffured like Einstein, from terror. So, do disembodied hands, flying trumpets, and ectoplasm photograph well?"

"Ectoplasm?! I'm wearing velvet! Scott better hope that stuff dry cleans out!"

James was laughing, but there was still a trace of the haunted in his eyes, so Jess volunteered tactfully, "James, I know this spook business is not exactly your cup of tea. If you want to skip it, Liz will be there for me. You could take a trip into Portsmouth."

"Don't be absurd," he insisted. "If I could parachute into occupied France, a staged séance should be a piece of cake. I'm with you."

Before Jessica could figure a different out for James, they were interrupted by a knocking on their door.

"Must be your sister," James decided. A glance at his watch and, "She's actually prompt? How did that happen? She usually can't even make Orlando's record of 'coming within an hour of his time.'"

Walking away to answer Liz's insistent rapping, Jessica laughed, "Usually, that would be the case, but Liz is dying to get down to tonight's business. And she hasn't taken the measure of Bill Carlyle yet! He had the nerve to stay holed up in his room and avoid everyone until tonight's event. No. My dear sister is champing at the bit to check this guy out."

Jessica opened the door on her sister, who wasn't literally champing. Instead, Elizabeth was elegant in a fitted silver lamé sheath number, her hair flawlessly upswept into rolls on either side of her face and captured long at the nape of her neck in a silver filigree clip.

"Ah, Liz, don't you look lovely," James pronounced.

"I'd say 'can the soft soap,'" Liz cracked, entering, "but I can't argue with the truth. Anyway, snap it up, you two. I want to get down there and give this Bill Carlyle the once over." To Jessica, she said, "I haven't seen Scott or Bev all day. How did those two take this new wrinkle? I'd love to have seen that!"

"I was surprised," Jessica explained. "They handled it much better than I expected. Bev said it took a few cases of smelling salts to revive Scott, but he called Madame Wanda and squared this guy's participation with her."

"So, what *was* her reaction? If she's so psychic, you'd think she'd have predicted this twist and warned Scott," Elizabeth decided while examining the slick magenta sheen on her nails.

Jessica shrugged and added, "Unfortunately, Bev didn't have time to chew the fat with me. That's all I know so far."

James slipped in, "Neither of you will know any more until we join the rest of your chums downstairs and get this show over with."

Liz allowed, "As much as I hate to admit it, James, my boy, you're right. Let's hit the road, kids."

They made their way down to the music room with surprising alacrity for having two women in high heels and long dresses, joined by Maura and Guy in the foyer. Apparently, Gerry had made a point of heading down earlier. Obviously, Scott, Bev, and the crew would already be there with the photographer. Jess expected the antagonistic Carlyle brothers to be waiting there as well; she hoped only *looking* daggers at each other. With these observations dancing through her head—and that dance more of a dervish's whirl than sedate fox trot—Jess was not able to offer Maura and Guy much help with their fascinated inquiries about the return of Bill Carlyle.

When their party reached the open doorway to the music room, Gerry's reason for getting there early was readily apparent. Jess, James, and Liz exchanged shocked looks. At an angle between the wall of windows and the wall separating this chamber from the next, two rows of chairs had been set up, with plenty of space for comfortable movement between the rows. In front of those chairs, Gerry was talking to a young, dark-haired woman in a long, nip-waist black velvet dress, its broad lace collar cloaking her shoulders. Her features were tense, uncertain. She was Jamie Blasko.

"She's almost the last person I would expect to see here tonight," Elizabeth commented, both eyebrows raised.

"Especially considering that trouble with her father after last week's broadcast," Jessica added. Making a quick survey of the room, she observed, "I don't see her father, not that I'd expect him, either. Still, I'd hardly think she'd leave him *alone* tonight."

"Maybe she hired a sitter," James remarked.

This was one of those times when Jessica wished she could raise a single brow. She settled for merely saying, "May-be."

Now she scanned the room to see whether everything had been set up as Scott had briefed them. Sure enough, a round table had been moved in for the séance, with a table mike rising like an electronic pine cone at its center. Five chairs circled the table where she'd only expected four. Jess had an uneasy feeling about the addition, but refused to let it rattle her. The wind outside shifted one of the heavy curtains by the back corner of the angled rows, making the sponsor shiver. *That's right, the heat from the equipment at the last broadcast had prompted Scott to dissipate it some by opening the window at the far right. Philip had also overseen all new fuses installed to avoid another power outage.*

Elizabeth interrupted Jessica's thoughts: "Say, I don't see my pal Jeanne Rivers anywhere. Does that mean we won't be getting any coffee and cake after the show?"

"That's why *I* came," James asserted.

"Relax, you two," Jessica advised, patting her companions' backs, "Scott told me he doesn't want any excess people around. Madame Wanda thought their 'vibrations' might interfere with her reception or something. Coffee and cake are being prepared in the kitchen for after the show."

"I know I'm relieved," James deadpanned.

Jessica started to give him a smart remark when Scott was suddenly with them, querying, "Ready to go, Jess and Liz?"

"Sure," Elizabeth answered for them both, "as long as Madame Wanda doesn't look at me as competition."

"Not at all," Scott grinned nervously. "Remember, she said you'd be there to boost her power."

"Like a supernatural amplifier?" James quipped.

"Oh, ye skeptics of little faith," Scott returned. He was still grinning, yet the possibility of his show turning into a walloping big flop lurked not far beneath that smile.

Jessica tried to reassure him, "Scott, no matter what, you and Bev have the smarts and creativity to pull something exciting out of this evening. I'm sure that Madame Wanda will give you a good show."

Yet, Jess also couldn't help thinking that this was all more than a show for Jamie, her father, and the Carlyle brothers. She focused back on Scott to say, "You've had a couple of big surprises, haven't you? I never expected to see Jamie here—and there's Mr. Bill over there, to boot. *Did* he have anything useful to tell you?"

Scott regarded Bill Carlyle a moment before answering, "He's a cagey one. I think he got more out of me than the other way around. But he is a wild card that'll knock the audience for a loop, returning from the dead. When we told Madame Wanda, she insisted he be in the room for the séance. Said because he was so closely connected to Felicia on her last night, his 'energy' was essential to making contact."

"Fatally connected?" slipped out of Jessica before she could catch herself. "Anyway, he can't be a welcome sight to Jamie, especially as he's been implying her father's guilt. I bet Gerry's not crazy about her being here. How did *that* come about?"

"Actually, Gerry and she came to me yesterday morning, before Bill Carlyle showed up. She wanted to be here if there was any chance to contact her mother—and to clear her father," Scott explained.

James inserted some pragmatism with, "Scott, this is the girl's life. Do you honestly think she's going to get the answers she needs here? What happens if Madame Wanda doesn't tell her what she's looking for or misleads her?"

Scott didn't have an answer, at least not right away. What he finally came up with didn't satisfy, not even himself. "She has Gerry to protect her, and we were on the level all along about what we are doing. Everyone went into this thing with eyes wide open, and was well paid, including all the actors who get to keep their jobs if this broadcast continues to boost our ratings. Now, excuse me. I've got to do an equipment check and set up the photo shoots."

He was gone.

James gave Jessica a bit of a sheepish look and apologized, "I guess I just put you in your director's bad books."

Shaking her head, Jessica reassured her husband, "No, you didn't say anything I haven't thought—even said. Liz can bear me out. But Scott is in a tough spot with the sponsor's brother-in-law over there," she nodded to the spectator's angled rows of chairs.

"Hey, you two, don't sweat it!" Elizabeth pronounced. "I'm on the job tonight. Madame Wanda probably figures she can coast on my ability. Don't worry. I'll bring it home."

"Bring it home?" Jess queried. "You don't actually believe we're going to raise a ghost, do you? You honestly think there is a spirit abroad?"

Liz looked at Jessica and questioned, "Did you tell James about my impressions? The presence around Jamie?"

"The 'presence'?" Doubt, uneasiness tainted James's voice.

"It's something I saw, or sensed—somewhere in between," Liz explained quietly, not wanting to draw too much attention from the others in the room. "Nothing evil, I think, but something troubled, attached to that kid. I think that's why her being here, and my being here, could make this whole shindig a success—of some sort."

James glanced at Jamie and Gerry, who were still speaking to Philip (himself keeping an eye on Bill). Facing his sister-in-law again, James asked skeptically, "You see her now, I suppose?"

"No," Liz replied. "It's been much less since Jamie's been with Gerry. But when the lights go down low and the ambience is right, I think something's going to happen."

"Maybe you should consider this, Elizabeth," James warned. "If the actual murderer is in this room or on the prowl from home, he may not be too thrilled at the thought of you calling up his victim to reveal him, even if this is all a hoax."

"Warm and reassuring thoughts," Jessica observed with an unhappy smile.

"Just play it cool, both of you," James advised. "Don't let on to anything that could get you into trouble."

"I don't think anyone's going to try and permanently silence me in a room full of people," Elizabeth insisted.

"You need to read more Agatha Christie," James advised.

"Or at least see more Charlie Chan movies," Jessica added.

Any pointed rejoinder from Elizabeth was forestalled by a knocking on the door.

"Must be our medium," Scott announced. All Jessica could think of was the ominous pounding on Macbeth's portal. She kept that dark thought to herself.

Scott and Philip both went to admit Madame Wanda, returning a few minutes later with her between them. The lady knew how to make an entrance. She might have been short on height, but she was long on style in a black evening gown that sheathed her in satin, a splash of jet-sequined material diagonally swathing her torso. Her hair, curly and honey-blond, almost to her shoulders, was held back from her cherubic face by jet clips.

"What? No galoshes," Liz muttered to Jessica. "I heard it might rain tonight. Some psychic."

Wanda's eyes fastened on Liz, and she mischievously told her, "I left them in the foyer."

"Hearing like a bat," Elizabeth smiled. "Helps you tune in the spirits more easily?"

"And I'm sure *your* spirit will provide any added boost I might need to receive calls from the other side," Wanda returned. Her answer was smooth but implied: "I'm the focal point, the one calling the shots, and don't you forget it!" She turned her attention to the other attendees, in particular, Bill Carlyle, who was now approaching her.

Jess cast her sister a quick glance, warning against carrying the verbal duel any further. However, she needn't have. Elizabeth was much more interested in watching Carlyle's meeting with Wanda.

The glamorous medium broke free of her escorts, Philip Carlyle stiffening warily as his brother neared. Wanda and Bill halted before each other. She warned, "You took a chance coming here tonight."

Bill sent his brother a piercing glance before commenting, "I don't need a psychic to tell me that. Or are you implying that Felicia's spirit might want to harm me? No reason for that. I'm innocent of her death."

"You may or may not have killed her, but you're hardly an innocent man, Mr. Carlyle. You have done her wrong in her life," Wanda pointed out firmly.

Jessica noted Jamie staring harshly at Bill Carlyle at those words. Gerry saw it, too, putting a hand on her arm, but she shook him off and came forward.

Catching sight of Jamie's approach, Bill, for once not being ironic, said, "Jamie Blasko. You have certainly grown into a lovely young woman, a credit to your mother. Do you remember how well you and I got on when you were a very little girl?"

Jamie stiffened. She seemed to struggle for words, finally retorting, "I'm not interested in what a child mistakenly believed. I am interested in what I'm seeing now. You tried to make my mother leave me, and now you're trying to pin all the blame on my father. You'd see my family completely destroyed. I despise you!"

Bill Carlyle protested, "Would you have me accept the blame when I'm not guilty? I can't help where the chips fall once I speak what I know. As for my trying to make your mother leave you behind, I leave it to you to think about who gave you that tale—and consider his reliability."

"That is as Gladys told me," Philip asserted triumphantly. "Are you going to impugn your favorite sister?"

Wanda's hand was on Philip's arm now. She cautioned, "Let it go, Philip Carlyle." She looked from him to Bill and back to caution, "I need an atmosphere of harmony if I'm to negotiate the eddies of the vale of spirits."

Jessica's brow wrinkled as she asked herself why Philip's claim about a sister no longer alive to support him rang true. Why she refused to trust Bill Carlyle's words. It came to her, then. The dream. Her last dream had played out what Philip claimed. The affirmation of that nightmare shivered through her.

"All right, Jessica?" James's whisper was in her ear.

Jessica nodded, assuring him, "Must be a chill from the window."

Her feelings were a little too complicated to explain under these circumstances—and why unsettle James even more when he was already uneasy with the evening's planned "activities"? That question became moot when Scott broke the tension by hurrying the players off for the "before" publicity photos.

Now, they were being seated at the table. Jessica enjoyed one last squeeze of James's hand before he and the rest of the audience were shooed off to the two rows of chairs. Wanda had one entire side of the table, her back to the audience to allow her to concentrate on Scott's direction and her own spirit-raising. Jessica was on her left and Philip to Jessica's left. On the other side of Philip was Liz, diagonal from Jessica, almost across from Wanda. At the moment, Jessica noticed her sister was carefully watching Jamie, completing the circle between Liz and Wanda. Jamie, herself, kept turning to share a gaze with Gerry in the first row, second seat, to the sponsor's left. At least James got to sit next to someone as nice as Gerry, though the sponsor's voice certainly could carry far enough to be annoying, like right now. Almost as bad, Bill was immediately behind James in the staggered second row. She'd expected that since Bill was a family member, he'd get a front row seat; but she'd heard him tell Scott where he wanted to sit to get a bird's eye view of the proceedings and ensure there was no funny business behind him. James had been a tad disappointed, since he'd had the same idea, but for reasons pertaining to Liz's and her safety.

Jessica's attention returned to the table to glance at Elizabeth. Her sister was frowning, still studying Jamie Blasko, who stared down at the polished table before her. Was Liz sensing Felicia's presence hovering nearby, already? Jess shivered, and Madame Wanda noticed.

"Don't be scared, Miss Minton," she brightly reassured her. "I'm here to protect you. Why, we haven't even begun yet!"

Deciding against cracking wise with, "I think Elizabeth and Felicia may have started without you," Jess, instead, offered a tactfully playful, "I ain't afraid of no spooks."

Jamie focused a sharp eye on Jessica and remarked, "You might at least pretend to take this seriously."

"I'm sure Miss Minton was only trying to lighten the tension," Philip Carlyle defended Jessica in a kindly voice. "I think she's much too considerate to intend any disrespect."

"And," added Madame Wanda, taking charge, "as I understand it, Jamie, your mother was a cheerful woman who enjoyed convivial spirits."

"So to speak," Liz added.

Wanda nodded her approval before continuing, "I'm sure a bit of humor would make her feel at ease enough to join us."

"Knowledge the benefit of your psychic powers?" Elizabeth queried "casually."

"No, Miss Minton, the benefit of researching my subject before I try to contact her," Wanda replied, refusing to be antagonized. "I have to know what to expect from her and how to make her feel comfortable enough to speak through me—perhaps even manifest."

Jamie joined in, carefully, looking at Elizabeth, "In my view, my mother would never feel at ease with such a skeptic lined up against her. Maybe we should replace her with someone who believes. Someone who wants to contact my mother. As much as I don't trust him, perhaps we should have Bill Carlyle at the table."

Jessica thought Philip Carlyle might shoot up like a V-2 rocket. More furious or horrified, she couldn't tell.

Before his words or actions answered Jess's silent question, Wanda put the skids on the whole conflict with a firm, even slightly irritated, "No. You don't understand what an asset Elizabeth Minton is. She has tremendous power, power that will boost my ability to override the doubts and resistance of those who want to bury the truth. Of course, her abilities aren't as refined as mine, but we need her. That's why she sits across from me, to create a direct line of psychic communication. As I suggested once before, I think Elizabeth has sensed your mother's presence."

Jamie faced Liz, surprised, and pressed, "Is that true? Did you see my mother? What did she say?"

"I said *sensed* not communicated," the medium set Jamie straight. "That takes the kind of training and discipline I have. But, as I told you, everyone at this table has some quality or bond to ease your mother's passage through the veil. Philip Carlyle was her friend and has experienced her presence. You know your own bond, Jamie. Jessica Minton is a sensitive young woman who had come close to your mother's soul, not only by her appearance but, more importantly, by immersing herself in Felicia's character to recreate her in the radio play."

Jessica sent Elizabeth a quick glance, unsettled with the memory of those dreams and her sleepwalking. Wanda's words cut much too close to the bone. Fortunately, Wanda's psychic powers hadn't tuned into the sibling telepathy. Still, the possibility that the invasive presence of her dreams might descend on her made Jess want to bolt from the table, but she wasn't about to chicken out. Liz gave her a subtle nod that said, "Don't sweat it, kiddo. You're tougher than this, and I'm here with you."

Scott joined them, asking, "Just about ready to begin?"

Wanda answered, "I think we're all settled now. If you could tell the audience to be completely quiet."

Jessica followed Madame Wanda's gaze to the sponsor's brother-in-law, painfully bending the ear of Guy Robinson behind him. Lucky for James, he had Gerry as a buffer between him and Edmund Ungerpreck, even if it put Bill Carlyle almost directly behind him. James had been talking to Gerry, but she could tell he still had one eye on her. She gave him a wink, which he returned.

Now Scott instructed them, "Okey-dokey, folks, as I explained in our afternoon run-through, Madam Wanda needs complete silence for her endeavor to work. To further aid her concentration, we'll cut all the lights except for this soft illumination on the table in front of the mike—and of course at the console where I'll be working with Chet and Vic."

"What? No crystal ball?" Liz quipped. "Not even a plantain?"

To clear up the looks of confusion around the table, Jessica interpreted, "Planchette. She means planchette."

"Planchette? I thought she was your hairdresser?" Liz puzzled.

"That's Blanchette, Liz. Blanchette du Val."

Appreciating the sisters' humorously breaking the tension, Scott joked, "Okay, Abbott and Costello, enough with the comedy routine. Let's get down to business. For mood, Bev will play a musical intro. We're going to shut down the lights, and when Wanda gives the signal, we'll start recording. Wanda's then going to describe her procedure, including her self-hypnotizing, then do it. We'll keep recording as long as it takes to get some material we can edit into shape." Turning to the audience, he warned, "So no comments from the peanut gallery. We don't want any side comments obscuring or interfering with our recording."

"What about the sound of the wind outside, through the window?" the sponsor questioned, surprising one and all by actually raising an intelligent question.

"We did some experimenting last night and figured out how to adjust for it, even use it for background atmosphere. We've got a handle on this," Scott answered.

Jess wondered if he were silently adding: "I hope."

Scott turned on the soft light, then crossed to the doorway to shut off the other lights in the room before closing the padded doors. Jessica barely noticed Scott retrieving a flashlight to guide himself safely around the equipment to his station with the technicians. She did notice that James was lost in the darkness beyond their soft table-glow. The underlighting before her likely made Wanda a distinctly eerie silhouette to the audience. To everyone at the table, she appeared like a ghost from a Universal horror film. They all must have taken on that creepy appearance, especially Philip firing a defiant look into the shadows cloaking his brother by the window.

Wanda gave Scott the A-OK to start, he pointed at Bev to play, and the mood of Satie's "Trois Gymnopédies' was turned by the situation from gentle and dreamy into eerie and ineffable. The intro completed, Scott nodded at Chet to start recording before focusing Wanda on him with a finger to his nose; then, with a sweeping point of that finger back at her, he signaled her to go!

Wanda began: "Tonight, we seek to penetrate the mysteries of the universe, to peer into the dark and backward abysm of time to find peace and justice for a lost soul. To give answers and peace to the loved ones she left behind. To liberate the quick and the dead."

Jessica considered that any unmasked murderer would certainly not feel much peace if he ended up liberated from life by the gallows. *Could it even turn out that Gladys Carlyle had dunnit? What kind of show Scott would pull out of that?!*

Wanda finished identifying the participants at the table and what each contributed to opening a path for Felicia, an eerier version of the same spiel she'd handed Jamie earlier. Now she was instructing, "Take one another's hands; build the circle of psychic power. Prepare to open a portal for Felicia."

Jess wondered if James was either getting antsy with all this hocus-pocus talk or wrestling down a guffaw at the portentousness of Madame Wanda's intonation.

A glance at the strained expressions of Jamie and Philip quashed Jessica's smarty-pants attitude. The clamminess in Philip's hand holding hers was a dead giveaway as to how much he had riding on this experiment. As much as Jessica hated the thought that Felicia's materialization might legitimize her own dreadful dreams, she also hated the thought of Madame Wanda making monkeys out of everyone from Scott to Jamie. *How in Sam Hill had they all gotten into this?* It was like recognizing what a mistake you'd made the second after your car on the roller coaster rolled away from the gate.

"To clear my mind and soul of all extraneous, interfering thoughts and encumbrances, I will now self-hypnotize. My unconscious will be open to the other realm, free to admit Felicia Saunders Blasko. I will become like an open soul."

Hmm, two misquotations from Shakespeare and one from Wordsworth. Literary gal, wasn't she? Jessica soothed herself with sarcasm—and a shade of resentment. *Where did this Wanda get off exploiting some of my favorite quotations to doll up her parlor tricks? Get your own metaphors, lady.*

Wanda was now speaking in a relaxed tone about imagining, seeing, being in a gentle, serene place. Of drifting away, of letting go of doubts and control. She was now becoming that open, living unperturbed soul, entering beyond the veil to provide a conduit. You could almost see the curling mists parting to reveal . . .

Jessica gave herself a hard mental shake. *What the heck! The lady's words were powerfully lulling! Darned if she drags me along into La-La Land!* Liz, her face creepy in the underglow, frowned at Jessica's reaction. Neither Philip nor Jamie appeared to have noticed, their attention focused on Wanda.

Their medium commenced calling Felicia to them, welcoming her, promising to give her voice, a voice that her haunting cried out she desperately needed for getting through. The room was silent with expectation. Even the groaning of the house under the taunting of the evening wind receded into the background in the glow of the table's light, in the lulling of Wanda's tones.

Wanda spoke softly, but not too softly for the mike to pick up: "Yes, I see her. She's speaking to me. Her words are soft, difficult to hear. The doubters block her. No, one doesn't want to hear because that person knows the truth. No, you will not prevail. Felicia is strong. The forces of the universe are strong. I hear her! I hear her!"

Jessica shook her head. That soft but intense delivery almost had her again! She quirked a skeptical smile at Liz, but her sister wasn't looking at her. Instead, troubled, Elizabeth was riveted on something across the room. *Maybe behind Guy or Maura . . . No, James!*

Concerned, Jess started to shift to follow her sister's gaze, but Wanda nailed all their attention with a sharp cry: "Yes, I am listening, Felicia! I hear! You were betrayed. Betrayed by someone who claimed to love you! Yes, may even have loved you—"

"Mamma," Jamie breathed, her dark eyes enormous in a white face eerily illuminated.

Wanda pushed on, her eyes blank to this world.

Or so she wants us to think, Jessica considered. But her hand did hurt from Wanda's bear-trap grip. *This woman must screw jar covers on for a side job!*

"He promised to love you, but not enough to let you go. He would never let you go. He made sure you could never go."

"Who?" breathed Philip agonizingly.

"Yes, I see him. You're showing him to me . . ."

Bravo! Jess mentally applauded, reassuring herself with skepticism, almost.

"Oh, my Lord! Yes, I see him. He's with us tonight. He's—"

Had there been a vague flash off in the corner by the audience just before a strangled mumble and a little squeak of pain and surprise escaped Wanda O'Malley? Almost simultaneously, Jessica felt Wanda abruptly squeeze her hand, before the medium fell forward on the table with an incongruous thump.

Every light, every bit of power went dark; the house shuddered under the hand of the gale.

A funny, vaguely familiar, acrid smell drifted across to Jessica, but she was too preoccupied thinking to try to place it: *Ouch! That thump on the table would leave a bruise you'd need a whole case of makeup to conceal.*

The medium's iron grip had collapsed limply in Jess's hand.

Wow! Helen Hayes-quality performance! Ha! Felicia's "psychic energy" too much for you, Wanda?

Jess started to give her sister a conspiratorial smirk, but Liz was still staring into the audience. Wanda still wasn't moving. Absently, Jessica realized that James had anxiously called her name, and she'd called back she was fine, but her attention was on Wanda. The unmoving Madame Wanda.

In the back of her consciousness, Jess could hear Scott cursing the control panel, the murmuring of the audience, Jamie whimpering into her hands, Gerry calling to Jamie, Philip questioning, "What is going on?"

It hit Jessica: the power out meant that the recording would be spoiled. This was no act cooked up by Scott and Wanda. Freeing her hand, Jessica poked the silent woman and hissed, "Wanda."

Nothing. *What if she'd had a heart attack or a stroke?* Immediately, Jess half rose, her fingers seeking out the carotid artery of the fallen medium.

Nothing.

Jessica straightened, horrified. That was when moonlight flooded the room. James and Gerry had completely pulled back the curtains.

Jamie shrieked and Philip burst out, "Good Lord!"

Elizabeth's intake of breath was sharp as a cutlass slice.

Jessica looked back down at the object of their attention: Madame Wanda, face down on the table, a stain spreading across the once lovely satin of her gown.

"Good God!" Jessica breathed, only now realizing that the acrid odor was from gunpowder.

Chapter Twenty-Six

"Jessica, *are* you all right?"

James was standing beside her, a hand on her arm as she nodded toward Wanda's slumped form.

"Jesus," escaped him.

"I believe I said something to that effect," Jessica remarked, beginning to recover from the horror of her discovery.

As James checked the prone woman's pulse, Philip Carlyle stared at them speechless. Jamie sobbed on. Only Liz had changed, looking from the body to Jessica and James as if suddenly awakening *into* a nightmare.

Steadying herself against her chair, Jessica could now call in a take-charge voice, "Scott, you need to get over here."

Barely looking up, Scott Zimkiewicz snapped back, "What?! Can't you see I'm trying to salvage this—"

"*Now*, Scott," Jessica commanded.

"She means it, buddy," Elizabeth added, having found her voice at last.

"On the double," James finished.

Scott stopped and really looked at the table. His irritation dissolved into horror.

"Good Lord! What happened?" Flashlight guiding him, Scott sprinted around the equipment and across the room. "Did she pass out? Oh boy!"

"Yeah, from a lead Mickey Finn," Elizabeth replied as Scott reached them.

The murmuring of the audience members was abruptly silenced and the attention of those around the table was riveted by the slow, measured clapping of Bill Carlyle. Crossing to the table, he pronounced, "Bravo! Bravo! A splendid performance! Kudos to you all! What better way to generate high ratings than feigning an on-air assault? And all this audience participation lends a beautiful verisimilitude. You even had a squib hidden on her back explode on cue to fake the bleeding. I have to admit that I don't know how you managed that cunning whiff of cordite. Remarkable!"

Carlyle's audacity in the face of their anguish left even the living at the table speechless, momentarily. Philip recovered first and, on his feet, verbally lashed his brother, "How dare you?! I knew you were low, loathsome, but this is below despicable! The woman has been killed. She came trustingly into our family's home and she was murdered! The only thing phony here is your status as a human being."

Bill took a good look at Wanda's form and reached toward the bloodstain on her back, only to be arrested by James's hand. Surveying them, shocked, Bill finally uttered, "This can't be real. I don't believe . . . No!"

"Well, it is," Scott said shortly, "and I want to know what happened."

Jess looked around the table. Philip glowered at the man he wished were still gone. Jamie whimpered. Liz was unusually quiet, studying her magenta nails on the table. James regarded the others speculatively.

Surprising herself with her self-control under the circumstances, Jessica began, "It happened pretty fast. You heard her starting to channel whom Felicia allegedly claimed her persecutor was, then WHAM! She gave a little squeak and fell forward."

"But no one heard a gunshot, right?" Scott frowned, looking around the table, the room.

"You wouldn't if your shooter had used a silencer, and we all smelled the gun powder," James quietly explained.

"Who would have a silencer on Birdsong Island?" Philip protested disbelievingly.

"You might not need a manufactured device," James noted. "Even a potato might do."

"Shall I have Jeanne Rivers check the root cellar for a missing spud?" Philip inquired sarcastically.

James ignored him.

Bill's practical question was more troubling, "You know an awful lot about this sort of thing, Mr. Crawford."

Uneasiness flared in Jessica as Bill's question poked into James's background, but they were all diverted when Philip turned the tables on his brother, "Mr. Crawford, however, was not sitting in the best position to hit Madame Wanda in the back at this angle."

"Unless he stood up," Bill countered.

"But he didn't," came Gerry's voice as he approached the table. "I sat next to him. He didn't rise—though I sensed someone behind me might have. Of the three of you back there, I hardly think Guy or Maura would be taking potshots."

"Well, yes, maybe I did rise when the lights went out. I was startled," Bill quickly protested. Then, his eyes narrowed and he coolly proposed, "Maybe you'd like to check me for a weapon."

"Perhaps we should," Philip called his brother's play.

Bill refused to fold, lifting his arms to allow a search, almost sneering at them.

"That's not necessary," Scott began.

James disagreed, "Perhaps not, but it would go a long way to clear Mr. Carlyle—and move us away from each other's throats."

"Be my guest," Bill Carlyle offered confidently to James.

James hesitated. Jess suspected he debated whether he should give away any more of his expertise in this area. But she nodded to him. What were the odds anyone would dope out he was good at a pat down from his S.O.E. years?

As Jessica expected, her husband was quick and efficient. An abrupt nod to Bill before he turned to the others and pronounced, "He's clear."

"What did I tell you?" Bill smugly challenged them all but specifically stared at his brother.

Philip narrowed his eyes to point out, "It was pitch dark. He had ample time to get rid of a weapon before he came over here."

"By all means. Let's tear the room apart and search for my phantom gun—and the silencer. Don't forget the silencer," Bill smirked.

"By all means, let's not," James responded. "What we need to do is *not* disturb anything, so the authorities can do their job. That means Philip Carlyle needs to get on the blower and call the police."

"And someone needs to make sure that when he does, he doesn't try to hang this thing on me," Bill demanded.

"Whom else should we suspect?" Philip retorted. "You have a stake in keeping Wanda quiet. You were placed at the right angle for this shot."

"With an open window behind me at the right angle as well. With someone else who has a good motive to silence the medium. Someone who was not in the room tonight," Bill argued, looking down at Jamie.

"What?!" Jamie blurted at Bill's insinuation.

Gerry sharply defended the Blaskos, "Don't go throwing out unfounded suspicions that can only hurt the innocent!"

"I'm innocent and I refuse to be hurt by my brother's insidious accusations," Bill insisted. "We all need to face the truth: Vitus Blasko is likely the person this medium was about to accuse. He has a powerful motive to shut her up. He had the opportunity to stand outside the window and make damned sure she didn't expose him. That heavy curtain on the open window would provide perfect cover."

"No, no," Jamie protested. "My father is home, with Danvers. It couldn't be he."

Gerry had an arm around Jamie's shoulder, but before he could add to her family's defense, Bill pressed, "If that's true, we can call the Blasko residence for verification—if we can rely on Danvers, himself."

Before Gerry could haul off and paste Bill one, James ordered, "Stop this baiting immediately. It's the job of the police to straighten out this muddle; we're not making it any easier for them with our bickering." Turning to Philip, James instructed, "You need to ring the police now. We'll stay put here—unless you'd feel safer if one of us accompanies you."

Jess smiled at James with respect, then winked at Liz. Her sister quietly nodded approval.

"Certainly, Crawford," Philip agreed. "You're entirely correct. But I'm just fine. I'll go across to my private line in the library. I'll also call down to Jeanne and warn her about what's happened."

"She could have gone outside, too," Bill posited.

"Except I left her in her room off the kitchen, doing the books," Philip undercut his brother. "Some of the help were in the kitchen preparing our post-performance refreshments. They certainly would have seen her exit the room. And just to save you the trouble of more half-baked conjectures, there are no windows or outside doors to her room."

"This guy just loves to accuse people," Liz stated with a toss of her head in Bill's direction.

Jessica tag-teamed her sister, "I hope Eleanor Roosevelt has an alibi."

Bill grumbled and returned to his seat even as Philip left the room.

Turning to Jessica, James wryly apologized, "I'm afraid the adventure is only just beginning."

"Adventure!" came the sponsor's excited voice. In the tension of the exchanges at the table, Jessica only now realized what a relief it had been not to hear a peep from Ungerpreck until this moment. Now, though, he was emerging from terrified shock for the prospect of making a fast buck. He rushed down upon them and pounced on Scott with, "You better have gotten all this on wax! Think of the ratings! A real live murder on the air! A real live dead corpse!"

Jamie gasped, but before anyone else could make an indignant peep, Scott blew his stack: "That sinks it! Do you have *any* sense of decency? A woman was murdered! This girl here (pointing at Jamie) is in near hysterics. We have a murderer running loose!"

"Our ratings—"

"You can stick the ratings where—"

"I think he gets the point, Scott," Jessica jumped in, hoping to save her director's job even as she inwardly applauded his blow-up.

"I get that while my brother-in-law is sick, I'm holding the purse strings for this show. Just remember, my sister turned over power of attorney to me! What I say goes," rumbled the blowhard. "I want all of this, the death, the arguments and accusations—"

"You may control the purse strings, but electricity controls the power that runs the equipment," Scott set Ungerpreck straight. "When the lights quit, everything quit. You got bupkis on wax. But cheer up, now you won't have to go toe-to-toe with Standards and Practices over broadcasting a murder. So, we have no show for this week. Your pulling the plug on me or anyone at this point is entirely moot. Go sit down and try to figure out how *you're* going to explain to your brother-in-law how *you* may have put the skids on his program. The stockholders won't be too happy, either."

Scott turned on his heel and rejoined Vic and Chet to see if the sudden power outage had damaged the equipment. The sponsor cowed under the disapproval of those around the table, like most bullies when you push back hard enough. He wandered back to his seat. At his departure, Jessica said, "I can hardly wait for the police to show, but can we at least move away from, um, Madame Wanda?"

That was when the lights suddenly came on to everyone's relief.

"I wonder if we should thank Philip," Jessica proposed. "I'm not sure, though, if it's easier to face Madame Wanda in the light or the shadows."

When Philip returned, he explained that the Chief of Police and a deputy would be here shortly; and that, when he and Jeanne had gone to the cellar, they'd discovered two of the replacement fuses had been defective. Replacing them had been easy enough. It was just bad luck they'd gone out when they did. It had been fortunate for the shooter, though, having the table light to silhouette Madame Wanda.

Reference to the late medium prompted those around the table to return their attention to the body. Jamie and Jessica both automatically shuddered. Thoughtfully, Philip suggested, "Maybe we should move Wanda's body to the settee over there, out of the way, and give her some dignity."

"No," James warned. "If possible, we don't want to make any changes that might queer the investigation."

"Yes, yes, of course," Philip concurred. "Good thinking. We don't want to antagonize the Chief. I can't begin to tell you how difficult it was to convince him this wasn't some kind of publicity stunt, considering the circumstances. I also discussed all this with Jeanne privately. It wouldn't be wise to let the other servants know what happened, just yet."

Philip moved off to talk to Guy and Maura, who seemed to have been lost in the shuffle of the tension. Comforting Jamie, Gerry helped her up and guided her to a chair. That was Jessica's cue to say to her husband, "I bet you wish you were still back worrying about just ghosts."

She looked down at Wanda's corpse and shivered.

Chapter Twenty-Seven

Jessica and Elizabeth were settled in two chairs pushed back against the right wall of the room, James standing by Jessica's side. There, they had a fine view of everyone else as they waited for the authorities. To their left, on a settee not far from the open, padded doors, Gerry still kept company with a somewhat more composed Jamie. Philip Carlyle was by those two, lending a steadying influence. Jess gave him points for that.

Bill Carlyle was back in his old seat, arms crossed, expression calculating, especially when his eyes lit on his brother. He had the look of a man checked but not checkmated.

The sponsor was now surprisingly quiet, likely more surly than quiet. Jess considered: *Is he worried about explaining his failure to the board of directors and his brother-in-law? Or is he plotting to get back at Scott for putting him in his place? It would be a damned shame if Scott ended up being made the goat for all this.*

In the center of the room, slumped on the table, remained the late Wanda O'Malley, who clearly wasn't going anywhere—at least not bodily.

James was quiet, watching the room, waiting to see what would happen next, reading the situation carefully. *And I've pulled him into this muddle. Yet he doesn't seem jittery, even upset, just on point. Hmm, was there something in the old boy that still craved the challenge of sussing out where danger lurked, outsmarting an enemy?*

Jessica's attention shifted to her sister. *Why was Elizabeth's elegant brow furrowed, studying the same corner of the room that had drawn her attention during the séance? Nothing special there: James's empty chair; Bill Carlyle behind, his seating somewhat staggered; next to him, Maura and Guy quietly talking. The heavy curtain billowing only slightly now that the wind was no longer so furious. Behind the seating, next to the windows, a painting on the wall. That's all she wrote.*

"Will I ever be glad when this night is over."

Scott Zimkiewicz's words jolted Jessica from her dissatisfying ruminations. He'd joined them without her even noticing. Scott continued, trying to lift them out of the evening's real horror, "Hope this police chief shakes a leg and at least clears things up enough so I can call in to the network and let them know our planned broadcast for tomorrow evening is out of the question. Carlyle told me Winston had ordered him not to let even a whiff of this get out until he'd had a chance to do some investigating. Anyway, I'm looking forward to talking to the brass about as much as getting a root canal without any anesthetic."

Jessica smiled tightly. No one wanted to give in to the implications of someone pulling a trigger on Wanda being unknown and at large.

Ever the pragmatist, James took up the conversational torch with, "This Chief . . . ?"

"Winston," Scott supplied.

"Winston, yes. Have you met him? Do you know anything about him? Do you think he'll be effective?"

Scott nodded, "Yes, I met him when he let us research the case in his files. Martha Royle at the historical society, who knows everybody and his brother, everybody's grandfather's brother for that matter, vouches for him."

"This is a Patricia Wentworth-calibre mystery. Mightn't it prove too much for a small-town constable?" James speculated.

"Oh, he's no hick from the sticks," Scott quipped. "No, Winston came here after he retired as a detective in our hometown, good old New York."

Something fluttered in Jessica's memory at those words. Something familiar pushing its way through the clutter of maybe four years, as well as the horror of the evening. Then Scott brought back Jessica from her pursuit of a flickering recollection with, "Actually, Jess, I think you'll take a shine to him. He reminds me of one of your favorite movie stars."

Her attention snagged, Jess brightly conjectured, "Ronald Colman?"

James laughed, "If that were the case, I suspect Jessica would confess just to spend some quality time being grilled by such a charming fellow."

Scott grinned, then replied to Jess, "Right hair color, but a little 'short' of the mark."

"Claude Rains?" Jess posited, hopefully.

"Closer to the mark," Scott replied mischievously.

However, the director's face clouded as he glanced over at Edmund Ungerpreck.

Following his look, Jess asserted sympathetically, "Scott, you did the right thing, telling him where to get off. Aside from the fact it was the moral route to take, you were on the money about Standards and Practices. They'd never let you get away with broadcasting an actual murder."

James added, "I can well imagine the legal nightmare that would ensue between hampering a criminal investigation and the families' fury at being entangled in yet another murder."

"Ultimately, it'd be a nightmare for everyone, including your sulking 'friend' over there," Jessica finished. She glanced at Elizabeth, expecting her know-it-all sister to put in her two cents, but Liz was studying her hands in her lap, shut off from them all. *This is not right.*

Scott ruefully concluded, "So, no matter what, even if I've put us all on relief, at least I took the high road to get us there."

Jessica would have said something to assuage her friend's, and her own, fears about unemployment; however, that intention was nixed by the knocker's demanding assault on the front door.

Scott looked toward the door and pronounced, "Looks like you're about to discover your dream actor's twin."

Yet the gravity of the situation dampened Scott's humor as he watched Philip Carlyle, himself, on his way to answer the summons of the police. A few moments later, two uniformed men accompanied a tense Philip Carlyle into the music room. The younger one, clearly the deputy, was fairly tall, about James's height, with dark hair under his crowned cap, a square jaw, and strikingly long lashes for a guy. That passed Jessica's consciousness in a fraction of a second, for she was riveted by the appearance of the police chief. He was a notably shorter and older man whose dark hair, lived-in features, and slightly stocky build all immediately coalesced into her placing the name Jim Winston. Only back in 1943, it had been Detective Winston.

Surprised, Jessica blinked. *Movie star, huh, Scott!* Well, Winston's resemblance to a screen player had certainly caused Jess and Liz a fair share of awkwardness during a murder investigation four years ago. No, the visage that looked more as if it should be on the receiving end of a cream pie than intently examining a crime scene belonged to Detective Jim Winston, the man with Moe Howard's face.

Liz started to point, but Jess quietly pushed down her sister's hand and whispered, "Don't make a fuss. We didn't really do anything wrong back then. He probably won't even remember us."

James caught the maneuver, even if everyone else was too preoccupied with either the murder victim or the investigators. He gave Jess a questioning frown, but she shook her head with an expression that he knew her well enough to interpret as, "I'll explain later."

Watching Jess's reaction, Scott gave her a quick grin and, knowing it would probably be his last chance to crack wise for a while, whispered, "Told you: a favorite movie star of yours."

Before Jessica could counter that she was actually more of a Larry fan, Scott had shoved off to join the police and Philip Carlyle, helping fill in the blanks about the evening's goings on. So, Jess settled back to listen unobtrusively, glad she was off to the side. It wasn't as if she'd been a viable suspect back then. Really, there was no reason to think Winston had retired because he'd lost the case when Dick Streeter and the Feds took it over. He'd have no reason to blame her. She was just being gnawed by darned Catholic guilt

After Chief Winston introduced himself and his deputy Jackie Hudson, Jess narrowly watched the chief take in Scott's description of the events: trying to raise Felicia to hear about her fate, the room conditions, the squeak and collapse when Wanda had been on the verge of a revelation, the silencer theory, but no weapon found. Through it all, Winston wore the expression of a man looking at someone with three heads. When Scott finished, he snapped, "Are you people nuts?"

"You've never heard of our mystery program?" Scott returned defensively.

"Never listen to that stuff. Classical music, news, educational programs—that's it for me. The rest is just one vast wasteland." Winston nodded toward the body and added, "A pretty reckless show, if you ask me."

"This isn't exactly a regular occurrence," Scott bristled. "Anyway, our show's not for real."

"Your victim is real enough," Winston returned. "Someone took it seriously enough to put a slug in her. Now, suppose you stop making speeches and answer some questions."

Scott's mouth went into a tight line, but he knew better than to dig himself in deeper.

Winston gave Philip Carlyle a thoughtful look. Jess wondered if the chief was about to chastise him for getting involved in this nonsense. He didn't, though. He might have thought it a waste of time, or he might have figured it impolitic to try and take to the woodshed a man with so much clout. Whatever the case, Chief Winston surveyed the room before facing Scott and Philip again to question, "This everyone who was in the room at the time? This where they were when she was shot?"

"This is everybody," Philip answered. "But some of us have moved around since. Surely, you can understand why no one wanted to remain at the table with . . . her."

Winston nodded, not saying anything at first. His studied gaze went to the corner of the room, almost directly behind Wanda's slumped form. Bill and Guy were in his line of sight. He snorted thoughtfully. Then the dark curtain billowed behind them slightly and the house creaked. Winston gave Philip a thoughtful look before asking, "That window behind the curtain open then, too? When she was shot?"

"Yes," Philip answered curiously. His eyes went quickly to Jamie and back again. Jess saw that Winston had noticed, but he only said, "A windy night to leave the windows open. Cold, wasn't it? And wasn't the wind a little noisy?"

"The transmitter and recording equipment raise a lot of heat," Scott explained. "We found that out at last week's recording session. As for the wind, we found a way to adjust for it, so it just added ambiance."

Winston nodded toward the body and commented, "Looks like you got more ambiance than you bargained for." Cutting off the affronted comeback forming on Scott's lips, he turned to the others in the room, especially those still in the chairs, and announced, "Okay, I want you all back in your positions when the victim collapsed and the lights went out."

"No!"

The sharp, terrified refusal had issued from Jamie Blasko.

Chief Winston exchanged a glance with his taller deputy before asking, "Something wrong—Miss Blasko, isn't it?"

Jamie anxiously tightened her lips, so Gerry spoke for her, "She was holding Wanda O'Malley's hand when she was killed. She's very sensitive. You can't expect her to sit down with a corpse. Hasn't she been through enough?"

Winston again shared a look with his deputy before observing, "I'd think that sensitive a soul wouldn't want to be involved in a spook show, even if that spook were her mamma."

"She wants to know the truth," Gerry shot back. "She wants her mother to have justice and her father to be cleared."

Gerry's reproof prompted Jim Winston to lean his head to the side speculatively and note, "Hmmm, that's funny. I don't see her father here, anywhere. Doesn't *he* want to hear his name cleared, to find out the truth about her mother, his wife?"

Jessica wondered whether the chief's unspoken implication was, "Or maybe he knew the truth and decided he'd better put a lid on Madame Wanda, permanently."

However, Winston only asked, "So, where is your father this evening, Miss Blasko?"

Surprisingly, the sensitive Jamie spoke up firmly, "My father hasn't been well these past few days. He's home, resting with our man Danvers there to care for him. I'm representing the family tonight. You can phone our home and check for yourself."

Wow! There was more steel in those words than I'd ever expected out of Jamie. Good for you, kid! Jess inwardly applauded. She looked up at James, who gave her a little nod to show he'd also been impressed by Jamie. Yet, there was a slight wrinkle to his forehead that Jessica couldn't quite interpret.

Winston certainly wasn't daunted, for he easily replied to the younger woman, "I'll just take you up on that, Miss Blasko." Turning, he instructed, "Jackie, I want you to call in Harvey Cagney; have him take a ride out to the Saunders' place and check on Mr. Blasko. Make sure Blasko's where he's supposed to be and has been all night. Tell Harve we'll be over to ask some questions once we're done here, so he should hold the guy there in the comfort of his house." Returning to Jamie, Winston queried, "Does that sound square to you, Miss Blasko?"

Jessica was impressed with the defiance in Jamie's eyes as she replied, "I've, we've, nothing to hide. Be my guest, though I'm not crazy about you disturbing my father when he's finally resting. You remember about his trouble earlier this week. He's still recovering."

Winston shrugged, "What can I say? Lady Justice makes demands on us all." However, he pondered momentarily before offering, "Tell you what, though. No sense making anyone keep close company with a stiff. For now, I want only the people in the audience to take their original seats. Zimkiewicz, you and your crew go back to where you were at the equipment."

"Smart move, Chief," approved the handsome young deputy solemnly.

"Jackie? You still here? I told you to put that call in and get Cagney back on duty. Shake a leg! Vamoose! I need you back here for questioning these folks."

Deputy Hudson fairly skedaddeled out of the room.

At least Winston hadn't called him a chowderhead, Jess mused. Still, she was more concerned with exactly what Chief Winston had planned for those around the séance table. He informed them.

"Anyway, the four of you who were around the table, sit tight on this side of the room." Winston pointed to where Jessica remained with the others, adding, "Wait a minute, I got Mr. Carlyle and Miss Blasko down as at the table. Who were the other two?"

"The Minton sisters," Philip supplied. "Over there, right where you want them. Jessica's husband will have to move, though."

Knowing she was being silly, Jessica's heart still skipped at being named to Winston. Happily, Winston looked squarely at them and said, "Yeah, those two. Okay." Not a shred of recognition as he signaled James and Gerry, "You guys, back where you were during the 'séance.'"

He didn't roll his eyes on the last word, but his tone was clear enough.

James squeezed Jessica's shoulder and said, "I'm sure it will all be over soon enough."

"Minton, Minton." The chief was unexpectedly rolling the name through his consciousness and out his mouth. He pivoted back to the sisters. "Actress. On the stage."

Winston was scrutinizing Jess and Liz. "1943, September. Frederick Bromfield. I remember you two. That was my case. Had to turn it over to the Feds. The biggest one I never got to solve. And here we all are again. And you never said a word."

"Well, son of a gun," Jessica decided to come clean, sort of. "If this isn't just a kick in the pants! What are the odds?! You say they took that case away from you, Detective, I mean Chief Winston? What a crying shame! Darned Feds! I wonder how it all came out?"

"And we had nothing to do with the guy's murder," Liz added brightly. "Not that you would think we had. How could we? Why would we?"

Jessica so wanted to throttle her sister, but she caught sight of James doing "the maths" to figure out how this reunion played into his own bait-and-switch gambit in the fall of 1943. He immediately pulled the Mintons' fat from the fire with, "Chief, I'm sure this is a lovely trip down memory lane, but can't it wait until after you've finished your investigations? It's late . . ."

"Who're you?" Winston cut James off with an appraising look.

"James Crawford. Just a guest," James answered pleasantly. "I'm married to Jessica Minton. Elizabeth is my sister-in-law."

"Your name's Crawford, and she's Minton? Some kinda modern marriage? Streamlined?" was Winston's doubtful assessment.

"If you like," James remained determinedly affable. "So, I'll just take my seat back with the other auditors."

"Yeah, sure. Make it snappy," Winston replied, turning away as Hudson returned to assure him that Cagney was on his way to the Saunders' place. James took advantage of the distraction to reassure Jess with a quick kiss before returning to his chair.

The auditors were all reseated as they had been during the séance, and Winston had each identify him- or herself, along with briefly explaining the person's connection to tonight's goings on. Jessica wasn't exactly sure why he skipped around rather than work his way through the order they sat in. Nevertheless, the process was quick and efficient; Jess could clearly perceive Winston's careful appraisal of each individual. He even put Ungerpreck in his place. Well, it was quick until Winston got to Bill Carlyle, who seemed to be stewing worse the longer he waited. *Or maybe that was*

Winston's plan. Cranky, impatient people had less control over their tongues.

Winston's first words to Bill were, "So, you're the long-lost brother I heard about. Twenty years is a long time for a vacation, bub, isn't it?"

Jessica glanced from Bill to Philip and back. Philip was more than a little pleased to see his brother on the spot, though he was too controlled to gloat.

Bill, however, refused to be rattled, even if he had been impatient, answering, "I was under the definite impression I wasn't wanted here when I left."

"But twenty years? So, what makes you believe you're suddenly welcome now? I don't see any fatted calf laid out."

"Let's just say by the time I got homesick, U-boats in the South Atlantic kept me from taking a cruise ship from Rio, and my luck was on too much of a downturn for me to afford flying. Before you ask, I'll add that a Carlyle has too much dignity to hitchhike or ride the rails."

"Mmm, and since you left under a cloud at Felicia Blasko's disappearance, maybe you were afraid to come back?" Winston suggested thoughtfully.

"Why should I be afraid, Chief?" Bill shrugged, again that lilting tone that always ended vaguely sarcastic, or menacing-sarcastic this time. "I left before she disappeared. You might as well blame my dear sister Gladys. She was the only one of us in the house that night. I'm sure Philip can offer evidence that he was in his office all night. Anyway, how can you accuse me of foul play when there's no body?"

Winston answered calmly, "No one's accusing you of anything, Mr. Carlyle. We're just trying to piece together all the facts. So, you'd say that you would have no reason to want to silence the medium if she came up with some new information on what happened to Felicia Blasko."

"I don't believe in this talking-to-the-spirits eyewash," Bill scoffed. "I only participated to make sure that no slander against me or my family was bandied about."

"I didn't say anything about talking to spirits," Winston corrected Bill in an easy tone. "I wouldn't be any surprised if an investigation of this Wanda O'Malley turned up that her contacts were all the earthly, not supernatural, variety. She may have come across some info in her travels that could put you—or someone else here—on the hot seat. Did you ever meet her before?"

The last question was slipped in so smoothly that it caught Bill unawares. He started, one might say, uneasily. However, Bill Carlyle was no chump. Channeling his unease into a facsimile of indignation, he retorted, "Certainly not! I may have been low on cash, but I have always had enough dignity not to chum around with carnival con artists."

"Wanda O'Malley was hardly that," Philip insisted. "She impressed me with her talents and honesty. She even had recommendations from prominent people in Portsmouth. Scott Zimkiewicz can testify to that. You can't trust a word out of my brother's mouth, Chief Winston. Just open your eyes and look at who is almost directly behind a woman shot in the back. Surely, it wouldn't be Mr. or Mrs. Robinson, two actors who scarcely knew Miss O'Malley. But Bill has every reason, I believe, to silence any revelations she might make. Everyone who knew him remembers how spoiled he was and how vicious his temper was. They also must remember how he pursued Felicia and lacked the self-control to react to her rejection with anything but murderous rage."

"You damned liar!" flared Bill with cold fury, fastening a Basilisk glare on his brother. But he transformed that look into something less deadly but no less powerful to face Winston. "Chief, why not ask my brother if his determination to vilify me has anything to do with a recently discovered will from our late sister that gives me controlling power over our family holdings. Wouldn't it be convenient for him to eliminate the competition via the hangman's noose? Rather casts shade over the credibility of his accusations, doesn't it? Besides, where's 'my' murder weapon? At his insistence, they 'frisked' me and found nothing. Only children believe they can kill with a finger gun."

"Zat so?" Winston asked Philip Carlyle. Jack Hudson was violently scribbling away through the whole interchange.

"Yes, yes, but he could have easily secreted the weapon somewhere in the room. The lights were out. It was pitch dark—"

"Did anyone see a muzzle flash?" Winston queried, his careful gaze scanning each face.

"No," Philip slowly admitted, "but with a silencer . . ."

Winston shook his head, and Bill Carlyle seized the moment, insisting, "We were so intensely concentrating on the séance that if the flash were from behind us and outside it might not have registered with anyone."

Winston paused to consider Bill's theory, so the prodigal Carlyle pressed his point, "Through the window. The open window behind us. The line of fire still works, I think. In the dark and in the excitement of being riveted to the performance, who would notice someone outside?"

"And just who do you think would have been hanging around on a night like this, waiting to plug the medium?" Winston drew Bill on, not without skepticism.

Jessica felt as if she were watching a tennis match, her head shifting swiftly from one man to the other as each volleyed arguments back and forth. Bill's turn.

"A desperate man," his words were level and cool. "An unstable man could have waited outside, thinking only in the moment, determined to silence the revelation of his guilt. We all know that man is the other significant suspect in Felicia's disappearance: Vitus Blasko."

"How dare you!" Jamie accused, her eyes fiery.

"You bastard!" Gerry hurled furiously, on his feet and turning around to lower over Bill Carlyle.

Jess saw James rise and put a restraining hand on Gerry's arm, even as the sponsor cowered and Bill stood up defiantly.

"Okay, simmer down. Sit," commanded Winston. Bill and Gerry hesitated, but backed down. Winston gave James a quiet nod to be at ease. James nodded back, resuming his seat. Despite the *sturm und drang*, Jess couldn't help a little smile of pride in him.

"Truth is ugly, but can't be denied," Bill stated coolly.

"You're forgetting," Jamie returned with steel in her voice, "that my father couldn't have been 'lurking' outside. He was home with Danvers all this time."

That was when Jeanne Rivers burst in, eye-catching in a fitted periwinkle-blue dress. But the dress was not nearly as attention-grabbing as her agitated words: "Chief Winston, your Deputy Cagney just called. You've got to get back to him right away! He says he's at the Saunders house. Danvers is out cold, drugged, and Dr. Blasko is nowhere to be seen!"

Chapter Twenty-Eight

Jamie cried, "No, that can't be!"

James raised both brows at Jessica, and she knew that as soon as this night was over he was going to try and hustle both her and Liz the hell out of town. She was 95% with him, but that other 5% wanted to know what the dickens was going on. That 5% wasn't any more convinced of Vitus Blasko's guilt than his daughter was.

Bill Carlyle was displaying the smuggest of smiles, which Jess would have loved to wipe off his pan. While Chief Winston was giving Jackie Hudson orders to call in the other off-duty deputy to bring in Blasko for questioning, Philip Carlyle looked grim. Now, Winston was grilling Jeanne: Who was she? Where was she during the murder? Had she or the other help seen anything suspicious? When he seemed fairly satisfied, if not exactly delighted, with Jeanne's answers, the chief instructed the rest of the group to wait in the drawing room while he and Hudson did a thorough search of this room. As the group was escorted from the room by Hudson, the coroner arrived to give Wanda's corpse a preliminary exam. Jessica had to practically drag off James, who, to Hudson's annoyance, lingered by the music room doors, betraying his penchant to discover some order underlying chaos.

Eventually, it was hurry up and wait to be interviewed in Philip's study, after Winston and Hudson finished in the music room. The folks at the table up first, Jess and Elizabeth were done and ushered off to their rooms fairly early in the game—no interchanges allowed with the others still waiting: a mingled blessing and curse. She could go collapse in her room, but she wouldn't see James until Winston worked his way through the audience to him. Jess had last glimpsed her guy by the French doors, lighting up a cigarette Gerry offered. Smoking was never a good sign.

So, here Jessica lay on her bed in her slate-blue pajamas, velvet gown tossed across a chair. The massive Carlyle mansion creaked under assault from a new battalion of winds blowing in the rain Elizabeth had predicted.

The crack of that rain on the windows set Jessica frowning. The people burned out by wild fires would have given their eyeteeth for this storm a week or so ago. Now, it only served to punish this old house. Maybe to punish Vitus Blasko if he wandered outside, if he hadn't been taken in by the local gendarmerie.

Jessica turned her face to the storm-splattered wall of windows and its distorted reflection of her room over the darkness beyond. Could she believe Blasko had killed his wife and then silenced Wanda to hide the first crime? *Poor job of it, if that had been his plan. Yet Jamie's anguished search for him a few days before certainly didn't make him appear all that stable, let alone clear thinking. Would he "go along quietly" if and when he was picked up? So, who had shot that silenced gun? How the hell should I know!*

But unhappy speculation continued taunting Jess.

Aside from James, three guys stood out with the military training to take an accurate shot. Philip had been at the table, ruling him out. For Pete's sake, he had wanted Wanda there in the first place. Gerry had sat in the row in front of everyone and definitely wasn't the killer type, even if he wanted to protect Jamie from devastating news. Vitus Blasko, however, could have motivation and could have been standing outside that window.

A glance at her bedside clock: *12:30, officially Halloween. Boo! Well, there's been enough trickery for a lifetime tonight. When do the treats start?*

A knock on her door. Jessica sat up so eagerly her exhausted head almost spun. *James? Back at last? Now that was a treat. But would he knock? Of course, you dope! When was the last time you didn't lock your door in this House of Dracula?*

"Jess? Are you still up?"

Elizabeth? Elizabeth with jitters in her voice, but definitely.

"Coming, Liz," Jess called, swinging her legs over the edge of her bed and hustling to open the door.

Elizabeth's hair was down, though never a mess, curling dark at her shoulders and pulled gently back from her face with combs. That face betrayed as much jumpiness as her voice. She moved swiftly through the doorway, the full skirts of her elegant royal-blue, quilted housecoat sweeping along. Before Jessica could say a word, Elizabeth surveyed the room and noted, "James isn't back, yet. Fine. Maybe just as well, considering."

Closing the door behind her sister, Jessica hesitated before pressing, "'Considering?' Considering what, Liz?"

To Jess, Elizabeth seemed to whirl around, but it was just the effect of her full skirts. Her words were dramatic enough without the sartorial emphasis, though she spoke levelly, "I have to talk to you, Jessica, about what I saw tonight. I knew *you* would believe me."

The possibilities jumbling in Jessica's head momentarily silenced her. *Had Elizabeth seen the murderer?! The flash of the gun muzzle? Had she told Winston already?* Finally, Jess managed, "Okay, Liz. Let's hear it."

"It's almost too incredible for me to believe, myself," Liz fretted, clasping and rubbing her hands before her like a *Vogue* version of Lady Macbeth.

"What?!" Jessica demanded.

"Well, it's—"

A rap on the door interrupted, followed by, "Jessica, it's James."

"What is this, Grand Central Station?!" Liz flared.

Jessica pushed out an impatient hand at her sister, muttering something about it being James's room, too! But, to be honest, she was dying to hear what Elizabeth was dying to tell her. So she dashed to open the door, nearly yanked a startled James Crawford into the room, then slammed the door behind him.

"Ah, hello, Liz?" James managed, unsettled.

Pointing a finger at Jessica, Liz warned, "If God, Himself, knocks, don't interrupt me!"

"This sounds serious," James noted curiously. "Odd, but serious."

Elizabeth ignored him, clearly ranking James far below God, and continued, "I saw something during the séance . . . peculiar . . . it frightened me."

"You told the chief?" James began.

"No," Elizabeth replied abruptly. "He'd never believe me. I know Jessica would. You might, if you weren't afraid."

James gave his sister-in-law a strange look, but bypassed her last statement to get down to practicalities: "Elizabeth, if you know something that might clear up this case, you have to tell the police. Aside from the fact it's the right thing to do, you don't want to get yourself in a fix by obstructing the investigation. Leo would tell you that. I'm afraid that you ladies have skirted the law too often for your luck to hold out now."

"I don't think what I saw will help solve the case," Elizabeth answered cryptically, "exactly."

"That statement certainly takes the biscuit," James frowned. "If it's irrelevant, then why have you gotten yourself in such a twist?"

Jessica ignored her husband's question. Knowing her sister's other other-worldly experiences on the island, she speculated carefully, "Elizabeth, was it when you kept looking past Wanda, toward that corner of the room and the windows near Bill and James."

"So you *did* see someone," James insisted.

Liz took a deep breath and coolly corrected, "Some*thing*."

"Some . . . thing? Oh, Elizabeth," James shook his head. "You're not trying to tell me you saw Felicia Blasko's ghost? Honestly? I suppose she pointed a spectral finger of accusation at someone?"

Elizabeth was too intent on getting her story out to notice the tinge of anxiety in James's sarcasm. Jessica caught it immediately. Her questioning eyes seemed to make him realize he'd revealed something he'd rather not have. He shut up.

Before Jessica could press him, Elizabeth was elaborating.

"It was fuzzy, no, I guess ethereal, like a wraith, and it wavered and flickered in that corner. It seemed to move toward Bill Carlyle, or maybe it was moving toward the window where Vitus Blasko could have fired a gun."

"Could you see a face?" Jessica questioned.

Liz shook her head, then answered, "No, just a fog, a misty kind of swirling."

James suggested reasonably, sarcasm gone, "If it was near the open window, it might have been a fog from outside—or a temperature discrepancy turning moisture into a mist."

"But *I* didn't see it, James," Jessica disagreed. "I saw Elizabeth looking. I followed her stare because I was curious—and I saw nothing. I might not have a spiritualist's vision, but I do know fog when I see it." Jess faced Liz and said, "When you sensed something before, it was always around Jamie.

Why wasn't it hovering over her at the table—not that I'm complaining that it stayed across the room."

Elizabeth shrugged, "Can't tell you that, kid. I just know it seemed determined to stick to that part of the room, then vanished right after the power cut out."

"It stayed in the same spot the whole time?" Jess questioned. "As if it wanted to draw our attention to someone or something? It never moved?"

"Well, not exactly." Elizabeth seemed reluctant to go further, but she finally added, "Just for a moment, this, I don't know, 'tendril' seemed to shoot out in a point . . . at him." She jerked her head toward James.

"Me?!" James was genuinely taken aback. But he quickly recovered to inquire coolly, "I suppose your ephemeral visitor is accusing *me* of being the murderer?"

"Don't be silly," Liz retorted. "You were in England when Felicia died. Solid alibi. Anyway, why would *you* need to put a lid on Wanda, permanently?"

"Why, indeed, Liz," James dryly concurred. "Now, maybe you'd like to hear my interpretation of your visionary experience. And I must give you credit for coming up with something that would put Coleridge's worser visions to shame."

"Oh, do proceed, Professor," Elizabeth replied with more than a touch of acid.

"Just this, Elizabeth." James began, his now patient tone suggesting he regretted antagonizing her. "You're a creative and imaginative person. You were keyed up by the heightened emotions, the music, the medium's incantatory words. You likely hypnotized yourself into seeing what you'd expected to see, what you've likely seen in movies. Please don't upset Jessica any more with such tales, considering the effect this place already has had on her."

Jessica couldn't help realizing that Elizabeth's description of the preternatural phenomena bore an unsettling resemblance to the sinister ghost in *The Uninvited*, a film both she and her sister had enjoyed.

Elizabeth read the doubt in her face and groused, "Swell, now you're siding with him, after all I've told you about what I saw before. You believed me then—and you've hardly been immune to mysterious influences here, have you, oh, beautiful dreamer?"

That last sentence was a sucker punch that left Jessica fumbling, "But you said, thought, it was all nerves causing bad dreams."

"I didn't want anyone around here getting the idea that Felicia might tell you something dangerous for you to know. I also didn't want to scare you," Liz revealed.

"You're doing a bang-up job of not scaring her now," James snapped, putting a much welcomed arm around Jessica as she reeled under her sister's words.

Liz fastened a fiery eye on James but pointed out coolly, "Are you worried about her or yourself? You can't completely hide it; all this ghost palaver gives you the willies. You try to act all logical-explanation-for-everything. But I can see in the back of your eyes that there's something about all this that gets to you. What are you afraid of?"

James dropped his arm from Jess and shot back, maybe more sharply than he'd intended, "I've been through a war, seen things that would still that tart tongue of yours, Elizabeth. Don't give me any guff about spooks or fake mediums being my secret fear."

Jessica's instincts kicked in and she took charge: "All right, both of you, knock it off this minute. I won't have the two people I love best at each other's throats. Remember what Ben Franklin said about hanging together or being hanged separately."

"Maybe an American revolutionary isn't the best choice to persuade a chap from across the pond," James allowed dryly. He extended a hand to his sister-in-law, asking, "Bury the hatchet?"

"Where?" Liz returned skeptically. Nevertheless, she took her brother-in-law's hand, shook it, and said, "I just don't want you implying I'm a nutcase. I know what I saw. I know this place is not a good place."

"That last statement is something we can all agree on," James smiled wanly. "Of course, if you both are interested in some intel on the crime, having nothing to do with visitors from beyond, I have something interesting for you."

"You do!" the sisters blurted together. They exchanged annoyed looks, then Elizabeth insisted, "Spill! What were you waiting for, an engraved invitation?!"

Jess gave her sister a backhand on the shoulder and cracked, "Maybe he needed a chance to get a word in edgewise." She smiled at James, adding, "But do spill, mister."

"When I was going into the foyer after my interview with Winston in the study, that Deputy Hudson . . ."

"The cute one with the long lashes," Liz confirmed.

James gave Liz a quizzical look but continued, "Yes, the very one, came rushing through, soaked to the bone. Before they could close the study door, I heard him say he'd found a gun outside, on the terrace."

"The murder weapon?" Jessica pressed.

James clarified, "He was circumspect, didn't make that claim. They can't know for sure until after a ballistics test."

"Sure," Elizabeth snorted. "The Carlyle crew is famous for strewing weapons around the grounds. I guess that closes the book on Vitus Blasko taking a shot from outside."

Jessica countered, "Unless Bill Carlyle took a shot from inside, then tossed the gun out the window in the darkness and confusion, just to create the suspicion you bought hook, line, and sinker." She asked James, "Did they say anything about finding a silencer on the gun?"

"Or a potato?" Elizabeth archly added.

Letting that crack slide, James answered his wife's question, "Not that I know of. They closed the doors, and I thought it wouldn't do to chance being caught with my ear to the door."

"That would take a bit of explaining," Jessica agreed. "So, if it is the murder weapon, they can get a set of fingerprints, unless the murderer wore gloves."

"I certainly didn't see any gloves on Bill Carlyle this evening. He'd have to be pretty slick to slip them on and off, then hide them without anyone noticing," Elizabeth insisted.

"You really want to hang this on poor Dr. Blasko, don't you," Jessica protested.

"You're awfully determined to defend him," her sister countered.

"All right, ladies, both of you, break it up. I'm sorry I brought this up," James stepped in, carefully. "It's late. We're all tired, done in by a ghastly evening." The wind howled past the window, and James tilted his head in its direction to acknowledge this proof of his assertion. "At any rate, it's time we all turned in. There'll be plenty of opportunity for useless speculation in the morning. Maybe our intrepid lawmen will have the case sewn up by then."

"That was irony, wasn't it?" Liz asked suspiciously.

"Yes, it was, Elizabeth. Now I'll walk you to your room," James replied.

"Oh, don't worry about me," she answered with a knowing smile. "I brought this along."

From her housecoat pocket she withdrew possibly the world's longest and sharpest hat pin.

Jess grimaced and James raised an eyebrow to comment, "Nevertheless, I'd better accompany you back. I'd hate to think a hapless guest on the way to the W.C. might startle you and end up impaled on the wall."

Elizabeth shot James a skeptical look but shrugged and kissed Jess on the cheek, saying, "Okay, good night, kid. Try to catch forty winks. We'll continue this tomorrow."

"Sure, Liz—and try to send my husband back to me unpunctured. I'm kinda attached to the guy."

"I'll do my best." Turning to James, Elizabeth said, "Okay, toots, let's hit the road. The kid needs her beauty sleep. Just try not to 'needle' me." She gave her brother-in-law an evil smile as she tipped the point with her finger.

James turned to Jessica and remarked, "Tell me again why I wasn't bats in the head to marry into your family."

Chapter Twenty-Nine
Monday, November 3rd

The sky was a brilliant blue, with wisps of white scudding across. No more grey billows of smoke hiding the sun, no more burning orange sunsets and dawns. But the smell of acres of incinerated forests still hung over them as Jessica and James sat together on a blanket on the small beach below the Carlyle mansion.

"The tide rushes in," James distractedly commented.

Jessica added, "I wish it would wash away our cares."

Silence hung over them again. To their left, the island jutted jaggedly into the choppy blue-grey of the Piscataqua. A flock of Eider ducks bobbed on the white-tipped, wind-rippled waters. An occasional Merganser or Goldeneye duck pierced beneath the waves to emerge unexpectedly somewhere distant. A red-tailed hawk soared overhead; circled; then, with a piercing cry, sought its lunch in the woods.

Leaning against her husband's lean body beneath his dark wool jacket, Jessica Minton tried to enjoy the riverside spectacle on this crisp autumn afternoon. She was glad of the warmth from her fawn wool jacket and dark brown slacks. However, something more than the lower temperature and the breeze off the open water put a shiver in her body and her spirit. When Jess tucked her head against James's cheek, he pressed back briefly but said nothing. He had been saying nothing, or next to it, ever since that late night confab with Liz in their room. This was his thinking, or rather brooding, mode. Despite her hopes, Jess hadn't been able to draw him out this afternoon. She knew that as much as he loved her, James would not speak until he'd thrashed out whatever was deviling him. Well, he'd certainly had a lot to digest these past few days after Wanda O'Malley's murder.

Vitus Blasko was under orders not to leave town. According to scuttlebutt, he'd appeared genuinely horrified on hearing of the medium's death, but the chief seemed to suspect that Jess and her colleagues weren't the only ones capable of putting on a performance. Worse, Blasko's explanation for the collapse of his alibi left a lot to be desired. He'd claimed that Danvers had fallen asleep before finishing his usual blend of after-dinner tea. Restless and melancholy over the anniversary of his wife's death, Blasko had left his snoozing butler to follow his yearly custom of visiting the cemetery. Unfortunately for him, there were no witnesses, not even a conscientious spirit trying to get the jump on the holiday-haunting crowd.

Still, Blasko had come up clean on the paraffin test, as had Bill Carlyle, after Philip used his family influence to put a rush on getting the results. Elizabeth, drawing on Leo McLaughlan's occasional indulgence in shop talk, had quietly pointed out to Jess and James that the results might work toward clearing Bill, but not necessarily Vitus. A meticulous scrubbing with soap and water could remove gunpowder residue, especially if the weapon was in good enough condition not to leave many powder particles. And that didn't take into account the possibility that the gunman had worn gloves. Still, no gloves were found by the police hidden in or around the music room. After Vitus Blasko had been completely cooperative about a search without a warrant of his home for gloves, nothing incriminating had been turned up there.

So now, Chief Winston was having a search done on the gun's history of ownership, while waiting for the ballistics test to confirm it as the murder weapon. It hadn't helped the foreign-born Blasko to have fought in the Great War with the Austrian-Hungarian forces, for whom that WWI-vintage Steyr M1912 was standard issue. However, with so many war trophies of various vintages floating around the country only two years after the last European conflict, it wasn't *conclusive* evidence against him. Philip had, apparently, used up his favors getting a rush put on the paraffin test, so he'd been unable to grease the wheels of investigation here. Further, Winston had widened his probe into Wanda's past for former "clients" who might be nursing a grudge against her. Nevertheless, no one was going back to New York until Winston was completely satisfied he wouldn't need them close at hand to settle this case.

All this info came via Philip Carlyle, whose prominence on the island made him privy to Chief Winston's reports. That must have stuck in Winston's craw, having to dance attendance on the island's big cheese when he had an important job to do. He must have longed for the days of big-city politics after this dose of the more personal corrosiveness of dealing with impatient small-town big-wigs.

An osprey suddenly plunged from the sky, snared a fish in its talons, then skimmed back into the blue. Survival of the fittest, according to Mr. Herbert Spencer. It was Nature, but that didn't mean Jess always had to like it, especially considering how a murderer had outsmarted everyone to snuff out Felicia, then done the dirty deed to Wanda O'Malley to ensure his survival.

"Cold, love?" James inquired, noticing the shiver Jess's thoughts had given her.

"He speaks!" Jessica tried to joke them both out of the blue devils.

"Tried" was exactly the right word, for James didn't follow his usual habit of kidding back. He appeared on the verge of saying more, but returned to his troubled silence. Jessica frowned. *This was different from his brooding over the war, when he tried to protect her from the trauma he'd known. This time, he seemed to want to tell her something but just couldn't.* Guiltily, Jessica recognized that coming to this place of unquiet spirits had stirred something inside him that did not want to be mastered.

"James," Jessica began, sitting up and shifting so he had to face her, "You need to tell me what's eating you. You and this ghost thing always used to be a kind of joke between us, but since you've been here, since the murder, especially since Liz talked about her wraith and you, it's escalated. You need to tell me what's going on. If you shut me out, I can't help."

"What makes you think you *can* help? How do you know if I open up that you'll *want* to help me?"

There was a glint of anger in her husband's eyes that Jess rarely saw. For a moment, it unnerved her, until she realized that it wasn't directed at her but himself.

"I know," Jessica said firmly. "I know how I feel about you."

"*Do* you know me? Everything? Maybe there are some things I've done, or failed to do, that might make you think differently."

"You mean like what you had to do in the war?" Jessica proposed carefully, not knowing exactly what James's dark secret was, only that he was not a man who was unforgivable.

James smiled bitterly, reflecting before answering, "In the war, I had reasons to do whatever I did. I had very little choice. Others depended on me. But this . . . I had choices and I made selfish ones, cowardly ones. Ones of which I'm ashamed. People died because of me, but I hadn't any higher responsibilities to excuse my actions—only my selfishness and fear.

"I really had managed to bury it, though, pretty well, for years. I just needed to avoid anything that would trigger emotions. I buried a lot during the war. But this place, these people just ripped down all my walls. Then there was your sister's vision: that made the whole damned thing clear to me. I can't bury my past, my guilt anymore. It's, they're coming back to confront me."

Struggling to make heads or tails of James's revelations, Jessica puzzled, "Wait. 'They' are coming back? James, are you saying that Elizabeth was right, that you are, well, haunted?"

"On the nose," James grimly replied.

"Well, I'll be," Jessica breathed, sitting back.

"I take it you don't believe me," James dryly commented.

"No, I believe you. I definitely believe *you*. It's just, well, so real, so immediate when you say it. I mean, with Elizabeth, I don't doubt her, but the concept is vague, distant. With *you*, though, you're my other half. It's like being hit in the stomach. But, wait, who on earth, so to speak, would haunt *you*? *Why* would anyone haunt you? You're such a good guy."

"Good guys do bad things, make unfortunate choices, delude themselves into thinking they aren't really hurting others when facing up would cost them more than they want to pay, especially when they're young," James quietly explained, guilt tensing his features.

"Okay," Jess allowed, "but you can't stop there. I need to know the whole story to help you."

James reflected before answering, "I imagine now that I've opened the door, hiding things now won't do any less damage than coming clean about why I'm not quite the prince you thought."

"I never said you were a prince, mister," Jessica said, trying to lessen his burden with a light touch.

"No," James smiled wanly, "that much is true." He squeezed her shoulder quickly, almost guiltily, then patted his jacket pocket to say, "This is the time a bloke could really stand a smoke, but I seem to have left them elsewhere. Ah well, I wouldn't want my wife hacking and coughing her way through my confession. Here goes."

Jessica put a hand on her husband's arm, and he gave her another resigned smile. He began, "You know I come from a mill town in the north, Milton Northern. You know I was a scholarship boy at University, thanks to the Thornton Fund."

Jessica nodded.

"I've told you a bit about my family; my Da was a mill worker. Ma Mère was an immigrant from France, a teacher who couldn't teach because no one would hire a foreigner when there were enough good Englishmen about. Once she married, the point was moot."

James paused, hesitating to take a more difficult step.

"And she loved roses," Jessica added, trying to put her husband at ease.

"Indeed, she did," James smiled. A bit sadly, he continued, "It wasn't easy to find beauty in a mill town. Her life was harder than I ever told you. She lost three children over the years until my brother Rob and I were all she had left."

"You never told me about the other siblings," Jess sympathized. "I'm so very sorry."

"It's not exactly a cheery topic to share," James answered. "That's not the worst of it, though." He paused before continuing, "But I'll tell you all about that."

Jess nodded encouragement.

James went on, "When my father died, one of us had to go to the mills full-on to support the family. I was the older brother. It should have been me, but my younger brother took it on."

The harshness in James's voice startled Jess. She started to reach for him, but he halted her with a raised palm, looking her in the eye to repeat, "It should have been me."

"Whose decision was it for your brother to go instead?" Jessica asked, looking for a way to ease James's guilt.

He paused, thought, as if seeing where she was going, finally replying, "The three of us sat down together. Rob and my mother told me to stay in school and work for the Thornton Scholarship. Rob would go to the mill since he didn't see much use in schooling."

"I imagine they also knew you were good at learning and how much you loved it," Jessica pointed out.

"Yes," James answered slowly, "but I didn't fight them. I was relieved to let them sacrifice so that I could escape that dingy town and pursue what I wanted. Maybe things could have been different for them if we'd both gone to the mill. Maybe, I could have saved . . . well, I didn't. I stayed at my studies, only taking millwork in the summer, until I could seize the opportunity of the Thornton Scholarship and escape to a nice Oxbridge education. I never looked back."

"Never? That doesn't sound like you," Jessica disagreed.

"Well, I won't say I *never* went home. I won't say I never wrote, but I could have done much more, kept track of my mother's health better or tried to settle down Rob. I couldn't wait to get out of that world, not that I was entirely accepted where I'd escaped."

James went silent now, thinking, turning away from Jess and watching the waves. Or was he only seeing the past? Blaming himself for mistakes he couldn't undo.

He was quiet for such a long time that Jess wondered if he'd reached the end of his tale. She finally suggested, "James, maybe, and it's a big maybe, because they wanted you to have that education, you were a little selfish, but no more than any kid that age. We all have dreams driving us, and if others want to support those dreams, believe in us, aren't we letting them down if we throw that help back in their faces? Besides, your dream wasn't your brother's. He wanted to leave school. Anyway, I can't imagine they'd really want to haunt you. I'd think that they'd be proud that you put their sacrifice to such good use. You've helped so many people."

Jessica's words were quiet but persuasive. James turned his head back to her, but he replied with a weary self-reproach that made her ache, "That might be true if there weren't more to the story. They have definite reasons to resent me."

"I can't believe that," Jessica insisted. "You'd better tell me everything. I can't let you torture yourself one minute longer."

James cocked an eyebrow and put to her, "I suppose you can erase nearly twenty years of bottled up guilt in one chat on the beach?"

"Just call me Dr. Freud. Seriously, though, talk to me, James."

James smiled, though it was hardly a grin. Still, Jessica could see that her tenderness spiced with humor had softened him. No, more accurately, strengthened him to open up. He took her hand, squeezed it and warned, "I hope I still have your sympathy after I finish. I'm not particularly impressed with myself. It's not every chap who can blame himself for his brother's and his mother's deaths."

That knocked Jess for a loop. But James was watching her; she wasn't about to let him feel deserted. She gave him a knowing nod and advised, "Never mind the melodrama, Mr. Crawford. Finish your story. I'll be the judge of who's responsible for what."

A glint of appreciation in his eyes, James resumed, "My brother was the first. I was in exams when word came to me he'd been killed in a mill accident. I knew he was never one to pay attention to what he was about, always getting himself into jams. I'd saved his skin more than once when I was working with him. I never should have left him on his own. He'd still be alive now, if I'd been a proper brother."

"I don't think so," Jessica disagreed. "Just working in the mills wouldn't have guaranteed you could protect him. You'd have your own work; you couldn't ride herd on him perpetually. Likely, he'd probably have gotten wilder with a big brother constantly on his back. Maybe you'd have even been the one hurt if you'd been distracted trying to perpetually keep an eye on him."

"Maybe that would have been a fair exchange."

"Not to me, and I doubt to your mother, either," Jessica shot back. "It certainly wouldn't have been so hot for all the people you helped during the war."

James admitted, "I've tried to convince myself of your last point. *That* I suppose is true. And I know you mean what you say about yourself. Yes, rationally, I know all that is important, but I doubt Rob or my mother see things the same way."

"Well, how in Sam Hill would you know? They're both dea . . . Oh? Oh!" The chill sweeping Jess paled the autumn wind's effects. "They haunt you? When? Since I've known you? When? What happens?"

"Hard to buy, isn't it?" James warily answered. "Now you know why I've never told you. Not exactly something a chap would be eager to admit to his bride, or anyone else. Not something a chap wants to admit to himself. So, I buried it. And I was doing damned well, until I came here."

Jessica sank inside at having brought James into a darkness he'd been trying to escape. At last, she said, "I'm so sorry for exposing you to all this. I'd never have made you so vulnerable if I'd known."

James raised a hand to quiet Jess, now comforting her, "It's not your fault. You had no way of really knowing how deep this goes. I was a little too adept for my own good at disguising it from you. Anyway, it's my sin. I was just kidding myself, thinking I could bury it forever."

Trying to understand, Jess questioned, "So, how often do they haunt you? I've never seen you react like this before."

"Before we came here, there were only two incidents. I didn't see anything when Elizabeth did, although now I realize there was something different about the cold in the music room that night."

"You think that what Elizabeth saw wasn't Felicia but *them*?"

James shrugged, "I can't say. I just know I haven't felt right since then. I've had a terrible sense of something reaching out for me, and I don't want to give it a shot at making contact. It's too unnatural."

"Does this place give you the sense of something threatening? Is that what you felt before with your experiences, a threat?" Jessica questioned intently.

"I'm not sure. I don't think . . . well, what happened before was more . . . intense . . . and I didn't stick around to see how it would play out."

"Hmmm," Jessica pondered. "Would you tell me about those experiences? The more I understand the more help I can be."

James quirked his mouth before replying, "I imagine if you don't already think I'm bats in the head, I might as well not hold out now. In for a penny, in for a pound." He paused, squared himself, then started, "You remember I said Rob was killed when I was up for exams?"

Jess nodded and James continued.

"I decided not to leave university for the funeral. I told myself I couldn't afford to fall behind the others or request postponement for personal reasons. I believed too many people already thought I didn't belong there, a scholarship boy from a mill town. I wasn't about to go ask for what someone might want to construe as special treatment. So, it ate at me not to go back to comfort my mother, but I made my excuses to her, and myself. Said I couldn't afford to jeopardize my place at University after everything everyone had done to get me there. True as far as it went, but I also didn't want to have to go back and look into faces that might accuse me of living when my brother had died in the hard work of the mills. I didn't want to chance seeing that look in my mother's eyes."

"Oh, James, don't do her that disservice. I'm sure that as much as she grieved for your brother, she was glad to have lifted another son out of a hard life," Jessica urged, heart aching for him.

'You may be right," James allowed. "However, the insecure, cowardly lad of twenty years ago didn't have the guts to chance it. So, I stayed away, buried my guilt in working to excel in those exams, and, when they were done, not long after my brother was buried, I had a visitor."

Jessica gnawed her lower lip intently when her husband paused. It seemed only now she realized that for the past few minutes the wash of waves, the seagull wails, and the mournful buoys' clanging had disappeared from her consciousness. She whispered, "Go on."

James did.

"I'd fallen asleep in my room, collapsed actually, when . . . I was, suddenly, just awake. It was the damnedest, strangest wakefulness I've ever known. All creation seemed to have condensed into one still point around me. The world had frozen, while I breathed and thought and felt with an intensity . . . I can't describe. I could move, I believe, but I didn't. It seemed wrong to try. And I felt I was waiting. Then I heard the tapping on the window. It took me a minute to realize that tapping was the code Rob and I used as kids to say 'let me in' when one of us would sneak out for a night-time lark.

"Jessica, I can't tell you the terror that overcame me, the sense that all the laws of the natural world had dissolved. Then there were those aromas, the ale Rob liked, the machine oil he and my Da would carry home from the mill. It was against all reason. I felt unmoored. God, so terrible, terrifying. I couldn't hide behind rationalization. And I thought, what if I have to see, to face, what the machinery did to my younger brother, the one I should have protected? I felt utterly exposed, that Rob would see me, did see me, for the selfish coward I was. He must have hated me for letting this happen to him. I couldn't stick it any longer. I pulled the strength from somewhere, broke the spell, ran from the room, and didn't return until just before dawn. I've been running from that memory ever since. That and what happened with my mother."

"Your mother?" Jessica breathed. "Her, too?"

James nodded. "There was a point when I was able to come home between terms. I worked up the courage to face her. It was no picnic."

Surprised, Jessica let slip, "She *did* blame you?"

"No, not exactly," James clarified. "She never said anything outright, but she did reveal Rob had wanted to talk to me before he died, perhaps delirious. He knew I was away, but he must have wanted to curse me badly for leaving. That's likely why he wouldn't let a little thing like death stop him. Anyway, I found out that my mother had become caught up in spiritualism. We had quite a row over it. I wasn't about to let charlatans take advantage of Ma Mère in her grief. I was at least a good enough son in that respect, or maybe I wanted to deny what I'd experienced. At any rate, I clearly wasn't good enough. She had a heart attack not long after and died. So, you might say I'm responsible for what happened to her as well. She must have felt so, too. Or maybe she sensed my shameful relief that I didn't have to worry about giving up my studies to support her."

Jessica started to protest, but James held up a hand. Jessica stood down, knowing it was painful enough for him to make these revelations without her interrupting.

"One night after her funeral, sleeping in my old bed, I had the same sensation of time and space coalescing around me. Then, there was the scent of roses, like the little ones she used to try to grow in her pots. True to form, I blew out of that room and never looked back. So, there you have it, and don't tell me it was all the delusions of my emotional state. I know the difference, and I've since researched others, people who aren't charlatans, whose stories confirmed my experiences. I've tried to keep my conscience from tainting my present for almost twenty years, but here, here it all seems to have allied against me. I don't know what will happen next."

"Oh, James," sympathized Jess before she hugged him close. Now he was crushing Jessica to him. They were both crying, and Jessica said, "I'm so sorry. I love you so much. I wish I knew what to say, what to do."

James leaned back, brushing Jessica's hair from her face to say, "This is good."

"But you blame yourself so much for just being human. None of these tragedies was your fault. You were even trying to protect your mother when you two quarreled. You've become a good man who has helped so many people. You've more than done your time in purgatory. Anyone who can't see that, living or dead, is on the wrong track."

"Maybe we should hand Elizabeth an Ouija board and see if she can get a conciliating message through," James responded with bleak humor. "Since I've been here, I've felt someone wants to contact me, but I'm not sure I want to get the message direct."

"I have a message for you. You have to stop punishing yourself. You always spoke about your mother as a giving, loving person. She would not turn on you. I can't believe she'd want you to suffer this way. As for your brother, I don't know him at all, but if he came from your family, odds are that he was a right guy, too. So, think about this: maybe they came to comfort you, to forgive, no, to get you to forgive yourself. It's your anguish and guilt that wouldn't let you see, that twisted your experience into something frightening. As much as I mistrusted Wanda O'Malley, she did say something that made sense: since we have mortal senses, our brains don't always accurately perceive something otherworldly. We translate it into what we expect to experience. Honey, you were so filled with self-reproach that it completely colored your perception. I don't know if you can take off those guilt-tinted glasses, but I'd like to help you try."

James straightened a bit and tilted his head thoughtfully before slowly responding, "I'd never really allowed myself to think of it that way: that they knew I was in pain. They were reaching out to forgive . . ."

"Not forgive. Let you off the hook," Jessica amended. "Surely, they knew you well enough to realize you'd be blaming yourself. Does that make sense, in the context of how your mother and brother had always been to you?"

James nodded slowly, allowing, "Yes, yes, it does. But it almost seems too good to be true."

"Sometimes the good is the true. Look at us. Who would have given odds in our favor four years ago?"

"You're a wise woman, Mrs. Crawford," James smiled tiredly.

"Mmm, Maybe I should hang out my shingle," Jess gently kidded. "You feel better, don't you?"

"I do," James agreed, "Somewhat. You can't expect a chap to be completely liberated from twenty years of repressed guilt in under half an hour."

"Well, we made a start," Jess replied quietly.

"I wish I'd opened up about this before," James admitted. "It was a barrier between us that I didn't like. But, yes, painful as this has all been it's better to have made a clean breast of things with you. It's better to know you think no less of me. Eventually, maybe I'll feel less a rotter."

"If anybody's been a rotter, it's I for dragging you into this God-awful place. Making you go through this confessional," Jessica admitted.

"A confessional that's made me love you more than ever. So, it's not such a bad thing at all for you to have brought me to this place and this moment," James disagreed. "Now, that's enough guilt for today. Hair shirts become neither of us."

James closed the conversation emphatically by taking Jessica tightly in his arms to kiss her with a passion that drove away all their demons, at least in this moment. Still, neither stopped wishing for the moment Chief Winston was ready to let them leave this benighted island.

Chapter Thirty
Thursday, November 6th

Jessica and Gerry were the only ones left at the breakfast table in the sun-brightened room. With a joking request that Gerry keep his bride out of trouble, James was taking a cigarette break. After all that had happened since he'd arrived, Jess wouldn't begrudge James this indulgence. Still, after letting his hair down, he'd been far less tense. It wasn't that she'd exactly convinced him he was back in his late family's good books; it was more that he started to forgive himself. Still, James wasn't wholly at ease. Jessica knew he wouldn't be until either the murderer was caught or he had her and Elizabeth off the island and back in the city. Boy, would it ever be nice to be back home with James and her number-one feline, if Dusty hadn't already changed the locks on them for being away so long. At least Lois Wong was there now to do Dusty's bidding and let them back in the apartment.

"Looks as if there's a lot on your mind," Gerry commented.

"Oh," Jess laughed, a startled hand going to the chest of her grey jersey dress, right where two wine-colored triangles converged at their apexes. "You caught me wool-gathering."

"You must have gathered enough wool for a whole sweater," Gerry teased over his coffee, adding, "I just can't get over how quiet it is this morning."

"As long as you don't say quiet as a tomb," Jessica warned.

"Anyway, it's so much less, um, lively with Winston letting some people he didn't need, like the Vic and Chet and the photographer, go back to the city. He even let Scott make a trip to try and square things with the station big-wigs. The music room looks so empty with all the equipment packed up and shipped back to the studio," Gerry elaborated.

The rest of that topic was interrupted as they heard the doorbell ring through the open dining-room doors. Gerry gave Jess a quizzical look before proposing impishly, "Mayhap our backwoods Sherlock has arrived to announce the solution to the crime."

The two waited, listening. Nothing. Concluding the interruption was only estate business, Gerry took up another thread of conversation, but a troubling one: "So, Jess, what do you suppose will happen to us, the show? After two weeks of repeats, are they going to dump us?"

Jessica tried to encourage her friend—and herself, "If anyone can save our professional skins it's that smooth-talking Scott. With the rebroadcast of 'Museum Piece No. 13,' we aren't missing a week on the air. Maybe Chief Winston will let us go back to the city next week in time to do another broadcast. I don't see him suspecting any of us, and he can't pump us for anything that we couldn't have given him this week. Anyway, he knows where to find us in the city."

"The unemployment line?" Gerry wryly conjectured. "We've got quite a scandal to beat here."

"As much as I hate to sound callous, it's the type of scandal that actually adds to the allure of our show," Jessica reflected. She took a sip of tea before responding to Gerry's grimace, "There is some good news, though. Mr. Wellstone will be back in the saddle sooner than expected. I guess you didn't hear from Scott that our pal Ungerpreck was called back to the city again and dressed down but good by his brother-in-law. And not just for bungling the show. There's talk about criminal charges by the Wellstone Company's board over his misappropriating funds."

"I thought there was much less mindless bluster polluting the halls recently," Gerry noted devilishly. "So, with Philip Carlyle off to the salt mines and your sister and the Robinsons on a Portsmouth day trip . . ."

"Authorized by Detective Winston," Jessica added.

"For the moment, that leaves you, me, James, Jeanne Rivers, and Bill Carlyle keeping company. Such a cozy bunch. Say, where is Bill Carlyle, anyway? He didn't join us for breakfast."

"I understand he's consulting with a lawyer in Portsmouth on his claim to the estate. Needless to say, Philip did not offer him a lift into town when he went in, himself. Made his brother call a taxi."

Gerry snorted, "Can't say I blame Philip. Jamie certainly hasn't any fondness for Bill, despite his claiming they were such good pals when she was a kiddo."

"Philip seemed to think that was just a clever way to worm his way into her mother's good graces," Jess concurred. "Fortunately, both gals were too smart for him." Here, Jessica paused, rethinking her conclusion: "Maybe not so fortunate for Felicia, though. Maybe seeing through him got her killed when she gave him the gate."

Gerry leaned back to check that no curious ears lingered outside the doorway. Satisfied, he quietly proposed, "So, you believe that Carlyle killed Felicia and took out Wanda to protect himself? Do you think she had some dirt on him, or that he fell for all this spook rigamarole?"

Jessica couldn't help reflecting that for some people, like James, the supernatural did not necessarily involve rigamarole. However, she wasn't about to blab his secrets. She only shrugged.

Fortunately, Gerry moved to another aspect of the case, "Much as I like Bill Carlyle for the murder, he was cleared by the paraffin test. No residue on him or his clothes."

"That's not necessarily conclusive, Gerry," Jessica answered, going on to explain what she'd learned from Liz about other factors affecting how much, if any residue, might be found on a person.

Dissatisfied at the prospect of Bill Carlyle's exoneration, Gerry reasoned "Bill didn't have time to wash up, so that's a point in his favor. As for the condition of the weapon? Since searching the music room didn't turn up another gun, the one on the terrace should be the killer's. But we don't know what the police know about the ballistics. Philip never gave us that dope, if *he* even knows. All in all, Bill's not entirely off the hook, but there's more than a reasonable doubt."

"Okay, Gerry," Jessica began cautiously. "You're not going to like this. There is someone else with similar motives for Felicia's and Wanda's deaths. I hate to say this, but Jamie's father has military weapons training."

Gerry scowled, not so much at Jessica as at the prospect she'd raised. He put directly to her, "Do you honestly think Vitus Blasko could commit murder?"

"Gosh, Gerry, that's a hard question to answer. I didn't know him twenty years back. The man I met in the cemetery, who'd be injured fighting a wildfire, he didn't seem that kind of guy. But has he been himself, lately? Or has he reverted to an earlier, darker self? I'd hate to think so. What does Jamie say?"

Gerry swallowed before replying, "Jamie doesn't know anymore. She wouldn't turn on her father, but I can see hesitation in her face, hear it in her voice. I think she's worried he's going off the deep end." He seemed ready to say more but stopped.

"That's not good," Jess quietly concluded, wondering what else Gerry might have said.

"No," Gerry hesitated, "but I also told her to consider another direction of the investigation: some disgruntled client gunning, literally I guess, for Wanda. One of them could have traced her here and handed her a payback, then dropped the gun in a panic. No one has been able to trace ownership yet, right?"

Jessica nodded, but remained silent. *Ballistics still had to show this gun was the murder weapon. Yet, what were the odds that someone happened to toss it on the terrace outside the room where a woman was murdered?* Not for the first time, it struck her that the killer would have to have been one hell of a marksman to pick off Wanda with one shot in a dark room. *Not entirely dark, though. The table light that had made Wanda look so eerie to those sitting with her would have turned the woman into a clear target for someone behind her, at the window. Something else niggled at the back of Jessica's mind, finding a path to consciousness through the track of this conversation. Knowing where to aim in this dark mansion, on that dark night wouldn't have been so easy without some inside dope. Dope from someone who knew which room and where everyone was sitting in it.*

"Gerry," Jessica drew out his name slowly, reflectively. "How about this: what if Bill had an accomplice take the shot? What if he'd teamed up with someone Wanda double-crossed in the past? He could have filled in his partner on the entire set up for the evening, then sat back through the whole thing and tested clean as a whistle because someone else did his dirty work."

"That's interesting," Gerry considered, then pressed, "So, how did Bill make contact? How did he know about Wanda or what she was up to or that there even was someone who'd team up with him?"

"Well, good grief, Gerry! Do I have to think of everything? Isn't that what the Chief of Police gets paid for? Still, do you think I should get on the Ameche and share my brainstorm with Winston?"

That prospect didn't appeal to Jess. All she had was a theory, one that probably had already crossed his mind, since he was a pro. Maybe she should hash this out with James before she said something that might earn her Bill Carlyle's suspicious evil eye. Happening to glance at her watch, Jess started and exclaimed, "Oh, gosh! Look at the time. That guy of mine could have smoked his way through a couple of cartons while we've been playing Holmes and Watson. How about we join him on the terrace and rescue him before all that puffing has him sounding like Sydney Greenstreet?"

Gerry chuckled, "Not a bad idea. This conversation's gotten a little too grim for me. Let's get ourselves some sunshine."

The two strolled toward the doorway into the foyer, with Jess commenting, "I'm surprised that one of the girls hasn't been in to check on us. Jeanne usually keeps them on the ball."

"Maybe the mice are taking advantage of the cat's preoccupation," Gerry kidded.

In the drawing-room, Jess was a little surprised to see the electric lights on and the heavy outer curtains not yet completely opened, though light entered through French doors ajar just enough to admit a person.

Gerry continued their conversation, "If you ask me, Jeanne's been dodging our pal Bill. I'd say she probably doesn't have fond memories of him from way back when, especially from some of the looks I've seen her shoot him when it seems no one's peeking."

"Really? I can't say as I blame her," Jessica responded. "He has called her a brat as a kid."

Jess caught a glimpse of a glow in the hearth from a weak fire. It was cooler today, but enough for a fire? A scrap of starter paper cluttered the hearthstone. She went to toss it into the fire and save some poor kid from Jeanne Rivers' wrath. However, Gerry distracted her with, "According to Jamie, Carlyle might have known what he was talking about."

Looking at Gerry as they crossed the room, Jess expressed surprise: "Oh, really? How's that?"

"Just that Jeanne was apparently a bit of a bold thing. Her mother was always getting her out of Dutch for being in places that a housekeeper's daughter should know were off limits."

"Oh, so she and Jamie weren't exactly playmates?" Jess queried with interest.

"Hardly. No upstairs mingling with the downstairs in this house."

Jessica was surprised that a regular guy like Gerry hadn't been put off by Jamie's being a bit of a snob, even if it had been programmed into her by her family. Since Gerry wasn't exactly of the 400, himself, hadn't he or Jamie seen the irony in their attachment? Oh well, maybe love blinded, if it didn't always conquer, all. Anyway, it could have been less snobbery than being a good judge of character that turned Jamie against Jeanne. Ever since the housekeeper had shown herself less than charming to James, Jess had been feeling much less sympathetic toward her.

Gerry threw open the French doors before them and Jess stepped out first—onto an empty terrace! Her forehead wrinkled as she uttered, "Where in Sam Hill is James?"

Right behind her, Gerry surveyed the area, concluding, "Hmph, he doesn't seem to be here."

"No kidding, Ellery Queen," Jessica grumped, more sour than she'd intended as uneasiness twinged her. A glance around revealed no one, not even on the green stretching into the forest, its brilliant foliage beginning to slip from flame and gold to maroon and umber.

"I don't get it. He said he'd be out here," Jessica muttered, walking slowly toward the balustrade.

"Maybe he decided to take a walk on the beach?" Gerry suggested.

"Without us?" Jessica swiveled to face Gerry. "No, he was supposed to be here. He said he would be."

"There is another, totally un-mysterious answer. Certainly nothing sinister," Gerry assured Jessica, walking up to her. "The guy did have about a quart of coffee this morning. He's not a camel."

"Oh." Jess rolled her eyes and laughed, "Can you blame me, jumping to sinister conclusions after all that's happened?"

Gerry grinned, "It'd be hard not to look for murder, mystery, and mayhem around here. Anyway, why would anyone target James?"

Jessica brightened, realizing that, for once, James was in a place where danger really had nothing to do with *him*.

Gerry continued, "I bet he'll be back in no time." He checked the sturdy military watch on his wrist and pointed out, "I have a little time to wait with you, before I have to get one of the guys here to drive me into town to meet Jamie."

"You don't mind?" Jess smiled. "I don't want to keep you from a romantic tryst."

"Hardly romantic. She's coming back from a meeting with her lawyer in Portsmouth." Gerry hesitated, but opened up, "Jamie's looking into getting power of attorney since her father's been acting, well, you know. It's more about my being a shoulder to cry on than anything romantic."

Jessica nodded sympathetically, then took Gerry's arm and started them walking around the terrace, adding, "You're a good guy, and she's a darned lucky gal."

Gerry shrugged, a little embarrassed. The cry of a hawk pulled their attention upward to a predator of the red-tail variety, circling with imperial grace.

"Think he's looking for breakfast?" Gerry quipped.

"At this hour? Brunch," Jess pronounced as they moved off the terrace onto the grass.

The wind rippled around them, making Jess glad of her long sleeves and her dress's warm jersey, not to mention the warmth of Gerry's presence. They managed to turn the conversation to mundane topics, for the moment leaving behind the shadows of unanswered questions in the crisp autumn brightness.

They had turned back to face the house when their red-tailed companion shot past in pursuit of a hapless pigeon—both crashing into a shuttered window on the far right of second floor, the floor of Jessica's room.

A startled, painfully empathetic, "Oh!" and wince escaped them both. The hawk dropped, pigeon in claw, but unexpectedly caught itself a few feet above the ground to make a low-flying escape around the rear of the building.

Another "Oh!" came from Jessica; however, this one expressed a sudden, puzzled realization.

Misunderstanding, Gerry reassured her, "No, it's all right. The hawk is fine. He's flying. I guess things aren't so hot for the pigeon, though."

"No, no," Jessica protested. "Not the hawk. The window. I never really looked up at it till the hawk drew my attention. What's a window doing there?"

Gerry gave Jess a confused look and asked, "The window? What do you mean 'what's it doing there'?"

Jessica waved a hand as if to clear away confusion and explained, "That's my floor, my room. But there's no window *there* in my room. I only have that long row of windows. *There*, that's in my closet. Believe me, I go in my closet often enough to notice a window, and there isn't one. Who puts a window in a closet, anyway?"

"Oh . . ." Gerry drew the word out knowingly. "Sure, it is funny, but not really. I can actually explain it to you, believe it or not."

"Well, give over, Professor," Jessica smiled.

"It's a *faux* window," Gerry clarified. "There's one like it at the other end of the house, where there's a bathroom for the rest of us peons without a star's suite. I asked Philip Carlyle about that some time ago. He told me he never had taken much interest in architecture, except that, as a boy, that anomaly got under his skin. I guess that scientific, engineering mind of his didn't like things to go unexplained. He asked his father about it, and the old man told him the *faux* windows were there to create a look of balance with the floors on each level. It appears that the father had quite a bit of knowledge about the house and its history, but Philip was never any more interested in it than the window business. So, he said nothing else got passed on to him. Bill, the artist, might have taken an interest. Maybe you should sit down and have a chat with him on architecture."

"No thanks," Jessica bristled. "The last thing I want to do is spend alone time with that shady character." But the thought of Bill possibly having a deeper knowledge of the mansion set her mind making connections. She knew someone else also seemed to have a history of knowing the way around that great building. What if . . . ?

"Holy Smokes!" Gerry blew apart her cogitations. He was looking at his watch again and worrying, "If I want to get to town in time to pick up flowers for Jamie, I'm going to have to shake a leg—I mean the good one."

"You nut!" Jessica laughed, her previous thoughts derailed by her friend's gregariousness. She gave Gerry a mock punch on the shoulder.

"Hey, no slugging the combat veteran, if you know what's good for you," Gerry kidded, heading them back to the house.

"She's very lucky, that Jamie," Jessica pronounced. "I hope she realizes that."

Gerry gave a snort, something between modesty and amusement, before changing the subject: "So, speaking of good catches, yours ought to show up any minute now. I think you can stay out of trouble till then. James shouldn't mind—"

"Go," Jessica ordered as they entered the drawing room. "I can stroll down to the kitchen, where it's broad daylight and way too many witnesses for foul play."

Jess didn't add that the tension she hid from him now was not over her own safety, but her frustration that she couldn't formulate with James a plan of action. Suspicions were coalescing into theory based on that *faux* window, Bill Carlyle, and Jeanne Rivers. However, that theory needed to be tested: the sooner, the better.

All these thoughts tumbled through Jessica's mind while Gerry explained something about Philip offering his family's lawyer to help Jamie take power of attorney. So, she was a little startled when he stopped and questioned, "Jessica, you look as if you were about to go into battle. Are you worried about James? I'm sure he's okay. I suppose I could wait until he gets back."

Jessica shook her head and insisted, "Don't be ridiculous. I'm fine, but Jamie will probably really need you after all that legal parsing of her family. Go ahead."

As if on cue, Lu Brown, Jeanne's second-in-command, rushed into the foyer, her uncharacteristically smudged face lighting with relief on finding Jessica. She poured out, "Oh, Miss Minton. I'm so glad I caught you. I'm so sorry about the delay. An emergency in the kitchen. I had to be stop-gap plumber. My Dad was one, you know—"

"Okay, Okay, Lu, just spit it out," Jessica calmed the other woman with a smile. Thank God that Lu was only excited, not distraught. So, it was unlikely anything had happened to Mr. Crawford.

"Well, your husband, he came through the kitchen, and then wrote you this note and went out the kitchen door. I would have delivered it to you right away, but those darned old pipes! We had a valve snap, and water everywhere, no time to call a plumber . . . I had to go work on it before we had a seven-years flood in there!"

Before Brown could hand over the message, Gerry said, "See, I told you not to worry, Jess." Next, he gave his attention to Lu, saying, "Miss Brown, Frankie's driving me into town this morning. Do you know if I should meet him at the garage, or will he be pulling the car up at the front door?"

Jessica's fingers fairly itched to tear the paper from Lu's hands as the young woman informed Gerry that Frankie was already waiting out front. Jess distractedly accepted a peck on the cheek and some form of "goodbye" from Gerry before he left, only to realize that Lu had started back to the kitchen, note still absently clutched.

"Lu! Wait! My note!"

Brown bobbed her head, embarrassed, and came back apologizing, "Ooops! Sorry, Miss Minton. We're in such a tizzy here. And on top of everything, Miss Rivers got a phone call on the kitchen line and out the door she went! Just before your husband came through the kitchen, wrote up the note, and left, himself. I don't know if it would have been better or not for her to have been around when the plumbing went haywire. Miss Rivers knows how to take charge in a crisis; but, lately, she's been blowing her stack every time something goes wrong. I think murder really upsets her. I guess it threw everybody off."

It was all Jess could do not to snatch the paper out Lu's hand. She finally burst out, "Yes, I know it's terrible. But could I just have my note?"

"Oh, Sure. Here you go!"

"Thanks," Jess automatically said, opening up the brief message:

> *Got to step out for a bit. Don't worry. See if Gerry can't stick around a little longer. Be back when I can. Try to stay out of trouble. J.*

What the dickens?! Jessica puzzled.

Jess looked up to ask Lu more about the letter, but the young woman had already bustled off to the kitchen, likely to battle further plumbing disasters.

Grumbling her frustration, Jess crumpled the missive in her hand. What was worse? Not knowing what James was getting into or not having him here to join her testing her theory?

Folding her arms, Jessica dug her fingers into the jersey of her dress. *James had left immediately after Jeanne Rivers went out. Following Jeanne? Why? He* didn't know about the speculations raised in her by that *faux* window and by Jeanne's childhood reputation for turning up unexpectedly all over this mansion. Those speculations only came together because, until today, she hadn't had reason to notice how that anomalous window did not square with the dimensions of her suite and her closet. And James would never have noticed, either, having never stepped in the closet when he had that roomy wardrobe for his duds.

So when was James coming back? How long was "a bit"? Even Liz was out of town. Putting her theories to the test alone would not be the smartest move she'd ever made, Jess knew. Here's where Old Scratch wiggled temptation under her nose: the people she mistrusted were nowhere around, either. Who knew when another such opportunity would present itself to explore her conjectures without having to worry about them? Here was her chance to prove her suspicions of what had been done to her and to Wanda, as well as how. All without Bill or Jeanne knowing what she knew.

But maybe she should call Chief Winston, first. *As if he would take seriously a gal who played at mysteries over the airwaves while he worked his tail off over them in the real world!* Besides, if anyone got wind of her suspicion before Winston could come out here, that person could clean up any convincing or useful, evidence. She'd look like a dizzy dame if she told him what she suspected without any better proof than a discombobulated sense of geometry.

However, if she could *prove* that her suspicions had a solid basis, without her having to delve too deeply, she could go right away to Winston and let the law do the rest. No one would have any idea that she needed to be silenced until it was too late to do her suspects any good. James couldn't fault her for being reckless if she came up with the evidence while Bill and Jeanne were out of the picture. But she'd have to act fast, before either returned.

So, Jessica set herself to test her theory *and* stay out of trouble. That's what she told herself, anyway.

Chapter Thirty-One
Same Day

Sunlight streamed brilliantly through the wall of windows in Jessica's room. Residing on a little table between the window and the closet were a measuring tape and a flashlight that she hoped she'd retrieved unobtrusively from the kitchen amidst its gradually diminishing chaos. Next to those items was a lighter and the wide candle in its decorative holder, taken from the room's mantel. Jess frowned almost guiltily at the flashlight. The lighter, she definitely needed for her initial testing, but the flash? Wouldn't she only require it if she intended to plunge over the threshold of her suspicions? No. She needed the flashlight to discern what lay over that threshold, even if she didn't cross it, which she would *not* do alone.

First, though, another visual test was in order, from the outside. Jess had already opened the closet, put on the light, slid her clothes over to the far left, then measured the depth of the closet along the wall. Now, she pushed open the long pane on the left side of the window nearest the closet. Despite the wind whipping her hair, Jessica leaned out to estimate the length of the building from where she looked, trying to square the position of the *faux* window with the closet's depth. It didn't square.

Jess thrilled with an odd mix of relief and fear. Suspicions were confirmed, but what suspicions! No, her experience as a night wanderer and haunted dreamer did not mean she was crazy; but, yes, she had been oh so vulnerable in the dark isolation of this room.

Pulling the window closed, Jessica sank back onto the window seat. Ought she wait for James? *How long? Would he be back before Bill or Jeanne?* She had no idea, and the thought of losing this opportunity stung. It couldn't hurt to take her testing just one step further, to locate the threshold that had betrayed her.

On her feet, quickly lighting the candle on the table, she returned to the closet. After pulling the chain on the overhead light to shut it off, Jess turned and closed the door behind her. By flickering candlelight, the far right wall, the outside one, was still visible. She remembered that the rear wall of the closet had vertical paneling from halfway up to the ceiling. Below, sections of wainscoting three feet long, each, extended across the closet's length. Slowly, meticulously, Jessica moved the candle flame near the wall, raising it and lowering it, watching it burn steadily as she moved left. The flame continued steady, undisturbed by the slightest breeze or anything more than her movement. It was a gradually growing letdown, a dismissal of her theory, but maybe this result was also a relief. Now she wouldn't have to wrestle with whether to take the next step.

That tainted relief was short-lived. About four feet away from where she'd started, the candle flame decidedly, consistently, wavered. Something was blowing the flame askew from beyond the closet wall, betraying one of the house's dark secrets.

Studying the paneling closely by candle light, digging into the seam with her nails, Jessica Minton detected the line, the faint line of a crack running down the panel! Excited, she struggled to disengage a thin cardboard sheet from her skirt pocket. *Darned clingy jersey!* Then it was free and, with shaking fingers, she at last wedged it in the crack.

Jess blew out the candle and had the closet light on to study the paneling. Yes, it was a tight fit, but if you knew what you were looking for and how to look, neither of which she'd had any reason to do before, well, there it was! The panel was wide enough for a person, or, people moving single file, to fit through. Jeanne Rivers, with that childhood reputation of showing up unexpectedly where she shouldn't, was the likeliest candidate to make use of it that Jess could think of.

The antipathy Jeanne and Bill Carlyle displayed sure made a smart cover for their partnership. They could have nursed resentments and greedy desire, for both had left the island under questionable circumstances. The two could have even sought each other out to form a partnership against Philip. While both had the motivation, Jeanne could supply a clever avenue to implement their plans.

And my resemblance to Felicia was why they dragged me into this beef! Given it was pretty clear Philip had cared deeply about Felicia, playing on that would have been an effective way to distract, weaken, him in in a fight for control of the estate. Then why had Jeanne insisted neither Liz nor I tell Philip about my wandering to Felicia's room? That certainly would have unnerved him. But Jeanne and Bill must have known the girl who'd found the dead roses would spread the word until the story reached Philip faster than War Admiral! Jeanne's silence would prevent Philip from suspecting her plans.

Still, why kill Wanda O'Malley? Had she somehow gotten wise to the plotters and threatened to out them? It was like a jigsaw puzzle with many pieces in place, but just enough important ones missing to keep you from recognizing the whole picture. *How many of those pieces might lie beyond this panel?*

Stepping back, Jess checked her watch. No sign of James, while the margin was shrinking for exploring in her enemies' absence. She looked at the panel again. Well, just opening it wouldn't expose her to any danger. It wasn't as if Bill and Jeanne would be skulking on the other side, waiting to pounce on her.

So, Jessica was tapping, pressing, pushing along the panels above the wainscoting. Nothing. The molding at the top of the wainscoting wouldn't budge, either, despite her breaking a red-painted nail and cursing the architecture's parentage. Next, Jess worked the same way at the molding. No dice moving anything, with another nail damaged!

Jess leaned back against the wall behind her. True, she had made an interesting discovery, but how important? *What if this was just storage space? All this inner* sturm und drang *over Aunt Minnie's hatbox and some broken chairs.* Or maybe awaiting her were answers that she suspected would reveal the missing pieces of the puzzle. She'd never know if she didn't open the panel. *Yet how?*

Wracking her brain for the next move, Jessica threw her head back in frustration—to catch sight of something interesting on the ceiling above. It was beautiful, painted, no, inlaid with mosaic to portray arrays of so many different flowers. She'd never noticed this before. *Well, who the heck looks at the ceiling of her closet? Boy, those rich people were something else, creating a gorgeous work of art that hardly anyone would notice. Funny, those yellow roses seemed familiar. Where did I see . . . ? Oh, right, the painting in Philip's study, done by his grandpa, the gent who'd built the house. Bill had come by his artistic talent naturally. Hmph, flowers on the ceiling of a closet seems a little over the top.*

Jessica pushed away from the wall and gave that rose a second look. Was there something shinier about the stone marking its center? She hastily left the closet, looked around, then grabbed a chair, dragging it awkwardly into the closet. With a quick prayer that the chair could support the extra serving of pancakes she'd scarfed down earlier, Jessica got up on the chair and examined close-up that center stone. It was metal, disguised with an enamel coat chipped in places by age, no, usage. Rough and recent usage. With only a moment's hesitation, Jessica pressed the suspicious stone.

There was a sound of moving wood, a trembling in the closet wall behind Jess, but it was not the sound of a panel unused for decades. Even before she turned and hopped off the chair, Jessica realized this was a well-oiled mechanism.

Before her was an opening into murkiness, not darkness. Perhaps that *faux* window wasn't 100% *faux*. Jessica shook a little with anticipation as she faced the gap where a panel had slid back into the wall. *A threshold to new answers!* Automatically, Jessica kicked off her pumps and stepped into a pair of walking shoes, lined up with the rest of her footgear. She didn't admit to herself that this action was a red flag that she'd intended to do more than peer into the opening all along.

Switching on the flashlight, Jess steadied herself and leaned into the opening. Her flash invaded the passage to reveal the not-so-*faux* window on the outside wall, only a few feet to her right. To the left, extending the length of the house, it was dusty but not terribly fretted with cobwebs. The brick chimney of her fireplace extruded into the passage, narrowing it there. Before you reached the chimney was what, from here, appeared to be a spiral staircase descending into darkness. *Charming*. An upward sweep of her light revealed a cord dangling from the ceiling, directly across from the stairs. After a sec, recollections of other older homes made Jessica realize the rope would pull down a set of stairs to the floor above—the floor with Felicia's room.

Jessica fairly vibrated with excitement, trepidation, and anger that her suspicions were being confirmed. But they could only truly be confirmed if she passed over the threshold, went down that hidden corridor, pulled down those stairs, and climbed to the next level.

No!

Proceeding would definitely not be staying out of trouble. Yet would James return before Bill and Jeanne? Once they were back, how safe would it be, even for both Crawfords, to explore the passage? And if they didn't check out this passage first how could they contact Chief Winston? Wouldn't he call them fools for trying to lure him onto a wild goose chase? After all, this passage didn't clearly connect to the music room where Wanda had been murdered. Winston already thought the program's crew a bunch of kooks.

Yet the longer she waited, the more time the culprits would have to clean up whatever mess they might have left behind, especially if they figured out they were no longer protected by ignorance of the dusty passage's existence.

Dusty!

Jessica had lowered her beam to the floor, noting that Jeanne wasn't such a swell housekeeper, after all. She had cleared away cobwebs to keep them from catching in hair or clothes, and thus avoid raising questions about their origin. However, she hadn't cleared the floor of dust. *Logical. Who would even conceive of looking for footprints in the dust of a passageway he didn't know existed?* Jessica, however, knew about the passage now and studied the prints in the dust attentively. Some were a bit blurred, marking a progress of coming and going, but others were darned distinctive. One set pretty much matched her size. Two other pairs accompanied, as if leading and guiding. Though a bit blurred, one was definitely from a man's shoe, but the other was a woman's. She'd bet her bottom dollar that Bill's and Jeanne's shoes would fit them nicely.

Beaming her flashlight down the corridor, Jess attempted to discern if the footmarks extended beyond the dangling cord. *Can't tell from here. If I go just a little down that way, to beneath the pull-down stairs, will I still be staying out of trouble?*

W-e-ll, no one is around. I'll be close to the opening. It's just a quick check. I might find loads of information to convince Chief Winston. And I have to have answers about those night wanderings.

First, though, Jessica tucked the flashlight under her arm, turned, and wrestled halfway through the opening the chair she'd stood on earlier. Carefully calculating, she positioned the chair to prevent the panel from slamming shut, as panels had been wont to do since time immemorial in books, plays, movies, and radio dramas. Much smarter than any detective's comic relief sidekick, Jess congratulated herself on having enough experience with mysteries of all ilk not to let herself get caught in a tight fix.

Now, Jessica confidently held her flash to illuminate the way and started down the passage, particularly careful not to smudge the footprints. That *was* creepy, following her own tracks, as if she were haunting herself! The creepiness dissipated as Jess became more and more convinced by this trail that she was now seeing how her "sleepwalking" had been under outside auspices. Yet how had they been able to move her into the passage and along it while she was asleep? The Portsmouth doctor's questions about barbiturates floated to mind. *Hadn't Jeanne Rivers studied nursing right after she'd left the island but been dismissed? Why had she been dismissed? Something to do with drugs?*

Fury seized Jess at the thought of being so violated, but it cleared as she was gripped by the striking evidence that the footprints ended in a kind of circle beneath the cord. The cord that dangled within easy reach of her hand. It wouldn't add much time if she pulled down the stairs, climbed up, and confirmed that they led where she expected. Old Scratch was working overtime with temptations today.

No! That pushes your luck way over the limit, kiddo! Get back! Send a message downstairs to have James shoot up to your room the minute he sets foot in the house. Then sit down and strategize together! You always work best when you work as a team.

A painful cracking, followed by a terrific crash forced Jessica to swivel around and stare, horrified, at the splintered chair, crushed by the panel that had slid powerfully back into place, closing off her exit. So much for being smarter than the average B-movie cliché.

Chapter Thirty-Two

It seemed an eternity that Jessica froze in place. Finally, a whispered growl escaped her, "Damned flimsy reproductions."

At least she hoped what was left of the chair was a reproduction. She knew darned well that the Crawfords' combined salaries couldn't afford to replace the real McCoy.

"What in Sam Hill am I woolgathering for?!" Jessica finally shook herself back to dire reality.

Swiftly, she reached where the panel met the wall, a chair crushed and jammed hopelessly there. Only now, the flashlight serendipitously illuminated a handle that would have easily slid back the panel, with a lever to lock it into place and keep it open. *Of course, if you were keeping people out of your secret passage not keeping them in, opening the panel from this side would be designed for easy use—unless some chowderhead jammed a splintered chair in there. Damn!* Why had she been so eager to look down the corridor and explore that she'd missed something so obvious?!

But maybe she could still get out of this one with a little elbow grease. Resting her flashlight on the floor, Jess gave a good college try to extricate the chair and unjam her safest portal to freedom. Nope, when she SNAFUd something, she did it up brown!

Though Jessica's knees might have had the slightest wobble, she didn't panic, exactly. Picking up her flash, Jessica shone it toward the spiral staircase. Then she turned it up to the cord dangling from the ceiling. Stairs going up and down indicated more than one passageway in the house and more passageways suggested more sliding panels. *Maybe even connections to the music room? No time for that now. You have to get out of here.*

Looking up, Jessica was pretty darn sure where the pull-down stairs would lead. She also had very personal reasons for seeking that destination.

Careful not to disturb the older footprints, Jess headed for the dangling cord. Still, she hesitated when she reached it, bedeviled by the question of who might lurk above.

C'mon, now, Jeanne Rivers must still be out if James hadn't returned from tailing her. Bill Carlyle? His lawyer would certainly have him tied up for some time.

It was musty. Jess's nose twitched and itched, but allowing a sneeze to echo down the passageway—possibly through the walls—seemed a really bad idea. Quickly, Jess got a handkerchief out of her pocket and gave her delicate little proboscis a gentle, preventative blow. Stuffing the handkerchief back in her pocket, she determinedly pulled down the cord and lowered the ladder from the ceiling above.

It came down smoothly with nary a creak. Someone had certainly been faithful about maintenance. A housekeeper for a man tied up constantly with work away from home would certainly have the time and opportunity.

Tucking her flashlight into the stretchy material of her sleeve, Jess proceeded carefully up the angled steps. Cautiously, the top half of her body emerged into the still murky light of the level above. Apparently, the windows up here also let in a limited amount of illumination through cracks in the shutters designed to make them appear fake.

Jessica put her flashlight down on the floor near the opening, careful to position it so it wouldn't roll and fall to the floor below. With no way gracefully to get off the stairs and onto the floor, she scrambled out, almost on all fours, retrieved her flash, then stood up, and turned to face the wall separating her from Felicia's room. Another cord, like the one she'd just used to lower the stairs, dangled overhead.

What was one floor up? *Oh, the attic cum studio—Bill Carlyle's den.* That was someplace she had no desire to explore!

The flashlight made clear that footprints like those below marked the dust up here as well. Careful not to disturb these prints, either, Jessica approached the spot on the wall analogous to the location of the lever release on the floor below. *There it was.*

Her relieved sigh was so enormous that Jess instinctively, anxiously, surveyed the passage on either side. Had she given herself away? Fortunately, there was no one to give herself away to. *Nothing except mouse droppings. Ugh! These people needed a Dusty patrolling their passages. Would that Dusty were here to take care of these rats!*

Jessica's hand went for the lever, but she hesitated. What if someone she feared was in there? She listened carefully, patiently, almost breathlessly. *Nothing.*

The lever moved beneath her hand; the panel slid back. This time, Jessica slipped the lock on the handle in place, then stepped into the room she'd visited with Liz and Jeanne, the room she knew from her "dream." A disquieting thought struck her. Was she locked in? Jeanne had said when they left the room that she was locking it up to prevent any more "practical jokes" of the dead-flower variety. Had the turn of Jeanne's key not only locked others out but Jessica in?

A determined stride across the room and an unsuccessful attempt to open the door dashed Jessica's hopes. She was, as Liz would put it, "Up the creek without a canoe."

Jessica sank into a plush chair. At least no cloud of dust rose and enveloped her. The maid, when Jeanne let her in, did a good job. However, waiting until Jeanne unlocked the room for maintenance hardly seemed practical, let alone prudent. Neither did pounding on the door and yelling to be let out—as appealing as those actions felt about now.

As things stood, there was another definite way out—almost definite. One flight up, if each floor's passages and panels matched up, she should be able to find a panel that would release her—into Bill Carlyle's attic studio. A gruesome option, but a better bet than trying to maneuver down a flight of spiral stairs in semi-darkness—leading she had no idea where— if they even led to an exit.

She knew that Bill was likely still away, but for how long? Time's winged chariot could easily be ferrying the Carlyle she feared most back to her. The longer she procrastinated, the likelier he was to return and catch her.

On her feet, flashlight in hand, Jessica determinedly disappeared through the secret panel, releasing the lever to let the wall slide back into place. The ease with which she could do so inspired a disturbing thought. *How simple it might have been for Bill Carlyle to slip into this room to murder Felicia after she'd spurned him, carry her away through the passage, then weight down her body for a permanent rest in the*

Piscataqua or even the Atlantic. And had the wandering child-Jeanne seen more than Bill wanted, only to form an unholy alliance with him when she became an exiled adult? Stop wasting time you don't have chasing question after question!

Climbing the ladder went relatively quickly. As Jess scrambled to her feet, she decided she was getting a little too much practice at this! You could really hear the wind whistling outside up here, rattling through the cracks. Before Jessica knew it, dust, must, and the autumn chill forced one hell of a sneeze out of her!

She froze, listening carefully. Was there any sound beyond the wall separating her from Bill's studio? *Nothing. Only the high-pitched wind circling and taunting outside the heights of Carlyle Mansion. Ah!* There was the lever, right where she'd expected it. Her tongue moved slowly over her lower lip. *No sounds. Nothing.* But a mental image of the cruelty in Bill Carlyle's eyes held her back—until it struck Jessica that more pieces of the jigsaw might lie beyond the wall, pieces that would give the puzzle's picture clearer shape. Besides, she wasn't totally defenseless with this super-sized flashlight in hand.

Jessica moved the lever; the panel easily slid back. Again, she fastened it in place before stepping into the studio. Terrifyingly, Jess found herself almost blinded by the flood of sunlight through the south-facing windows after all her time in the murky passageways. Praying that nothing she couldn't see threatened, Jessica forced herself to keep cool and squeezed her eyes shut, gradually squinting them open to adjust her vision.

What Jessica saw was like a slap in the face. Though the studio windows had been a surprise, the wall papering, the furnishings, the room lay-out, and the door to her left seemed to solidify into the setting of her last "nightmare." The dream where a figure she seemed to recognize now as Bill Carlyle had pleaded, even threatened, for her to leave with him. To escape . . . Vitus? Inside her rose a deep dread of something terrible impending. But was that Vitus or Bill?

Jessica shook her head clear. Of course, it all seemed familiar, real. They'd spirited her through the passageways to this place, just as they had to Felicia's room. Didn't the footprints indicate that? Hypnotized or drugged, maybe both, she *had* been here before.

Anger flamed through Jessica at being used as a pawn against Philip—or maybe against Vitus. He had also been terribly disturbed by the stories about her being haunted by Felicia, by the radio program—though why Vitus might be Bill and Jeanne's victim, Jess couldn't say. Before she could pursue that avenue further, her eyes lit on a canvas-covered painting on an easel by the window. *Hadn't Bill once said something about another portrait of Felicia he'd been working on, one he claimed was a "truer portrait"?*

Jess wasn't sure why, but she felt that portrait might add another important piece to the jigsaw. She crossed to the painting and pulled away its covering. So much flooded Jessica's head that her mind and body stiffened at the overload. The soft velvet of the olive-green dressing gown worn by the woman in the portrait, she could suddenly feel its plushness under her fingers, against her skin. But the expression, the attitude of this Felicia struck even deeper. Gone was the neatly coiffed hair, the sad but dignified expression. This woman, captured from the waist up, twisted tensely to face Jessica from a chair that seemed to imprison. Then there were those eyes! Her expression! Both revealed her beauty, but a beauty tortured by trepidation and defiance: a woman preparing to confront something terrible.

That was what Bill Carlyle saw as truly Felicia? Or was it how he wanted people to perceive her? Whichever, the image spoke to what Jessica had felt in the dream of this room.

In the last dream, there had been another man approaching: who? Vitus? Jessica shook her head. *These dreams were what Bill and Jeanne wanted her to see—or were the dreams entirely under their control? Had a part of Felicia capitalized on Jessica's twilight mental state to slip in and convey her own message? Perhaps her fear of Vitus?* Jess's head whirled, trying to figure out whom Felicia feared most.

Or what if she had it all wrong about Jeanne's partner? *What if the housekeeper had been working with Vitus all along? He certainly could have been caching an enormous storehouse of resentment against the Carlyles for, he believed, destroying his family. Jeanne could have sought him out at her return to plot a blow against Philip. After all, she had brought the article to Philip with the picture showing my resemblance to*

Felicia. Perhaps Jeanne and Vitus *had engaged Wanda's help. Still, exactly what had been in it for Wanda and why the need to silence her?*

After all, *Jeanne* had sent Jessica to the old cemetery precisely at a time when she would run into Vitus Blasko. She only had Jeanne's word for it that she didn't know he went there. A little too coincidental for Jess's taste, considering all she was learning now.

Yet, what she'd seen in Vitus Blasko, herself, made her want to believe in him. Whereas, she'd felt Bill Carlyle was no good from the moment she'd laid eyes on him. Unfortunately, gut feelings weren't always the most dependable, especially when you knew you were biased in favor of one and against another. Instead of clarifying her perceptions, this portrait only led to more whirling conjectures. This extra piece of the jigsaw didn't seem to fit in one distinct place.

Jess dropped the canvas back over the portrait and gave herself a good mental shake: *You can't afford to hang around here letting your thoughts chase their tails!*

Yet the possibility that a little deft snooping might produce a key to this Rosetta Stone of possibilities tempted. Unfortunately, snooping was Liz's forté; deftness James's. She wasn't sure where to look first, and she wasn't certain she'd be adept at covering her tracks.

Those worries became moot. The sound of a tread on the stairs beyond the door to her left, too heavy for any of the housemaids, told Jessica Minton that the jig was up! An iceberg had nothing on the temperature of what crept up her spine.

Could she get out in time? What would Bill Carlyle do if he caught her? Damn, why hadn't she listened to James!

The tread stopped, even as Jessica started moving toward the open panel. But she halted at the sound of a woman's voice she couldn't quite place, hissing in anger, while Carlyle responded, low but threatening. For a moment Jessica strained to listen. *No dice.* Then her better judgment, finally, kicked in.

Get the devil out of here, you dope!

Jess scurried to the open passageway, trembling as she thought she heard Carlyle again climbing the stairs. Once more in the passage, she fumbled with the latch as the voices sounded closer to the outside door. *Yes!* She got the latch up and slid the panel back in place, hiding her from that dreadful room. For a moment, Jessica stood, waiting. Nothing came from the room from which a single panel protected her. Now a doubt taunted her: had she dropped the canvas back over the painting? She must have! She was sure she had . . . pretty sure. Jess took a step toward the panel. *Was there time to go back and make certain?* No, she needed to get the devil out of here!

Slowly, quietly, she turned to the open, drop stairs, but she looked back at the panel. She could stay and listen, try to learn something. *A tempting thought. No, a terrifying one!* One or both of her adversaries might have reason to enter the passage and find her standing here with her mouth hanging open!

Jessica looked down the drop stairs and frowned. Descending was always so much more difficult than ascending. As if she had the luxury of preference. She started out—only to half-slip, banging her back against the stairs and nearly launching her stomach out her mouth! Those steps pressed uncomfortably against her, but she leaned back into them for safety, the rest of her body stone still. *Had sounds of the commotion penetrated up into Bill's studio?* Jessica listened, motionless. Tensely, she waited, and waited. *Nothing.*

Slowly, Jessica finished her descent. Thank God, she'd switched out of her slick pumps into these sturdy shoes. If she hadn't, instead of only having a bumpy slip, she'd have ended up a painful lump on the floor below. *Lovely thought!*

Jess carefully, slowly, pushed the stairs back up, praying they wouldn't join the floor above with a bang. *Eureka!* They connected with fairly little sound. *Ha! Bill and Jeanne had outfoxed themselves.* Putting these passages in smooth working order to cover their surreptitious escapades had now served her nicely. Well, *something* had gone right since she'd gotten herself into this pickle!

Descending to the level of her room proved a little less stressful, perhaps because Jess knew she was putting another whole floor between herself and whoever was in that attic studio. However, that damaged panel painfully reminded her she was still in a jam, kind of like the one caused by the crushed chair.

Her flashlight illuminated the metal staircase spiraling down to . . . *What? Where?* Jess looked back at the eighty-sixed panel to her room.

Maybe she should stay put, listen for James, then pound and call to get his attention. But how long before he returned to the house, let alone their room? Did she want to see the look on his face when he finally released her? Well, it beat being discovered by Jeanne and whoever her accomplice was, should they decide to stroll through the dark shadows of these passages.

Her flash's light returned to the spiral stairs. They could very well lead her to more clues. But she'd have to get a move on. Who knew how long those two upstairs would stay occupied arguing?

Maybe she'd made enough discoveries on her own for the day. Maybe she'd just get herself the heck out of harm's way. *Hmm, if the upper floors are linked to the lower ones, somewhere below would likely be a panel enabling a soul to get out?*

Jessica sighed: *In for a penny, in for a pound*, and started for the staircase. *Yup, really not such a swell job of honoring James's advice to stay out of trouble.*

Chapter Thirty-Three

In full sunlight, Jessica Minton had never enjoyed descending a spiral staircase: vertigo city. With only the illumination of her flash and one hand on the twisting railing—*Bro-o-ther!*

Fighting off the trembles, Jess proceeded at a crawl, though it still felt as dangerous as riding a car without brakes down a twisting mountain road. Why in the name of all that was sacred hadn't she just stayed put and waited for James? Why did she have to keep pushing her luck until the mousetrap snapped on her?

Breaths came abruptly, anxiously, as Jess descended, never knowing when she'd miss a step and tumble into . . . what?

Suddenly, under the illumination of her flashlight, a landing appeared below. The stairs still spiraled further downward, but a landing did extend over some distance to what she believed to be the outer wall. It was hard to tell within her flashlight's illumination, but, if she wasn't mistaken, the passage turned to the left, revealing there was an extension not just behind an inner wall but behind the mansion's outer wall, where the buttress was. If she had the layout of this house accurately in her head, she was looking at a kind of interstice between the drawing room and the music room. That brought Jessica up short. Around the turn, the passage continued perhaps as far as the music room windows. *If it has some sort of secret opening into the music room, a person might take a shot at Wanda, and the bullet might appear to come from outside, through the window. Bill and Jeanne clearly knew about these passages! Just one or two problems, smart gal. Bill had been sitting in the audience, while witnesses put Jeanne in her room with no way out but past them. Yeah, but if these secret panels are here, couldn't Jeanne have one in her room? Maybe. A big maybe. Besides what in Jeanne's background said the lady could successfully pull off such a difficult shot? Shallow, girl, shallow.* Not *a maybe was the fact that Vitus Blasko, a man with military training and no alibi might have been shown the passages by Jeanne.*

Jessica sighed heavily, leaning against the rail, trying to push sweat-plastered hair away from the back of her neck. The heat of anxiety clashed miserably with the chill of the uninsulated passage. Perhaps she needed to check this out. She started to step into the passage but caught herself. Ever since she'd entered this not-so-fun-house portion of the mansion, she seemed to have made bad choices, been flummoxed, messed things up. It was time to think before she leaped into a worser mess. If she blundered down that passage behind the music room, any evidence there would likely be destroyed or contaminated. For once, today, she would use her head and wait until she could get an expert in, like Chief Winston. Consulting with James first wouldn't be the worst idea she'd had, either.

The thought that around the corner might be a way back into the sunshine taunted her, but Jessica wasn't about to chance doing any more damage. She did make a sweep with her flashlight of the wall backing the music room, just in case there was a panel-release close enough to allow her to enter without disturbing evidence. *Nothing. Well, the next floor down would be the cellar. Wouldn't that be a good bet if you wanted to hide ingress and egress to a house?* Screwing her courage to the sticking place, Jessica pressed onward, down those creepy spiraling stairs.

An unexpected slip shoved Jessica's innards outwards. She barely managed not to lose her flashlight as she banged the backs of her legs on the metal! *Ouch!* she dared only think. *Wait, any sounds? Thank God, no. Jeepers, that's going to leave black and blue marks. But if that's the worst . . . Oh, my Lord, no!* Jessica was horrified to feel a ladder shoot up her leg from the hole in one of her nylons. *Darn the Carlyles and Blaskos en masse!*

Nevertheless, Jessica soldiered on until the stairs straightened out, and she saw a door not quite closed flush, several steps down in front of her. *A door, not a panel. Maybe that meant this was the last stop! Wait.* A dim light leaked through, into her hidden space, killing her exhilaration. Was someone on the other side of the door standing between her and liberation?

Could she have come so far to be stymied now? After a few minutes of anxious waiting, it gradually seemed to Jessica that whoever was out there was awfully quiet. Maybe it wasn't even a room, but a corridor illuminated for someone not nearby, not even a person she need fear. Someone could even have just forgotten to put out the light.

Jess ran her tongue speculatively over her lower lip. She couldn't, wouldn't, wait for someone to find her. Jessica hefted the flashlight in her hand: big, heavy, and more than adequate for cracking a hostile noggin—as long as that hostile noggin wasn't attached to a hostile body holding a gun. Well, she couldn't stand here all day. Bill or Jeanne could decide to check the passages and find that jammed panel to her room.

Slowly, carefully, Jessica pushed on the door. *Thank God no creaking! It's good not to live in the* Inner Sanctum. *No sounds from beyond, either.* The door opened just enough for one terrified blue eye to peer out into what lay on the other side.

Nothing—well not *nothing*. It was a storeroom filled with all kinds of detritus of the past one-hundred years or so of Carlyle habitation. *But no one.*

What was *that light?* A lamp set on a desk left of center of the wall facing Jessica—and on the wall left of that was a door. *A door!*

Jess's heart sang! She all but cast caution to the wind, shooting out of the imprisoning passage! Then, only a few strides into the room, she suddenly took a flyer over some dad-blasted thing that sent her careening against a tall wardrobe—all that kept her from a painful date with the dirt floor. A door of that wardrobe sprang open under her impact, revealing a surprisingly modern-looking garment bag hanging within. A bag that clearly was not empty.

She could make out the lettering on that bag as "Beausoleil de Québec: Quality Period Reproductions." *Period? What period? Maybe twenty years ago?* Anxious as she was to escape, Jess also knew she needed to accrue as much ammunition as possible to back her suspicions of what had been done to her. Almost savagely, she yanked down the front zipper, finding what she both dreaded and desired: olive green, gold brocade on the front and belt. She fingered the velvet, plush as she'd "dreamed." Their gaslighting had been a complete sensory illusion: tactile as well as aural and visual.

Jessica clenched her fists at the thought she'd been dressed and put through madness; used as a pawn, no, an elaborate prop, to drive either Philip or Vitus to . . . to what? Madness?

Slowly unclenching her fists, Jessica realized that she no longer held her flashlight, lost when she'd almost fallen. *Damn!* She couldn't afford to leave behind any clue to her presence. *Where?* Her eyes scanned the room. *Okay! Under the desk with the light and that medicine bottle, journal, and leather case. What's* that *all about?*

Though Jess fairly flew over to the desk, she was careful not to take another tumble. She even managed to dodge the ten-foot standing mirror, but how could you miss such a gorgeous piece with its frame, a carved wooden rush of leaves and fruit encircling the heavy glass. At least the perilous crack running down it was someone else's seven years of bad luck. She'd had more than enough of her own today. Could it be turning now? She was in line for some answers that would crack this house's mysteries wide open. Maybe sometimes you needed to get yourself into a little hot water to win the highest stakes. Maybe she needed to grab her flashlight and try to blow!

Nevertheless, when Jessica straightened up from retrieving her flashlight, she couldn't help taking a good look at the objects on the desk. She wasn't going to miss a shot at finding more pieces to the puzzle; she just wouldn't linger doing it—even though a part of her brain screamed: "There's the door! Get the devil out of here, you dope!"

Unfortunately, what Jessica found on the desk was as confusing as it was illuminating. She recognized a dispensary bottle, reached for it, but halted. Better not to move it or smudge anyone else's prints with her own. She could still read the label, though, from where she stood: sodium amytal (amobarbital). Capsules of amobarbital, capsules that could be opened and poured into a specific individual's evening coffee, a barbiturate that would make her more pliable to hypnotic suggestion—especially if the drug was administered by someone with the nursing background to calculate the dosage to avoid any suspicious aftereffects like addiction or withdrawal. Someone like Jeanne Rivers. And who would be more adept with spinning those hypnotic suggestions than Wanda O'Malley? So, what she'd learned from Pat O'Brien's travails with narcosynthesis in *Crack-Up* had been educational, after all! Still, this discovery opened up more questions than it answered: if Wanda and Jeanne had been in league, why was Wanda killed? What had gone sour?

Well, at least they hadn't been using scopolamine on me. Now that was nasty stuff! She'd researched its effects when playing a character on her program being drugged with it. The effects were scarier than the episode! And her symptoms hadn't matched those effects. Thank heavens for small favors.

However, something else caught Jess's attention, puzzling her. Two pictures in expensive frames, one of Felicia, in that same olive gown, holding a baby Jamie, and one of Felicia, alone, in her wedding dress. They were carefully hung on the wall above the desk, so that if you sat here, you might easily rest your eyes on them. Someone venerated Felicia, but who? Certainly not Jeanne or Wanda. Had Bill really cared for *someone*, after all? If that were the case, would he degrade his guardian angel into an agent against his brother?—if that's what this was all about.

Or, much as Jessica hated to admit, wasn't it more likely that Vitus was keeping Felicia's image before himself as an inspiration to punish the Carlyles for ruining his life? Jeanne could easily have clued him in to the secret passageways and surreptitiously set him up in here. Still, he'd waited an awfully long time to act. Then again, the opportunity had only presented itself with Jeanne's return and her discovery of a look-alike for Felicia.

Jeesh! Now I know what Dusty feels like when she chases her own tail! Why won't the pieces make this jigsaw clearer? It's worse than one of those pictures that shift from one image to the other, depending on how you look at it! Well, how about taking a gander right in front of you, Miss Genius?

A relatively small leather case, maybe eight inches by five, zipped up; next to it, a journal. The front cover of that journal bore a title in perfect, graceful script: "Experiment."

Scientists performed experiments, yet the script revealed the grace of an artist.

Jess tucked the flashlight under her arm and reached for the journal, but caught herself. Lord, she was sorely tempted to read what might be this plot's history, but Jessica knew better than to contaminate the journal with her prints. Unfortunately, her anxious scan for some sort of cloth to stand between her and the surface of the book was frighteningly halted.

Keys rattle beyond the outside door of the room.

Panic razored through Jessica. She knew she'd never make the passageway before the right key found the lock. A lightning fast survey of the room shot her one hope: the huge mirror. Flashlight firmly in hand, Jessica managed to slip behind the mirror, even climbing onto a fortuitously stored chair to hide her legs from sight, before the outer door groaned open.

There was a rapid, light tread of a woman entering and crossing to the desk. *A woman. Thank God it would be Jeanne not Bill!* That was a relief, but not enough to keep Jessica from silently praying, *Please, God, don't let her hear me breathing! Oh, jeepers, the door! The passage door! It didn't close behind me!*

Jess gripped her flashlight determinedly. If she were caught, she was going to come out swinging!

The woman beyond was muttering softly, even here feeling the need for secrecy. Dared Jess peek through the cracks between the frame and the stand? Maybe it was better not to move and make the old chair creak beneath her.

There was a flurry of movement; the outer door complained again, then slammed. Keys rattled. The door was locked.

Jessica half expected to slide bonelessly down the chair to the floor, like a cartoon character. Instead, she pulled herself together and hopped down. Coming around from the mirror, she regarded the outer door. *Was it one that needed a key to unlock it from either side?* She fought mightily not to let her spirits sink, knowing this door was likely her last shot at getting free without anyone else's help. Returning to the jammed door in her closet and waiting for James seemed to present way too much of a risk that someone dangerous would confront her. That was when her eyes came to rest on the desk—the empty desk. Jess rushed over. Well, not entirely empty. The pictures of Felicia were still there, but the barbiturates, the leather case, and the journal, *Damn, the journal!* were all gone! Scooped up by Jeanne Rivers, but why? Why would she think this obscure cellar room was no longer safe? Did she know Jess had discovered the passageways? Was she planning to take it on the lam?

Would that she could have grabbed at least that journal when she'd had the chance. Well, maybe not. Rivers would certainly have torn this room apart searching for it. Cold comfort in a cold, damp cellar. Still, she might as well thank heaven for small favors, although you might need a microscope to find this one.

The lock on the outside door rattled again, as if someone were testing it, freezing Jess. But she jerked herself into action, hot-footing it back to the old hiding place, knowing she didn't have time to reach the passageway. *Here we go again!* But she wasn't laughing.

Chapter Thirty-Four

Jessica managed to get herself safely behind the enormous mirror and atop the same old chair—prompting the familiar plea: *Please don't collapse under me!* A desperate wish that James might appear to get her out of this one fleeted through her mind, but she knew she was on her own. It struck Jess that this person was having more trouble than Jeanne getting in. That still didn't bode well, for the only other person who'd likely want to get into this forgotten storeroom would be someone who knew its secrets, Jeanne's partner. Whether Bill or Vitus, the outcome of being discovered was not good, leaving Jess too afraid even to risk exposing an eye through the crack between frame and stand to peek.

The door opened, a moment's hesitation—checking for intruders like her? The entering tread was definitely a man's, light and cautious. Bill's tread on the stairs had been heavy, she remembered. How much of a twinkle toes *was* Vitus Blasko?

Holy Cow! Why did her nose choose now to once again itch and twitch in the dust and must. *Fortitude, girl! Will power!* Quietly giving her nose a pinching rub did the trick, but it wasn't any help with her terror of being discovered by . . . whom?

Listening intently, Jess could discern the new arrival's moving cautiously toward the desk. *Cautiously? Why would Jeanne's partner need to act cautiously on his own turf?*

A growing suspicion, curiosity, maybe even relief she would barely allow herself, freed Jessica to let one blue eye take an extremely careful peek. *Holy Cats!*

"Hi there, handsome," Jess purred seductively, leaning around the mirror and bracing herself with her left hand on the elaborately carved frame.

James Crawford whirled on her, one hand reaching for his shoulder holster, or where Jess knew it *would* have been had he been on active duty instead of vacationing in New Hampshire.

Hands raised, Jessica called, "Hey, fella, stand down. I'm on your side."

His eyes raced from attack mode to relief to fury. Fearing what he might have done if he hadn't recognized Jessica, James snapped, "Jesus Christ! Don't you realize that I could have hurt you?"

Jess tried to calm the situation with a shaky attempt at humor: "With what? Your imagination? I know you're not carrying."

James bit out, "You know I don't need a gun to do damage."

Lowering her eyes, Jessica nodded, regretting she'd allowed relief to outweigh her better judgment. But, as the alarm passed out of both of them, they cocked their heads curiously and burst out simultaneously, "What the hell . . . ?" "What in Sam Hill are you doing here!?" The more genteel exclamation issuing from Jessica, of course.

Jessica recovered first to point out, "I wouldn't even be here if you hadn't gone traipsing off to God knows where."

"I left you a note, and, as I recall, I closed it by asking you to stay out of trouble," James replied, crossing his arms.

"You wrote 'try to stay out of trouble.' Lord knows I *tried*."

"Apparently not hard enough."

Jessica narrowed her eyes and, coming toward her husband, growled, "Why, you so and so . . ."

Before she could finish, they were together and in each other's arms.

After hugging each other tightly with relief, Jess smiled up at James, "I am so glad I found, no you found . . ."

"We found each other," James smiled back, before he went almost stern, "Which leads me back to my earlier question, *sans* expletive: what the deuce are you doing here?"

"Ditto," Jessica insisted, adding, "And you go first. I have a feeling your explanation is far less complicated than mine."

"I doubt it," James stated skeptically, "but to get to the point, I was following Jeanne Rivers. I take it you were well hidden so she wouldn't spot you when she came in here."

Jessica bypassed James's statement, pulling back to question, "Why were you following Jeanne?"

"I'm afraid the answer isn't as simple as you expect," he began. "But to make a long story short, or shorter, anyway, when I was on the terrace having a smoke, I saw her come rushing into the drawing room holding an envelope, part of the morning mail, I imagined. She ripped it open and read it as if her life depended on it."

"She didn't see you?"

"She was too preoccupied, and the curtains had been only partially opened. From where I was, I could see her without her seeing me. Her anxiety over that piece of mail made me decide to keep things that way."

"You were spying on her?"

"Do you want to hear the rest of the story or provide annotations?" His tone was tinged with impatience.

"Okay, sorry. Go on. Go on. I should know better than to expect an old dog to give up his old tricks."

James frowned a little at Jessica's canine characterization of him, but wasn't about to waste time. He continued, "I think you'll be glad to know I kept an eagle eye on her goings on when I tell you about what she was prying into. After Jeanne finished scanning the two sheets of paper inside, she started a fire in the hearth, ripped the sheets up and started to toss them in. Unfortunately for her, one of the help, that Lu I think, interrupted her. Something about a plumbing emergency."

"Snapped valve in the kitchen," Jessica automatically supplied.

With a nod, James then cut to the chase, "She left and I stepped in. The sheets weren't entirely consumed; she'd been ushered out in such a hurry. It was the medical report from your doctor's visit, including the results of your blood tests."

Jessica took a quick glance at the desk where she'd seen the bottle of barbiturates. Before James could continue, she surprised him with, "Did it show traces of sodium amytal?"

"How did you know?" James questioned curiously.

Jessica almost spilled everything she knew about the items on the desk and the passages, but that would have drawn them down a rabbit hole before she'd have a chance to find out what she needed about Rivers. She only said, "I'll explain after you fill me in more on your Jeanne story. It'll all make more sense."

"I could see that you'd been tested for exactly that substance, along with a few others, but the results were burned."

"So, there must have been something there Jeanne didn't want me to see," Jessica surmised uneasily. "If I were clear, she'd have no reason to destroy it."

"Rivers might if she was afraid you'd discover the letter had been opened and demanded to know who had violated your privacy," James pointed out. "Once she opened it, she might have thought it would raise less suspicion to just act as if the letter never came or had been mislaid by a servant."

"Well, whatever the results, I have good reason to think Jeanne may have been working with someone to drug and hypnotize me into having those dreams and my midnight rambles."

"Hypnotize you? Who? How?" James puzzled.

"I think Wanda O'Malley was on Jeanne's team, but let me go on."

James nodded and Jessica continued, "I know that kind of drugging can make a person pliable to suggestion. But did *you* know that Jeanne was a nurse at one time who lost her job over what Annette Risdon called 'some funny business' at a hospital? Could have been related to stealing and selling drugs. She might still have some contacts."

James thoughtfully mused, "That is interesting. But why do all that to you?"

"When we get to my story, it will make more sense," Jessica answered, though it killed her not to pour out all she'd discovered.

James looked at her a bit dissatisfied with being kept in the dark, if only temporarily, but agreed, "All right. At any rate, her agitation over the letter decided me that I'd better follow her to see what she did next. When she was in the kitchen, I saw her get all flustered over a phone call and dash out. I jotted down that note for you," a raised eyebrow told Jess he was considering how she'd definitely not stayed out of trouble, "and tracked her. She met someone, and it wasn't anyone I'd expected."

"Really? Who? What happened?"

"She went to the old family cemetery through the woods to meet Jamie Blasko."

"Are you kidding me?" Jessica protested. "That can't be. Jamie was supposed to be in town seeing her lawyer this morning, then meeting Gerry."

"Maybe she finished early and made this stop before she saw Gerry. Or maybe Gerry better double-check her alibis," James answered. "I know I saw Jamie rendezvousing with Rivers."

"All right, all right, go on," Jessica relented. "I don't want to stay here any longer than necessary."

"We could walk out the door," James pointed out. "It's probably not exactly brilliant to while away the afternoon in a dangerous sort's secret hideout."

"No, we can't. I have a few things to show you that mean we have to stay. Don't give me that pained look. Finish your story. It will all make better sense when I tell you after you finish this story," Jessica sighed.

"Right then," James continued, a look in his eye telling Jessica he was not happy that she was holding out on him, even temporarily. "Rivers met the Blasko girl in the section out of the main graveyard, a mausoleum in a pocket of the woods."

"I know the place," Jessica affirmed. "So, what did you hear?"

"Not as much as I'd have liked. I couldn't get near enough without being seen or heard with those dead leaves crackling underfoot. Most of the time, the wind came up and either roared too loud for me to pick up much or carried their words away. But I could hear Jeanne threatening Jamie to stay away from the Carlyle house and to stop getting chummy with Philip Carlyle. There was also something about watching out for Bill Carlyle's bad side. And that maybe Jamie had better watch out for her loony father, too. She didn't know him as well as she thought."

"Ouch," Jessica winced for the berated Jamie. She speculated, "Maybe that crack about Bill meant she'd sic him on Jamie, or," here, Jessica hesitated, not happy to offer the alternative, "perhaps Jamie's not knowing her father meant that *he's* Jeanne's partner."

Viewing Jessica curiously, James observed, "You keep talking about Jeanne having partners: first the medium and now Carlyle or Blasko. What haven't you told me?"

Jess opened her mouth to reply, then reconsidered coming completely clean just yet. She finally explained, "Is there anything else to your story—because mine's a complicated doozy."

James looked as if he wanted to press the issue, but he knew her well enough not to. He finished, "A little more. I was impressed with Jamie showing a surprising amount of gumption. She came back at Jeanne by accusing her of sending a poison-pen letter to her father; but Jeanne, the bold one, laughed in Jamie's face."

"Oh, yes, I know about that," Jessica shook her head. "What a piece of work is Jeanne! She even tried to hang it on some poor girl she'd fired. Come to think of it, the whole story about a vengeful ex-servant could have been a fairy tale. Who would take the time or have the temerity to check it out with Philip or the other servants? But I guess that clears Vitus as her partner. Who would try to make her own partner look unstable to everyone?"

"Unless she was aiming at creating just the perception you described. Misdirection is the con man's most essential trick, love," James countered.

Jess was beginning to think that if she had just grabbed that journal, they'd have the answer to so many of these questions. However, James riveted her attention with, "I followed Jeanne back here, and she seemed a bit shaken, despite her fierceness to Jamie Blasko. She had seemed to waver when they started arguing about 'packages' or 'passages.' Maybe 'packages.'"

Jessica smiled at this perfect transition for relating her experiences. Finally, she could feel her misadventures in the honeycomb of the mansion hadn't been a colossal foul-up.

"They said 'passages,' James. I *know*. While you were trailing the nefarious Miss Rivers, I was exploring four floors of *passages*, secret ones, starting from the panel in my closet."

James's mouth didn't drop open. He was too British for that. Still, Jess could read him inwardly debating whether to read her the riot act or press her to spill what she knew. Before he could decide, Jess harnessed her excitement to carefully relate a description of the panel in her room, the passageways with their suggestive footprints in the dust, the rooms so much a part of her nightmares, the dressing gown she'd found here, tying them together with her theories about how Jeanne had worked with either Bill or Vitus, and at one point Wanda, to make her live those nightmares, all likely part of a vicious plot against Philip or Vitus, depending on who Jeanne's partner was. Jessica saved for the penultimate her revelation of finding the sodium amytal, the case, and the journal, cursing the paradox that grabbing the diary could have answered all their questions, while setting Jeanne searching the room with fatal consequences for Jess.

Jessica had saved for last revealing the passage that might have hidden Wanda's murderer. However, before she could spring that gem, James startled her by cursing, "Damn, I saw Jeanne rush out of here when I was nicely tucked behind the furnace waiting for her to make an exit, so I could comfortably nip in for a little peek at what she was hiding in here. I didn't even realize she was slipping her secret away right under my nose! I should have continued following her instead of playing master cracksman with the locked door. I'm a blasted fool!"

"Well, your choice did rescue me," Jessica offered, not sure how thrilled she was that he'd forgotten that little fact. Nevertheless, she softened to add, "So, I wouldn't say that was completely a foolish choice."

His look sheepish, James frowned again, grousing, more at himself than at her, "And we've been standing here chattering away while she's made off for God knows where to destroy her evidence. It's too late to try and find and stop her now. We've come up completely empty."

Jess put a hand on James's arm and said, "Not completely."

She told him about the passage that ran behind and around the corner of the music room: the perfect spot for murdering Wanda O'Malley. James didn't complain she hadn't told him earlier. He was all business now.

"Did you give the landing a canvassing? See any evidence?"

Certain she'd done right, Jessica answered, "I shone my light in the passage, but I made a point not to go in there and risk contaminating any. I couldn't discern anything, but that doesn't mean someone with better lighting or professional equipment couldn't. Also, I couldn't get around the corner. That's where I think you might find something. Gunshot residue on the wall? Shell casings? Anything?"

James nodded and smiled, "Nice going, Mrs. Crawford. I think Chief Winston will find this quite interesting. However, before we give him a ring, I'd like to see this space. I want to know exactly what I'm talking about when I contact him. Hand over the torch, would you? I can find my way by myself. You look all in. Why don't you go . . ."

Jessica shook her head, "No dice. I'm okay, and I can show you the way. Anyway, we're in this together, buddy."

She didn't add that trying to find her way out of the cellar alone, with no place in this house feeling safe, was not exactly on her hit parade of smart ideas.

Chapter Thirty-Five

Jessica Minton stood tensely on the spiral staircase above the landing that backed the music room. On the step below her, James Crawford used the limited illumination of the flashlight to scan the passage extending beyond and around a corner. They'd scarcely spoken in their ascent, then only in whispers. They had no proof that Jeanne had entered these secret ways to find a new stash for her incriminating materials, but no assurance she hadn't. Better to play it safe and keep quiet.

"Anything significant on the floor I might have missed?" Jess whispered, aware her eye was not as trained as her husband's in such matters.

James answered, still, staring down the way, "Nothing I can see by this light, but that doesn't rule out this spot, especially with the passage angling for a prime shot at your medium. There could be some kind of sliding panel there. Not big enough for a person to pass through, but effective for getting off a shot at a victim—and with all the excitement and concentration on the table, who would notice a panel sliding back? I have to admit I didn't. My attention was entirely on you."

"Well, thank you," Jess replied, momentarily pleased by his admission. However, she was all business for, "Still, whoever did it would have to be some kind of a crack shot, even with Wanda silhouetted."

"Hmm," James looked up at Jessica, the flashlight illuminating him with far too much eeriness. "Who arranged the seating at the table and the placement of that light?"

"Oh, I don't know, exactly. Probably Scott or Beverly," Jessica considered. "They gave directions, but implementing them would have been Jeanne or one of the girls under her. Gosh."

"Gosh, indeed," James ruefully concurred. Then he decided, "I've seen enough for now. Let's get out of this fun house and decide the best way to present our case to Chief Winston."

"Aren't you afraid Jeanne or whoever her partner is will come down here and 'tidy up'?"

"As far as I can tell, neither she nor her partner is wise to what we know just yet. We may have a little time, though maybe not much. After all, it's not as if they can make the passages just disappear."

James had guided Jessica down the spiral stairs; into and out of that dreadful storage room (making sure the door was relocked); through the cellar. To her surprise, though, he took her away from the stairs ascending to the kitchen and toward those leading to one of the bulkheads opening up behind the mansion.

He explained as they started up the steps, "The kitchen is our friend's domain. The last thing we need is to come up from here and run smack into her with you looking as bedraggled as Dusty after chasing a mouse around the cellar. Tell me that wouldn't arouse her suspicion."

That "bedraggled" characterization did not go over well with Jessica; however, she only commented, "Dusty never had rats this big to contend with."

She could tag him later.

After slowly lifting the wide bulkhead door and cautiously checking to ensure the coast was clear, James led Jessica out into the fresh, cold autumn air. Finding herself hustled across the packed dirt space between the mansion and the garage, Jess thought, *Thank goodness, no one seemed to be around to notice.*

As they reached the grass, far enough from the house to permit the muted beginnings of conversation, Jessica questioned, "Why didn't you get on the horn to Chief Winston and tell him to get himself out here *tout de suite*?"

"Which phone, love?" James answered with a glint in his eye. "The one in the kitchen with all the help around, perhaps even Jeanne? Or maybe in the telephone vestibule, where you can't see who's lurking around the corner?"

"Point taken," Jessica allowed. "There is a private line in Philip Carlyle's library, but the room's usually locked. Three guesses, and the first two don't count, as to who has the key."

Jessica was shivering in the cold wind as she spoke, which James didn't miss. Taking off his jacket as the wind wreaked havoc with his own thick, dark hair, he put the garment around Jess and asked, "Better now?"

"Yes," she smiled up at him, his care erasing much of the past hour's direness, "but you're going to freeze your patoot!"

"You forget: I'm the rugged sort. My patoot is just fine." He grew serious again. "Jessica, we must get into town right away. But before I see Winston, I want to make sure all my ducks are in a row. So I need to check if the post office box I set up has Dick Streeter's report yet."

"Oh, that's right. You set that up when we came back from seeing the doctor in Portsmouth. Really good idea to take that precaution, considering what happened to my medical report," Jessica concluded. "I'd say that maybe I should have done the same, but it looks like Jeanne's getting her mitts on that report worked out better for me than her. Anyway, do you think Dick was able to find anything yet?"

"I do if I know Mr. Streeter. But when we passed the garage, I noticed neither of the cars was there," James observed sourly.

"That's right. Philip drove himself to work in the sedan, and Frankie drove Gerry in to meet Jamie . . ."

Jess trailed off, again flummoxed by what Jamie had been doing in that cemetery with Jeanne when she was supposed to be seeing Gerry. But James was talking now: "It's a long walk into town."

Jessica brightened, smiling: "True, but it's only about fifteen minutes by bicycle. It's not as fast as a car, but it beats hoofing it. Even better, we won't need to ask anyone's permission or get any keys. Follow me. I know where the bikes are kept."

"Why didn't I think of that," James shook his head, following his wife.

Jessica smiled sweetly and said, "I guess being as bedraggled as a mouse-chasing cat makes a body smarter."

Tagged!

James just grinned.

They'd flown through the woods with the speed of Assault pursuing his equine nemesis Armed, Jessica being the pursuer. Pedaling for all she was worth, figuring that hair and hose were already past all salvation, she could still barely keep pace. And she sensed that James wasn't even going full throttle. All that pedaling from pillar to post while undercover in France certainly gave him the edge on a girl who'd only been taking joy rides through Central Park.

Soon they were out of the woods, literally if not figuratively, and James stopped at the edge of the main road to ask, "Need a breather, love?"

"No . . ." a quick couple of pants. "I'm fine." Deep breaths.

"If you say so," he smiled, despite the seriousness of the situation. "It's under a mile to the village. At least now we'll be on tarmac."

"Smooth sailing," Jessica winked, then pushed off on the lead, though not for long. Yes, she did realize that James's little inquiry had been designed to let her catch her breath.

When they passed the white building housing the police, Jess was relieved to see one car parked there. *God forbid Winston was out. Unless he had taken another vehicle. Don't think like that!*

Shortly later, they glided to a stop outside yet another white-clapboard building, the post office. As they started to hustle in, Jessica tried to shove her wind-tousled hair into some kind of order. She knew her hose were beyond redemption, but she had to do *something* to keep from completely looking as if she'd just fallen out of a tree.

Activity at the post office had settled down after the lunchtime rush. One clerk was on duty, but she seemed maddeningly preoccupied with sliding letters into the right slots while trying to chat up James on where he came from and what he thought about the weather. Jess's urge at this point was to grab the older woman by the lapels of her suit and pull her over the counter to demand James's mail. Her nerves-of-steel spouse, however, managed to turn on the charm and inquire about a rush mail delivered to his P.O. Box.

"Sure thing, Mr. Crawford," the old gal smiled. "It just come in late this mornin'. I was gonna call to the house to let you know, but it got way too busy. Here you are." Before she could hand over the envelope, the woman got a good look at Jessica, frowned, and questioned, "Honey, you all right? You look like you just fell out of a tree."

Jessica bit down her annoyance and forced herself to reply patiently, "We bicycled in, and I forgot to wear a kerchief over my hair. Heck of a windy day, isn't it?"

While the woman was giving Jess a doubtful look, a gust corroborated her claims, rattling the roof. Then, to doubly test the patience of both Crawfords, the woman absently pulled back the envelope from James as she instinctively looked upwards. To Jess's mind, a crack definitely appeared in her husband's nerves of steel.

"The envelope, please," Jessica smiled sweetly, nodding toward James.

"Oh, yes, certainly. What am I thinking?" the woman stammered, at last putting their prize in James Crawford's hands. To his credit, he did not snatch it away, but smiled graciously, thanked the older woman, wished her a good afternoon, and then as calmly as possible hustled Jessica out the door.

The screen door closed behind them, and Jessica pressed, "Well, aren't you going to open it?"

Her husband glanced about at the passersby on the sidewalk, deciding, "Not right here." His eyes settled on the green island running down the main street, with benches situated at intervals.

"Over . . ."

". . . there, the empty bench," Jessica finished, her eyes already settled on the same spot.

"We make quite a good pair, don't we," he grinned, escorting Jessica across the street, after an instinctive check for traffic.

"A marriage of true minds," Jessica playfully agreed as they reached the bench. "Now let's can the small talk and see what Mr. Streeter has to say. Start with Wanda, since she's the murder victim."

Sitting together, they were close enough for Jessica to read along with James after he opened the envelope.

"Well, we knew that," Jess muttered at the information of Wanda's working all over in vaudeville, and then in some fancy supper clubs. However, it was where and with whom she'd worked about two or so years ago that made Jess utter, "Bingo!"

"It does look promising," James understated, ever circumspect.

"Promising, my Aunt Fanny," Jessica insisted. "Sure her partner didn't go by Jeanne Rivers, but look at the description: the hair, the eye-color, the build—and the name. *Jean*ette Brooks? Brooks/Rivers? And one of her acts, for Pete's sake, was as an exhibition sharpshooter. Sure. It all makes sense that she brought Wanda up here to work on Philip, and maybe Vitus, too. You know Wanda told us this yarn about having a 'premonition' that she should drive to the island and knock on the Carlyle door, which just 'happened' to be when Jeanne and Philip were talking about Felicia's hauntings. Some coincidence."

"One manufactured by Jeanne?" James rhetorically inquired.

"A surer bet than Stymie at a mile and a three-eights," Jessica nodded. She added, "I'll let you in on another bit of info. See that about them working in Rio until mid last year? That's one of the spots Bill Carlyle said he'd been holed up for years."

"Rio is a big city, Jessica," James cautioned.

"I know, but it's still a significant coincidence."

"Why don't we see what Dick found us on Bill, then," James proposed thoughtfully, flipping back through the pages. Before Jess could get a good look at what he saw, James uttered a reflective, "Hmm." When Jessica did get an eyeful, she realized that had been a "hmm" of disappointment.

"Next to nothing on the chap," James frowned. "It does report on him working in Rio, but nothing on a connection to Jeanne. Then there's something about his re-entering the country in Florida late in 1946. That would be not too long after Jeanne got the housekeeper position, but before your producer set up plans for the broadcast, correct?"

"Yes, why?" Jessica questioned as she mentally juggled dates, trying to follow where her husband's cogitations were leading. "I think Scott heard from Philip in January of this year, which would give Jeanne, Wanda, and Bill plenty of time to do something about the passageways."

"Without Philip knowing?" James doubtfully raised the question.

"Philip? You're suspecting Philip? That's absurd. Why would he be involved in all this shadiness? Anyway, they *could* slip something by him concerning the house. Remember, he spends almost all day at that factory. I also understand he travels for his business quite a bit," Jessica pointed out.

"Jessica, I know that you never like to think ill of people you feel have acted kindly toward you, but we have to consider all possibilities," James advised gently. "Let's look at what the report on Philip says before we jump to any conclusions one way or another."

"You even had Dick Streeter check on Philip?"

"I even had him look into Danvers," James wryly answered. "Ah, Philip *has* done quite a bit of business travel, especially to Washington. Well, this is interesting."

Jessica followed James's reading and blurted, "He lost a major contract in '44, then again with the cutbacks at the end of the war. No wonder he jumped at the broadcast. Scott gave him a helpful cash infusion, though, knowing our budget, it can't have been *that* much help. Is it relevant, though, really?"

"It does suggest that brother Bill will be in for a bit of a belt round the head if he wins his case to get control of the Carlyle holdings," James concluded.

"He could sell the property to developers who've been scouting the island," Jessica suggested. "I don't think Philip wants that. It seems to me he has too much sense of tradition. Bill, on the other hand, he's the materialistic type; and in his present financial state, any chunk of change would be a significant incentive for him. Still, why kill Wanda? Unless he didn't want to share."

"Then Jeanne should be more than a little nervous," James concluded. On reflection, he added, "When I saw her in the cellar, I think she was, likely between Jamie suspecting her and Bill's tendency to terminate partnerships fatally."

Jessica proposed, "At least this all seems to point away from Vitus Blasko. That should be a relief for Jamie."

James remained silent a moment before saying, "We'll see."

He flipped to another page and pensively exhaled over the information that Jessica skimmed and summed up out loud, "Vitus did serve as a *sharpshooter* in the first Great War. But that was thirty years ago. Rifles are quite different weapons than handguns, right?"

"True," James allowed. "Nevertheless, we don't know that he hasn't extended his expertise over the years. It's time to turn over all our findings to Chief Winston. Then let him do his job."

Jessica agreed, "Yes, you're right, of course. No more amateur sleuthing for me. Let's drop all this in the good police chief's lap. Then we can find ourselves a room with a good solid lock and NO secret panels!"

Chapter Thirty-Six

They'd quickly reached the police station by bike, but before taking a step on the path to the building, Jessica stopped her husband to ask, "I was thinking: how are you going to explain getting all this dirt from Dick Streeter and still keep your involvement in the cloak and dagger biz on the q.t.?"

James nodded and answered, "Yeah, I gave that some thought, myself. I have an idea. I can't say it's brilliant, but I think it will do."

After James succinctly laid out his plan, Jessica added her two cents, and then the two headed up to the station's entrance. Except, as they faced the glass door leading inside, Jess's excitement faltered at the thought of facing that world-weary kisser of Winston's with their fantastic tale. Well, they did have an honest-to-goodness reliable source to back them up. Still, when James held the door for her, Jess couldn't help resenting the decorum of "ladies first" meaning she had to go first into hostile territory. Worse, between her wind-tangled hair and stair-savaged hose, she dreaded what her appearance would do to their credibility.

They entered a large, open room filled with the smell of stale cigarettes and coffee initially brewed to take the chill off the first Ice Age. A wooden rail separated them from the main body of that room. Directly across was a metal door, probably leading to the cells. A desk was to their left, file cabinets were pushed against the walls, and a somewhat more prominent desk sat at the far left corner. From here, Jessica read the desk plate: James H. Winston, Chief of Police. But that desk was vacant. Was she disappointed or relieved?

All this ran through Jessica's mind before a voice to the right asked, "You people need help?"

A woman on the downhill side of middle age sat at a desk, paperwork before her, a radio dispatch console to her left, under a window. She was the dispatcher, of course.

"Yes," James smiled to the woman's jaded, over-worked expression. "We need to see Chief Winston. It's extremely important. I believe we've come across information that will be highly useful to him."

James had the warmest of smiles. Hard for even someone who wasn't as nuts about him as Jess to resist. The world weariness of the dispatcher thawed enough for her to ask, "Important, huh? What's it about?"

"We're from the Carlyle mansion," James elaborated. "I believe we've found something that might aid Chief Winston with the O'Malley case. It is terribly important. We want to be of help."

"Lord knows he could stand some. Well, you don't look like a couple of crackpots," although she did hesitate saying that after giving Jessica the once over. "Just go on over to his desk. There's a couple of chairs there. Chief stepped out for a minute." She jerked her head to a short corridor behind her. "He'll be right back. I tell them guys not to drink so much coffee, but do they listen?"

"Men!" Jessica sympathized. James raised an eyebrow, while the older woman agreed, "You got that right, honey."

When they passed quickly through the gate and over to Winston's desk, Jess had the peculiar feeling she was being watched. A glance over her shoulder revealed the dispatcher frowning at the ladders up the back of her stockings.

The woman caught her eye and commented, "Honey, you fall out of a tree or something?"

"Or something," Jess replied, "But that something I fell into could be a big help to your chief."

The dispatcher shrugged, "Fine by me. Like I said, Jim can use all the help he can get."

As James pulled out a chair for Jess by the desk, he whispered to her, "I can see why she's only a dispatcher not a detective. Not the right kind of curiosity with too much tongue-wagging of other people's business."

Jessica glanced back to assure herself the older woman was oblivious to them now, then answered, equally softly, and not without disapproval, "Fat chance of a woman with ability getting to be a detective. Too many people with clout think women aren't good for anything but being a housewife and mother. I do know lots of gals were glad to go back to the 'normal' before the war, but I also know plenty others who were frustrated and, well, lost, because the independence they'd found working on their own was taken away from them."

After a quick glance 'round to make sure no one would hear, James reflected, "I have to say a large percentage of the field agents in the SOE were women, and damned good. But I don't think they'd be eager to go back to that line of work, not any more than I would."

They were quiet a moment until James changed the topic with a nod toward a closed bakery box on Winston's desk: "What do you suppose the good chief has there? I must admit I'm beginning to feel a bit peckish."

"We're in a police station. There's a pot of coffee and the box is from a bakery," Jessica grinned. "Classic stereotype. Donuts, of course!"

The sound of a door closing across the room and a subsequent mutter of voices drew their attention. Winston and the older woman were looking them over, the Chief not appearing thrilled to recognize them. Then again, Jess wasn't sure she could ever remember seeing Winston looking any way that might be remotely construed as "thrilled."

"You two, Crawford and Minton, huh?" he said, starting toward them. "Yvonne says you have some info for me on the O'Malley case?"

Definitely not excited. Not dismissive, exactly, but dubious just the same.

James rose, beginning, "Yes, good of you to see us, Chief. I suspect we've come across some facts that you can use."

"You have, huh?" Winston merely observed, a downward motion of his hand indicating James should sit again.

Jessica compressed her lips to control her impatience as Winston stopped to pour himself some coffee, giving a querying nod to her and James. She shook her head in a manner that expelled some of her impatience as James said, "No thanks, but we do need to talk. You'll want to hear us."

Where did *James get his patience?* Jessica marveled.

A patience she just did not possess. In fact, she had to bite her lip to keep from snapping at Winston as he came over, sat down, and responded, not particularly impressed by James's words, "You'll have to excuse me if I don't get too excited, Mr. Crawford. You'd be surprised at the crazy leads I get that don't pan out. A guy doesn't want to get all het up till he knows what he's getting. Anyway, at least you two don't seem to be like the types who claim the Hound of Hades did it."

"Thanks for that much," Jessica couldn't help saying. A sharp look from James calmed her annoyance sufficiently for her to proceed according to plan. In deference to Winston's annoyance with the nutcases wasting his time, Jessica said, "I know some of this is going to sound a little crazy, but the basic fact is, I discovered these passages in the Carlyle Mansion. I explored them and . . ."

Sitting up abruptly, Winston interrupted, "Look here, lady, after what I just told you, are you pulling my leg?"

With powerful self-control, Jessica refrained from informing Winston that *his* appendage was the last one in the world she wanted to yank. Instead, she forced herself to respond calmly, "No, I'm dead serious. Don't I look like someone who got stuck prowling through the recesses of an old manse?"

"You look as if you took a tumble down a flight of stairs," Winston conceded, reflectively. "Okay, go on. What's so important about your secret passages?"

"A lot," Jess answered, focusing on his interest rather than his wisecrack. "But, more importantly, I found a passage behind the music room. It hooks around to next to the windows, where everyone seems to think the shot that killed Wanda came from."

Jim Winston leaned back in his seat, regarding Jessica, gears clicking behind his eyes. After a moment, he turned to James to question carefully, "And you were wandering around with your wife? Kind of a funny date, in my book."

James corrected, "That's not precisely accurate. After Jessica finally got out of the passageways, she told me what she'd seen. So, I had her take me back to show me."

Winston scowled, then grumbled, "I suppose the two of you tromped all around the floor and made a nice little hash of any relevant evidence?"

"Not at all, Chief," James answered, refusing to be ruffled. "We didn't set foot in the passage by the music room for precisely that reason. I only scanned the area with my torch. I couldn't see anything definite that might be useful, but I only had a standard light. And I'm not a professional, like you. However, I can assure you that, as my wife said, where the passage angles to the left could match the position from which the medium was shot."

Winston gave James a speculative once-over, then looked down at his desk. The box of bakery goodies caught his eye and he reached for it, but Jessica could see he was still mulling James's words.

Manners seemed to halt Winston's speculation, for he turned to Jess, nodding to the box with the inquiry, "Would you like one, Miss . . . Mrs. . . . ?"

There was something disarming in Winston's inquiry. So, even though he might be trying to lull her, she decided it best to meet his gallantry halfway. Jess smiled. "Having a professional name gets confusing. Just call me Jessica. The first name never changes. Thanks for the offer, but I couldn't handle a donut after my big breakfast."

"Oh, it's not donuts," Winston replied, digging into the box to pull out a delectable. "It's croissants. This bakery does some job on them. Light and flaky. Donuts are too heavy for me. They do great pies, too. Do you like cream pies, Mrs. . . . Jessica?"

James eased in, "My wife and I do have a warm place in our hearts for banana cream—but I have more to tell you, though not precisely about the passageways."

"Yeah, well," Winston replied, "a guy like me has to wonder why a nice gal like your wife, here, was playing Nancy Drew in her rich host's mansion. Sounds a little screwy, don't you think?"

That query raised not only Jessica's hackles but the fear that her strange dream experiences would come out to make everything else they said sound screwy. She interjected, "I'll tell you what I was doing. When I was outside the mansion with Gerry Davis, we noticed that where one of the windows was placed would actually put it inside my closet. I knew that wasn't right. To make a long story short, I went into the closet and figured out there was a secret panel that led to a passageway."

"So, you went snooping around without permission, in your host's home, just for the hell of it?" A casual but clearly skeptical tone.

Jess could see that James was about to rise to her defense, so she stopped him with a subtly raised hand and replied, "I got stuck in the passages when the panel shut, okay? Granted, it was not exactly my shining hour, but that's what happened. I searched through the floor above and the attic level to get out, but no such luck. Anyway, I found that landing next to the music room, which I did not disturb, before I finally found a way out through a room in the cellar. Good enough for you?"

"Curious gal, aren't you?" Now he grew more serious. "You know what curiosity did to the cat."

"I know information brought her back," Jessica countered steadily.

"Well, sister, this kind of information could get you bumped off if someone knows you're even looking for it, never mind that you have it."

James moved in here: "I have some additional information that may help you keep my wife safe—and close your case."

Winston took a bite from his croissant, brushed away some flaky goodness from his shirt, then regarded James curiously before ordering, "Shoot the works, fella."

James pulled from his inner jacket pocket the envelope containing Dick Streeter's report and convincingly fibbed, "During the war, when I was at Washington Irving University, a chap from the F.B.I. came to me for some information on individuals I'd known at University back home. I can't tell you anymore, and I'd prefer you keep even this much under your hat. But he owed me for some favors, so I collected. I decided if my wife and her sister had to stay here with a murderer on the loose, I'd better do what I could to end the danger."

"Mighty uxorious of you," Winston observed. "Mighty considerate of you to lend a hand, too. Okay, pal, hand it over."

Not too convinced, not too pleased, Jessica assessed the Chief. She really had to hand it to James for remaining unperturbed by Winston's attitude.

"Take a look, especially at Wanda O'Malley and Jeanne Rivers," James advised levelly. "You'll find it interesting."

"Well, let's just see," Winston casually replied, extracting the report. "But if you don't mind, I'll take it from the top here instead of skipping around. Get the full effect that way."

"Suit yourself," James responded, keeping much cooler than Jess knew she felt. But James had the right idea: Winston was not a guy to be rushed. She also had to admit that they were expecting Winston to swallow a heck of a lot from them. Plus, he clearly had to tread carefully when dealing in a case concerning the big families of the island.

Without looking up from his reading, Winston commented, "Yup, we knew all about Blasko's sharp-shooting background. Came out when we were questioning him." Now looking up at them, he remarked, "Even here in the backcountry, we can conduct an investigation. Oh, let's see, yup, knew all about Philip Carlyle's financial troubles—though I can't see how bumping off a phony psychic, even a real one, would help him." A bending of the page to read about Bill and he added, "Nope, nothin' new here. Maybe a little more specific on where and when he was working as a sketch artist."

James directed, "Now take a look at the intel on Wanda O'Malley. Rather interesting, isn't it? Especially in terms of where she worked in South America and the description of her assistant, originally a female sharp shooter. Does that assistant sound like anyone you know?"

Winston's expression was reserved, but he followed James's suggestion. He sat up, giving James a narrow-eyed glance before shaking out the pages in his hand and frowning as he finished. Finally, Jim Winston observed, "You know, I put in to the Feds for information like this and haven't gotten back my report. You must have some clout to get all this dope before me. That interests me."

"More than finding evidence more tightly linking Jeanne Rivers, perhaps even Bill Carlyle, to the murder of Wanda O'Malley?" James countered, *now* embroidering a bit on his report's suggestion of Bill's connection to the women. "Look, I explained my 'in' earlier. If you want more detail, fine, we can have a lovely chat over whiskies in the local pub some night. But I'm giving you a chance to have a suspect in custody right this week."

Winston's eyes narrowed. Then, unexpectedly, he suddenly shook his head, grumbling, "How could I be such a dope. It won't wash. Remember, Rivers has an air-tight alibi: locked in her room with kitchen staff right outside her door. You and your smart theories."

"It will wash," Jessica countered. "We had the same doubt until both of us made the logical leap: if there's one set of secret passages, what's to say there aren't more, including one in Jeanne's room? Everyone who knew Jeanne as a child remembers how she would unexpectedly show up all over the house. Doesn't knowledge of the passages explain why?"

The Chief gave a thoughtful, even acquiescent frown, saying, "Okay, I'll grant that. Let me think about a motive. Rivers pretended not to know O'Malley, but then killed her once she got her in. Hmm, maybe a scam to bilk Carlyle and some of you radio people went sour? Then there's Bill Carlyle. Yeah, he could have lied when he said during questioning he'd never seen either gal when he was south of the border. But what's his connection to their plot? There *is* that lawsuit against his brother, but how does killing O'Malley help him out there?" He looked hard at Jessica and James, "Anyway, blaming Rivers all falls apart if she can't be placed behind the panel at the time of the murder. You, Mrs. . . . Miss . . ."

"Jessica," she repeated, warm with hope that he *was* taking them seriously.

"Yeah, okay, Jessica, can you show me the passage behind the music room? The bullet's trajectory from there would make more sense than through the window. Let me do a preliminary check before I call in the crime scene boys from Portsmouth."

"Certainly," Jess beamed. "Let's go now before Jeanne figures out anyone is on to the passageways."

"And how would she get wise?"

Jessica's enthusiasm cooled into sheepishness as she admitted, "Let's just say you should always check the durability of an antique reproduction before you use it to prop open a secret panel."

"I'll make a note of it," Winston returned dryly. He reached for the phone on his desk and said, "But now I have to know who else of your chums is around the house at the moment."

Jessica explained, "None of the actors or crew, and my sister's in Portsmouth. You knew that. Philip went to the office; Bill was in the attic studio, last I knew; and we're not sure about Jeanne. Most of the indoor staff is probably still contending with rambunctious plumbing."

"Well," he snorted, "not too many busybodies around to watch us, though we might have to keep our eyes peeled for the suspects. So, I'm just going to give Mr. Philip Carlyle a jingle; I'll try him at home, first, to ask his permission . . ."

"Whoa," Jessica insisted, her extended hand signaling Winston to stop. "You can't do that. You can't tip him off. He might try to protect Jeanne. He thinks a lot of her."

It surprised Jess that James hadn't joined her protest, until Winston calmly pointed out, "I can't *not* do that. Ever hear of a little thing called the Fourth Amendment?"

Jessica's eyes shot upward as she mentally ran through the amendments until she got to number four, causing her to blurt, "Illegal search and seizure. Got it."

"On the nosey," James smiled, and their eyes shared recollections of their trying to stay on the right side of that one in adventures past.

"You're right," Jess agreed. "We're not a bunch of Nazis here."

"No one in his right mind would want to be," Winston added. Then he was back to business. "So, let's give Philip Carlyle a jingle. Try him at the office, first, if that's where you think he is."

James put a calming hand on Jessica's arm, and she smiled weakly back, but she couldn't be calmed, not entirely. What if Rivers were taking it on the lam even as they sat here? Would Bill Carlyle hightail it out with her?

"Hello? Yes, this is Chief Winston on Birdsong Island. I'd like to talk to Mr. Carlyle. I need his help on something. Yeah, sure, I'll hold."

Waiting, Winston put a hand over the speaker of the phone and remarked to Jessica and James, "I wonder how many layers of secretaries I'll have to wade through to get to the big cheese—Yes, hello. Oh? Really? Left for home some time ago? Well, thanks, I'll try . . . Oh, you can put me through from there? Swell, thanks, doll. Oh, sorry. No disrespect intended, Ma'am."

Jessica leaned over to James and explained, "That's right. With his separate line in the study, he can call out, and they can patch you through from his office without having to go through the town operator."

"You know a lot about this guy's phone business," Winston observed, waiting for his call to go through. "You moonlight for Ma Bell?"

"No. No big secret. Philip told me when he was showing me around the study—"

Winston's hand came up, silencing her as he heard Philip Carlyle pick up. "Good afternoon, Mr. Carlyle."

My, what lovely, warm tones you have when you want to charm someone into giving you what you want—especially if that someone has the influence to decide if you keep your job, Jess mused.

"Sorry to bother you at home, but I've just come into some new information about the case, and I really need to shoot over there to discuss it with you. I know you're a busy man, but your input is critical. I know you want me to wrap things up as soon as possible, save your family from all the scandal, and put things back to normal for you. Like you were telling me the other day. I aim to please. Yeah, sure, about five or ten minutes. Swell. I'll see you."

He hung up and smiled at his visitors, "Catch more flies with honey than vinegar."

"And it's always harder to turn down a request to person's face," James added knowingly.

"You said it, professor," the Chief agreed, standing up. Taking up his dark jacket and his hat, Winston gave one slightly longing look at the box of croissants. Duty, however, prevailed and he gestured for Jessica to precede the two men with, "Shall we?"

When they reached Yvonne at her desk, Winston gave her a succinct account and a suggestion to keep her lips buttoned about anything she might have overheard. His tone told Jess that Winston had the chops to master even the most headstrong of what James dubbed chin-waggers.

They were in the patrol car outside, but before pulling out into traffic, Winston turned to Jessica and her husband next to him and instructed, "Look, you two. We're playing in the big league here. Carlyle has a lot of juice, and he might not want to believe his housekeeper hornswoggled him or even that his brother is further besmirching the family name. So just let me do the talking. More important, I don't want to walk in there and be blindsided, so is there anything else you haven't told me?"

Jessica turned to her husband, asking with her eyes if she should risk coming completely clean about the drugging and her nightmares. James nodded. Right he was. If Winston did know what Jeanne, and likely Bill, had done to her, if he knew about Jeanne's secret room and the materials she'd taken, it might clarify how she and a partner had conspired together—Jess hoped. Anyway, it was too late for Winston to turn back now.

Chapter Thirty-Seven

The black and white pulled up at the front entrance of the Carlyle mansion. Before Jessica or James could move a muscle, Winston warned, "Like I said, I'm bringing you two in on this coz I can use you to keep things on track. But make no mistake about it, I do all the talkin'—or most of it. Just in case you do hear something that doesn't sound right, I don't want you to butt in. Just, maybe, raise your pinky, like so. That's all. *Capisce*?"

"No argument here," James agreed. "We're not here to get in your way."

Jessica added, "Anything to help."

"Fine. You can do that by following my lead. Okay, let's go."

They were out of the car and almost to the door when Jessica had a disturbing thought. Arresting Winston's hand as he started to knock, she sprang her concern on him, "What if Jeanne answers the door? What should we say? I just hate the thought of looking that woman in face, knowing what I know. I'd love to crown her . . ."

Winston cut her off, "That wouldn't be very helpful would it? You're a hi-falutin' actress, ACT. Play it nonchalant. Now let me do my job."

James gave Jess's arm an assuring squeeze, while whispering in her ear, "I know you're a trouper. I've seen you make nice with the devil."

Jess ruefully agreed, "Okay, Chief Winston. I'm game. Let her rip."

The door opened under Winston's businesslike rap, but only after a pause. It was a toss-up which side of the doorway felt the greater surprise.

"You usually answer the door yourself, Mr. Carlyle?" Winston asked.

"I do when the help are all at sixes and sevens in the kitchen, and my housekeeper is nowhere to be seen," Philip answered, exasperated, before giving Jessica and James a quizzical once over at their accompanying Winston.

"You don't say?" Winston inquired. "No idea where she is?"

"Not at the moment," Philip replied, still puzzling over Jess and her husband's presence. Then he remembered himself and offered, "But, please, come in—all of you. I'm anxious to find out . . . be of help."

"Tell you what, Mr. Carlyle. I just remembered I have to get a message out to Deputy Hudson. Why don't you take the Crawfords in and I'll be right back. Think about a good place where we can talk in private."

"All of us?" Philip asked uncertainly. He was *not* pleased with Jessica and James's involvement.

Winston didn't answer that question, instead replying, "Be back in a jiffy, and we'll have a profitable talk."

His back to Philip Carlyle, Winston tapped a silencing finger over his lip to Jessica and James to reinforce his earlier instructions.

Philip was speaking, "Well, please come in. I must say this is all rather confusing." Jess entered with her husband, as Philip continued, after closing the door, "I am eager to have Wanda O'Malley's murder cleared up. A killing in one's house is hardly conducive to maintaining the family reputation, not to say how it makes me look in the business community. Of course, I want to see justice for the poor girl, too. I say, Jessica, what happened to you?"

Now that they were inside, Philip got a good look at Jessica's sorry sartorial state.

"Um, let's just say it has something to do with what you're about to hear from Chief Winston," she evaded.

"But you look as if you'd taken a fall down a flight of stairs, out a window, and into a tree," he blurted. "And you, Crawford, you allowed this to happen to her? A woman like her should be protected. Why I would have . . ."

"Put her on a leash?" James finished mordantly.

Philip started to glare, and Jess could see this was pretty darned far from Winston's advice. However, she knew that Philip had struck one of James's few sore spots: not always being able to keep her out of harm's way.

She plunged in, "Knock it off, both of you. When I get into a tight spot, it's nobody's fault but my own. Anyway, we shouldn't be at odds. We're here with Chief Winston to help settle this case. Isn't that all the matters?"

Philip looked curiously from Jessica to James. Her husband regarded him with that coolness he always adopted when he really wanted to take a poke at someone, but he knew he'd be sorry later.

"Yes, yes, of course you're right, Jessica," Philip admitted. "I apologize to both of you."

James gave a nod that marked a truce with the other man.

Still puzzled, Philip questioned, "But what's your connection to Winston's information?"

"That's something best to let Chief Winston explain," James answered reasonably.

On cue came a knock on the door, prompting Philip to move past the Crawfords and re-admit Winston. After closing the door again, Philip told the Chief, "I trust you've taken care of your business so we can get down to cases."

Winston smiled to reply, "All hunky-dory. So, how about we move somewhere more private, where none of your help can overhear?"

"Yes, yes. This way to the study," Philip instructed. His expression grew troubled as he added, "I just wish I knew what happened to Jeanne. This is not like her."

Of course, the three gentlemen allowed Jessica to go first, but not before she exchanged an uneasy glance with James. *Why wasn't Winston off trying to bring Jeanne back for questioning?* Her husband seemed to read her mind, for he signaled her with a subtly lowered hand to hold tight and trust Winston to know his business.

Philip brought them into the study, closed the door behind them, then got each seated. He settled in his own chair behind his desk, under the painting of roses that had clued Jessica in about accessing the passageway behind her closet. Was Philip curiously regarding her fascination with the painting? Jess dropped her eyes.

Winston gained all their attentions by asking, "Mr. Carlyle did you realize your house is riddled with secret passages?"

Winston's tone had been calm, but Philip Carlyle still straightened in his chair, bemused. Then he almost laughed. "You can't be serious! My house? Secret passages? That's absurd! This is hardly the Castle of Otranto. Where did you get that fantastic idea?"

"From this young lady over here. Right, Mrs. Crawford?"

Jessica confirmed, "I'm afraid you were partially correct when you asked what happened to me, Philip. No windows or trees, but I did slip on some stairs in the passageways that run behind my room, up to Felicia's on the next floor, and to your brother's in the attic, then down to your cellar."

Before Jess could say anything about the space behind the music room, Winston subtly lifted a hand to quiet her. Jess watched Philip look from one to another of the three. At last, he spoke: "You are serious, all of you? Chief Winston, I'm sorely dismayed to see a man I backed for his job come up with such a fantastic tale."

Jessica winced for Winston, but he remained impassive. And how did she feel about Philip's dirty crack? Well, the guy had clearly been knocked off kilter by this revelation. Throwing his weight around might be a defensive response.

Philip now seemed aware of his ham-handedness, for he apologized, "Forgive me, Winston. I'm under such a strain lately, and I'd hoped you had something more solid. I do see how suspicious secret passages sound, but I don't see a clear connection to the murder in the music room."

"That's because Mrs. Crawford didn't tell you about all the passages she discovered. Apparently, she found an off-shoot behind the music room that seems to line up with the angle the murder weapon was fired from."

"What? But how relevant is that fact?" Philip questioned, confused. "You found the gun outside. You even thought the assassin might be some enemy of Wanda O'Malley who snuck onto the property, then dropped the gun outside."

"We still don't know for certain that gun is the murder weapon. There's a big jam of cases in the Portsmouth lab that even you couldn't speed up. No reason the killer couldn't have left the gun there to make us think it was fired from outside. That outside angle never did line up right. Anyway, the gun might even have been left before the séance, unless you know for certain the grounds were clear," Winston calmly explained.

"No, of course I wouldn't know that. We'd hardly be checking the terrace for weapons," Philip grudgingly replied.

"Nope," Winston continued, "this looks to me like, literally, an inside job. That's why I'm asking your permission to search the passages. I'd also like to see any blueprints you have of the house, so I can check if there are any indications of them."

Philip Carlyle's forehead wrinkled as he processed all he'd heard. Finally, he said, "Yes, of course, you may search. We've got to get to the bottom of all this, but I can tell you now that the blueprints I have won't help you. I had some work done on the house, though not where you mentioned, and there was nothing in those blueprints remotely resembling what you described."

"But there may be another set somewhere that do show what you're looking for, Chief Winston," James broke his silence. "Perhaps hidden away and forgotten in an older part of the house."

Winston started to scowl at James but relented when James added, "Or comparing blueprints with the actual physical dimensions of the house could also be of help."

The Chief nodded, "Yup, the professor's on to something. What do you say, Mr. Carlyle?"

"I say of course," Philip replied. "Whatever is necessary to bring the murderer to justice. But, one question, Winston. You said you suspected an inside job. Who do you think was the murderer?"

"I'd rather not say until I've had a chance to do more investigating, if you don't mind," the Chief answered reasonably.

Jessica could see Philip thinking carefully before he spoke, "Wait. You stepped out to make a call on your radio right after I said Jeanne was missing. In fact, you, Jessica, even had something of a startled reaction. You people are accusing Jeanne, aren't you? You think she's guilty, and you sent out a deputy to arrest her."

"Just to bring her down to the station for questioning," Winston said almost soothingly.

"And then what?" Philip lowered. "Hasn't Jeanne had a hard enough time? Won't people let her live down her past and turn over a new leaf? She's been a Godsend to me here. I won't let her be railroaded just so you can close this case." Then Philip's expression shown with triumphant recollection and he finished, "But you seem to be forgetting that she has an airtight alibi: behind the locked door of her quarters with several others outside. Crack that if you can."

"If there's one set of hidden passageways, there could be more," Jim Winston stated simply. "That's another reason I need to see some blueprints—and search her room, with your permission as owner of the property."

Philip frowned before replying, "I could say no and make you get a warrant, if you could find a willing judge."

The two men locked eyes, and, to help Winston, Jessica worked up her nerve to buck his instructions, "Philip, if the Chief finds nothing in her room, that would go a long way to clearing Jeanne. Don't you think cooperating with him will help her?"

Carlyle thought that over, finally suggesting, "And if she is cleared, perhaps you'll take a closer look at someone else, like my brother."

"Your brother was cleared by the paraffin test, and he was sitting in the music room, not behind the wall," Winston pointed out.

"Yes, but he could have hired someone. Someone who knew how to fire a gun, unlike Jeanne Rivers," Philip proudly insisted. The knowing looks on the three before him pricked Carlyle to question, "What aren't you telling me, Winston? I'm entitled to know. It's my home, my employee; no, my friend. What aren't you telling me?"

Jess wondered what Philip would say if he knew that his "friend" had formed an alliance against him, most likely with the brother he fiercely detested.

Winston shrugged, then said, "Okay, Mr. Carlyle, I'd hoped to break it to you more gently."

Jessica watched Winston, thinking, *No, Mr. Chief of Police, you don't regret this at all. You've been maneuvering Philip into making you hand him this revelation from the get-go, making him think it was his idea.*

Winston "broke it to" Philip: "I've been investigating everyone involved, relying on my contacts with the Feds."

Jessica noted James smile at this appropriation of his endeavors, but he said nothing.

Winston continued, "I found out that your 'friend' Jeanne Rivers has an interesting history in the time between her leaving New Hampshire and her return to take a job with you. Did you know she had an act in night clubs as an exhibition sharp-shooter, that she later partnered in the Brazil club circuit with Wanda O'Malley's mind-reading act? How about that a bit over two years ago, she and Wanda performed at several of the same places where your brother Bill was working as a nightclub sketch artist?"

Philip's face collapsed, and Jessica's heart went out to him. It took him a few moments, but he did face Winston to say in a hopeless voice, "So, the three of them were in cahoots? Of course. Wanda showed up when Jeanne was talking to me about the ghost of Felicia. It was all a damned setup. And who knows when Bill really got back in the area? A snake in the grass like him would know how to keep a low profile while they put their devilish plan into action. That fraud Wanda probably helped him to hide out."

Jessica wondered why Winston hadn't sealed his case by revealing how Jeanne and Bill had manipulated her with drugs and hypnotism. *Would that just complicate the issue?*

Philip, pain evident in his features, pressed, "Why would she do this to me? What could she hope to gain? And why kill Wanda?"

"Maybe she and Bill were planning to oust you from the company and the estate. It ties in with this business about a new will," Winston proposed. "They might have thought getting rid of Wanda would increase their splits. We won't know until we talk to both Rivers and your brother. But I don't want to do that until I have a look-see in that passage and in Jeanne's room. That copasetic with you, Mr. Carlyle?"

Philip raised his chin to reply, "Let's get to the bottom of things."

Chapter Thirty-Eight

The wind insistently rattled the French doors of the drawing room, as if trying to burst in on Jessica and Philip. Jess's thoughts were on the tense and silent Philip Carlyle, sitting across the low table from her by the hearth. No, that wasn't entirely accurate. She was actually wondering what James and Chief Winston would find at that spot behind the music room. Winston had wanted Philip with them, as owner of the house, but he'd been too upset by all the revelations. So much so that Winston feared the nervous Carlyle might inadvertently contaminate or damage evidence. So, with James showing him the way, the Chief had left Jess and Philip drinking tea—or at least sitting in front of said tea.

Jess listened carefully, wondering where the two gents were between the walls. She heard nothing, but then again, no one had noticed the rat in the wall on the night of the murder. Jessica certainly chafed at not being able to join the guys in their investigations, but she just wasn't needed. Winston had also sternly warned them that if Jeanne or Bill should come by, neither should be challenged. Jess should just slip away to knock a pre-designated signal on the music room wall where James and Winston were investigating.

Unfortunately, the past fifteen or so minutes had been congenial for neither Jessica nor Philip. Aside from ordering the tea and telling Lu Brown she was now top sergeant, he hadn't uttered more than a peep to Jess. If he hadn't sat there so morosely, she might have thought Philip a bit cold-blooded, already writing off and replacing Jeanne. Yet, in all fairness, given what he learned, what could he do? Whatever the case, what wouldn't Jess do for a hot shower and some fresh clothes!

Maybe Philip read her mind, for he surprised Jessica by breaking the silence, "Poor Jessica Minton. What a day you've had for yourself! Those two may be gone quite some time. Why don't you take a break and do a quick change? I can hold down the fort until the others return."

"That's so thoughtful of you, Philip," Jessica smiled, genuinely grateful. "But, to be honest, I don't cotton to the possibility of running into Jeanne or Bill, alone."

Philip nodded, suddenly opening up, "I'm entirely devastated by Jeanne's perfidy. Lies and plots I expect from my . . . I shudder to call him . . . brother. I can't say I'd put murder past him. I've always leaned towards him being the one who took Felicia from us."

"Do you think that's part of why Bill and Jeanne killed Wanda? Maybe she had proof Bill was Felicia's murderer and was going to put him on the hot seat unless he forked over a bigger cut of your estate?"

Philip hesitated, reluctant to explain, "I'm afraid the joke's on the whole conspiracy. I don't think you know this. I've kept my financial concerns under wraps, to keep up appearances. If a businessman doesn't *look* successful, his business will be in trouble—even if he has good, solid plans to revive it. Investors, bankers, they'll desert you like rats off a sinking ship."

Having seen Dick Streeter's report, Jessica found Philip's admission no news. Still, that admission had cost Philip so much, Jessica wouldn't slight it. With sympathy she didn't have to fake, Jess asked, "Is the trouble very bad?"

"Bad enough to make Bill's felony fraud with this will business or Wanda's murder hardly worth trying to cheat me out of the family holdings."

But there was another motivation that Philip hadn't considered, so Jessica put it to him: "Maybe it's not the business or the money he's after but the property right here. I've heard quite an earful from the island grapevine that some off-islanders would love to get their paws on this land and throw up a bunch of lucrative developments."

Philip flared, "Yes, he is low enough to go for something like that. Bulldoze over nearly one hundred years of family history. This beautiful mansion, this exquisite architecture, all for the filthy ducats from a herd of nouveau riche! Over my dead body!"

"Yikes, Philip! Don't give him any ideas!"

Philip must have seen her embarrassment at provoking him, for he leaned forward, put a hand over hers, and reassured, "No, please. Forgive my outburst. To be honest, I'm less upset by Bill than by Jeanne. I've always known what a dastard he is, but Jeanne, I thought she was almost my friend. And to know she was allied with *him*? How the two must have laughed, knowing they'd pulled the wool over my eyes."

"Please, Philip, don't beat yourself up on that account," Jessica tried to comfort him, while unobtrusively freeing her hand. "She fooled me for a time as well." Jess wanted to add, but knew better, "At least she didn't drug you into thinking you were haunted or nuts or use you to torture the Blaskos." That made her pause: *Why* had *Jeanne and Bill used her against the father and daughter? To deflect suspicion for Felicia's murder onto Vitus? Sure, that made sense.* Jess added, "Elizabeth and James had Jeanne's number. I guess I'd better learn to be more cynical."

"Never give up one of your most endearing qualities," Philip insisted gently. Too gently, for it gave away too much, especially after his covering her hand with his.

Jessica looked quickly away, mumbling a "thank you" for kind words, feeling bad that she could only disappoint him. *Like Felicia?*

The sound of James and Winston in the foyer filled Jess with relief. She was immediately up to greet them. Her awkwardness with Philip Carlyle's revelatory mien, she hid behind eagerness to hear the two explorers' report. The Chief's features gave away nothing. *Darn the old stone face!* But James, carrying Winston's powerful portable light, seemed quietly satisfied as he followed Winston into the room.

"C'mon you two," Jessica pressed. "Give over. Was it a success or a bust?"

James nodded his head in deference at Winston. It was, after all, the Chief's show.

"Whelp," Winston began calmly, "If you go around the corner of the passage, it ends right before where the window would be. The outside buttress there is hollow, fake. Wouldn't you know we found a slider panel that lines up nicely for nailing the victim? It's not big enough to notice from the room, but it's large enough to get off a good shot. We can check it for powder residue, later, but it's been a week."

"Did you find any shell casings?" Philip questioned.

"Nope," Winston replied. "Someone was fairly careful, but not careful enough."

Jessica and Philip exchanged perplexed glances until the Chief reached into his jacket pocket, adding, "I did come across this, caught on a rough patch of the wall."

Winston pulled out an evidence envelope, which he squeezed open and invited, "Jessica, would you take a gander inside and tell me what you think? I removed it with a pair of tweezers."

Uncertainly, Jessica came forward. Peeking inside, she tilted her head and revealed, "It looks like a small piece of bluish cloth. Something snagged from the shooter?"

Winston nodded. "It was on the wall across from the slider, like someone caught it there from leaning back after taking a shot. Maybe killing another human being was a little much for our shooter, and she sank against the wall to pull herself together. I gotta give your husband credit for that conjecture. He's a smart fella, the professor."

"Don't give him a swelled head," Jessica quietly kidded. "But what do you guys make of that chunk of material?"

"That's what I thought you could help us with, Jessica. Have you ever seen anyone with this color, maybe a dress or a blouse?"

"It's hard to tell color and texture with it stuck in that envelope, Chief Winston. Could you take it out for me to get a better look?" Jessica requested.

"Can do." Winston brought out a small case from the same pocket and, nodding to James, instructed, "Grab the tweezers and take out the cloth so your wife can see it, while I hold the envelope. I'm a police chief not an octopus."

The tweezers held before Jessica a small, jagged patch of soft, periwinkle-blue material. It took a moment, but she recalled seeing that striking color in a dress that had impressed her as rather expensive-looking for a humble housekeeper.

"It's from one of Jeanne's dresses; the one she wore the night Wanda was killed," Jessica asserted. "I could never forget material like that."

Philip came forward and concurred, "Yes, yes. She's right. I've seen Jeanne in a dress of this color. I don't remember if she wore it the night of the séance, but this definitely looks to be from one of her dresses."

"Well, it didn't waltz in and snag itself in that passage," Winston summed up. "Putting this evidence together with Rivers' recent behavior and with the verifiable background information I can provide, I'm asking you as agent-in-charge for permission to search Rivers' room for the dress in question, in addition to any other incriminating evidence of her involvement in the murder of Wanda O'Malley."

"Of course, of course," Philip agreed. "You don't have to put it in legalese. I want the whole truth now."

"I've been in law enforcement long enough to make sure I cross all my 't's' and dot all my 'i's.' No way anything I do is getting tossed on a technicality," Winston replied easily but firmly.

"Yes, yes," Philip assured the Chief. "I just want that traitor to my house in custody—and my brother, too—before they can do any more harm."

"First things first," Winston answered, unperturbed. "Now, let's take a little stroll down to her room. I need you, Mr. Carlyle, since I'll bet the door's locked. My guess is that you have the master keys."

Philip nodded.

To Jessica, Winston said, "You, I need to identify the dress. But you, Crawford, stay here. I don't need you, so there's no sense raising the help's suspicions by having more people than necessary going into the room."

Jessica gave James the ghost of an impish smile, now that he was the one left behind. James tried to give her a stern look but the corner of his mouth quirked up. He only said, "I'd tell you to stay out of trouble, but I know better."

"There'll be no trouble on my watch," Winston stated before pointing Jess and Philip to head out.

Two or three women were still in the kitchen, the flood there having been recently mopped up, when Philip led Jessica and Chief Winston to Jeanne's quarters, just off the capacious room. Lu Brown was giving directions for the evening meal, but no one of those under her could resist a curious glance at the three outside Jeanne's door.

Lu and came over to Philip to inquire, "I hope you don't mind my asking, sir, but any word on Miss Rivers? She was out, then back, then off again. We haven't seen her since. It's not like her."

"I know, Brown," Philip reassured her. "We're trying to find out what might have happened. Perhaps there's something about her mother. The old woman hasn't been well. If she should come back, would you send her to me? But don't mention our being here. I don't want to seem to impinge on her privacy, but if she has some trouble, I'd like to help."

Lu readily agreed, "Of course, sir."

Hmm, Jess considered, *quite a display of compassion considering what Philip had been saying earlier, but maybe it wasn't acting.* She knew that even in the face of proof, it was hard to flip her feelings like a light switch—unless she was dealing with Nazis. Those creeps she had no sympathy for.

The room was dark until Philip Carlyle pressed the button on the light switch by the door. That door closed behind them, and Jessica mused, surprised, "A room with no windows? Really?"

"There are windows all over the house," Philip stated matter-of-factly. "You don't need windows for sleeping or doing accounts."

"I guess," Jessica ruminated as she surveyed the Spartan quarters, deciding that maybe Philip hadn't been quite so much of a friend. The room was good-sized with white walls. A desk and a filing cabinet were directly across from her, backing the house's outer wall. The bed was perpendicular to the wall on her left, with a nightstand and lamp next to it. Far from a lumpy cot, but not exactly a fluffy canopied number, either. There was a lighter spot over the bed in the shape of a cross that had been removed after long residence. Mrs. Rivers certainly was a good Catholic, but Jeanne had ditched that influence—as her participation in fraud and murder certainly indicated.

Now a few framed pictures or paintings of tropical settings hung on the wall. This woman had dreams that did not include burying herself forever in harsh New England winters.

Her plot with Bill would surely have bought her escape to the tropics if it came off. Across the room, on the wall to Jessica's right, was a table lamp next to a fairly new recliner. No windows, but Philip had sprung for a comfy chair. Practical of him. Next to the chair was a wide sliding door for what Jess guessed was a closet. *Sure, a closet.*

Jessica observed, "The architect who put in the passageway to my room hid it in my closet. Bet your bottom dollar, Chief Winston, if you check this one, you'll find how Jeanne got out undetected on the night of the séance."

"How about checking there for that dress, first?" Winston tamped down her enthusiasm.

"Sure thing, boss," Jess saluted him. She crossed the room, slid back the closet door, and entered. As the two men waited outside, Jessica pulled on the overhead light by its string. *This certainly is a darned big closet for a room this size.* Then it struck Jess that this might have been where the child Jeanne had slept: good-sized for a closet but claustrophobic for a child to sleep in. Yes, there were a child's scrawled drawings on the wall and areas rubbed by a bed's placement.

No wonder Jeanne had burst through the physical and class barriers to infiltrate her "superiors'" lives, to make this place her own. Perhaps even spy on what had happened to Felicia? Did she hold power over Bill Carlyle, not the other way around? Likely, she would just adore seeing developers bulldoze this elegant prison.

"Find that dress, yet?" came Winston's voice from outside the closet.

"Uh, not yet. Still looking!" Jess answered hastily.

Jessica flipped rapidly through the long row of dresses. *Hmm, this was not a wardrobe you'd easily come up with on a housekeeper's salary. Maybe Philip Carlyle's anguish was over the betrayal of someone more than a friend. How far had Jeanne gone to advance her and Bill's plans?*

Jessica's hands rested on a startlingly periwinkle silk dress. Grabbing the garment by the hanger and marching into the center of the room, she announced, "Got it!"

"I believe that is the one I've seen," Philip concurred, his voice reluctant.

"Fine as far as it goes," Winston decided, coming over to Jessica, "but it doesn't really help if you can't find a hole or a repaired patch that matches this piece of cloth."

"Okay," Jess considered. "If she leaned back, it ought to be on the back somewhere, especially in a spot you wouldn't notice, wearing it or putting it on."

To the men's quizzical expressions, Jessica explained, "If she snagged the dress, as you conjectured, in the heat of the moment or when she was upset, she wouldn't notice the problem right away. But if she were putting it away or putting it back on later, she'd notice the tear, unless it weren't in an obvious spot, like—right here, behind the shoulder blade. You can't see back there, especially the way the material drapes a little. And especially since the zipper's on the side seam not the back. She could take it off and never notice. Come to think of it, I don't think I've seen her in this dress, since the séance."

"Guilt, likely. She associated it with the murder and couldn't bear to wear it again," Philip sadly conjectured.

"Could very well be," Jessica agreed. "Now, let's see that little scrap again."

"Like I told you, a woman's touch is what we need," Winston pointed out as he got the envelope, then the case with the tweezers, relying on Philip's help to take out the fabric since he still wasn't an octopus.

"And there's our match," Jessica asserted.

"There it is," Philip repeated, far less sanguine. "You'll forgive me for not sharing your cheer at seeing someone I trusted irrevocably damned—Hello, what's that?"

He'd dropped his eyes for those disconsolate words. Following Philip's gaze, Jess could barely discern something poking out from under the bed: brown, leather, not terribly big. Recognition made her suck in her breath. Before she could say a word, Philip Carlyle had crossed the room and pulled out the leather case she'd seen in the cellar, the one she'd extrapolated Jeanne Rivers had dashed off with.

"Carlyle! Put that down!" Winston commanded. "On the bed! Now!"

Philip automatically obeyed, but his features grew stern when he retorted, "I'm not used to having others use that tone with me."

Jess almost expected Carlyle to add, "Especially not a town employee." Nevertheless, when it came to doing his job, Jessica could see that, come hell or high water, no one interfered with Jim Winston.

"You don't want to risk messing up the evidence, Mr. Carlyle. Let me handle this," Winston said, carefully replacing the fabric in the envelope, which he returned to his inner jacket pocket. However, he kept out the tweezers, using them to pull the zipper open on the case.

Winston looked up at Jessica and said, "Is this what you saw in the cellar room? What disappeared right after Rivers left the room?"

Getting a good look at the contents, Jessica felt a chill: a syringe and an empty ampoule designated scopolamine, not the sodium amytal they'd used on her. Before she could answer, Philip demanded, "You saw Jeanne with this, in the cellar?"

"That and a journal," Jess answered, immediately regretting being forthcoming when Winston glared at her for talking about evidence.

However, Philip had center stage, demanding, "A journal? You mean my brother and Jeanne wrote up a journal of their plot, and you let them get away with it?"

Jess returned coolly, "I didn't think Jeanne would have exactly handed it over to me if I asked nicely." She turned to Winston and explained, "This is the same case. I never saw the contents, though. Scopolamine, huh? That's nasty stuff. It can rob you of your will and it has devastating side effects. What they show in movies is nothing compared to reality."

"You're remarkably knowledgeable about drugs for a radio actress," Philip remarked.

"I researched it for a show," Jessica retorted. She caught her temper, though, remembering the strain Philip was under. Besides, she couldn't help wondering why the ampoule was empty, and neither could Winston.

"Looks like she may have used this fairly recently," the Chief noted. "The syringe and little glass aren't dry as a whistle, like you'd expect with something not used in a while. But on who?"

"Do you think Jeanne might have committed suicide?" Philip reluctantly proposed. "That would explain why she didn't destroy this evidence."

Thinking back to the last she'd heard from Jeanne, also the last she'd heard of Bill, Jessica pointed out, "In the passageway behind his room, I heard Bill Carlyle arguing outside his door with a woman. Must have been Jeanne. Maybe one of them used this drug on the other. She's the one with a nursing background; she could have injected him and taken a powder. Still, Bill's a powerful guy. He could have turned the needle on her, then left the case here to make her look bad. He may even have the journal up in his room, now."

Winston went into action, hurrying them to the door as he spoke, "Yeah, if Jeanne's alive, we need to bring her in. And we need to have a talk with your brother, now, Mr. Carlyle. I've got to get the lead out and have an APB put out on Rivers after we make sure your brother is all right, not on the lam. We'll collect Crawford and take him with us, in case there's trouble."

"Right!" Jessica chimed in.

Jim Winston stopped short, looked her square in the eye, and ordered, "Oh, no. You stay put in the kitchen, Agatha Christie, where there's plenty of people around to keep Rivers from thinking you might be easy pickings."

"But . . ."

"No buts."

"He's right, Jessica," Philip gently reasoned. "You need to be where you can stay safe."

"Fine," Jessica agreed, "but that wasn't my caveat. I just wanted to say that if you're worried about people Jeanne is on the warpath for, watch out for Jamie Blasko. I heard she and Jeanne had words earlier, and one of the words was 'passages.' Jamie even accused Jeanne of sending her father an anonymous poison-pen letter."

"And you're just telling me now? Never mind, we've got to check out Bill Carlyle. So, while we're at it, Jessica, you get on the horn and tell the dispatcher I said Deputy Hudson needs to shoot over to the Blasko place and keep an eye out for either Jeanne or Bill. When you're in the kitchen, ask that Lu to send a servant up to us on the q.t. if Rivers comes in while we're in Bill's room." He turned to Philip and said, "Okay, Carlyle, let's roll." Back to Jessica: "You stay out of trouble."

They were gone even before Jessica could throw her hands up and question the universe, "Why do people keep telling me that?"

Chapter Thirty-Nine

Jess finally had a sip of the tea that she hadn't been able to drink with Philip. The ceramic pot had kept it reasonably warm, even after she and it had been moved to the kitchen. On the other side of the room, the cook, Mrs. Trask, and her staff were confabbing on how to resolve the crisis of what to do about dinner when it wasn't clear who would even be here. Jess sensed the undercurrent of backstairs insight that the evening meal was the least of the household's worries.

Raising her eyes, not so much heavenward, but roughly in the direction of Bill Carlyle's studio eyrie, Jessica listened. No shouts, no gunfire. How much *could* she hear through the floors and walls of this house? Yet, she could attest that those walls were not nearly as solid as people believed.

Jessica turned to the sandwich Mrs. Trask had prepared for her lunch, her cover for being in the kitchen, just as Lu Brown came in from the main house. In a snap, Lu decisively settled all questions from her subordinates. Jess briefly amused herself with the prospect that Lu had engineered a brilliant frame job on Jeanne and Bill just to secure this position.

Her eyes returned upward. *How long would it take them?* She wished Chief Winston could have handled Bill by himself or at least waited for a deputy to get here. However, to make sure neither suspect got away or to see if they needed to save someone from a drug overdose, they couldn't wait around. Though she wouldn't want anything to happen to Philip, her real worry was James. Yes, he could handle himself in tricky situations, but she still preferred he didn't have to handle anything trickier than annoying administrators, plagiarizing students, Liz in a bad mood, or Dusty with her claws out. James was experienced and cautious, but what she had seen in Bill Carlyle was a hard heart with no compunction about whom he hurt. Sure, Winston was there, but what if Philip did something that triggered Bill, getting James hurt in the crossfire or while trying to protect the others?

The back door opened, and Jessica nearly jumped out of her skin. Nope, no Jeanne Rivers. Just one of the help returning with some pots that Mrs. Trask had sent over to the garage to have the dents beaten out.

Jess looked down at her watch. Almost fifteen minutes now. *What was going on up there? It was so tempting to slip out of the kitchen and up several flights to the attic studio.* Except, might she foul up an interrogation or, worse, tragically tip the balance in a Mexican standoff?

Attempting to distract herself, Jess stared down at her sandwich with more concentration than any ham and cheese should ever be forced to endure. Somehow, some instinct told her to look toward the doorway leading to the main part of the house. James was there.

Quieter than any mouse only detectable by Dusty, he raised his head slightly, his eyes signaling she should unobtrusively join him. *What else did his eyes reveal? Why weren't the others there?*

With a silent grace surprising herself, Jessica slid around the table to join James. Giving no more than a quick nod, he gently moved her to stand behind him.

James surprised Jess by calling pleasantly, "Miss Brown, Lu, would you be kind enough to come with me for a moment? Mr. Carlyle needs to confer with you on some household business."

Lu nodded, broke off from Mrs. Trask, promising to return directly, and came to James. All the while, Jess's forehead wrinkled with consternation at this odd request. Still, she trusted James to know what he was up to and remained in his shadow, for the moment.

James gave Jessica a bit of a nudge and started them down the corridor toward the foyer, closing the door between the kitchen and the formal part of the house behind them. Once the three reached the foyer, James made a quick survey before admitting, "Afraid I told you something of a fib, Miss Brown. The Chief still wants to keep this quiet from the rest of the staff, but would you continue to keep an eye open should Jeanne Rivers return?"

"Why, okay, yes," Lu answered. "Is she in trouble? What's this all about?"

In Lu's expression, curiosity conflicted with her inculcated loyalty to the Carlyle family.

"The Police Chief only needs to talk to her, clear up some things," James assured Lu. "If she does come back, just quietly send a girl out to us. We'll be outside the front entrance. If Rivers tries to leave before we come, no need to detain her, just note where she goes. Could you help us out that way? It would be a right good thing all 'round. I know Mr. Carlyle would appreciate it."

Lu nodded and agreed, "Certainly, if it will help Mr. Carlyle."

The second the kitchen door closed behind Lu, Jessica was on James like Dusty on Polish ham, "Okay, mister, spill. What happened? Does Winston have Bill outside in cuffs?"

James deeply inhaled, only to give Jessica a cryptic, "Not exactly."

Folding her arms in front of herself, she pressed, "Exactly what *does* 'not exactly' mean?"

James tipped his head toward the front door and replied, "Let's step outside where we can talk more freely. The walls have ears."

Jessica returned, "Don't *I* know *that*. Okay, hon, lead on." As they traversed the foyer, ironically bright with sunshine even as the house's secrets seemed to grow darker, Jessica added, "You know you're lucky it's me and not Elizabeth you're putting off. She'd have the truth out of you in a snap."

"Bloody likely," James allowed ruefully. "I was only trained to resist Nazi interrogation."

Humor glinted momentarily in his eyes as they reached the door. Here, James took off his navy wool blazer and put it over Jessica's shoulders, saying, "You'll need this. Quite a nip out there."

Jessica smiled up at him. "How could a girl resist a swell guy like you? Anyway, I'm just glad that you came back from upstairs in one piece. You all did."

James's hesitation shook her. Before she could question who was on the casualty list, he'd opened the door and brought them into the cold November afternoon. Titmice in the trees buzzed warnings, chickadees countered with cheery peeps, an off-beat soundtrack to Jessica's fear. Off to her right, Philip Carlyle was looking down. Thank God he was unharmed. Chief Winston, where was he? No, there he stood by the police car, putting in a call on the radio. So, Bill Carlyle must be in the back, behind the screen, probably cuffed, hunched, and glowering. But he wasn't. He wasn't anywhere.

"The meat wagon's on its way," Winston's voice cut into Jessica's thoughts as he approached.

"Mea . . . Meat wagon? Not ambulance or paddy wagon?" Jessica blurted, pulling James's jacket closer about her. Had Bill killed Jeanne in their argument and fled? The other way around? Finally, she managed, "Who's dead?"

"It was ghastly, just ghastly," came Philip's voice, shaken.

Would Philip show this much feeling for a brother he'd despised? Who'd plotted against him? Yet Bill was still his brother.

Jessica looked up at her husband: "Who was it, James?"

Before James could answer, Philip put a hand on Jessica's arm, turning her to him to reveal, "It was my brother. Sitting in front of Felicia's portrait in that chair. That terrible image he'd created of her. The way he wanted her to be, under his control. Good lord, that expression on his face, I swear she must have reached at him from beyond the grave . . ."

James pulled Jessica away from Philip's horror, toward himself, and cut off the other man: "Nonsense. It wasn't any ghost that did in your brother. It was an overdose of one of the nastiest of drugs: Rivers' scopolamine. He had a heart attack from the overdose. That's what put that look on his face."

"Jeanne?" Jessica repeated. "Well, she does have the know-how, but Bill's a big guy. I can't imagine him sitting still for a jab of something fatal."

"Gotta give it to your husband there," Winston put in. "It sure did look as if the painting had really scared the living daylights out of him. Yep, he was sitting in that chair, paints out, touching up the portrait. Not that I really buy into that spook malarkey, but it might have actually passed for a heart attack, at first. But your husband checked, under the poor stiff's . . . guy's hairline. Someone he trusted enough to turn his back on jabbed the needle right there, in the back of his neck. The examiner would have picked up on it, especially since we know Jeanne has the drug and the know-how to use it, but your fella saved us a little time. Yup, Carlyle trusted Jeanne until it was too late. Gotta say he looked as much surprised as horrified."

"Surprised by sin," James quoted Milton, though not in context.

"Yeah, well, sure," Winston allowed, not exactly sure what he was agreeing to but not particularly caring. He had more important things to deal with. "All right, as I said, the meat . . . the wagon is on its way. I'm going to do a more thorough examination of the room. We have an APB out on Rivers, not just here but in Portsmouth and with the state police."

Philip burst forth, "From the look on my brother's face, I believe he realized that he was being paid back for his treachery for more than one murder. Chief, when you examine my brother's room, you must look for evidence that he murdered Felicia and disposed of her afterward."

Jessica moved even closer to James, away from Philip's cold intensity. Chief Winston's reaction was to somewhat cast oil on the churning waters of Philip's insistence: "Mr. Carlyle, I've got my plate full trying to nab Jeanne Rivers and tie this all into a solid case without going back to an ice-cold one. Even dropping your name, I can't get the crime scene guys in here until Monday; they're so backed up now. But don't get yourself in an uproar. I'll keep my eyes open."

At the law officer's words, Philip pulled himself together. "I'm sorry. You must forgive me. I'm not myself. I've had more shocks today than a man ought to. What can I do to help *you*, Chief?"

Jess wanted to reach out sympathetically to Philip, but she was just too emotionally burnt out.

"Happens to the best of us," Winston replied. "If you really want to help me, just stand back and let me and my guys do our job. Like I said, I put out the APB on Jeanne, and I called in Deputy Pinder to keep an eye out at Edna Rivers' place. I don't know if Jeanne has much cash, so she might try to hit her mother up for some dough before she blows town."

Jessica offered, "It sounds as if Jeanne's pretty good at dropping off the radar. Look at the gap in her history between leaving New Hampshire and showing up in Rio." However, Winston's "Don't tell me how to do my job expression," prompted her to finish with a more laudatory, "But I'm so glad that you sent someone to watch out for the Blaskos, especially Jamie. Jeanne might be crazy enough to go after them."

"Yeah, I been meaning to ask you about that," Winston said. "How did you know she was on the warpath for them, Jamie in particular?"

Jess scrambled for an excuse that wouldn't reveal the awkward fact that James had been tailing Jamie. Her husband even started to speak—

when they were saved by the bell, or more like the buzzer, as the car radio signaled a call for Winston.

The police chief dashed to take the call, and it wasn't long before he had another bombshell for them. Pinder had called in to report Edna Rivers was dead.

Philip broke the shocked silence with, "You can't tell me that Jeanne poisoned her own mother. I could believe she might do in Bill out of self-preservation, but . . ."

"That's not what I'm telling you," Winston calmed him.

"Then what did happen, Chief?" James asked.

"You may know the old gal's had strokes before," Winston began.

"Oh, it was something natural." Jess was relieved, though hardly pleased. "I used to talk with Mrs. Rivers after church. I'm afraid a few times she even called me Felicia, but she didn't mean anything screwy by it. I suppose it's fortunate that she didn't live to see what her daughter came to. That would have just killed . . . oh, sorry, unfortunate figure of speech."

"Umph," Winston grunted. "I wish I could say you were right, but Jeanne likely precipitated that stroke. Seems the old gal got a call from her daughter earlier this afternoon. Annette Risdon walked in on the conversation right as the old gal said her daughter's name over the phone and collapsed. Annette says she lost her own head, screamed, "Edna, you're dead!" and rushed to her side. She tried to get Jeanne on the line, but the daughter had hung up. So, Annette called the operator and had her send for the doctor, just in case. As it was, the old lady did come to—"

"I thought you said Mrs. Rivers was dead," Philip puzzled, surprised.

Jessica glanced at Philip and nodded, confused herself.

"Well, let's just say her recovery was brief. Annette got her upstairs, into bed. Then she went to answer the door for the doctor. They heard a crash upstairs and found Edna on the floor by the bed, definitely gone this time. They figured the old lady must have gotten up, confused by her attack, tried to get back into bed but couldn't quite make it."

"Tragic," sighed Philip. "But perhaps, as Jessica said, she didn't grasp precisely how low her daughter had sunk."

"That's not exactly what I said," Jessica protested.

"No, maybe not," Philip amended. "However, I'm afraid I'm not thinking straight after all that's happened today."

"I wonder if Jeanne knows about her mother," Jess considered.

"Good question," Winston observed. "It might make her careless or distracted."

"Or desperate," James warned.

"Yeah, that thought crossed my mind," Winston admitted. "I've called in some of the boys, off-duty, to help search the island for her. Thanks, Mr. Carlyle, for tipping me to some of the sites on your estate that would make a good hiding place. I've put a lock on your brother's door, and we disabled the sliding panel to the room. It should be safe enough for me to take some time to help you make sure this joint of yours is locked up tight."

Jessica interjected pensively, "What about panels we might not know? Maybe we can't keep Jeanne locked out."

Philip countered, "We can always check our rooms to ensure there's no secret ingress—which means we'll be moving you and James to new accommodations. I do have some firearms for protection. If your husband can handle a handgun, we should keep everyone safe, especially if we can also rely on Mr. Robinson and Mr. Davis."

"I don't like to see civilians get too free and easy with the hardware," Chief Winston warned. "I don't think you should worry too much about running into her, though. From what I know about your housekeeper, she's probably too smart to hang around here when everyone's got an eye out for her."

"Of course," Philip reassured him. "We all have good heads on our shoulders. Both Mr. Davis and I are even veterans. At any rate," including Jessica and James now, "I believe Chief Winston is correct that Jeanne won't come back. She's not a maniac but a practical woman who killed out of what seemed like necessity at the time. I wouldn't be surprised if my brother hadn't threatened her. Though I've been disabused about how well I knew Jeanne, I'm still certain she would want to get as far away from here as possible."

James looked at Jessica uncertainly to propose, "We could go into the village and stay at some lodgings there until the Chief no longer needs us."

"And take Liz, Gerry, Guy, Maura, and Lord knows who else with us? Are there rooms enough?" Jessica disagreed.

Winston added, "The little lady's right. We're still full up—even into Portsmouth—with refugees from the fires. No, sit tight. You should be fine, especially with the precautions we talked about."

James didn't look exactly pleased, but Jessica offered him the cold comfort, "At least you won't have to tell Liz she'll have to pack and leave her comfy surroundings for a tiny hotel room for the three of us!"

James acquiesced, though not thrilled. Jess's glance at Philip told her that he was relieved not to be left alone with the dark secrets of his house. *What a day for him! For us all!*

"Okey dokey, that's settled," Winston concluded.

Philip smiled weakly and said, "Good, then. If you don't mind, I'm going inside to sit down for fifteen minutes—get myself grounded. Then I'll join you in making sure we're properly locked up."

"Sure thing, Mr. Carlyle," Winston assured him.

Jessica offered Philip a supportive smile, but James only gave him a tight nod.

After Philip had closed the front door on the other three, Chief Winston told Jessica and her husband, "It's a good thing you'll be here with Mr. Carlyle. I know he and his brother were anything but pals, but all this must have knocked the poor guy for a loop. And don't you worry about that Rivers dame. If she's still around, we'll find her. It's been a rotten day all around."

"I guess it's not been so rotten for Vitus Blasko," Jessica proposed, wearily trying to find a bright spot. "Jeanne's guilt clears him of Wanda's murder, maybe even Felicia's. He should rest easier, knowing he's been vindicated all around."

Winston raised his brows, querying, "All around. Like I said to Mr. Carlyle, I can't speak to a case that happened twenty years back when I've got a modern one to close out."

Jessica wanted to argue, but James headed her off at the pass with mischief in his hazel eyes: "We should let Chief Winston do his job—and I'm getting cold. Either you and I go in or hand back that jacket."

"Smart guy," Jessica rejoined with a twinkle of her own. "Okay, you win. I could use a shower, a change of clothes, and some hosiery without ladders you can climb." To Winston, "Coming, Chief?"

"Nope. Expecting another call, so gotta stay by the radio for the moment. Then I'll be in to help you check around."

"We'll send you out a sandwich and a cup of coffee," Jessica promised. "It's the least we can do after tearing you away from your croissants."

"Much appreciated, Ma'am."

Entering the house, James encircled Jess with his arm. He didn't say a word, but she could feel his relief that he had her safe and sound. Her arm around James's waist signaled her appreciation.

Chapter Forty
Friday, November 7th

Hitting the hay early, Jessica had managed to dodge a third-degree from Liz on all the excitement that had transpired while she was in Portsmouth. With the new room given her and James, Jess had indulged in a soothing shower, a change of clothes, and a thorough examination of the new place for secret panels. As the old saying went: the couple who checked their room for secret passages in creepy murder mansions together stayed together.

Anyway, talk around the new day's breakfast table was much more upbeat. Chief Winston had given Guy and Maura the green light to return to New York. Most of their bags were ready to go, with a few to be shipped tomorrow. Today, they'd be going to Portsmouth to catch a train out of New Hampshire. Sitting next to Jess, Elizabeth had finally taken a break from grilling her sister to explain in detail how she could have done things better than everyone else yesterday. Jessica tactfully refrained from telling her big sister that *she* could do with a dose of scopolamine. As if the drug could even begin to slow down Elizabeth!

Surveying the table, Jessica also couldn't help thinking about the people who weren't there, even more sadly, why they were missing. Philip Carlyle had actually taken a weekday off from work for a task far more difficult than running his business. If he hadn't left already, he'd be making arrangements for his brother's funeral after the autopsy. Gerry Davis? He hadn't come down to breakfast. Maura and Guy reported that he'd come in late last night, around the time that they had, finally receiving word from Jamie. No explanation where she'd been yesterday, only that she couldn't, wouldn't see him until she got things squared away with her father. The Robinsons were both concerned that he'd been pretty cut up.

The absence that concerned Jessica the most was her husband's. He was still upstairs, snoozin', which in itself was not bad. It was the reason why that gave her some trouble. Perhaps it was the release of tension over present events. On the other hand, maybe it was the opposite: present events had triggered his wariness, bred in his war years, of not letting himself rest until he knew all threats were completely neutralized. Whatever the case, in her own fitful sleep, Jess had caught James sitting up nearly all night. Any attempt on her part to stay awake to keep him company, James had nixed. *Well, he was making up for lost time now.*

"So, is Professor Dreamy still upstairs sawing wood?" Elizabeth cut into Jess's thoughts.

"Lady, you must be psychic," Jessica returned, knowing her sister's teasing was intended therapeutically.

Guy piped in, "You don't need to be psychic to know we'll all be thrilled to get back to the city. When do you gals and James get to return?"

"Chief Winston says he should be done with us before the coming week," Jessica explained. "Of course, we're on call whenever he needs us."

Maura asked Elizabeth, "You're free to go, aren't you? I mean, it's your sister and James whom the Police Chief really needs."

"You think I'd leave my baby sister here in this Castle Frankenstein?" Liz returned, putting an arm around Jess's shoulders.

"Actually, Elizabeth, Frankenstein didn't have a castle. He did have an attic," Jessica corrected. "Or were you thinking about the movies not the book?"

"Either way," Maura interjected, "I'm glad to get out before I come down with a permanent case of the willies. For heaven's sakes, this past month we've been *living* our program. Take me back to the big city, strikes, red scares, crimes, and all."

"Say, it's not all bad, now," Guy laughed. "Everything's finally turned around. They figured out the murderers. Scott and Bev have made nice with the network, our real sponsor is back in the saddle and feeling better, and his brother-in-law just got arrested for embezzlement."

"You don't say!" Jessica bubbled.

"Yep. Bev phoned from town last night while you were wrapped in sweet dreams. The D.A. flipped some of Ungerpreck's buddies to whom he'd been bragging about how much smarter he was, being able to 'appropriate funds,'" Guy explained. "What a dope, huh?"

"I'll say," Jessica cheerfully agreed. However, she sobered to add, "I guess most everything is tied up, except, well, we still don't know who killed Felicia. She'll probably never be at peace."

"There you go again, thinking too much," Elizabeth shook her head. "You need to get out of this gloomy joint—and do some shopping!" Elizabeth turned to Maura and Guy: "I know one of the help was going to drive you into Portsmouth. How about Jess and I take you in? We can all have a nice chatty drive and lunch there, while I get my sister out of this place for a few hours?"

"Sounds great," Maura replied. Guy nodded agreement.

"Not a bad idea," Jess agreed, "but I don't want to be too long. After we drop Maura and Guy, we could have lunch in town. I just don't want to be gone long enough for James to wonder about us."

Liz snorted. "Why? The murders have been solved."

"Jeanne's still out there," Jess noted.

"Oh sure," Liz quipped. "Every girl who's on the run for double murder loiters about her hometown. It's the best way to avoid getting caught."

Maura teased, "You never know, Liz. She could be hiding near the road, and when you drive by, she could pretend to be injured on the pavement. When you two stop to help, she'll grab you!"

"Don't worry, Maura," Elizabeth deadpanned. "If I see any bodies on the road, I'll just drive right over them."

"Gee, Liz. That seems a little harsh," Jess suggested dryly. "Couldn't you just swerve around them?"

"If I *must*!"

Guy decided, "Ah, maybe we'll have Jessica drive."

Their chuckles greeted Philip Carlyle when he entered the room, apparently not yet having gone out. Everyone immediately sobered.

However, Philip smiled quietly, reassuring them, "No, please. There's been enough unhappiness in this house, especially caused by my brother. I won't let him continue to hurt people even in death."

Their nods were wordlessly sympathetic. Jessica broke the awkwardness, "Will you be joining us for breakfast, Philip? Lu is doing a nice job taking over . . ."

Jessica cut herself short, realizing what a bad choice it was to accidentally bring up Jeanne's absence and, by extension, her perfidy.

Yet Philip put Jessica at ease: "Yes, yes. She's doing rather well." Speaking to the Robinsons, he added, "You two will be leaving us today. I'm sorry that you'll have to use the station wagon, but I'm afraid I will need to take the Olds, myself, for . . . business."

"Don't apologize," Guy assured his host. "Jess and Liz are going to drive us in and make a day of it. We'll actually have more room, with the station wagon, for our luggage."

"And Elizabeth will have more room for her shopping," Jessica added. "There may be a few antiques left in Annette Risdon's shop for her to scarf up. I only hope that when we hit the rails for home, we don't have to hire a baggage car for all her booty."

"Wise guy," Liz muttered, though she loved it.

There was more talk, thanking Carlyle for his hospitality and his apologizing for the bizarre tragedies his guests had experienced. Jess arranged with Philip to let James know that she'd gone off with Liz, since he'd likely be up and about before the sisters returned. Probably the best medicine in the world for James was a solid rest and for her to escape the darkness of this house into the open air.

It was cold. So, as Jess and Liz stepped out of the café several hours later, Jessica was glad to be wearing her fawn wool blazer over a long-sleeved light orange blouse and chocolate brown slacks. Elizabeth was shrugging into her own olive, wool jacket over a striped blouse and tan slacks, while remarking that winter was on the way.

"Not quite yet," Jessica disagreed, leading her sister briskly up the street. "No slate-colored juncos."

"Huh?"

"You know, those slatey, blue-grey little birds that make a sound like castanets when they scatter," Jess explained without slowing a whit.

"Oh, yeah, sure," Liz returned with a touch of sarcasm. "The ones that hang out with the red-bellied sapsuckers."

"Yellow," Jessica corrected.

"Huh?"

"Yellow-bellied *sapsuckers* and Red-bellied *woodpeckers*," Jess smiled, moving rapidly.

"Fine, Mrs. Audubon, but could you slow it down? Your name's Jessica Minton not Jesse Owens."

Jess put on the brakes, slightly, explaining, "Sorry, Elizabeth. Service was awfully slow today. I guess it had to do with the staff putting together food for the refugees. I can't kick about it on those grounds, but I do want to get back to James."

"James is a big boy. He can get along without you for a few hours," Liz advised.

"I know, but with all that's happened, and Jeanne still on the loose, he could be wondering about me."

Trying to kid away her sister's concern, Liz queried: "Oh, and what about me? I suppose James thinks I can go to the dogs—Oops, poor word choice, with the Hound of Hades out there."

They'd dashed across the street to their car, parked in front of Annette Risdon's shop. Elizabeth urged, "Seems a shame not to pop in after we parked right here. There's this darling set of jade earrings and matching bracelet! You know how I adore jade! And I saw a lovely gold stick pin with a lapis lazuli head that would just do for you."

Jessica fished the car keys out of her shoulder bag and unlocked Elizabeth's door, laughing, "What! No solid-silver water bowl for Dusty?!" She opened the door for her sister. "Besides, you ought to leave something for other customers."

Liz gave Jess an acid smile, which she puckishly returned before circling the car to the driver's side. All kidding aside, and refreshing a day as it had been, it was time to get back. Liz leaned across the front seat to unlock her sister's door, saying as Jess opened it, "Okay, you don't have to hit me with a two-by-four *many* times. Let's get back and see what the big lug is up to. For all your concern, he's probably put away a couple of sides of beef by now. For a wiry guy, he sure can chow down. But I guess that's one of the many fine qualities you lovebirds have in common."

Jess was on the verge of giving her sister a smart comeback, when the shop door flew open and out rushed Annette Risdon, calling, "Oh, Jessica Minton, I'm so glad I could catch you! You saved me a world of trouble, not having to go all the way out to the Carlyle place to give you . . ." Her hand extended a narrow white envelope ". . . this letter from Edna."

Receiving her envelope, bewildered as to why Mrs. Rivers would have written her, Jessica managed, "Oh, Mrs. Risdon. Thank you. I'm so sorry to hear about your friend, Edna Rivers. I really liked her." Jessica absently slipped the envelope into her jacket's left pocket, finishing, "How are you doing?"

"Well, all right, I guess. I'll miss Edna, but at least she won't have to face the worry and shame over Jeanne. She did the best she could with that girl."

"I know," Jess condoled. "At least Mrs. Rivers had a good friend in you. As I said, I really liked her. She was frank and warm. So, do you know why she wrote me a letter?"

"Well, my dear, I guess you could say it's a sign of how much Edna liked you, too, even if she couldn't always get your name straight. You'll see she addressed the envelope: 'To the Felicia actress.'"

"At least she saw that I was only 'acting' Felicia," Jessica added with gentle humor. "How did you come across this, anyway?"

Annette explained, "Well, this morning before I opened, I stopped by Edna's cottage to do a little more cleaning up. Wouldn't you know, I came across this on the floor, almost under the dresser in her room. Guess that's why I didn't notice it sooner. So, when I saw the estate wagon here, I figured it'd be easier to wait for you to come back—and here you are."

"Well, thank you," Jessica smiled. "I'm glad some things work out serendipitously."

Leaning out the window next to Jess, Elizabeth interjected, "So, what's it say?"

"Land sakes," Annette scolded. "It's a sealed envelope. How should I know?"

Jess wagged her finger at Liz. "Interfering with the U.S. Mail is a federal offense."

"It's not stamped and hasn't even seen a mailbox," Liz reasoned. "Fair game in my book."

"That's my sister; just loves to kid us out of our blues," Jess assured the skeptical older woman. "But thank you so much, Annette. I appreciate your getting this to me. I'll read it when I get back to the house. I promise to let you know if Mrs. Rivers says anything that you might need or want to know."

"Oh, never mind that. Edna wasn't always so clear in the head these last several years. Who knows but it might just be a lot of nonsense."

"Okay," Jessica replied. After exchanging a few quick pleasantries, the older woman returned to her shop and Jess slipped behind the wheel. Now, Elizabeth pounced: "So rip it open and tell me what the old gal had to say!"

"Down girl!" Jessica laughed. "You heard Annette Risdon. It's probably just a lot of confusion. You'd think it were the key to a big mystery. News flash: mystery's been solved."

Jessica got the car started and in gear before adding, "We'll be home in two shakes, so just hold your horses. Now, don't distract me while I'm driving."

"If you pull over, kid, and switch places, I can drive and you can read. Perfect solution!"

"Right," Jessica smoothly countered. "I'm going to trust the wheel to someone who earlier proposed to run over anything—or anyone—in her way. For the sake of motorists, pedestrians, bicyclist, and small mammals: No."

Elizabeth snorted, "You know what I'm suggesting makes perfect sense, with the added advantage that I'll stop needling you."

"Look, Elizabeth," Jessica opened up. "I liked Mrs. Rivers and she liked me. Did it ever occur to you that there might be something personal in the letter? Maybe it's not all a crazy quilt. There might be something that's really for *my* eyes and heart?"

Elizabeth relented, "I hate it when you go all humane and *right* on me. Okay, okay. But the minute we get back, I expect you to rip that sucker open and let me know everything you see that is not *entirely* none of my business."

"Deal," Jessica agreed with a smile. "We should be back in under ten minutes, anyway."

True to her word, Jessica had them home about eight minutes later, without mowing down anything human or otherwise. Pulling into the garage, Jess noted Philip's sedan gone. *Of course, taking care of his brother. What a rough deal for the poor guy.*

The sisters stepped out of the garage into the sunshine, Liz trying not to prance with anticipation. Jessica, on the verge of telling her sister to take a tranquilizer, recollected her own nightmare experiences in that department. She let her sister continue to prance.

Pigeons were murmuring in the eaves of the mansion as Jess noted the painful writing on the envelope: "To the Felicia actres." Had Mrs. Rivers' abilities degenerated that badly? Could it have been written when Annette left her to admit the doctor? Had Edna Rivers fallen trying to get back into bed not out of it? Would she need to show this to Chief Winston? Oh, she was probably letting her imagination get away from her. Anyway, she'd better snap things up before Elizabeth had a stroke.

Jessica quickly ripped open the envelope, then pulled out and opened the sheet. Her mouth dropped at what she read laboriously scrawled there.

Chapter Forty-One

"Holy Mother of God!"

Elizabeth Minton might have occasionally dropped a ladylike imprecation from time to time, but she was not normally given to taking the Lord's, or any of His relatives', names in vain.

Vaguely aware that she ought to be mad at her sister for snatching away this unnerving missive, Jessica had to grant that the look on her own puss but definitely justified Liz.

"Jess," Elizabeth breathed, shaking the page in front of her. "Do you know what this means?"

Getting a grip on herself, Jess replied, taking back the letter, "It means, if we can believe this, we now know where Jeanne's crime journal is—and more."

"Do you believe it?" Elizabeth pressed.

"I don't know," Jessica shook her head. As she re-read that message scratched out on the threshold of death, Jess understood James's description of haunted time distilling into a single point:

"Felicia's truth Jeanne book truth study window seat hid big folder brown 84 find it"

"Is that it?" Liz demanded. "Does she mean Jeanne's journal? The one you saw in the cellar room?"

Jessica came slowly back to herself, finally answering, "Maybe. Maybe, Liz. It kind of falls into place, now that I think of it. I mean, Chief Winston told us that Mrs. Rivers was on a call when Annette found her, and they thought it was Jeanne. Maybe Jeanne told her this as insurance, but Mrs. Rivers was so shocked she had another stroke."

"So, you believe this is the real deal?" Liz questioned excitedly. "The journal is actually hidden in the house, in the study's window seat?"

Jessica took a deep breath to gather her thoughts before answering, "Gee, I'm not 100% sure. I mean, this was written by a woman whose brain had just been scrambled, and why would Jeanne tell her mother where she'd hidden the journal for insurance, but leave it hidden when her mother died? Some insurance if the person who's supposed to take care of it is dead."

Elizabeth let loose, her arms akimbo: "What really gets me, Jess, is that she heard her mother having a stroke over the phone and didn't lift a finger to help her. I told you she was no good from way back. But why hide it here and not at her mother's?"

"Maybe she reads Edgar Allen Poe, you know, the purloined letter? Hide it under our noses, in the master's own study. It's too obvious for us to guess. Who'd expect Philip to have it?" Jessica conjectured. "But, Liz, when she left, when she knew everyone was after her—and after she'd killed Bill—why not take it with her and destroy it? With Bill gone, where was the need for leverage?"

"That's not an issue if she killed Bill after she called her mother and hid the book," Liz reasoned. "With him dead, over whom did she need leverage? Maybe killing him was a desperate response when telling him she had insurance against him failed. But listen, kid, we can stand here arguing the 'whys' and 'wherefores' till the cows come home. Meanwhile, if Jeanne hasn't split this island, she could sneak back, grab the incriminating book, and lam out. So let's get the lead out and nab it first."

Elizabeth was hustling Jessica by the elbow toward the kitchen door even as Jess protested, "Wait, Elizabeth. Hold on! If this is legit evidence, shouldn't we call Chief Winston and see what he thinks?"

"No dice!" her sister insisted. "That guy's busier than a one-armed paper hanger, though why anyone would make a hanger out of paper is beyond me. The clothes would just fall right off. And arms, hangers don't have . . ."

"Elizabeth!" Jessica interrupted, digging in her heels and abruptly halting them at the back-door steps.

"Okay, Okay," Liz relented. "My point is that Winston is tied up with a mountain of work on the case, never mind his regular responsibilities. For the love of Mike, you remember what Deputy Hudson said today when we ran into him at the café. Then, here you come with a disjointed letter from a sick old lady who could just be rambling over some words her daughter *might* have said. Not a very reliable lead, in my book. Even if he does rush out, what happens if there's nothing to find? Considering the old girl's condition when she scrawled out the note, you know as well as I do that's a genuine possibility. I wouldn't want to be in your shoes if you throw a monkey wrench into Winston's investigation by wasting his time."

"You know, I *know* there's a hole in your logic somewhere, Liz, but I'm just so bushed from everything that's been happening, and the rest I haven't been getting, that I see your point—even though I realize I shouldn't."

"Good," Elizabeth agreed with an emphatic shake of her fist. "Let's get to it!"

"Just hold your horses, Eddie Arcaro," Jessica warned. "We'll look, but we'll bring James in on it. You know he's a maestro at doing a search without contaminating evidence. And if he thinks the whole deal is a bad idea, we'll listen to him. Copasetic?"

"Don't pull that jazz lingo with me, missy. I was hep while you were still in pigtails and pinafores, but, okay."

And into the kitchen they went.

Mrs. Trask, her helper, and the day maid Regina were taking a well-deserved break before laying out the goods for the evening meal. Seeing the two guests come in through the kitchen entrance, the rather surprised cook asked, "Miss Minton, can I help you?"

"Maybe you can," Jessica answered, her iron grip on Elizabeth's arm barely subduing her sister's impatience. "You wouldn't happen to know if my husband is up or where to find him?"

The older woman put down her capacious blue-willow teacup to answer, "Well, he's been up, all rightie. Ate himself quite the breakfast. But where he got himself to, I couldn't say. An awful lot of work keeping the kitchen going, you know."

"Oh, I'm sure," Jessica managed to smile. After all, antsy as Jess was to get at the truth, Mrs. Trask was a busy woman with no idea of why impatience sizzled inside the Minton gals. Jess did have an idea of who could be of help and asked, "Would you know where Lu Brown is?"

"Certainly do, Miss. She's off in the drawing room, double-checking this one's (nod to the day maid) work. She's darned tootin' going to make sure Mr. Carlyle thinks she's up to the mark, takin' over for that one as left us all in shock."

"You got that right," the day girl grumbled. "If she isn't careful she's going to be twice the tartar—"

"Thanks so much," Jessica smilingly cut short the girl's complaint. There was no time to get caught in stirring up a backstairs hornet's nest. Jess gave her sister a nudge and, before Elizabeth could complain about going off on a side trip, had her out the door with a quick whisper, "Lu can tell where to find James."

From the drawing room doorway they saw Lu, standing arms akimbo, by the fireplace, frowning at the maid's work there. Looking up as Jessica and Liz as they approached, Lu sighed with a disgusted gesture, "Would you take a look at that?"

Liz impatiently piped up, "Never mind the housework—Whoa! That *is* a disgrace! What? Does she think heaps of ashes are the latest thing in *Homes and Gardens*?"

Before Lu could be sidetracked, Jessica smiled at the young woman, gave her sister's arm a silencing squeeze, and inquired, "Lu, we just got back, and I'm dying to see my guy. You don't know where he's keeping himself right now, do you?"

Lu took a moment to switch gears before answering, "Oh, yes. Actually, I do—but he's not keeping himself here. He went out. To see the Blaskos."

"The Blaskos?" Both Jessica and Liz questioned, surprised. Recovering first, Jess pressed, "To their home? Why did he go there, Lu?" Her words grew concerned, "Nothing's wrong, is there?"

"No, I wouldn't worry," Lu answered. "I mean, I don't know the whole story. No one told me directly." Here she seemed embarrassed to admit: "I just happened to hear as I went by the drawing room. Mr. Philip seemed to have taken a call from Jamie Blasko. I didn't hear the phone; she must have called his private line. Anyway, there was something about Mr. Crawford going there." Lu's embarrassment gradually lessened as she saw that her information was helpful to Jess. "Neither he nor Mr. Philip seemed upset. So, I wouldn't worry."

"But you didn't hear why he went?" Jessica asked, Liz piping in, "Or when he'll be back?"

Lu shook her head, "I can't say. Like I told you, I just happened to be passing by. I wasn't trying to find out."

"Of course," Jessica assured Lu. "We understand—and you've been a great help. Thanks."

"All right, then," Lu bobbed her head, "I'd better get after that Patti to do a better job in here, but maybe I'll let her finish her tea before I light into her."

Offering a pleasant expression, Jess approved, "Good idea, firm without being a tartar." She started to let Lu pass, but delayed her with, "Lu, I don't suppose James left me a message. Maybe you forgot to tell me?"

"Not that I know of," Lu answered. She looked at her watch and said, "That was about fifteen, maybe twenty, minutes ago. He'd have to go through the woods on foot since the cars were out and there's no good bike path. So, he's probably not quite there yet."

"All right," Jessica replied, keeping the lid on her frustration.

As soon as Lu was gone, Jess turned to her sister with: "Now what? Maybe I can call over there—"

"And say what?" Liz countered. "'Hon, hurry home. We've found the journal that tells the whole story?' What about an operator overhearing? What if James isn't even there yet? Are you going to leave a message: 'Tell my hubby to hoof it home pronto so we can pour through a secret record of the crimes?' Aside from blabbing what we know, it will take another chunk of time for James to get back. Do we have time to wait? Anyway, Lu said neither James nor Philip seemed upset."

"All right, already," Jessica retorted, putting her hands up to tamp down her sister's floodgate of words. "So, what do you propose, Liz?"

"*We* go ahead and check out the journal. You told me before that Carlyle said his study was open to you."

"To get a book, Elizabeth, not to poke and pry amongst the hidden contents, like in a window seat. Maybe if he were here, we could ask him . . ."

"But he is not here. James is not here. Only we are here. Who knows if and when Jeanne might sneak back and grab that journal right from under our noses!" Elizabeth pointedly argued.

Jessica compressed her lips, finally starting, "I hate poking where I don't belong—"

"Like in the secret passageways of your host's house? In rooms the passageways lead to?" Liz archly countered.

"I didn't intend to go exploring. I got stuck."

"You got stuck after you poked your nose into checking out that passageway," Elizabeth checkmated her sister. "Besides, you're only bending a little rule of etiquette to help a more important rule of justice. Finding that journal could tie everything together for Jim Winston. Prove once and for all what those two did to you. Prove they killed Wanda, maybe even pin Felicia's murder where it belongs."

Jessica's sigh was tremendous. This endeavor wasn't nearly as left of the law, let alone as dangerous, as the time Liz and Lois Wong got her to dress up as a maid to sneak into a hood's apartment to find and retrieve a stolen gun used to frame their friend. It would do, though. And it seemed it would have to be done.

"Look," Liz advised, "all we'll do is slip in now that nobody seems to be looking, take a quick peek in the window seat (being careful not to disturb anything), grab the journal, and split. Use your handkerchief to pick it up, so as not to mess up other fingerprints. Piece of cake!"

"Never say that, Liz," Jessica growled. "Don't jinx us."

"So, we're on?" Elizabeth proposed, brightening.

"All right. I know I'll regret this, but, okay," Jess relented. "There's sense in there, *somewhere*. Here's what we'll do. Even though I've been given borrowing rights, to be honest, I'd rather that no one knew I was in there. It makes me feel bad, poking where I shouldn't, especially if there might be nothing to find. So, I'll close the door to hide what I'm really up to. You'll lounge around on the threshold of the music room, maybe grab yourself some sheet music to peruse. If anyone other than James comes down the corridor, especially if that person looks interested in the study, find a way to knock on the door. No! Pretend you have something to put back in the room. Since I won't toss stuff out willy-nilly, when I hear you at the door, I can replace everything in a snap and . . . Yes! slip out the window over the window seat."

"I should be the one doing the search," Elizabeth disagreed. "You've seen what I can do unwrapping and rewrapping Christmas presents to me—or rather, you *haven't*!"

"Yes," Jess argued back, "And I also know I can't trust you not to get distracted into other business; then, Bob's your uncle, the whole household's back and we still won't have the journal—if there is one."

"You've got to stop listening to that Brit husband of yours. I can't make heads nor tail feathers of the slang you've picked up from him! But, okay, you win. Let's go."

Leaving the room, Liz added, "Wait, does he keep the study locked?"

"Always looking on the bright side, aren't you, Liz?" Jess responded quietly as they headed down the corridor. "I know Jeanne told me ages ago, but I don't remember. Well, let's hope the window isn't locked."

A few minutes later. Jessica was trying the study door. *Damn! It was locked! Looks like it's the window for me!*

However, the undaunted Elizabeth insisted, "All rightie. Never mind the window, kid. Stand back and let someone who knows her stuff take charge." She pulled two hairpins from her elaborate coiffure and went to work on the lock, saying, "I see them do this in movies all the time, and I've always wanted to try it."

"But, Liz, that's just in movies—You did it!" Impressed, Jessica added, "Maybe you and James should get together on this lock-picking business— and *he* needs special instruments, not going in much for hairpins."

"Never mind that, kid," Liz commanded. "You wanted the job; now get in there and do it."

Jessica slipped into the study, closing the door behind her, surprised at the room's unexpected chill. *Ah, the open window. She wouldn't tell Liz that her demonstration of B & E skill had all been for naught. Anyway, it wasn't smart, locking the door but leaving the window open. Still, poor Philip had been through enough lately to excuse any degree of absent-mindedness.* Jess just hoped she wouldn't have to capitalize on his mistake for a quick exit.

She quickly crossed the room, immediately kneeling down before the window seat. *Thank God! It's unlocked!* Jess eagerly lifted the lid. A stack of black notebooks was jammed into the right side by rows of rust-brown, pasteboard accordion folders, making sense of the letter's reference to a folder.

Jessica reached toward the folders, but hesitated. *There was a heck of a lot of them, but not 84, the number Mrs. Rivers had specified.*

Something seemed to creak behind her, toward the desk! Jessica jerked around. *No one. What did you expect? The ghost of Felicia waltzing in to bop you with the right file?*

Jessica's eyes rested on that painting of flowers behind Philip's desk, the one that had tipped her on how to open the panel in her closet and pass into the dark interstices of the Carlyle home. *Interstices? Had she really just said interstices? Who uses a word like that? Only someone afraid to plunge back in and risk finding nothing, after all.*

Okay, here's the first folder. No, too light to hold a journal. The next one felt heavier, though. *Holding a book?* Jessica hurriedly fiddled with the old knot, so tempted to just rip it. *Right, a dead giveaway that someone had invaded Philip Carlyle's sanctum.*

The string unknotted! The folder spread open and presented Jessica with . . . a manual on manufacturing-machinery and a pad of notes.

"Damn!" Jessica muttered, immediately twisting her head to scan the room. *Of course, no one heard. And Elizabeth hadn't given a single warning. Get back to work!*

The next few folders were far too light, leaving Jessica to flip swiftly through that row and into the next without coming to anything of interest. She didn't have all day, so what was the fastest way to eliminate the duds? Jessica gave the outside of the folder in her hand a careful once over. Wait, in the lower right-hand corner, where she'd generally had a finger or thumb holding the folder, a number in black ink! They were all numbered and in sequence, but with gaps in that sequence. Jess flipped rapidly through the row, praying 84 would be there.

77, 79, 80, 82, 83, . . . 84!

Fingers trembling on the thread, Jessica realized, hopeful, that this thread had recently been retied, was even a little loose from haste.

Her hands plunged in and paused with dread-tainted hope; she felt the top of a notebook. Swiftly, she removed her hand to pull a handkerchief from her pocket. She wasn't about to smear up someone else's prints with her own! As if ripping off a band-aid, she yanked her discovery out by its edges.

It was a familiar object, though hardly an old friend. Jessica started to get up, but hesitated. The last thing she wanted to do was run half-cocked with this thing to Chief Winston if it didn't actually prove anything. She was also blazingly curious, and hadn't what Jeanne and Bill done to her earned her the right to know how to fill in all the puzzle's pieces? Yet, if she hoofed it out of the room to examine it with her sister, could she keep Liz's paws off the book so she could have a careful look-see? She had to know *now* what she had her hands on, literally and figuratively. Anyway, Liz wasn't signaling danger, and everyone ought to be out for quite some time. She had to know.

Jessica sank onto the floor, sitting back against the bottom of the open window seat. Careful not to smudge or add prints, she opened the book. An envelope slipped out. Catching it, Jess noticed at the top of the page the logo of the developers reviled by so many of the islanders. At first, she wasn't surprised. Certainly, Bill and Jeanne would have been in contact with the firm, having no love for the land and the mansion, only caring about the cash that the destruction of both would bring.

Except when Jessica fully opened the letter and read the name of its addressee, she was shocked into a disbelieving double take. *It couldn't be!* She'd defended this person, believed in this person. But there it all was, in black and white: how the combined sale of the Blasko and Carlyle properties was what the developers really wanted, was all they'd settle for, and for such an enormous price that this person would be sitting pretty for life, and then some. Not wanting to believe her eyes, Jessica rapidly flipped through the book's pages with the tip of a pencil left in the bottom of the folder. *Please show me something to disprove the facts of this letter!*

Sure, it was all there—all she'd known before, all she'd hoped would explain Felicia's fate. But none of it was what she'd wanted to find. There was confirmation of what she already knew or figured out about Jeanne's drugging her and Wanda's using hypnosis on her drug-weakened state to induce the nightmare visions. How Jeanne had sabotaged the car and then paid off Nathan Jones to pick up Liz and her to "accidentally on purpose" drop them at the Blasko place. How Jeanne had sent Jessica to the cemetery to meet Vitus Blasko, all to so shake up the family that their property would be easy pickings for someone wanting to make a bundle selling the land of both families. How Jeanne's partner had gone to pay Wanda O'Malley an unexpected visit that afforded the opportunity, unbeknownst to Wanda, to eavesdrop through an open window on a phone conversation. Listening covertly, the writer had learned that Wanda would betray her cohorts to a rival for a bigger cut of the action by naming that eavesdropper as Felicia's murderer at the séance. Wanda O'Malley had been sentenced to death even before the writer had slipped away without her being aware of that person's presence.

But the journal also filled in missing jigsaw pieces, creating a picture Jess wanted to deny. She wasn't surprised at the details of Jeanne's working secretly with her ally to repair the passageways while the servants were fast asleep in the dorms over the garage. She already knew that Jeanne and Wanda had teamed up with Bill in South America, but not that the three of them had worked that circuit to con nightclub customers. And she hadn't known that Jeanne's meeting Bill again had triggered the curse of nightmares for which Wanda used hypnosis to unlock the source. For buried deep in the unconscious of this one-time child rover of secret passageways was the memory of a horrible sight through a crack in the panel, the sight of Felicia's murder. That memory provided a powerful incentive for Jeanne and Wanda to return with blackmail on their minds, until the prospect of the real estate killing had turned a victim into an ally. *But this person? How could I have been so wrong?*

Distraught with these revelations, Jessica couldn't think any further, for the moment. Finally, staring at the floor before her, she gathered her thoughts and blurted, "Good Grief! James is at the Blaskos! I've got to get him back here!"

Scrambling to her feet, Jessica automatically turned to close the window seat. *Sister, getting caught prying is the least of your worries!* The house creaked and settled again, but she thought nothing of it until she turned around. A panel had slid back behind the desk where the painting hung. The painting that was repeated upstairs and had opened up all the other passages to her. Before Jess could recover herself, a voice she knew too well spoke softly enough to elude Elizabeth's sonar but loud enough to halt her, "Jessica, stop right there."

The speaker remained in the shadows of the passage, but his weapon with its silencer was clear enough. She opened her mouth but was muted by that quiet but forceful voice, "I can drop you before you can say a word, though I certainly prefer not to. As for your sister, I'll take her down the minute she comes through the door, so don't even try to warn her."

Yes, it was the partner named in the journal, and that partner seemed as cool now as he had been kind in the past.

Chapter Forty-Two

The startling flames and lush, soft apricots of October were largely gone from the trees. The leaves were mostly decayed and fallen to the ground or dangling rusty or muddy brown from the branches. Of course, there was that one exception from time to time, like Coleridge's "one red leaf, the last of its clan,/ That dances as often as dance it can,/ Hanging so light, and hanging so high, /On the topmost twig that looks up at the sky." That was just fine with James Crawford this afternoon as he bustled along the shortcut to the Blasko home to which Philip Carlyle had directed him. It was cold. Still, with the sun out, the walk was pleasantly brisk. James also had to admit he enjoyed being out of the Carlyle Mansion. Last night had been a rum one. Despite, or maybe because, the tension was wrapping up, his anxiety had burst out, leaving him restless, unable to sleep. Once the need to hold everything together had passed, mind and soul had collapsed for a little bout of hell.

But that was last night. This morning, exhaustion had nicked him and put him down for several hours. After that snooze and an enormous breakfast, he felt, well, maybe not precisely right as rain, but close enough, all things considered. So, he hadn't been worried at all when he'd heard that Jessica and Liz had gone off with the Robinsons, but would meet him here. Chief Winston seemed to have things well in hand now concerning Jeanne Rivers, while Bill Carlyle was past worrying anyone. Yet, what was that odd little inkling in the back of his head? An echo of the old days when he'd learned never to relax, never to believe there mightn't be an eleventh-hour twist? But he wasn't on a mission. He was in the States, where a perfectly capable constable had charge of things.

James forced himself to think about Jessica, how glad he was that she was having some time off with that sister of hers. *Jessica took things too much to heart, cared too much about what happened to others. It was time she had some fun, and maybe got this worrywart of a husband out of her hair for a few hours, but not for too many.* He picked up his pace to shorten the separation.

Anyway, Elizabeth would take good care of her. Liz really was a good egg and a smart cookie—Good Lord! Her criminal mixing of metaphors was rubbing off! Truth be told, though, as much as James loved to cheek his sister-in-law, he got a kick out of her cheeking him right back. More important, they both loved Jessica so much. He couldn't bless Liz enough for calling him in when his girl needed him. In her own smart-aleck way, Liz had let him know that she blessed him for being Johnny-on-the-spot at her S.O.S.

He just hoped this visit with Jamie would turn out to be more of a social call than a Lonely Hearts Festival. He felt sorry for the girl, what with losing her mother, nursing an unstable father, and the rocky road all that caused with Gerry Davis. However, there were limits to how much you could commiserate with some people before they pulled you down with them. He'd certainly benefited from his wife's tender heart, but he'd seen her take on too much. Still, her hard-headed sister was there to put the brakes on things if necessary.

As James came out into the driveway, a few yards up from the building, he was a little surprised not to see a Carlyle vehicle parked out front. Then again, the drive turned around the left of the house, so likely the auto was parked there. *Damn, the habit of suspicion was a devil to buck!*

Chuckling at himself, James made brisk work of traversing the distance between himself and the door. It would be a treat to see his wife again after a whole morning apart. Of course, he had no idea what the mood might be with the Blasko tribe. So, maybe he was going to be Jessica's prince, riding in on his own two feet to rescue her from drowning in lugubriousness.

James reached the front door and knocked, only to see the door swing open under his first sharp rap. Automatically, he stepped back and to the side, making himself no longer a target in silhouette against a sun-filled doorway. James Crawford silently cursed as once again he instinctively reached for a Colt in a shoulder holster that wasn't there. Anxiety surged at what all this could mean for Jessica and Elizabeth. Now, James was more than glad when old habits of cool calculation slid into play. A glance to the left set him figuring on the usefulness of the window there: could he slip over and check out the lay of the land inside? That consideration was abruptly scotched by a woman's distraught voice calling from within, "Is that you, Mr. Crawford? Please come in, now!"

Jamie Blasko appeared in the doorway, disheveled, pale, strained. She stayed only long enough to say, "Quickly! Someone's been hurt!"

"Jessica? Liz?" escaped James as he followed the young woman inside. In the foyer, he grabbed Jamie by the arm and demanded, "Tell me what's happened."

Jamie pulled her arm free. Shaky, she answered, "Not your wife. They haven't arrived yet. It's my father. Please, in here, in the drawing room."

James let her lead him into a room on the left, the same one where Jess and Liz had waited the first night they'd come to this dark island.

Vitus Blasko lay face down on the floor before the hearth, a vicious cut on the back of his head where someone had clipped him a nasty one. James immediately knelt by the man to discern if that clip had been fatal. Even as he did, Jamie was explaining from just inside the room, "I found Jeanne Rivers over him, with a pistol, like the one that killed Wanda."

James looked up and replied, "He's still breathing. Have you called an ambulance?"

He really wanted to ask, "What the devil was Jeanne Rivers doing here?" However, a man was down: that was his first priority.

"What? I don't know. It all happened so fast. She left. Why *would* she come here?" Jamie fretted, standing by a little table near the door. "Can you help my father?"

"Yes, I think so, perhaps," James replied, turning back to the injured man. "We've got to be careful about moving him, with this head injury. But you've got to call an ambulance—"

James never finished his instructions, for Jamie said in an unexpectedly calm voice, "We won't do anything of the sort."

He turned sharply. Jamie was holding the island's most popular gun, the Steyr-Hahn. A drawer in the little table near her was open, from whence the weapon had been removed.

"Put your hands up and stand *slowly*," she instructed tightly.

James calculated the distance between them. She'd been smart enough to stay sufficiently far away to make rushing her a bad proposition.

The capable way she held the gun, her alert regard of him, made James realize that his best bet, for the moment, was to play for time.

Complying, James nodded at her weapon and queried, "A fire sale on Steyrs recently? Two-for-one bargain?"

"More like three-for-one collecting war souvenirs," she returned, just a trace of tension starting to seep through her smugness. James could read that she was not an old hand at this.

He cocked his head quizzically and asked, "Mind explaining, since you hold all the cards, anyway?"

Jamie raised her chin and worked up her nerve to answer, "I would say that it will all make sense, eventually, but not to you. You won't be here."

Deciding to work her ego, James observed, "I don't think a chap need be Sherlock Holmes to extrapolate that Jeanne Rivers was never here, that you did this to your father."

"Jeanne Rivers hasn't been able to do anything since Thursday," Jamie replied, pleased with herself on that one—*or was she just trying to psyche herself into being cold-blooded?* Despite Jamie's surface composure, James sensed that killing did not come naturally to her, which he fully intended to work to his advantage.

James had already noticed the couch a few feet behind him: with a little luck it could offer temporary cover or even an advantageous spot from which to disarm her. Playing for time, he questioned, "So, Jeanne Rivers has escaped, after all, and left you behind?"

"Not in the way you think," Jamie replied, pleased with knowing something James didn't.

As curious as he was to get to the bottom of Jamie's enigmatic statement, James was more concerned with whether Jessica and Liz had fallen victim to Jamie. He still managed to sound merely curious with, "And my wife and sister-in-law were never here, either?"

"More like your widow." Cruel, but she seemed to force down a flicker of doubt.

James appeared merely to shift his stance, but he'd taken an imperceptible step back as Jamie focused on his face. He calmly asked, "And is the third Steyr intended for Jessica?" So hard to stay calm asking that question.

Jamie raised her chin and smiled, superiority a trace forced, "Not if she plays ball. If she's smart and takes my partner's offer, she can live long and prosper as a merry widow."

"Your partner?" James queried, portraying affable interest. "You really are a clever one, full of sly surprises. I'm impressed. But how do the two of you expect to get away with all these murders? Even for you, that ought to be quite an accomplishment, with the bodies piling up like cordwood. Chief Winston is bound to nick the two of you as the only ones left standing."

"That's where my partner and I have so much more on the ball than you, Crawford. This isn't supposed to read like part of Jeanne Rivers and Bill Carlyle's spree. My father has been acting quite unstable lately. He's not really, but I've been spinning a neat little web to make him appear that way for some time. And so had my partner, with a similar agenda, as well. Sometimes, enemies start at cross purposes; then become allies when circumstances shift and old alliances fail. We all knew how much your wife resembles my late mother and my father's fascination with her. His instability of late has been helped by a little chemical assistance from me. I learned quite a lot about medication and side effects when I wasted my life coming back and nursing him through his illness."

"This is all quite lovely," James's words and pointing hand briefly directed his wired captor's attention to her prostrate father, while he took another quiet step backward, "but I still don't see how all this is going to help you get away with murder, literally and figuratively. It'd be a pity if no one understood to acknowledged your cleverness, if only briefly."

"Simple. You came here to meet your wife. My father wandered down from his sickbed, fought with you because his addled brain told him you were a rival for Jessica Minton's double. In the struggle, sadly, you were fatally shot, but you survived just long enough to crack him on the skull—also fatally. I know because I witnessed everything, frozen with horror, of course. I'll call for the doctor 'immediately.' After I see that you're both quite dead. I might have to hit him again, to be sure." She gulped at that prospect. Then she pushed herself to conclude. "But what must be done, must be done. That's how we planned it this morning when you all gave us the golden opportunity, with you sleeping late and your wife going out with everyone this morning."

Seizing on Jamie's hesitation at striking her father once more, James pressed, "You'd do that to your own father? *Can* you really stand to feel his skull crack, again?" Her glance went to the man's body, helpless, shallowly breathing, while James shifted yet closer toward the edge of the couch. Then, she was watching him again, so James pulled something from the heart to reach her humanity, "Are you fully prepared for that, for taking responsibility for the death of someone in your own family? A person who gave you life?"

"Life?" Jamie flared. "What life did he give me? Neglect, ruining my chances for happiness when my fiancé found out about him? Chaining me here to take care of him? Damn him! It's his fault my mother is dead! He deserves all he gets from me—and more! No, the killing we'll make selling this and the Carlyle property together will only begin to pay off his debt. The proudest day of my life was when I turned on my partnership with Bill to cheat Philip and agreed to join forces with Philip Carlyle last week!"

Vitus Blasko groaned, moving his head, half-rising before collapsing again—and drawing Jamie's full attention, her gun reflexively pointed at him now. Seizing the distraction, knowing the distance too much to rush his captor, James dived behind the couch. Jamie fired twice. The first shot went high as James dropped low. The second hit home, searing into him like a red-hot poker as the name Philip Carlyle reverberated in his mind.

Chapter Forty-Three

Philip Carlyle stepped out of the shadows. Without raising his voice enough to be heard across the room and through the door, he stated, "Fortunate that I had come to this room *now* to double-check that no evidence was left behind from hiding Jeanne's body in the passage before I disposed of it. I heard the two of you outside, and it was simple to close myself in the passageway and see what you were up to."

Genuinely startled by his revelation, but still mindful enough to play for time, Jessica stated, "You killed Jeanne."

"Yes, Jessica. I did, while you and James Crawford were poking about the chamber behind the music room. I, unfortunately, had to eliminate Jeanne. I'd thought I'd gotten away scot-free, slipping from the panel, grabbing the phone, garroting her before she could say my name to her mother. The icing on the cake was hearing that busybody Annette Risdon scream, 'She's dead.'"

"You must have had a coronary when Winston said she hadn't died right away," Jessica concluded, stringing the moment out. She'd weathered the old cracked-villain-has-to-bloviate-on-his-mastery routine more than once, but this was Philip Carlyle's first rodeo. If only James would hurry up and figure out that Philip had sent him on a wild goose chase to the Blaskos'. She couldn't risk an unarmed Elizabeth coming to her rescue, but James would know how to take down this guy.

She had to keep Philip going. He'd just said something about it all working out for the best. So she played on his egotistical need to control the story, "If Jeanne was your partner, why kill her? I saw the money they were offering if you could get your hands on the Blasko property. There was plenty for you both. By the way, clever move: using me and the séance to drive Vitus over the brink so that to support her Dad's care, Jamie would have to sell out cheap to you. You and Jeanne had her on the ropes. Your high-powered lawyers, eventually, would have kayoed Bill's 'new will.' You and Jeanne would have been home free, especially after you'd gotten rid of Wanda for trying to sell you out to Bill. You're too intelligent to kill indiscriminately, Philip."

"Jessica," he set her straight. "I never act indiscriminately, though I may adapt to changing circumstances swiftly. Poor Jeanne had lost her nerve and was becoming a liability. Even though Wanda was a double-crosser, I'm afraid killing her took more out of Jeanne than she'd anticipated. They had been friends, you know. When Jamie had that little talk with Jeanne about the panels, she panicked. She took the journal, the drugs and tried to use her mother as a shield and hide them under my nose, thinking I'd never suspect. I'll give her that for cleverness, quite Poesque."

"So, you let her live long enough to do your dirty work, injecting Bill with the scopolamine," Jessica surmised coolly. Only her professional skill at dissimulation enabled her to hide her disgust.

"Oh, no, I wish I could take credit," Philip admitted. "Before I acted on my decision to eliminate Jeanne, I'd formed a more efficient partnership. My new partner had gotten sick of Bill's greed and pressure to make their alliance something, shall we say, more physical. She knew about my plans from Wanda and sought me out with a proposition to eliminate the deadwood and combine forces. Experience giving her father injected medications proved useful."

"Jamie?!" Jessica breathed. "Why would she partner with you?"

"Jamie hadn't read Jeanne's diary. So, all I had to do was tell her that Bill killed her mother. That Gladys had told me on her deathbed, when it was too late for me to do anything about bringing the murderer to justice without shaming my family. Of course, we both knew that her father deserved to suffer guilt and suspicion for all the pain he'd caused her and Felicia. So, she did exactly as I wanted to Bill. It wasn't easy on the poor girl, but unlike with Jeanne, I believe she'll get better with practice. Jeanne never had Jamie's rage stewing for twenty years."

Jessica looked Philip square in the eye to challenge, "But we both know Bill didn't kill Felicia. The journal makes that clear. That night, Jeanne was in the passage. *She* saw that you didn't spend the night in Portsmouth. You went to Felicia after Bill had passed out in his room and begged her to go away with *you*."

"Because I loved her," Philip argued, revealing unexpected vulnerability. But memory hardened him. He finished, "She rejected me. I tried to hold her, convince her, but she struggled against me, hit me. I hit her back. She fell, struck her head."

"Then it was an accident, Philip," Jessica tried to soften him. "You could have—"

"Shamed the family? Gone to prison? Let my place go to Bill?" His brother's name was fairly spat. "No. I would not have that. It is unfortunate, though, we may have three more deaths. Or, perhaps only two, if you will be reasonable dear Felic . . . Jessica."

"Two? Three? Oh, James is with Jamie now. She's planning to kill him?" Jessica couldn't help charging forward, stopping abruptly at the desk between them, the pistol halting her. "You can't have her kill him. You can't. I don't believe she'll go through with it. She hasn't a reason, like finding justice for her mother. You can't let that happen, Philip."

A rap at the study door startled them both, but not enough for Jessica to chance going for the pistol. It had to be an impatient Elizabeth. Philip's eyes signaled Jess to quell her sister's curiosity, even as Liz called, "Kid, find anything? Need some help in there?"

No dumb bunny, Jess all too well remembered Philip's warning of what he'd do to Elizabeth if she came in. *No doubt he figured to pin that on Jeanne Rivers, too.*

She raised her voice to reply, "No, Liz. Keep watching. There's a lot to plow through. Keep running interference for me."

"Okay." Her tone was definitely irritated.

Liz, you'd be a hell of a lot more irritated if I let you walk in and get plugged.

"As I was explaining," Philip recommenced, "if you play your cards right, the deaths may only total three, Fel . . . Jessica."

Not understanding Philip, Jessica scrunched her features. Still, she took careful note of his tendency to merge her with his lost love. She'd make it useful.

"Ah, I see I've piqued your interest. Perhaps you won't reject my proposal out of hand. You are so much like her. This is a second chance for me, to start over with you, Felicia."

Minus a pesky husband, Jessica sourly reflected. *Figuring on Jamie taking care of that little bump in the road for you?* Keeping her counsel,

Jessica continued to listen carefully for an opening to play Philip into revealing a way out of this deadly jam.

"This time, I can give you everything the others couldn't. With the money I clear from the sale of all this land, we can go wherever you like and have a whole new life. I know you are in there, Felicia. The two of you couldn't look so much alike by coincidence. It must have been more than drugs and hypnotism that enabled us to guide her in your footsteps. Forget about all the others who stood in our way. Those who aren't gone will be soon."

He spoke almost pleadingly. To think she'd once sympathized with Philip! *Not now. How easily he'd killed to get his way!* This guy had conjured up and pretty much pulled off his elaborate plan and now was going completely crackers on her. But maybe she could use his mental fracture to her advantage. Yet how much time did James have? He shouldn't be any pushover for a kid like Jamie, but the way Jamie had taken them all in proved she was no innocent "kid"—and she had the element of surprise. Still, Jessica had an idea that just might get her to James in time. Nevertheless, she recognized that though Philip Carlyle had taken a ride around the bend of normal, he was still no sap. *If I give in too easily, he might get wise.*

Folding her arms in front of her to hold the journal against her chest, Jessica summed up, "So, you're offering me my life if I keep my mouth shut about the murders. But how could you ever trust me if I turned my back on my husband's murder?"

"A wife can't testify against her husband," he replied. Jessica wisely resisted the urge to correct "can't *be made* to testify"—discretion being the better part of inexact language just now. Philip went on, "I can offer you so much more in culture, in travel, in wealth, and in devotion. I have a lifetime to make up to you. I'm also sure you're smart enough to realize it's better to be a live woman than a deceased widow. Besides, once you've made the bargain, you're part of the group. There's no turning back."

"Is that last part what you told Jamie? I mean, that's why you trust her not to double-cross you?" Jessica asked, making her tone start out defensive but end awestruck at his cleverness. A nice distraction by stroking his ego.

"Jamie and I do share a pact of mutual guilt. Neither one of us can implicate the other without destroying himself," he agreed. Then his voice softened to promise, "But you, Felicia, if you'll just pledge yourself to me, I'll never betray you. I owe you that after my, my *mistake* twenty years ago. Just pledge yourself to me, and I'll give you all the devotion I promised you before. Everything will be as it should always have been."

Fear of being caught? Guilt at what he'd done? Brooding over a lost love? All three? This guy has gone around the bend and into the next county. He really thinks I am Felicia now. That conclusion made Jessica hope she could play on a convention expected of even the doughtiest heroine on the screen or page.

"Oh, this is so much," Jess breathed, starting to wilt, dropping the journal to the floor and putting her hands to her forehead. *That should play into Philip's cracked idea of Felicia as a tender flower desperate for his nurture.* "You're asking so much of a girl. You're offering so much, to make up for the past. I mean, I feel sorry for that poor sap Crawford, but to make the world as it should always have been matters more. And I feel Felicia is such a part of me. I just . . ."

Jessica slumped forward with a heavy exhalation, falling towards the desk. Bracing herself there, she could see Philip put down the gun a distance from her. She felt his hand touch her left arm and, with unexpected speed, she delivered a sharp elbow jab to his ribs; a crushing stomp on his instep with her heavy-duty walking shoes; and, as he doubled over in pain and shock, a fierce chop to the back of his neck. Philip Carlyle was reduced to a heap of dazed pain on the floor, courtesy of two maneuvers Liz had taught her as protection against mashers and a *coup de grâce* thanks to James's instruction against fifth columnists. At last, she'd gotten to use all three at once!

"Elizabeth! Get in here on the double!" Jessica yelled as she sprinted around Philip, moaning and down for the count, to grab the pistol.

Liz burst in, took in the scene, and exclaimed, "Jesus, Mary, Joseph, and the rest of the gang! What the . . . ?!"

"Never mind 'what the . . .' I've got to get to the Blasko place to save James's bacon. Don't ask questions. Just call Chief Winston and an ambulance or doctor, or both. Tell them to meet me at Vitus Blasko's, pronto." Jessica was already dashing to her approaching sister and handing her the gun. "Someone may have been shot. Tell Winston that Jamie and Philip are behind the whole deal. It's in the journal, on the floor." Pausing at the door, Jess added, "And don't let that crazy son of a so-and-so get away. Tie him up if you have to!"

"But . . ."

Too late! Jessica was tearing down the foyer to grab the station wagon keys in the kitchen. She never heard her sister yell, "Wait! Come back! You don't even have a weapon!" Or maybe she did hear but couldn't stop. Maybe she'd decided she'd figure out something. *Cars had tire irons, right?* She had to get to James before it was too late!

The gun she'd retrieved from the desk trained on the dazed Carlyle, Liz got on the blower for Chief Winston.

Chapter Forty-Four

Four years behind enemy lines in France, nearly two years undercover in the States, and James Crawford had never been shot by an enemy. He'd been cut, sprained, ligament-torn, and close to concussed, but nary a bullet wound, except for that staged graze of his arm four years ago. It took a petite girl on a New Hampshire vacation island to put him on the serious receiving end of a bullet. It hurt like a bastard. And it was bleeding.

He was sure she'd, fortunately, missed an artery, or he'd have been swimming in blood by now. He was also sure the bullet was still in there. *Yeah, no exit wound.* That left him in no position to leap up and make a charge—so he'd better figure out where Jamie Blasko was and how he could take her by surprise with a game leg that hurt like hell.

She was talking—had been talking, muttering to herself with anxiety, uncertainty—all while those thoughts had flown through James's head. Yet he still heard every word, adrenalin finally kicking in to suppress the pain, to keep his mind on track.

"Damn! He's down? Is he dead?"

Did the girl even know she was talking, not just thinking, her words? Good. Disorientation was something he could use. He had to marshal all the advantages he could scrabble together.

"Philip promised it would be easier the second time. It isn't. I don't want to kill this man. *He* didn't murder my mother. I don't want to." James could hear her moving slightly toward the couch. "But I have to kill him. He knows too much. It's too late."

She stopped advancing and conjectured, hopefully, "Maybe he's dead. He could be. I don't hear anything. Maybe it's all over and done."

Jamie paused. *Listening for me.* James held down his breath, biting back a groan at a sudden vicious throbbing in his left thigh. The adrenalin pound of fear and fight gave him strength.

"No! I have to make sure. I have to see if I need . . . if he needs to be finished off."

James could hear her moving reluctantly forward. He could hear her breathing raggedly with dread, still trying to gin up her nerve with mutterings about Philip and her need to be strong. He recognized that those preoccupations had led her unwisely to approach the couch head-on to the center rather under cover of the corner behind which he'd dived. Maybe that's what kept her from firing through the couch to finish him off. Or maybe Philip had warned her that too many shots would smash up their neat little scenario. A man with too many bullet holes would have a hell of a lot of trouble jumping Vitus Blasko and cracking his skull once, let alone twice.

These thoughts were fleeting, barely recorded as James Crawford carefully shifted position to brace his back against the couch, bringing his hands back and under it, all under the cover of Jamie Blasko's distracted mutterings. He tensed, feeling the same adrenaline surge that had gotten him through fighting and dodging capture in the war. *Bless the Lord for the click of those high heels on the polished wood floor, ever so cautious as his adversary attempted to be! Come on. Just a little closer, ducks, right up the center of this bloody couch.*

Now!

With a tremendous heave that almost left him dizzy, James mustered leverage and strength to shove the couch upward and back.

A scream, a shot, a clatter of the gun hitting that polished wood floor. Pain sent clouds of black laced with purple and magenta before James's eyes. *No! Time to press the advantage! But how far away had the Steyr fallen from the woman moaning with pain and shock, pinned under the couch?*

One more burst of adrenaline. That's all I need!

With a tremendous effort, James Crawford managed to hoist himself up. Bracing himself on the couch, his weight made Jamie Blasko cry out. His right leg was good enough to carry him around the edge of that couch, even as an eagle-eyed scan revealed the pistol near enough to Jamie's reach if she could only pull herself a little freer.

Past the couch on his good leg, James collapsed, the blackness threatening to engulf him. *No! Not after all this!* He pulled himself to his good knee, the blood soaking through his trouser leg in his desperate exertion. His eyes only saw that weapon, Jamie's fingers drawing closer, straining for it. Consciousness circling down the drain, James battled to hold on! But Jamie was also driven by a fierce instinct to conquer and survive. Her fingers nearly reached the stock. James was crawling now, pain almost buried under his overriding drive to beat his would-be executioner to the weapon.

Jamie's hand grasped the stock. James gathered himself for a desperate, last-ditch effort to throw himself forward—when Jamie's hand fell away with her soul-wrenching wail of, "Oh, no! Not you!" and James felt himself overwhelmed by that familiar power of time distilled into one point.

He knew he could move. He managed to pull the Steyr beyond Jamie's reach, clasping it in a hand that didn't seem quite part of him. It seemed like a dream, his body detached from a soul that existed outside time. Jamie Blasko was weirdly past caring about weapons and killing now. She stared, tears streaming down a face filled with terror, awe, shame, regret. It shuddered through his soul that he knew how that experience could sear your psyche. What *had* brought all this anguish to Jamie? Her gaze was directed behind him. What terrified her as he had once been terrified was behind him. This time he was too weak to run as he had twice before. He felt himself bitterly smile, realizing he hadn't the strength even to crawl. Or maybe it was just time to stop running. He looked behind.

For a brief moment, James thought it was Jessica, but the clothes were wrong, familiar, but wrong. *Oh, yeah, the portrait.* They were the same as in the portrait, not the one of terror imprisoned in Bill Carlyle's studio. The other one, the one showing a woman sad yet tender. At least, that was how he thought he remembered her. Through the haziness of his weakened vision, she seemed to shift in focus. Sure, that was it: a hallucination. No, that was wrong. Hell, hadn't he seen something like this in a movie? Paulette Goddard dressed as an ancestress in an abandoned mansion to spook, so to speak, thieving villains. *That was it!* His clever, theatrical wife was here to rescue him in a cracked-brained plot that they'd both seen in a revival-house theatre! He tried to chuckle, to urge her, "Come off it, love! Take the gun here! Hope you brought the coppers." But words wouldn't come out of his mouth. Only thoughts. Only thoughts had any purchase in the quiet, still moment. They'd laugh later—after he gave her hell for pulling such a dangerous stunt.

James closed his eyes, but they drifted open when he heard Vitus groan with pain. Somehow, James knew it was more emotional than physical. Without really feeling it, James had shifted his head so that he could see Jessica kneeling by the man.

What?! What are you doing over there with him? I'm over here! Why aren't you saying even a single word to me?

But there were words, though not for James. And he realized that he could apprehend her words though he wasn't exactly hearing them. He perceived those words in bunches, as if he were a wireless receiver, not tuned precisely to the broadcast station.

". . . forgive you . . . peace . . . me . . . all past . . . care . . . child . . . together . . . family . . . care for her . . ."

Funny how this daze made the voice sound different, not Jessica's. Funny how the voice seemed far away.

He hadn't seen her move, heard the rustle of her long skirt, but now she was with Jamie. *Again, there were words of love and forgiveness. Or were they words? Wasn't it just a sensation?* Then the hand that rested on Jamie's brow sank into her forehead as a wisp of kindness that brought such peace and release to Jamie's features, all while his mind again picked up words about releasing the innocent.

Wait a minute? Sank into Jamie's brow? Not metaphorically! James realized now that there was a kind of softly shifting glow to the visiting form, that there was even a hint of transparency to the folds of her dress. *Jessica did not have these kinds of special effects at her disposal, and Jamie Blasko would hardly be sharing a bullet-induced hallucination with him.*

The haze of warmth between mother and daughter was drowned out by all the terror and anguish of his own visitations, all the memories of his dreadful life in the war; James Crawford could not move. His mind began rearing stony walls to surround and pen up those dread feelings of the unknown, the uncontrollable to protect his soul from being overwhelmed by a touch from beyond the vale.

Then her eyes, her sad eyes, were on him. He felt her warmth encompassing the protective wall around his soul. Her words penetrated, nonetheless: "I tried to stop her with Bill, but her sense of outrage was too strong. She couldn't hear me. You, you are innocent. I couldn't let her take another life when it was neither a misled sense of justice nor pain that controlled her. But you have a sensitive soul. That helped me reach her now."

He felt her words and traces of her gentleness: "You don't need to be afraid. You don't need to be angry. See what anger and the desire to punish and guilt have done to these two? Let go of it all."

The warmth from her seemed to flake and chip away at his walls, even create cracks.

James resisted what felt like her invasion of his secret guilt, his darkness. It was his. No one else should see all that he was, had done, had failed to do.

"They don't forgive you."

Those words sliced inside, as if a sword had materialized inside his stone wall to strike. And yet . . .

The wound was healed in a breath with her words: "They feel they have nothing to forgive. They love you, your humanity, your ideals, your mistakes. They only want to release you. They only wanted to say goodbye. To leave you with their love."

The wall cracked, gaped, but not so much under the pressure of her words as from the responding warmth of long-suppressed hope within.

The thought drifted from him: *But I didn't want to punish anyone.*

"Not even yourself?"

The inner warmth glowed with inner recognition.

"Let go. Your wife released your mind; now you must release your soul. Have the courage to let go and open yourself. They want to reach you. They tried again that night at the séance, but the darkness of those surrounding souls, of your own fears, blocked them. Do you have the courage and humility now to give up hiding, to open yourself fully to them?"

James Crawford was a man of courage. He closed his eyes and opened himself to possibilities.

Chapter Forty-Five

A searing pain in his thigh ripped James Crawford back from the peace that had wrapped him in quiet for Lord only knew how long. He groaned.

He realized that, kneeling by his side, Jessica had wrapped his leg to staunch the bleeding. Her face was strained, but a glow of relief shone through her blue eyes. He only just realized that she'd elevated his leg with a cushion and put a smaller one under his head.

"How you doing, cowboy?" she grinned, one hand gently pushing dark hair from his brow, the other holding his. "Bet you're glad now that when I took those Red Cross classes during the war, I had a tartar like Liz for my instructor."

"I think I'll pull through, though I suspect I'll have to give up jitterbugging and high jumping for a day or two," James weakly replied, irony still intact—until his mind cleared enough for him to remember Philip's plans for his wife.

"Philip!" he burst out, trying to get up. "Did he hurt—?"

Jessica pushed James gently back down, quieting him with, "Down, tiger. I'm here, aren't I? Between the defense maneuvers you and Elizabeth taught me and his inability to realize that all women are not delicate little flowers, well, let's just say they'll be taking Philip away in an ambulance not a paddy wagon. So, relax. I had Liz call Chief Winston and an ambulance to meet me here. But I got the whole truth out of Philip Carlyle."

"Before you beat him up?"

"Darned tootin'. But what in Sam Hill happened here, James Crawford? Talk about 'you should have seen the other guy.'"

"Mr. Blasko? Jamie?" James questioned, regaining enough presence of mind to be anxious about the others.

Jessica glanced back at the two in question before returning to James with, "Jamie is out cold—and she's *under a couch*? As for Vitus, right after I fixed you up, I checked him. He's still out, but he's breathing okay. I didn't want to leave you to get him a cold cloth while you were still out, but the ambulance should be here any minute. So, let's try not to worry."

He nodded, then closed his eyes for a moment, saying, "Poor Vitus was a victim of his daughter's acrimony over her mother, but she wasn't quite as adept at killing a chap who'd done her no wrong as she was at punishing the fellow she thought had done in her mother."

Jessica pointed her chin at James's leg and observed, "She wasn't entirely a bust, though." A pause, then she added, "Philip admitted he, not Bill, killed Felicia. I guess Jamie ended up playing Laertes to Philip's Claudius."

James quirked a sad smile of agreement, closing his eyes. Ought he to have been shocked to discover Philip had been Felicia's executioner? Maybe, though, it wasn't all that much of an eleventh-hour twist, all things considered. Anyway, he was too tired to dwell on others' perfidy. Instead, he wanted to relish the lingering peace of his preternatural encounter. To share it with Jessica. He opened his eyes and let the gleam of his happy place shine out to her as he said, "You know, you were right, what you said to me the other day on the beach, about my mother and Rob. I know it now. I saw it. I feel so free."

Jessica blinked, confused, finally speaking: "How? Nearly getting killed?"

He smiled, "Felicia was here."

"Wha . . . ?"

"She stopped Jamie from grabbing the gun and finishing me. I know how crazy this sounds, but it's true. She stopped Jamie. She's the reason Jamie's lying there, passive. She comforted Vitus—and she came to me and opened the door to let Ma Mère and Rob through. This time I let them in, Jessica. You were right, and I feel so free."

Jessica just stared. *What the devil?! He must have dreamed it, right? Some delirium of pain and crashing adrenaline. That had to be it.* Except when she'd come in, Jamie had been mumbling "Mother, thank you" over and over before passing out. And Liz had had those sightings—one of which had been next to James at the séance.

"I can see by your expression that even my imaginative wife thinks I'm a bit bats in the head," James remarked wryly. "Well enough. I know what I know. I know what I feel. And I feel liberated, at last, of those old chains."

Jessica allowed, "Hmm, well, there are more things in heaven and earth, et cetera." She paused before adding, "And, just think, now you and Elizabeth have something in common: spook sightings. Anyway, all I care about is that you're happier."

"You know, Jessica, you aren't exactly correct about what Liz and I have in common. There's one other little point," he teased.

"Oh? Don't tell me you're going to take up shopping."

"No, Mrs. Crawford. It's that we both love you very much."

"Wise guy," Jessica managed after a grateful little sniffle. She bent down to kiss James, and he mustered the strength to make it worth her while.

That's when the constabulary made its appearance.

Jim Winston surveyed the room, shook his head, and said, "Sure you two lovebirds need us? Looks like you have the situation well in hand, so to speak."

As Deputy Hudson rushed to help Vitus Blasko, out in the woods, a hound howled.

Epilogue
Saturday, November 15th

The colors of November are grey, brown, maroon. Trees barely hold a leaf, and most of those remaining are crusty and curled on grey branches scratching against a faded sky. This day, the wind-roughened waters of the bay that the island park curved 'round were slatey under fierce white crests. And it was much colder. Yet Jessica Minton and James Crawford, sitting on a bench overlooking that bay, were warm. They were together.

Resting against the bench, next to James, were a pair of crutches. A bullet wound and surgery wouldn't heal in a day, but Mr. Crawford was coming along nicely. His arm around Jessica, he squeezed her shoulder again. She leaned into him, closing her eyes, content.

"I know November seems drear to most people, but there's something lovely, peaceful about it for me," Jessica finally said, playing with the collar of her fawn fall coat. "All the exciting splash of autumn color and activities are done; it's time to rest and catch your breath before winter sets in."

"We could all use quite a breather after the last few weeks," James wryly agreed. "And we're both looking forward to a big turkey dinner and lots of pumpkin pie."

"There is that," Jess smiled, snuggling closer to her husband's warm, grey wool coat.

A cracking twig to their left made them both start.

"Sorry, folks," came Chief Winston's voice. "Didn't mean to sneak up on you."

"After what we've been through, Chief, you really *ought* to know better," Jessica chided, tongue in cheek.

"Yup, well, I get you. But I was driving through the park; and, when I saw you two, I thought you might like the official word on the case now that you'll be heading home. Why make you wait until the Portsmouth D.A. calls you back?"

"So the lawyers' strategy to get them off on insanity pleas didn't pan out," James surmised.

"Nagh. Insanity's not going to work. They had to be pretty darned competent to work out their intricate plots. No, they're both up for murder one, though with Carlyle's connections and Jamie Blasko's pretty face and sorry back story, I don't think anybody's going to the gallows."

The wind whipped Winston's dark police jacket, but the cold hardly bothered him.

"Does that disappoint you, Chief?" James asked. He tightened his hold on Jessica's shoulder, remembering all the threats against her.

Winston shrugged, "I ain't bloodthirsty. We got 'em off the street. They aren't gonna have no picnic when they get life. What about you, Crawford? You and your wife almost became part of their tally."

James looked thoughtfully out to sea before answering, "They showed me what a cancer nursing vengeance and resentment can be. Jessica is safe, I'm safe, they're in the hands of the law. That's good enough for me."

Jessica gave James's chest an approving pat, even as Chief Winston nodded.

Brushing strands of wind-tossed hair from her face, Jessica pointed out, "What's crazy is that if this crew had used the kind of genius behind their complicated plots for a positive goal, think of all the good they could have done themselves and others."

"Yep," Winston agreed. "The plots those two teams cooked up were some humdingers. To think I might not have gotten wise if you two hadn't poked your noses where they didn't belong."

"That's nicely put," James laughed.

"Yeah, well, just don't make a habit of it, you two. Next time you might not be so lucky."

James and Jessica both thought: *You don't know the half of it!* However, James agreed, "Point taken, Chief."

"This was a humdinger all rightie," Winston reflected. "I thought when I took this job, it'd be a breeze. I even patted myself on the back for turning down the other two places up in Maine as being hinky."

"Oh?" Jess inquired.

"Oh, yeah," Winston elaborated. "One place, along some cove, people kept dropping dead around this English teacher. The other, this fishing village way up the coast, the local big-wig family had all kinds of peculiar skeletons in the closet, way more than here."

James assured Winston, "I expect things will settle down considerably now."

Winston shrugged, hopefully.

Jessica, however, had sadder thoughts to express: "I feel for Vitus Blasko. His whole family is lost. Worse, he has to realize that the rapprochement he thought he'd found with his daughter was all a horrible lie fabricated to destroy him."

"Funny thing," Winston mused. "As soon as he got out of the hospital and found out the whole story, he sold all his property to get her the best mouthpiece he could find. It's like saving her became his whole purpose in life. I hope she appreciates what the old man is doing, how he's trying to make things up."

James quietly stated, "I think she does now. I think she's a different person."

Jessica licked her lip, reflecting on what James had told her about the visitation, hoping it was for real. Yes, she believed it was.

Winston continued, "'Course Philip Carlyle had to sell everything he had to pay for his lawyers, what wasn't already mortgaged to the hilt. Funny, ain't it? He came up with his criminal plan to make a killing with developers, and he ended up selling out for what he could get to try and save his skin from being punished for that plot."

"Which means that beautiful mansion and that lovely grotto will be completely obliterated," Jessica concluded. "That's sad."

"Not so sad, considering all the misery and psychosis that festered in that house for twenty years," James considered. "Maybe it's better to tear away the past so young people can build a new future."

"Perhaps," Jessica sighed.

Winston revealed, "It's not all going. The historical society used its clout in zoning to make the developers preserve the grotto as a public park. They like history, but they're no dopes when it comes to beefing up the tax base and bringing in new business."

"Rather ironic, isn't it?" James posited to Winston. "All that will remain of the Carlyle legacy is a monument to Philip's nemesis, Bill."

"Ain't irony a scream," Winston shook his head.

413

James added, "Just think: if Bill, Wanda, and Jeanne hadn't met up in South America, perhaps none of this tragedy would have occurred."

"Yeah, I guess it's a coincidence for the books," Winston agreed. "If Jeanne hadn't seen Bill again, it might never have triggered her memory and given her and Wanda the idea for blackmail or changing their minds to hook up with Philip. If Bill hadn't found out from Jeanne that no one was after him for murder, he wouldn't have realized his brother had pulled a fast one, promising to tell him when the coast was clear. He'd have never gotten the idea to find out what really happened and search out Jamie for a little profitable revenge."

"Well, anything with that many moving parts is bound to fall apart, eventually, right?" Jessica conjectured. "It's just terrible that so many got crushed in the debris."

"Hey, enough with gloom," Winston changed the subject. "Where's the other gal, the tall one, your sister? Back in the city?"

"Liz? You mean Liz?" Jessica supplied. "She got an important long-distance call at the inn today, and she has to do some tall thinking about a decision. She's taking a walk in the woods over there to figure things out."

The wind teased strands of Liz's neat upsweep and chignon. So preoccupied was the tall woman that she scarcely noticed, as she followed the narrowing path through crinkling, crackling, crunching leaves under bare, swaying branches. Only the perennial-bushes hugging the trail she traveled, buried in thought, retained their brilliant red berries. She had one hell of a decision to make before returning to New York and Leo McLaughlan. The call from him this morning made her realize that she really loved the guy. That terrified her!

After her train wreck of a marriage and what had happened with Larry Sanders, how could she risk his happiness? Still, she couldn't keep him dangling forever. It wasn't fair to a right guy like Leo. So, she'd have either to let him go or jump feet first into marriage. Did she have the nerve? Maybe it would be safer, kinder to him, to let him go.

Somewhere, several yards back, the leaves and underbrush rattled under rapid movement.

"It's a squirrel, just a squirrel," Liz muttered, looking behind but discerning nothing. She tightened the belt of her wool coat about her waist. "They always make a racket like a moose with a glandular condition."

It didn't help that Elizabeth realized the sound came from between her and the head of the trial. The trail! This narrow track wasn't the wide path she'd started on when she'd left her sister and brother-in-law to think things out. How'd she manage to wander here? She'd better try to find her way back, pronto!

"Aroooooo!" shattered the stillness, a few yards closer, still between her and the way back. The bushes mightily shook and rattled.

"Yikes!"

Elizabeth took off down the narrow trail to God knows where faster than Dusty hearing the call, "Tuna!"

The brush rustled even more furiously behind her!

"Aroooo!"

"The Hound," Elizabeth breathed, her life beginning to flash before her eyes. The crackling drew closer!

Then, a foot went wrong and Liz, trying to save herself, twisted to the side and tumbled down a slope of crunching, crumbled leaves. Rolling uncontrollably, all Liz could think was what a fool she had been if this was the end. For just one last chance to see Leo again! The Hound's wail echoed in her ears; the leaves on the slope crackled the menace's approach.

She thudded into the bottom of the slope. The wind knocked out of her, Elizabeth realized with horror that she couldn't move, even as the thudding and crunching told her the hound was bounding down upon her. Unable to look, she screwed her eyes shut, with one last thought of Leo.

Then it was on her. Something heavy hit her shoulder. She managed to raise a hand, hoping to fend off snarling fangs from her throat and face. Too late! Liz felt the most thorough face licking she'd ever experienced from a dog. An encouraging nuzzle and woof were followed by the return of that affectionate tongue. Liz's eyes flew open on a sweet, if bedraggled, standard red dachshund, whimpering and snuffling for joy at having captured a human.

Liz sat up as the dog climbed onto her lap, receiving her pets now that he was satisfied she was unhurt.

"So, fella, you have a collar but the tag's missing. Have you been lost all this time? Poor pup. No one came looking for you? Looks like we'll have to find your home. And if we can't, I have a place for you. I just hope Leo always wanted a dog."

Chief Winston happened to glance across the green to the trail emerging from the woods.

"Say, I'll be!" he exclaimed. "There's your sister with Old Lady Amadon's dog."

"What?" Jess uttered as she and James followed his gaze. There was Liz, leading a large Daxie on a leash, make-shift from her coat belt. Seeing them, Liz waved while the dog uttered the familiar, if now happier, "Arooooo!"

"There's your Hound of Hades," James laughed.

Winston gave James a puzzled look and corrected him, "Huh? Nagh, that's Mrs. Amadon's pooch. He got lost after she died some weeks back. Welp, looks like he's found a home."

Knowing what had been her sister's conflict, but now seeing the content, even joy, on Liz's face, Jessica observed, "That pup isn't the only one getting a permanent place with Liz." Turning to James, she teased. "Looks like you might have to don a monkey suit, after all, hon. I expect Leo will want his brother-in-law-to-be in the wedding party."

The End

This 'n That

When I first got the idea for *Shadows*, I wanted to set it on the Maine coast as a tip of the hat to one of my favorite trips into the Gothic, *Dark Shadows*. Unfortunately, I cooked my literary goose by setting the story in 1947, generally known as "the year Maine burned." That October horrific forest fires incinerated huge swaths of forest, farms, and even towns, including Bar Harbor, Wells, and Kennebunk. Now, the fire itself would have proved an effective backdrop for fiction (and apparently already has). However, that was not the story I had already planned. So, when I refer to the devastation of those fires in *Shadows*, I'm writing about the real thing. If you're interested, check out the sources that I used for research, *Wildfire Loose, The Week Maine Burned* and the following websites. Martha Fowler's report for the Rochester Historical Society[1] and "The Fires of 1947 Nearly Destroyed Newfield" in *Fosters Daily Democrat*, Staff Writer.[2]

After perusing a map of the Northeast to find a site that would be somewhat isolated, yet not too far from civilization to make travel there and remote broadcasting infeasible, I settled on an island where the Piscataqua River, off Portsmouth, empties into the ocean. I fictionalized this island into Birdsong Island (tip of the hat Supremes-ward) to include a rustic cemetery, three family mansions, a ghostly lady, and a Hound from Hell. The Stone-Throwing Demon is an actual legend, though (New England Historical Society.[3] For details of the real island, not the one in my novel, check out these sites: "Daytrip to New Castle Island"[4] and The New Castle Historical Society.[5]

---

1 https://www.fosters.com/article/20080124/gjnews04/243156442
2 https://www.fosters.com/article/20121025/GJNEWS03/121029538
3 https://www.newenglandhistoricalsociety.com/stone-throwing-devil-new-castle-new-hampshire/
4 https://mappedbymegan.com/day-trip-to-new-castle-nh/
5 https://www.newcastlenhhistoricalsociety.org/

Knowledge of sodium amytal and scopolamine initially came to me through forties *film noir*. Check out *Crackup* and *The Fallen Sparrow*. Nevertheless, I'm more meticulous than to rely on the text of old films, so my best professional source was: "Truth Drugs in Interrogation" by George Bimmerle.[6]

As inaccurate as I usually find Wikipedia to be, I did discover useful information on weaponry. So blame them if I got the murder weapons wrong.

Knowledge of radio programs, again, was initially inspired by golden era films, but I rooted most of what I wrote in some well-researched writings. Leonard Maltin's *The Great American Broadcast* is one of the most thorough, intelligent, and fun histories of radio programs from their inception early in the twentieth century to their fading out in the late fifties/early sixties. Particularly useful to writing about suspense and horror programs are *Terror on the Air* (Richard Hand), *Tales Well-Calculated to Keep You in* Suspense (Darryl Shelton), Michael Samerdyke's *A History of* Suspense: *1942-1962*, and Inner Sanctum *Mysteries: Behind the Creaking Door* (Martin Grams, Jr.). Listening to programs like *Suspense, Lights Out*, and *Inner Sanctum* further shaped my crafting the types of shows that Scott Z. produced with Jessica and company. Finally, I have to admit that Rupert Holmes's series on AMC, *Remember WENN,* inspired me with the humor and excitement of creating live radio! When IS that series coming out on DVD?

---

[6] https://www.cia.gov/static/a56eb9be08868b6e14c6ff838ae77087/Truth-Drugs-in-Interrogation.pdf

Acknowledgment

Acknowledgments never seem to cover all the people who deserve thanks, but here goes my attempt to express my genuine gratitude for the many who helped make this novel possible. First, thank you to my posse of readers who helped me keep my facts straight and not say anything too dopey: Ruth Haber, Kathy Healey, Judy Jeon-Chapman, Amber Vayo, and De-Ping Yang. A special thank you to Philippe Telemaque at the Dinand Library at the College of the Holy Cross for setting me up with microfilm and showing me how to use the machine so I could use the *New York Times* to figure out radio broadcast schedules, train schedules, and all the juicy stuff in the news that Jessica and Liz had to be up on. Loads of thanks to all the friends, family, librarians, fellow authors, and readers who have supported and encouraged me. Special thanks to Jean Grant, Janet Raye Stevens, Lorraine Sharma Nelson, Cheryl Marceau, and Mary Small for guidance and advice in republishing this second edition once my rights were returned. Extra special thanks to Kim Coghlan.

Above all, thanks to my husband, Yang, my fact-checker and best pal. This book is dedicated to him.